GODFIRES

Also by William Hoffman

Novels

THE TRUMPET UNBLOWN
DAYS IN THE YELLOW LEAF
A PLACE FOR MY HEAD
THE DARK MOUNTAINS
YANCEY'S WAR
A WALK TO THE RIVER
A DEATH OF DREAMS
THE LAND THAT DRANK THE RAIN

Collected Stories

VIRGINIA REELS

GODFIRES

A NOVEL BY

William Hoffman

VIKING

WITHDRAWN

VIKING
Viking Penguin Inc., 40 West 23rd Street,
New York, New York 10010, U.S.A.
Penguin Books Ltd, Harmondsworth,
Middlesex, England
Penguin Books Australia Ltd, Ringwood,
Victoria, Australia
Penguin Books Canada Limited, 2801 John Street,
Markham, Ontario, Canada L3R 1B4
Penguin Books (N.Z.) Ltd, 182–190 Wairau Road,
Auckland 10, New Zealand

First published in 1985 by Viking Penguin Inc.
Published simultaneously in Canada

LIBRARY OF CONGRESS CATALOGING IN PUBLICATION DATA
Hoffman, William.
  Godfires.
  I. Title.
PS3558.O34638G6 1985   813'.54   84-21910
ISBN 0-670-80329-4

Printed in the United States of America by
The Book Press, Brattleboro, Vermont
Set in Plantin

BT 16.95/9.32 - 7/85

For George

GODFIRES

1

I lie bellydown on the rasping cot, my chain clanking as I shift to gaze out the crooked doorway of the cabin toward motionless briers, tangled kudzu, and drooping swamp weed blooming yellow. I await the precise tread of the master.

I am hungry and anxious to be fed. The crooked doorway, against which ancient sun-kilned bricks crumble, is a frame fronting the wilderness growing around a long-abandoned pond and grinding mill. Those who lived here were mill slaves, the blacks who loaded wagons, operated levers and gears of wooden machinery, and adjusted the water's speed through the earthen race.

Now that race is silted and choked by glistening lilies. Algae as richly blue-black as wet night films the pond's surface. Trees whose roots have eroded clog the stream—dusty birches, pale willows, and broken sycamores that lie toppled and decaying. The mill itself is gone except for random hand-hewn beams among grasping weeds and a sheet of rusted, lacy tin that creaks in the wind or pings and pounds during rare summer showers.

My stomach rumbles, and I sink back to the cot, causing my chain to jangle. The chain is new, its steel unblemished, and is fastened around my left ankle by a padlock, also new. To prevent abrasions, the links are fitted daily to other parts of my body: the right ankle, my wrists, my waist.

The chain leads to a great millstone crudely chipped and shaped from a boulder, again the work of slaves. Mules would have dragged it from the stream. The millstone lies tilted against a broken hearth.

I remember Rhea laughing and lifting a hand to touch the cleanness of her strawberry hair.

I stop remembering to listen to crows who roost in the swamp. They perch atop trees whose shade is not solemnly dark like the upland oaks' but diluted, thinned by sunlight penetrating the leaf, causing a green pall over the wild growth, that tinted light seeming to come not from up or down but everywhere, as if I'm submerged in a turgid, fervid sea.

The crows squawk their three-note alarm, and a hawk voices defiance, a red-tail whose shadow I've seen scythe the underbrush. There are frogs around the pond and along the stream, great jumbo bellowers whose bassos of an evening roll over the low ground like belches of satiated gorgers. These too become silent, though an occasional craven plops into the stillness of slimed water so thick it could be worn over the shoulders as a shawl.

I see the master walk from among bulrushes and marsh elder, the step soft, yet long and sure. The military figure is erect and wears a camouflaged hat draped with mosquito netting, a khaki work-shirt that has its sleeves rolled down and buttoned, and boots of rubber and leather, the kind local hunters order from L. L. Bean up in Maine. Tan brush pants are faced with leather to give protection against thorns.

On the right of the master's belt is a revolver, a Smith & Wesson .38 police special. A strap across the hammer holds the pistol securely in an oxblood leather holster. On the left the master wears a sheath knife, the sort used to skin deer. The master carries a red plastic thermos of fresh water and a paper sack of food.

I stand from my cot. I have some range on my chain, though I can't reach the door. There are needs I have to satisfy by using the old-fashioned white enamel chamber pot.

The master stops just outside the doorway, stares at me through yellow shooting glasses, and enters to place the thermos and food on a table built of raw lumber at the center of the room. The sack is leaned against the thermos. The master draws the revolver before fitting a key into the second padlock and freeing me from the millstone.

I am still a dog on a leash. By this time I understand the rules of my captivity. As the master holds one end of the chain, I cross to the chamber pot and carry it out among swamp grass to the pit I have dug while under supervision. I empty the pot into the pit, shovel on soil, and walk to the suffocated stream, where I dip the pot under algal water. I leave the pot in sunlight to dry.

It is exercise time, the drills prescribed by the master, who holds an end of my chain. I perform deep knee bends and side-straddle hops. I am quickly sweaty and of interest to insects. They buzz around me as the master watches without expression. I try an ingratiating smile, but it has no effect.

Next we cross to the well, an old well, the stones retaining it rounded and licked by moss. The master has replaced the frame of two-by-fours above it on which is hung the pulley, draw rope, and a bucket. The pulley has been oiled. The bucket and draw rope are new, the latter garish yellow in sunlight. The bucket drops fast and booms against the surface deep below.

The well water is not for drinking. It hasn't been inspected and carries a slight scent of sulphur, but it's all right to wash in. I unbutton my shirt, lay it over the frame, and out of the bucket scrub to the waist. I am handed soap and a clean towel. I shave, using a safety razor and a metal mirror served up to me. I prop the mirror against a two-by-four and bend to it.

Finally there is food, which I eat at the cabin table while the master watches, gun drawn. The master likes me to eat and has brought snap beans, beaten biscuits, and cold chicken aplenty. I am gaining weight.

After the meal the master attaches the other end of my chain to the millstone and locks it. I sit on my cot, my feet together, my hands on my knees. The master uses the single wooden chair, careful to stay separated by a good body's length. Even if I am brave and strong—neither of which is true—there is no way I can move quickly enough to seize the gun.

It is time for our lesson.

Master: Are you comfortable?

Me: Yes.

Master: What is sin?

Being the Commonwealth's Attorney in Howell County, Virginia, I was soon to hear. Two brothers named Hensley, ages twelve and fourteen, were float-fishing down our local Wye River in an aluminum jonboat bought from Sears, the boat propelled by a current as indolent as the late-June morning. Even the buzzards seemed to be drowsing on sluggish thermal updrafts.

For bait the boys used minnows and night crawlers, and when the river bumped the boat gently against spongy earth of the southern bank, they believed the man to be sleeping. They rose to stare.

They might've grinned except glittering flies sped across the man's face and in and out of his slightly parted mouth. As the boys realized what they saw, they boated their fishing poles, grabbed for oars, and pulled wildly to the opposite bank, where they ran among pines to a secondary road and up the dirt lane to their home.

Their mother, a spare woman who wore a poke bonnet to shade her face while suckering tobacco, called my office on the second floor of a courthouse built by the WPA during Franklin D. Roosevelt's administration. My window gave out the front to a concrete Ionic column and a brass bell from which a rope dangled, the bell to be rung on lawing days. Arrogant breasty pigeons who kept residence under the eaves had become used to the clanging and did not rouse at summonses to the bar of justice.

My secretary, paid for by the county, received the call, her name Florene, though I addressed her as Mrs. Epes, a hardy, compact woman forty-five or so, which made her a good ten years older than I. An unswerving Baptist who sang in the Shiloh Church choir, she suspected I had desperate longings for her body and never came around but always stood in front of my desk.

"You'll want the sheriff," she said. "And your sunglasses."

I reached for the phone as if it possessed fangs. On this stillborn summer day in Howell County, all I wanted was to be closing the office and slipping away from the courthouse. So far I'd gotten through pretty well. I knew I was about to be bit.

"How about we go in a county car?" the sheriff said.

I stood, reached for my seersucker jacket, and adjusted my sunglasses. My fingers were slick on the frames. No office in the courthouse was air-conditioned. We needed rain bad, though while it fell, the drops were as heavy and sticky as soup.

"I'll hold the fort," prim Florene said as I left the office. She'd mothered two vigorous children, yet surely she'd never suffered anything as earthy as intercourse to conceive them.

The sheriff's territory was a one-story brick addition at the rear of the courthouse, a dim, hot lair made up of an office, a squad room, and a shadowy cell block where black hands grasped bars. Usually country or gospel music rattled through the place, provided by a tri-county radio station which operated during daylight hours. Street talk had it that the renowned Buster Bovin, dynamite preacher and presently Howell's most famous son, owned a majority interest in WPAL.

The sheriff sat at his oak desk, a man whose flesh was so loose it seemed the only thing holding him together was his rumpled tan uniform. Unbutton his shirt or drop his pants and he would've flowed across the floor like lard melting in a skillet. He moved no more than he had to, and when he had to, it was with a slow, rolling gait, as if he perpetually paced the deck of a pitching ship and needed to compensate for rough weather.

He was in his fifties, balding, his eyes faintly blue, washed out, weary. He'd been sheriff four terms, and by now most of his deputies were kinsmen. His kin lived up practically every dirt road in the county, and on election day they turned out like rabbits. He also had a nephew about to finish law school at William & Mary, and I was aware the sheriff was weaving plans for him.

The sheriff, his name Burton Pickney, did the driving as we rode out in a police cruiser, the steering wheel creasing his belly, though he'd shoved the seat back as far as it would go. No lights flashed, no siren shrilled because we could do without curiosity or excitement. Once away from Tobaccoton, however, he drove fast and efficiently, enjoying the mastery of his fingertips over the souped-up Ford. It was the only thing he was enjoying.

"What about Doc Robinette?" I asked.

"A deputy's bringing him to the river."

Weeds at the side of the road were dry, the crops bedraggled, the fields ruptured under dust. Howell County wasn't yet in a state of drought, but at the edge of it, what little rain we'd had, the steamy showers, just teasing us with the hope of lushness, keeping alive the vision of corn and wheat upspringing, making us dream that the oaks, poplars, and hackberries wouldn't draw in like men

grown old. Yet the pines endured. No matter how scorching the
heat, how killing, the loblollies weltered, a slow, sensual nodding
in air itself too torrid to stir.

The Hensleys lived on a lane grown up with Queen Anne's
lace. The unshaded plank house was built around a central chimney
and reared at the corners on rocks dragged in from the fields. The
siding had recently been painted white, the window frames a dark
green. At the rear were an equipment shed, stacked hay bales, and
a chinked log barn where the dark leaf was cured.

Both Clyde and Ruth Hensley waited on the porch, he a lean,
weathered man bent from stooping to his rows, she straighter, more
alert, full of that long-term, enduring strength of country women.
They had cleaned themselves up as if the event were special enough
to require company manners.

"Boys," Clyde called behind him as Sheriff Pickney and I
walked from the car toward the porch.

The two young brothers sidled out the screen door, their eyes
lowered, and moved in behind their father. They too were washed,
combed, and changed into freshly laundered denims. The boys had
a quietness about them as if what they'd found on the riverbank
had elevated them with the speed of light into the responsibility of
manhood.

"Like to take them," Sheriff Pickney said.

"I'll come too," Clyde said and shifted his weight to walk down
the steps.

"Well thanks for the offer, Clyde, but it mighten be better if
you didn't right now," the sheriff said. "How about we hollering
if we need you?"

Clyde's face tightened with disappointment. He wanted to see,
as did his wife. Death transcended even kin or crops. Still, Clyde
was too polite, too naturally law-abiding, to protest.

Sheriff Pickney, the two boys, by name Amos and Aaron, and
I started away from the house. Clyde spoke once more.

"They think they recorgnized him."

"Anyhow, we'll know in a minute," the sheriff called back. "I
mean for sure we'll know something."

He directed the two boys into the rear of the car, listened to
their instructions, and drove toward the river along what had once
been a timbering road. Weeds stroked the underside of the Ford,
and dust rose twisting behind us. The sheriff used his radio to give

his location to the dispatcher in Tobaccoton.

The road stopped at pines, and we left the car to walk among them on a path laid down by the delicate hoofs of deer. When I got home I'd wash down with kerosene to rid myself of chiggers and ticks. I was number two in line, following the older boy, Amos, and I remembered it was always supposed to be the second person that a startled copperhead struck.

The aluminum jonboat had been jerked onto the bank and abandoned, fishing poles sticking out, oars thrown to the bottom. The night crawlers had buried deep into the gallon paint bucket of red soil, attempting to escape the heat of the sun and its deadly dryness. Both boys pointed across the river.

Amos did the rowing while Pickney sat in the stern, weighting it deep, and Aaron and I balanced the bow. Amos was a towhead with a long, serious face like his father's. Like his father also he was lean and sun-cured. The homemade oars, carved from pine, dug in, and the boat left a murmuring wake.

The boy knew the river. Instead of angling upstream to allow for drift, he crossed directly and when near the far bank rowed against the current where it was negligent. Pollen coated the water a yellowish green. Sunlight exploded between trees. Aaron, the boy beside me, trembled and was ashamed of it. He held his legs as if they were frightened hounds attempting to escape, but they bumped mine.

Willow branches trailed into the water and disturbed the flow's patient fabric. The branches were coated with dried brown mud from the spring flood. A sunning turtle slipped from grass and sliced into the river. A heron squawked and flapped into shadows.

Amos pulled the jonboat toward a white oak so large it overpowered all space around it. Running cedar, blue lupine, and ferns grew in its blanketing shade. The jonboat slid onto the bank with a smooth sibilance.

The man lay in wild grass near the rocks. His body was turned on his left side as if resting, his knees were drawn up, his hands templed beneath a cheek. His ankles were crossed. Had not the emerald flies been at him, he would've appeared serene, the face at the threshold of a smile.

He wore a blue summer blazer, a lemon shirt open at the neck, wine slacks, and polished loafers. His feet were sockless, his ankles tanned. He was large, physical, his tan not country but of the links, pool, and beach. His dark-blond hair appeared recently combed and waved. He was graceful in repose.

When the four of us got positioned in front of the body, we became hushed. Then the sheriff raised his thick heavy hands to lay them protectively on the boys' shoulders as his mouth moved in a whispered curse. We all recognized the man. Any Howell County citizen would have. The governor of Virginia would have. I was once so envious of the person on the ground I wished him to be uglied in a car or plane crash.

His name was Vincent Fallon Farr.

2

Me: Sin is the conformity unto, or transgression of, any law of God, given as a rule to the reasonable creature.

Master: No!

Me: I thought—

Master: You didn't think. You're just speaking words. Do it again.

Me: Sin is the conformity—

Master: Sin is any want of conformity unto, or transgression of, any law of God, given as a rule to the reasonable creature.

Me: What I meant.

Master: Do it!

Me: I don't understand—

Master: You don't need to understand yet. You must first have the knowledge.

Me: Sin is any want of conformity...

———

No bridge existed by which the Howell County Rescue Squad could drive to the other side of the river, so the helmeted men rowed across in a boat, their own, carried lashed to the top of the squat white ambulance. Two of Sheriff Pickney's deputies also arrived. One named Carl took pictures with a Polaroid camera belonging to the department.

The men from the Rescue Squad, all volunteers who wore white coveralls as well as the silver hardhats, laid Vin's stiffened body gently into their boat, treating him as if still alive and able to feel any rough handling. They rowed him to the other bank, where they unstrapped a canvas stretcher.

"Need a report from the medical examiner," I said and adjusted my sunglasses.

"Where in red hell's Doc Robinette?" the sheriff asked. "Maybe they lost."

He and I rowed over in the aluminum jonboat. The Hensley boys had been sent home. The Rescue Squad arranged Vin's body on the stretcher. "Take him to the funeral home but tell them not to touch anything till after Doc's examined him," Pickney said.

"They're not to talk to anybody about anything either," I said.

"Rhea," Pickney said. "She ought to be notified before finding out some other way."

"You tell her," I said. Rhea was Vin's wife.

The sheriff disliked it. He hoped I'd do the dirty work, yet didn't argue. Being the Commonwealth's Attorney, I was the county's top law officer, but I'd never had more than a working relationship with Burton Pickney. Soon as his nephew graduated from law school, the sheriff would start drawing in his numberless kin to undercut me at the polls. His will was that of running water, a placidly determined force which could be slowed, even diverted, but never long blocked.

The Rescue Squad carried Vin away under pine boughs. The afternoon light was baffled by trees except for gaps where blades of sun slanted into the flowing water. A ragged flight of noisy crows fled through the woods.

We tied the jonboat to a willow and drove back to town. For a minute the sheriff and I sat there in the asphalt parking lot behind the jail, Pickney resting his fleshy forearms on the steering wheel. He shook his head as if I'd asked a question.

"And it's my birthday," he said. "Hell of a damn present. I was about to take my vacation. Going down to Carolina and catch me some fish. I ain't caught a decent eating fish in two years. Mr. Payne, you ever get the feeling things are working agin you?"

"Only all the time," I said as I leaned to the door to open it. I didn't intend to return to the courthouse. Too much excitement, too many questions. I'd wait for Doc Robinette's report. I walked to my car, which was parked in a reserved slot behind the jail, a three-year-old Chevy Malibu, a vestige of the life I'd lived with Jeannie. It'd been hers, but in the settlement she'd taken the Porsche as well as most of the bank account and an Irish setter named Kelley.

I drove west from Tobaccoton, passing a state historical marker and crossing an iron bridge. There'd been a Civil War battle for the bridge, though books didn't tell why, and surely this bridge didn't lead to much of anywhere. The battle must've been an accident, a skirmish between Rebs and Yanks out foraging for yams, hams, and scrawny fleeing chickens.

As I unbuttoned my collar to allow air to blow down my shirt, I glimpsed blacks hammering a new tin roof on their church. Howell County was tick-infested, chigger-infested, but most of all it was religion-infested. If religion were oak trees, we would've been living in a primeval forest instead of a thirsting land where the red soil of fields flowed into the sun's glaze like rivers of dust.

Exactly seven miles by the odometer, I slowed and turned right onto property that belonged to my father and had been owned by three generations of Paynes before him, a languishing farm of some 140 acres whose fences sagged and whose pastures had given over to acidity and whisping broomstraw.

The lane from the highway was laid straight between flanking locust trees, the trees each spring sweet with tiny white blossoms that fell like perfumed snowflakes, but the locusts were past their prime—some splintered by lightning, others wind-broken, the rest merely exhausted with too many years of striving to endure. They should've been cut for firewood, but who was around to do that?

The house appeared in fair shape, fundamentally sound, if incomplete. At the beginning it'd been only a two-story frame box to which a grandfather added a wing. A second wing was intended to provide symmetry, yet nobody in the family since had gathered enough cash or acumen to finish the job. I'd kept the siding painted, though the English boxwoods of the formal garden were overcome by creeper, wisteria, and honeysuckle. Still there existed nothing desperate about the place, no air of panic or rout.

Eddie Blue, the great All-American mechanic, was fooling with my gasoline lawn mower on the turtle-backed walk in front of the house. He held a screwdriver and stared perplexed at parts he'd laid out on the bricks. He glanced warily at me as I drove around the house to the garage.

Carrying my seersucker jacket over an arm, I returned to the front. Eddie Blue was a muscular black of eighteen who had been a tackle on Howell County Consolidated High School's football team, the Hornets. He wore shorts cut from jeans, his bulging thighs about to bust them, and a red short-sleeve jersey with the number 76 on it. He'd poked a glistening black index finger into the mower's carburetor.

"At it again huh?" I asked.

"Mr. Payne, why don't you buy us a good mower? This thing ain't worth horse apples."

He hated cutting grass. He pushed the mower as if the job were beneath his station. Give me a man's work, his attitude said, a challenge. Let me hew oaks.

"It's not a cheap mower, Eddie. Cost me almost two hundred dollars, and I do recall I requested you not to think of yourself as a master mechanic."

"But it's old and tired," he said as he lifted the spark plug to examine it for fouling. The tips of his fingers were blunt and oily.

"Two years old, a span not ancient in the life of a good lawn mower if it is handled with care, its innards not tampered with by persons who understand little of the internal combustion engine's principle."

"I understand! I took four years of shop at school and got an A in mechanics."

"You may be the greatest who ever lifted a wrench, Eddie, but what I know is I come home to find you with parts all over the yard and the rattails not getting cut. In order for lawns to be mowed, the parts have to be in the mower, and it has to be running, and I am a little put out at paying you for the time it's not running."

"You tough to work for, Mr. Payne, you know that?"

"You accomplish so little of what might be termed work around here I don't see how you're able to make that judgment."

Resentment expanded Eddie Blue outward and upward. He became hot tar. His cheeks puffed, and he almost boiled.

"You don't want me to work for you no more?" he asked.

"Work, yes, that I want, but fooling around with the innards of my mower I do not want. Slights against my two-hundred-dollar mower I do not want. Excuses I do not want. What I desire is long clean swaths cut from my lawn in a reasonable time and at a reasonable cost. Think you can handle that assignment?"

He didn't answer but kept expanding, roiled tar about to overflow. I should have fired him off the place long ago and would have except he was Aunt Lettie's grandson. I had to keep her happy. She believed Eddie Blue was one sweet boy and would quit me if I ran him away.

He curved above the mower and began to replace parts. Sullen tar. I walked to the rear of the house and up the steps to the screen door. I heard my father's phonograph, the music coming through the house not only to my ears but also to my feet, the boards carrying it. I crossed the buckled green linoleum of the kitchen. Above the stove was an electric wall clock that didn't work and a Bank of Tobaccoton calendar which was outdated, kept there by Aunt Lettie, who liked the color photograph of Holstein cows grazing among the vivid buttercups. The kitchen smelled of onions, home-baked bread, and country meats.

I walked through the unused dining room with its lace curtains, crystal in a china cabinet, circular mahogany table, and silver tea service on the sideboard. In the hallway I hung my jacket on a brass coatrack. A stained-glass fan window above the front doorway tinted the afternoon light to a spectral dullness.

My father stood at the head of the steps. He leaned over the railing and held his white-ash cane as if he would use the crook to reach down and hook me up.

"I could die and nobody would know," he said.

I returned to the kitchen, where Aunt Lettie had fixed his plate, covered it with a paper napkin, and stuck it into the cool oven. On the plate were fried ham, English peas, butterbeans, and a buttered slab of cornbread. Normally she would've served my father, but she was off at her big meeting, the annual gathering of sisters and brethren at her church—The Healing Springs African Pentecostal. She led the singing.

I set the plate and a tall glass of mint iced tea from the refrigerator on a tray and carried them to my father, who waited by leaning both hands on his cane. He straightened to bang the steel ferrule against a pine board of the floor. His white hair was combed straight back and contrasted with the alcoholic ruddiness of his skin. He wore a clean white shirt, khaki pants, and flimsy bedroom slippers.

He backed away tapping his cane. He would no longer allow me in his bedroom but had ordered Aunt Lettie to set up a card table in the hallway, where he did his eating, the table placed under a light fixture converted from gas, the ruby-red shade etched with entwined roses. On the table were a steel fork, knife, and spoon, GI issue, meant to be used with a mess kit in the field but kept by my father to remind himself of his hardship and sacrifice during war.

"When you're running late, you ought to telephone so I can prepare my stomach," he said. He now limped at attention, on parade, as if hearing the "Stars and Stripes Forever" instead of what played on his phonograph, which was Glenn Miller's "When Johnny Comes Marching Home."

"My apologies to your stomach, and I trust the commander had a pleasant day," I said. He didn't like that. Tapping of his cane against the floor changed to rattlesnake speed. He'd been only a sergeant.

"Oh, you think you're a cutie," he said. "What do you know? What does anyone who hasn't faced it know?"

I went downstairs to my bedroom, the master bedroom on the first floor, where I stripped off my tie and sweaty shirt. After washing up and dabbing myself with kerosene, I reached for the June copy of *Sail*. I walked to the pantry and knelt to the cabinet under the counter to set aside jars of snaps, greens, and okra which hid my brown bottle.

I carried the bottle to the kitchen window and held it to the light to check its level against the crease I'd made that morning with my thumbnail at the edge of the sunburst label. No liquor filched. I poured a two-finger measure into a highball glass at the sink. After what I'd gone through on the riverbank that day, I felt justified in quick and thorough fortification.

I gagged, spat into the sink, and stood bucking. I rushed to the foot of the steps, where I shouted at my father.

"It's for your good," he called back.

"I don't need you to do-good me! You again put vinegar in my bottle and I'll burn down the house while you're sleeping!"

"You need something. Think of your liver all swollen and diseased, like what comes out a hog. God, I'd hate to see it all blue-black and pussy. Turn a man to stone."

"What about your liver?"

"It's too late for me, but I can't help trying to do right for you, though it's probably no use the way you're going. You're already ruint. The hope of the family!"

"If you can sneak downstairs to poison my liquor, you can get your own food from now on."

"For your own good I endured the suffering and pain, to try to help you. Last night I dreamed about what an awful thing your liver looks like. Your mother would've wanted me to try."

It was no use, we went around in circles, his circles, with me just running slam bang into myself. The truth was we both drank too much, way too much, only we kept it to floors, split-level boozing so to speak, his up, mine down. Eddie Blue was his source of supply, coming once or twice a week with bottles from the state ABC store and delivering them when I wasn't home.

I left the house, walked down the back steps, and unlocked the trunk of my Chevy. Inside was an unopened half gallon of J. W. Dant sour mash, which I carried to the kitchen. I dropped four large cubes of ice into a tall insulated glass, poured four ounces of whisky over the ice—Lord, that lovely first gurgle from a new bottle—and topped it with a shot of water from the tap, well water cold and without chemical additives to envenom the taste.

Just as I raised my glass, the phone rang. We had two phones in the house, one upstairs in my father's bedroom, the other on a table in the downstairs hall. I waited to hear whether or not he would answer it, and when he didn't, I stomped through the hall, yet hesitated before lifting the receiver. After the day's events at the river, telephone could mean only mess.

"What about Vin Farr?" Burley Speas asked, Burley the owner of the twice-weekly Bannister *Bee & Messenger*. Bannister was in the next county. Tobaccoton had no paper. "It is Vin, isn't it, down at the funeral home?"

"Do me a favor, Burley, don't ask till tomorrow. Tomorrow I think I can help you out."

"But, hell, you can tell whether it's Vin or not. There's no reason you can't tell me that, is there?"

"You see, Burley, we don't know much yet, but we're going to hold meetings tomorrow, after which I'll be right on the phone to you. That's a promise."

When I got shut of Burley, I left the phone off the hook because in another few minutes everybody in Howell County would be ringing my bell. News spreading was like a blister rising. Vin had been prominent, known to many business associates, and had served a term in the legislature. His was the death of a prince.

I carried my drink and the copy of *Sail* to the grape arbor, where trellises were shaky under the weight of unpruned vines. The place was quiet and cool, the evening air moving up over fields from the river, causing the broomstraw and locust leaves to murmur.

I sat looking in the river's direction, my seat a tubular aluminum chair bought at Howell County Mercantile and bound by multicolored plastic strips. The Wye, more than a mile distant, couldn't be seen. I ordered my mind to keep Vin Farr on the slab at the funeral home. Plenty of time to wrestle Vin's ghost.

I swallowed a first sip of the drink, allowing the sour mash to slide slowly over my tongue and seep down my throat. The beast quieted, knowing its thirst would be slaked. Yellowness had bled from the late-afternoon sunlight. Insects droned around blooms, and mockingbirds spun dazzling intricate tunes as I opened *Sail* across my lap and coveted a Swan 42, a Finnish sloop that had a 23-foot beam, an 8-foot draft, a displacement of 22,000 pounds, all powered by a 40-h.p. Perkins diesel. The question was, Could I, who'd never been in a sailboat, single-hand one? Did I possess the courage to tread the sea?

For the moment I would skip courage and pretend to cast off from Yorktown, run between Cape Henry and Cape Charles, and set a compass course for the Bahamas, for the blue water and sand beaches the color of purity itself, a whiteness that stunned. I'd allow the vane to steer while I stood forward watching dolphins play in the bow's turquoise wash and flying fish arc, iridescent, before the chrome pulpit.

As long as I dreamed, I might as well supply a woman, a young girl deeply tanned, like new copper and maybe slightly oiled, wearing a two-piece white bathing suit that nipped her satiny skin. On my teak deck she lay with a knee pulled up, an arm under her head, a hand on her rippling stomach, her face turned to the side, her lavender eyes looking out toward island palms. Her blond hair would be unbound and spread about her, the strands thickened by salt water. She'd have salt of the sea all over her.

"You better eat!" my father hollered, he a silhouette in his upstairs bedroom window. "Think of your rotten liver!"

In my chair I felt the surge of sea, heard wind among shrouds and the lapping of waves against the hull. Several times I returned to the kitchen and held my eyes half closed to maintain the vision, to suspend and restart it while I opened the refrigerator for ice or poured from the brown bottle. I really sensed the earth rising and falling among long ground swells. I made a slight adjustment to my course, somewhat south of east.

The feeling was so realistic that later in darkness when I tipped slowly from my chair and sprawled face downward against the dry grass, I heard the eternal running swish of the sea passing my ears.

3

Master: Do you understand now?

Me: It's the word "reasonable" that confounds me. To be truthful, a lot seems unreasonable.

Master: You're not trying.

Me: I am, but I can't seem to grasp it, just as some people can't do math. I'm sorry, I want to answer right, but for me God is like algebra or long division.

Master: You're not giving your best. We'll go through it again. What is sin?

———

I slept poorly and woke dreading the day. My skin was hot and sticky. The first thing was to have a bath. There were no showers in the house, their absence further evidence of hope deferred.

For breakfast I drank orange juice over ice cubes and ate a cold biscuit spread with grape jelly. My father wasn't yet moving. Aunt Lettie arrived to clean and cook, but she'd again leave early to continue her churching, this the one time of year when blacks returned from their northern diaspora in their finest clothes and vehicles, the latter polished to outshine Heaven's glories.

She was piqued because of my fussing at Eddie Blue about the lawn mower. She passed in the kitchen as if she didn't see me. She prepared my father's breakfast, carried it up to him, and I heard them talking as I attempted to steady my mind on the approaching unpleasantness involving Vin Farr. I wanted to skip this day, wind time ahead a couple of weeks so that everything would again be easy.

"What's church got to do with it?" my father asked, baiting her. "You all could hold your meetings anywhere—a barn, the fairgrounds, the stockyard. The meetings are socials."

"The Lord Jesus calls us into His presence to bless us and fill us for another year. He pour love into us like milk into a jug."

"Tell me this, how can He be in all those churches at the same time? Does He split Himself up and stick a toe, say, in the Methodist church, a leg in the Baptist, a hand or elbow in The Healing Springs African Pentecostal? How does He have enough of Hisself to go around?"

"God can't be put no end to," Aunt Lettie said.

When she came downstairs, I had on my tinted glasses and was counting money in my wallet to make certain of enough for lunch. Again Aunt Lettie passed without seeing me, her chin up, her mouth pouted. She was a small woman, very nearly a dwarf, yet she never in her life had any idea of smallness about herself. She walked the earth as if it were her private patch. She wore wire-rim glasses too large for her fierce triangular face. Her skin was dark loam. Her dresses were hand-me-downs from people she worked for—cut, hemmed, and altered countless times, yet some retaining a surprising smartness. Even at the stove or sink, she wore hats, this morning a yellow straw platter with artificial flowers on top. Her cow had bitten off most of the blooms.

"I'm writing you a check," I told her.

"I could make twice as much in the shoe factory," she said. She stood on a three-legged wooden milking stool to reach the faucets. Her hands sopped dishes in suds.

"You'd spend most of the increase getting to Bannister and back," I said. "Besides, starting right now I'm raising you ten cents an hour."

"Whoopee, I'll buy me a Cadillac car and a swimming pool. I going to order a Paris gown."

"You hear anything in town?"

"Don't have to go to town to know big's lying on a hard bed at the funeral parlor," she said, stepping down from her stool as she toweled a plate.

"How'd you find out who?"

"Whos is for owls," she said and dragged her stool to the stove, where she turned her back to me. That was all she was going to say. I signed her check and left it on the table. They could put the phone back on the hook.

I walked down the back steps to the garage. During the night the earth had cooled, though new heat was already building. I drove out the lane and toward town. Men, women, and children stooped in fields to work rows of coarse luxuriating tobacco. Harnessed mules plodded.

Ahead was Tobaccoton's skyline, church spires like ship masts against a pinkish-blue horizon, though the town was 200 miles west of the ocean. We had no factories in Howell County, only the rolling mill and two brick warehouses; yet a community of less than 3,000 people supported 23 churches, one for every 130.4 human beings. The only things lacking churches in our town were dogs, cats, and waddling pigeons around the courthouse and on the roof of the mill. Two men could stop to light a cigarette or spit and a church would spring up.

I parked in my space behind the jail, put on dark glasses, and slipped through the side entrance to the courthouse. I was relieved no reporters were about. I climbed to my office, where Florene worked at her desk, puzzling over a warrant and scratching the crown of her head with the sharpened point of her yellow pencil.

"You sure ran out on us yesterday," she said. "The sheriff's coming with Doc Robinette."

The doctor was an old man, his hands palsied, his vision blurred, who kept bits and pieces of a general practice going among the aged. He'd been on the payroll so long as county medical examiner it never occurred to anybody he could've been replaced by a younger, more capable physician. His was the tenure of always being around.

I stood at my window smoking and looking out at the street, the one-block row of stores and shops, most late nineteenth-century buildings whose façades had been modernized. Men using ladders belonging to the volunteer fire department were stringing a

WELCOME HOME BUSTER streamer between power poles. People stalled on sidewalks to shake hands, chat, and glance toward the courthouse. They had to be talking about Vin.

Vin had indeed been important to the county, the owner of a number of businesses, including a sawmill, a pallet factory, and a charcoal plant. He owned shares of the New Tobaccoton Bank. He'd been a speculator shrewd enough to buy parcels in the southwestern section of the county before the Corps of Engineers proposed a flood-control dam and paid high dollar for land condemned and immersed.

I'd known him since I was a boy. He'd once roughed me up on the playground behind the elementary school while we were having team footraces. Toward the finish line he jerked on my shirt to hold me back and pass. Words were traded between us. I ended up stumbling home holding a bleeding nose and attempting not to cry.

In years since, he'd whipped most people, not on a playground or by use of his physical superiority, but in the arena of business and money. I hated him. He always called me Tone, from Tu-tone, caused by the fact one of my eyes, the left, was pale green and the other aqua, that is, sliding off green to bluishness. He'd been the first to use the nickname on me, and it was picked up by most everybody, including girls and even some of the teachers at Howell County Consolidated High School. Way back then I'd begun to wear dark glasses.

Vin was a man blessed, elected to health, intelligence, and beauty, predestined to pick the golden apples of this earth. No sweaty footballer, but a pole vaulter, holder of a state record—his soaring body arched and rigid in grace so emotional that even I who despised him felt pierced and as if he had somehow used me sexually, violated my manhood. When we met on the street, my genes deferred to his.

During the Vietnam madness, which I avoided by my year in the seminary and then law school, Vin was a fighter pilot. No stinking Nam mud for him, no dysentery or blood-sucking leeches, but flight boots, shimmering pinks, and a dashing leather jacket, his jet cockpit smelling of Lifebuoy and Aqua Velva at Mach 1.

I heard Florene in the outer office talking to Sheriff Pickney and Doc Robinette. The doctor, listing because of his medical bag, shambled in and bumped my bookcase. He seemed to bounce from it to desk to chair. Had he wiped his glasses, he would've discovered a new day.

The sheriff closed the door, and I got Doc turned right and seated. Pickney's uniform shirt collar was open, and he sat, positioned the yellow legal tablet on a rolling thigh, and lifted an ankle to rub it. He wore white socks which had a rayon sheen, the whiteness startling against the sallow hue of his soft flesh.

"I told Rhea," Pickney said. "Drove out yesterday afternoon, and I'd appreciate it if you didn't put a job like that on me again. She was dressed for a party. She thought Vin was coming home to take her to a party."

"Poor suffering woman," Doc said, his voice wavering.

"Poor in some respects, though not bank accounts if what I hear is correct," the sheriff said. Sweat had formed on his temples and above his loose mouth. "She staggered when I told her. I took off my hat and spoke as kindly as I could, but I had to tell her straight out. I don't know no other way. It was like wind blew her."

I thought of Rhea dressed for cocktails, at first hearing and not believing, not able to set the words in her understanding. I should've gone out there. It was more my job. She wasn't one of Pickney's people. She wasn't one of mine either, though as a boy I'd hidden in the pine woods to watch her ride her horse.

"What you have for us?" I asked Doc.

He scratched a cheek, his fingernails long and curved, the sound like sandpaper. He hadn't shaved. He sometimes forgot to shave as he forgot which of his patients he'd visited, going twice to a person the same day and writing them a second prescription for the same medicine. Doc licked his lips, but his trembling tongue didn't wet them. The bottom lip had a vein in it, a tiny forked streak very blue.

"I have been unable to locate any immediate cause," he said as his head bobbed. "No wound, snakebite, anything of an outward physical nature."

"Heart attack?" I asked.

"There's no way I can make that determination by listening to a heart that's no longer beating."

"Care to make a guess?" Pickney asked.

"No, I would not."

"Insects, spiders?" Pickney asked. The index finger of his right hand was creeping up his chest. He'd been well named, for that finger itched to go to ground in his nose.

"No indication of irritation, swelling, or distension," Doc said.

"How long had he been dead?" I asked.

"Fourteen hours give or take a couple by the time I got to him. He died late the Sunday night of June twenty-ninth or early Monday morning, June thirtieth."

"What else?" I asked.

"Nothing else," Doc said, his palsied hands fluttering around his medical bag.

"You?" I asked, turning to Pickney, whose finger had found the nose and squirmed into it.

"I'm trying to figure how he got to the other side of the river," the sheriff said. "Had to be by boat or else he swam, but if he swam his clothes would've been wet, which they weren't. They might've dried on top but not underneath."

"Could he have gone fishing?" I asked. Vin had been a sportsman, particularly a hunter, merciless with a rifle, which became an extension of himself like a finger of death reaching out.

"Not the way he was dressed, and there wasn't no fishing gear, no boat even." Pickney paused. "Course it might've floated off, and we're looking downstream."

The sheriff withdrew the finger from his nose and sighed as if he'd just risen from heavy labor. When his holstered pistol clunked against the chair, he reached to the heavy blue-steel revolver and touched it as a man might quiet an unsettled dog.

"Anything else?" I asked.

"Grass on the bank's been crushed down, but Vin could've done that hisself," the sheriff said. "Grass rises too."

"The Hensley boys add anything?"

"They didn't go ashore till with us. I'll talk to them some more when they not so shook. Nothing to dust for prints. Can't lift prints off stones."

"Wallet?" I asked and thought I should've checked that yesterday on the riverbank. An alert Commonwealth's Attorney would have. A friendly sheriff would've seen to it he did.

"Gone," he said. "All pockets empty."

"Well, hell, Burton, you getting around to tell me he was robbed?"

"Don't have to be robbery. Vin was a man who didn't need to carry money. He was walking credit. And empty pockets don't explain how he died. If it did, I'd be dead too."

"Okay, let's put robbery aside a moment and see if we can piece together a likely explanation. It's a hot day, Vin goes out in a boat to cool off, maybe take a dip. He feels pain, rows to the bank, and suffers a stroke."

"No evidence of stroke," Doc said, ashes from his dangling cigarette falling onto his dark crumpled tie. The tie had become mottled gray from smeared ashes. He looked about to go to sleep.

"Hair wasn't messed," Pickney said. "And he was smiling."

"The smile could be a muscular reflex, couldn't it?" I asked Doc.

"A smile can be anything," Doc said.

We sat feeling the heat push in off the street and hearing the blasting diesel exhaust of an eighteen-wheeler hauling pulpwood through town. I realized I should be doing more, yet couldn't seem to get my mind focused. I felt removed, out of it.

"Allergy?" I asked. "Something he ate or touched?"

That was so stupid they didn't bother answering. I pursed my lips and attempted to appear thoughtful. I fingered my dark glasses. I wished I were still in bed.

"Another thing, down at the funeral home they want to know when they can put Vin in the ground," the sheriff said.

"Not when we don't know how he died," I said. "You don't even have enough for a death certificate, do you, Doc?"

"No way around an autopsy, which I can't perform," Doc said. "We'll have to send Vin to the Capitol District medical examiner in Richmond."

"Oh, my Aunt Minnie's fanny, ain't there no other move we can make than to get mixed with those bastards in Richmond who'll treat us like we're cross-eyed two-headed morons?" Pickney asked.

"You're talking about the state crime lab?" I asked.

"They think they invented brains," Pickney said. "Going to save the bacon of us poor-ass country boys. Get more publicity than a movie star with three tits. What they don't give out is how much they fail to finish, the cases they file as pending."

"Hold it a second, are we talking about a crime?" I asked.

"I'm saying once it gets to Richmond those piss-peckers down there will nose in on it. They'll want to grab any credit lying around so they can holler for a bigger appropriation from the legislature."

"But are we even suggesting this is a crime?" I asked.

"Got to consider it when you find a body you don't know what's happened to in peculiar if not suspicious circumstances. Let me ask you a question. When's the last time anybody saw Vin Farr on the river instead of chasing a dollar?"

"An impulse," I said. "This heat anybody could be out on the river."

"I'm making no judgments," Pickney said. "Just trying to line things up."

"I'm with you about keeping everything here in Howell County if possible," I said.

"Vin's body has to go to Richmond," Doc said.

"But not right this minute," I said. "Burton, maybe you could drive back to the river and take another look."

"I been twice and plan to go again," Pickney said. "Might have been somebody there besides Vin. Lots of wild grass crushed down. Some of it right beside the body."

"You're suggesting?" I asked.

"Kind of a depression beside the body," Pickney said.

"Let me see if I understand what you're giving us," I said. "You think it's likely somebody was lying on the ground with him."

"I can't go as far as likely. Maybe Vin was rolling around doing something."

"Screwing?" Doc Robinette asked, and his using the word shocked Pickney and me. Doc usually spoke in either mannered or medical language, and for him to say "screwing" was comparable to hearing a lady break wind.

"At least a possibility," Pickney said. "We talked about his expression. Agreed, that smile could have been caused by muscular contraction. But he sure looked like a satisfied man to me."

"The crime lab can tell whether or not he had been copulating," said Doc. "Semen is easy."

"But I hate them getting into it," Pickney said. "They think we so dumb. They think we don't got brains enough to find our way around turds."

"Tell the funeral home to hold the body," I said. "They can refrigerate it, can't they?"

"Sure, Tom Berry even stores deer meat in that cooler," Pickney said. "Damn if I could eat it knowing what it'd kept company with. You?"

Tom Berry was part owner of the funeral home, and I had no idea the sheriff possessed such sensitivity. I considered his question rhetorical.

4

We have finished a theological discussion. The master has asked how I can look at the sun, the moon, and the stars and not believe the world has been created to a purpose, that is, that the world and man are not linked in a reasonable design.

I pretend to ponder but do not answer. To me there is nothing reasonable about the sun, moon, and stars. Only a mad inventor could have conceived and flung them up there, down there, or however He flung them. But I do not tell the master.

The master leaves me well fed, cleansed, and morally instructed. I am again on my cot facing the ceiling and pine beams. I think of escape. How long have I been here? I am uncertain of the first days. I wish I had used my thumbnail on the leg of the cot to mark each sunrise, faintly of course to prevent the observant eye of the master from noticing.

I expect somebody to appear, a search party, a coon hunter, boys roving through the woods and swamp, but only the master has come. Surely I am still in Howell County, yet I don't know that absolutely. It feels like Howell County. The trees, the undergrowth, the odors are familiar. The sun has the same unforgiving heat, and mosquitoes sing the same tune.

The mosquitoes rise at dusk, the scummy mill pond the perfect nursery. The master has thought of me and brought two aerosol cans of Bug Shot, and during the night I lie spraying my face, neck, and arms. I rub the spray over my shins, causing the chain to clank. I hear the disappointment of the mosquitoes—their first enthusiasm, their veering off, their complaint. What, after all, is a body for if not blood and feast?

I will ask the master to bring me netting. Then if the master will loosen an end of my chain I'll collect three limber swamp saplings, bend and bind them to the cot with twine, and thus have a frame for the netting. No longer will I lie coated with the sweet stink of the spray, its sticky glaze, which I have come to hate. I taste it each time I swallow and am tempted to allow the mosquitoes to party on me, let them fill and stagger away bloated.

I have tried shouting. I stood and screamed till the effort tore my throat. Once I heard an answer and hollered, "Yes! Here! Help!" but realized the answer was only echo, my own voice bouncing back from the cabin's shell. I shook my chain and kicked over the cot, though I straightened things before the master returned. I have learned the master insists on neatness.

I tug at the chain. The millstone pulls back with the unyielding weight of the immovable. I check the locks, the first fastening the chain to my ankle, the second that connects a loop of the chain to the millstone. The locks possess the impervious superiority of steel.

I search for an instrument to pry with, a nail to scratch, a tool to bang, but the master has thought ahead of me. In the end I shout and rage as if anger can free me. Then I again collapse on the cot, gasping, cursing, weeping. When mosquitoes come, I reach for the aerosol can of Bug Shot to spray myself, laying the sweet puke on me like shellac.

———

I rose in court to argue the Commonwealth's case against a thirty-two-year-old woman who had beaten her husband so badly he needed to be carried to the Bannister hospital. She wasn't a large woman, hardly an inch over five feet, and appeared fussy, even prudish, the kind who would send back a salad if the lettuce wasn't fresh.

"He was pig drunk!" she said when I questioned her. She sat

in the witness stand to the left of the judge's glossy bench, Judge
Gareet, who tapped his walnut gavel against the soft palm of his
pudgy hand and was reared back in his great chair to gaze benignly
at the lighted but ineffective brass colonial chandelier. Because
shades of the high windows were kept drawn, it was always dusk
in the courtroom.

"Is that when you hit him?" I asked.

"Falling down pig drunk!" she said, a brunette, her stiff hair
pressed to her skull as if vulcanized. "He turned over my kitchen
table, broke jars of my watermelon pickle, kicked a big hole in the
screen door. He'd spilled the soup. I work, I—"

"Ma'am, please answer the question."

"I work hard over at the shoe factory, ten hours a day counting
travel time, and what do I ask except he keeps the weeds out of
my garden and milk the cow, and I come home worn to bone to
find him alaying on the floor laughing like a crazy idiot, alaying
right on my kitchen floor with a bottle set on top his chest, laughing
and kicking like he was dancing on his back."

"You're volunteering more information than I'm inquiring
about," I said, seeing the smile of portly John Price, her lawyer,
one of Tobaccoton's three attorneys, the smiles too of spectators in
the shadowy courtroom, which smelled of pork barbecue because
the big shaded windows were open and receiving exhaust fumes
from the fan of the Southside Cafe next door.

"My house looked like wild Indians had run through it!" the
woman said. "And him laughing on my kitchen floor like an idiot
moron. That man's lucky I didn't kill him!"

To speak the last, she leaned toward her husband, who sat at
the state's table, a pleasant clumsy fellow who would've made two
of her. He wore the one suit he owned, a dark go-to-meeting outfit
of coarse wool put on summer or winter. His round, shiny face was
still bruised and swollen. He looked fearful she might get at him
again.

"Is that when you struck him?" I asked.

"Killed him is what I should've done the way he tore up my
house. He hadn't milked neither!"

More smiles in the courtroom, particularly among the deputies,
the town police, the bailiff—all beefy country boys in uniform who
were the main audience and always appreciative of a good line,

ready to nod, wink, or slip out into the corridor to laugh and slap a shoulder.

"You struck him while he was helpless on the floor?" I asked, adjusting my tinted glasses.

"I stood him up out of his mess, stripped off his filthy clothes, and hosed him down in the yard before I took him to the bed. I laid him on that bed, and when he was snoring, I pulled the sheet around him and tied the corners. Then I poured it on him."

"What'd you strike him with?"

"My fry pan. I two-handed him with my fry pan."

Laughter in the courtroom, but Judge Gareet did not discipline anybody. He smiled to himself and tapped the gavel against his palm. Deputies grinned and shook their heads. They were gleeful at the picture of her shaggy, good-natured husband who just liked a swallow of shine now and again—how he must've come up out of that drunken sleep unable to free, much less defend, himself because of the sheet as the little woman whacked away at him with a fry pan big as a banjo.

"How many times did you strike him?" I asked.

"Till my arms wore out, and I wish I could've done it some more. He pulled down the living-room curtains and burnt a hole in the sofa not even paid for yet. I mean I could've killed him dead!"

The husband cowered at the state's table, a man trying to escape into himself, as if his battered body were a hole and he wished to crawl down into it and bury himself. Deputies, bailiff, and the town police grinned as did the shuffling old men who had come in off the street to flee the sun and see the show.

"You're admitting you almost crippled him with that fry pan?" I asked.

"You can't hurt a mule! You ever heard of a mule being hurt by being hit? And he's king of the jackasses!"

Laughter cut loose all over the courtroom, people not bothering to walk into the corridor or cover their mouths. Delighted Judge Gareet sat forward with a guffaw. I might have laughed myself except I was thinking of Vin's body being on its way to Richmond and the Capitol District medical examiner as well as the fact many days had passed since I won even an insignificant case for the Commonwealth.

The judge tapped the gavel once, and the courtroom quieted. He was pink as shrimp, jovial now, and his stomach growled for lunch. He would never bring in a judgment against this pious, upright, hardworking little lady who knew when and what-for to give a drunk-as-a-pig husband that'd wrecked her neat house.

"What I think is you got off lucky," the judge said to the husband, who by now would've hidden under the state's table if allowed. "Burning holes in sofas and tearing down curtains. Worst of all, breaking those jars of watermelon pickles when everybody knows your wife won a prize for them at the Five-County Fair. Why, I ought to send you to jail for that alone, but I'm going to go easy. Just don't let me hear of you not milking the cow or keeping the garden free of weeds. Above all, you suck up no more happy juice. You do and you going to be having a thirty-day party out chopping brush with the road gang." Judge Gareet rapped his gavel. "Case dismissed. This court's adjourned for food."

I gathered my papers to leave. The husband had already fled. His wife walked out, her posture stiffened by righteousness and justice done. John Price crossed the aisle to shake my hand.

"Maybe you should have introduced the fry pan as evidence," he said, laughing. "Clean the hog fat out first. Don't get discouraged, Billy. One of these days you going to win a big one."

"What I should've done is stayed home," I said.

"Just hang in, son, you going to do it. But listen here, what can you tell me about Vin Farr? Rumors been whistling around the county like bullets."

I admitted only that Vin was dead and his body had been transported to Richmond and the basement office of the medical examiner. I'd called and attempted to persuade the examiner to drive to Tobaccoton, but he, a Dr. Clayborne Gaw, said he needed his assistant and lab equipment to make a determination as to the cause of death in an unviolated corpse. That's what Vin had become, an unviolated corpse.

I walked from the courtroom to my office, where Florene appeared both harried and peeved.

"The phone's been ringing off the desk," she said. "Am I supposed to make up a tale or what?"

"Never tell a lie," I said and closed the door on her fuming. I opened it again. "No calls."

Before I got seated, there was a knock, and in came Burley Speas. He was slim and bony, the flesh run off from hustling to keep his little newspaper going against the pressure of Danville and Lynchburg competition lapping at his door. He could be sitting still and appear on the move, his corpuscles racing around inside.

"You're supposed to call me," he said, speaking even before he was within talking distance.

"Sit, Burley."

"Oh, I'd like to sit and wiggle my toes except I have a paper to put out, and it's already got enough typos to cross-eye you. If I allowed myself to slow, I might figure what a fool I am trying to make a living bringing print to this Baptist backwater. I'd see the smartest thing I can do is light a match to my plant for the insurance. Now don't try to slip me aside. The Richmond papers been calling and treating me as if I work for them. They never in their life shared anything with me, but they want to know what I got. What I got is bills and flatfeet. They asking me, mind you, whether they should send reporters. Me they ask!"

"Burley, we don't need reporters or anything else from Richmond."

"Why do we not?"

"Because we've not determined yet what happened," I said, sitting back as he roamed in front of my desk and pulled at slips of paper in various pockets.

"You don't know how he died?"

"Correct."

"Just give me everything you got," he said. He held a pencil and a pad jerked from the pocket of his white shirt. He wore no jacket, and his ratty brown tie looked as if it'd been dragged through printer's ink.

"The facts are few and simple. Vin died sometime night before last. We not only don't know how or why, we can't even conclude the reason or means of his being where he was. His body is now in Richmond, where it is undergoing a medical examination by state authorities."

"That's all?"

"For the moment. I realize you have a duty to inform the public, but as a favor and courtesy to me, don't hurry things. Allow us to do the best we can here in Howell County. If and when we find answers, we'll give you an exclusive you can trade to the city newspapers."

"I can't hold back long. Rumor is his death wasn't natural."

"Now wait a minute, nobody has a right to say that."

"You've decided he died of natural causes?"

"That's the point, I, we, the sheriff's department, we haven't decided anything because we're still investigating. In time the facts will be uncovered and revealed."

"But there's a possibility of homicide?"

"I can't say yes or no since we haven't made a determination, but I can tell you I don't want to be tripping over Richmond reporters every time I come into the courthouse, and I think you should show some consideration for the family."

"For Rhea, you mean," Burley said and stopped roving to eye me.

I reached to my tinted glasses. Burley and I'd known each other as boys, and he'd observed my feelings about Rhea. I didn't get the shakes any longer at mention of her name. I'd learned to control my demeanor through the practice of law. I was able to stand expressionless before a jury or the stern redress of a judge. Still Rhea's name could cause a surge of blood.

"For Rhea and anybody else who can be hurt," I said.

"Okay, Billy, I'm for Rhea, Tobaccoton, and the county too." He slid his pad into his shirt pocket and reached to the door, yet hesitated. The tone of his voice changed. "Hear you lost one today."

"Another one you mean."

"You haven't had much to display your legal talents on."

"You worried about me, Burley?"

"Maybe. You got to be aware the sheriff's laying down shoe leather in behalf of his nephew. In no time that boy will be out of school and practicing law. It's eighteen months till elections and that may seem far off, but it's not. All the while the Pickney clan will be multiplying like mice in a grain bin."

"You're telling me I should do good on this thing with Vin."

"That's it. Do it right, you'll look like a hotshot, especially with stories and pictures in the state newspapers."

"I'm trying to do it right."

"Just reviewing the bidding. I won't bother with goodbyes."

I stood at my window and watched Burley rush out the front of the courthouse to his car. Virgil, a town policeman, was about to ticket Burley's Ford, but when he saw whose car it was, he smiled, slapped shut his book, and reached for Burley's hasty hand.

Florene tapped on the door and stuck her head in. Her face was agitated.

"Your father," she said. "You told me not to lie."

I sat in my chair and faced the wall before I lifted the phone.

"I heard," he said. "You lost another one. You're making a great reputation for yourself."

"I appreciate your interest," I said and wondered how he'd learned so quickly about the morning's courtroom debacle. Aunt Lettie must've told him. Aunt Lettie knew everything.

"The hope of the family," my father said. "That's what we all thought you were. A man with the highest SAT scores of any graduate from the Howell County school system. Now six in a row. I just pray your mother can't see it."

"Call me anytime and thanks again," I said and hung up.

The rest of the afternoon was no better. There were ringing phones and people jammed at the door. I sneaked out the back first chance I got, leaving furious Florene to fight off the Indians.

When I reached home, I found Eddie Blue had again been at the lawn mower. Parts lay on a stone border around a neglected flower bed. Cursing, I tried to reassemble the mower myself but couldn't. I had no ability for things mechanical. In that respect Eddie Blue and I were alike.

From the garage I fetched a cardboard box that had held cans of oil, laid the parts inside, and set the box in the trunk of my car. Tomorrow I would take the box and gutted mower to Pugh's Garage and have the engine resurrected. Aunt Lettie or no Aunt Lettie, Eddie Blue was finished around the place.

In the kitchen I scrubbed grease from my hands, fixed a drink, and thought of myself on a boat far away, a place like Tahiti, so distant that trouble could not reach it, where blue water slid over immaculate sand, breadfruit dropped into my lap, and languid dusky girls used palm fronds to fan flies off me.

Such a vision was childishly stupid. Likely I was going to need a job after the next election. I might try for a government position. As I walked out into the evening light, which had the quality of molten iron, I heard my father's phonograph playing Artie Shaw's "Indian Love Call" and assured myself that the government could always use another lawyer. I carried on a little internal dialogue.

"What branch of government should I work for?" I asked myself.

"The Department of Interior," I answered. "I can sue crippled Indians for the United States."

"The United States doesn't sue crippled Indians," I said.

"That's the job for me."

5

Master: What is God?

Me: God is a Spirit, in and of Himself infinite in being, glory, blessedness, and perfection; all-sufficient, eternal, unchangeable, incomprehensible, everywhere present, mighty, knowing all things, most wise, most holy, most just, most merciful and gracious, long suffering and abundant in goodness and truth.

Master: Almighty.

Me: Almighty?

Master: Not merely mighty but almighty.

Me: Right. I can see there's quite a difference between mighty and almighty.

Master: Satan is mighty. God is almighty.

Me: I don't know what I was thinking.

Master: Further questions?

Me: Incomprehensible. If God is incomprehensible, how can we know Him?

Master: You're being serious?

Me: I am, absolutely.

Master: We can know aspects of God, experience them, but that knowing and experience are like tiny drops in an ocean. God is too immense to comprehend. We see through a glass darkly.

Me: Thanks for clearing that up.

Master: Does anything else bother you?

Me: Not about the lesson, but I wonder if anybody's looking for me.

Master: They are.

Me: Glad to know I'm missed.

Master: You must give up hope of being found. There's only one trail through the low grounds, it's difficult to follow. Most of the way is swamp or land flooded by beavers. You're not too uncomfortable, are you? You have the mosquito netting.

Me: But I can't help wondering how long you're going to keep me here.

Master: That hasn't been decided. Let's get back to the lesson. What are the decrees of God?

Me: God's decrees are the wise, free, and holy acts of the counsel of His will, whereby, from all eternity, He hath, for His own glory, unchangeably foreordained whatsoever comes to pass in time, especially concerning angels and men.

Master: I am impressed.

———

This morning notices about Vin were in both the Lynchburg and Richmond papers. The obituaries listed his clubs, accomplishments, honors. No reason was given for his death.

At the office I prepared bills of indictment for the summer term of the Howell County Grand Jury. There wasn't much—the theft of a John Deere bailer, a destruction-of-property charge against a drunk farmer who'd driven his pickup through a cemetery wall and knocked over tombstones, and an assault complaint brought on behalf of a black woman whose redbone hound had been shot by a neighbor.

I heard marching music and looked out the window. Drums thumped, horns blared, clarinets shrilled. The high school band flashed into view under the banner honoring Buster Bovin's return from Africa. The high-stepping white boots of the majorettes arced, silver batons spun upward, and tubas, great golden blooms, lurched side to side.

Buster himself followed seated in a convertible furnished by the Bannister Plymouth dealer. He still wore his sand-colored safari suit and dashing bush hat. He gestured to the crowd as if dispensing alms of salvation. I half expected native boys to tread behind carrying trophies he'd collected, not ivory or slain lions, but souls he'd saved, demons he'd laid low, each mounted to be hung on the wall of his church study. I could hear him: "Brought down that fine specimen in Capetown with the only word of God."

The parade over, people returned to stores, offices, the banks. I again studied the indictments I expected the Grand Jury to certify as true bills. I should win all three cases, but the drunk busting up the cemetery and the bailer theft were certainties. They would break my string of losses. Afterward I'd get out on the road more, shake voters' hands, sit on the stoops of swayback country stores, maybe dip a little snuff, discuss blue mold and the price of feed.

"How are you, sir?" I asked, attempting to sound hearty and sincere.

"What?" Florene asked. She opened the door to look in at me. "You did say something, didn't you?"

"I bumped my knee."

"I thought you spoke."

When she closed the door, I stopped rubbing my knee. I had to beware talking to myself. Florene was loyal, yet gossiped, especially with her old-maid sister, and first thing I knew town folk would be saying the Commonwealth's Attorney was not only failing to win his cases but also losing control, gibbering in his office, his brain disordered by liquor.

I leaned back in my chair, closed my eyes, and thought how the mighty had fallen. I'd returned to Howell County from Richmond, where I'd lived in an opulent section of the city. I'd been making payments on a Georgian house which had an attached two-car garage, a slate roof, and a backyard fishpond. Jeannie and I attended the Monument Avenue Presbyterian Church, belonged to the second best country club, and were patrons of the Virginia Museum. I had membership in the Bull & Bear.

I worked for a corporation newly listed on the American Stock Exchange, a manufacturer and exporter of textile machinery with sales exceeding $55 million a year and rising. My office was on the nineteenth floor of a bluish building that had shaded plazas, splashing fountains, and linden trees poking from terrazzo pavement. It wasn't a corner office, but my view looked west to the James River rippling like green champagne around ancient rounded white rocks.

I'd been hired as legal counsel, a golden boy they were bringing along on the fast track and considering for a management appointment, which would have provided me the key to the money machine, an even larger house, hunt-club membership, all those blessed apples of the earth right there before me to be picked up.

Only I was smashed by a vision. Just about everybody from Howell County had them at one time or another. Visions were our local malady. Mine struck on my big day as lead attorney in the corporation's case, my time to shine. I sat in the courtroom listening to the opening keen-witted remarks of a plaintiff's attorney, a man even younger than I, but a person of such natural grace and ability that my genes did obeisance. They became abashed before him as he moved in front of the jury, his demeanor that of royalty who could conceive only victory. Fair he was, his smile the lifting of a curtain and the revealing of rightful, innate superiority.

I'd worked hard to reach that courtroom, all those gray greasy days during school in Howell County, all those dateless dreary nights at the University of Richmond. Slaved I had, sweated, schemed. I'd used to the full the last iota of talent, mind, and invention granted me, and because of that concentration of small powers I was able to fool a lot of people, including myself.

Until that moment in the courtroom and the vision where I came face to face with true excellence as real and blinding as the sun's rising. Under that searing light I saw what lay ahead for me wasn't glory, understood I had no greatness within, that I was a mere grub disguised by the borrowed mantle of judicial majesty. I panicked in that august chamber and was whipped before opening my mouth.

I did open that mouth but not to form words. In terror of my vision I fled into disgraceful escape. My throat already choked, I clutched it and gasped. I staggered about in the best sophomoric dramatic tradition. Other lawyers gathered around to pat my back and support me. Realizing I was about to wet my pants and to avoid further shame, I collapsed on the floor in front of the judge's bench.

Bailiffs carried me out. For a time I was able to fool everybody, though the doctors probed, frowned, tapped, tested. They circled my hospital bed and held solemn discussions using Latinate discourse. My father, who then still believed in me, gripped my hand and tried to keep his fear from showing.

When I returned to the corporation, people were solicitous,

never pressing or asking how soon I'd be ready for the fight, the legal wars. They treated me as if I had broken bones. Patience was official. I played the part six weeks. Finally Mr. Sydnor called me into his corner office.

Mr. Dwight Sydnor was nearing sixty and had the most perfectly groomed hair I'd ever seen—like burnished silver of a helmet, each precise strand giving off a sheen as if exclusively stroked and fondled. He smoked a bulldog pipe, wore English tweeds, and nipped his words. Behind him a snow shower blew in over the frozen river.

"Billy, we can no longer delay those patent-infringement actions. Are you able to handle it or should I farm them out?"

"There's an alternative," I said. "We can settle."

Mr. Dwight Sydnor believed in economy of emotion. He lifted his chin, tightened his admirable teeth on the stem of his pipe, and allowed his left eyebrow to slide slowly upward, all simple gestures, yet he gave them such elegance I felt I'd been unclothed.

"That's not the way you saw it previously," he said. "Is it your opinion we mightn't prevail?"

"I've restudied our case. It's possible we have inadvertently crossed into the plaintiff's terrain on the multiform knitting machines. Certainly we are innocent of intent to violate, but the patents are complex, and it may take years to clear ourselves. On the other hand I think we could escape liability rather cheaply. I would estimate under $100,000."

"You regard $100,000 as being cheap? Billy, I'd be careful whom I mentioned that to around here."

I was looking past him to the river, where seagulls sailed updrafts into snow as if bathing in it. At that instant I wanted to be in a boat on an ocean, alone, warm, maybe even naked, feeling the eternal lift of the sea and a huge distance between me and where I sat.

"You see we have to worry about the bastards in the wings," Mr. Sydnor said. "If we compromise, they come at us in swarms. They take us to the bank and empty our vaults. As my granddaddy told me, you stomp a snake before its fangs grow long."

"I don't know what I was thinking," I said.

Though I did further research on the case, I never carried it to court. Suddenly I developed pains in my chest, and my throat would close until I wheezed. Mr. Sydnor, gentleman that he was, arranged a leave of absence from the corporation. I was covered by an employee hospitalization policy and lay in bed a month under observation. My wife, Jeannie, brought me all the boating magazines she could find.

The second time I returned to the corporation, I found I had little to do. My office was smaller, the legal work routine and not involving courtroom presence. Perhaps they expected me to show fire, but I kept the door shut and waited. Again Mr. Sydnor was patient. Not until early summer did we have another conference, this one at Richmond's privileged Commonweal Club, a watering place where I'd once hoped to win membership.

We drank at the side terrace of the converted Victorian mansion, our table among potted flowers and under a scalloped green canopy with the initials of the club on it in white English script.

"Billy, we have this feeling you're not really happy with us any longer," Mr. Sydnor said.

I sat stirring my scotch and praying I wouldn't become sick in public.

"You've had to notice we're moving up a man junior to you," Mr. Sydnor said.

I'd noticed, a youth named Gordon, a suave hotdog right out of the University of Virginia who possessed complete dedication to corporate monasticism. If he cut a vein, figures from the company's balance sheet would have flowed out, not blood.

"I thought my research was satisfactory," I said, too shaky to lift my drink.

"Your research is impeccable, but it's not exactly what we desire from you. Research is relatively easy for us to secure. What we need is a warrior, like Gordon, who's very ambitious and a hell of a fine attorney, a man who believes right always stands at his side."

"Who'll attempt to win at any cost."

"Billy, winning's the American way, and at this time in this company you can't want it too much. What is deduced in the executive suite is that the scent of the kill doesn't excite you."

"Does it you?"

"I'm almost out of the wars. I'll take my pension and move to Florida, where I'll fish, raise tomatoes, and have a fling or two on the market."

"Your advice?"

"Look for another situation. The company will be tolerant,

make you a nice severance, and allow you to use your office a number of days. I expect they'll even throw you a party."

"I think I'm dying," I said.

"The feeling will pass," Mr. Sydnor said. "Now have another drink."

I had many of those all right. Over the next six months I drank plenty more while Jeannie and I sold our house, gave up our memberships, and moved to Tobaccoton to live with my father.

I didn't face until later that the young lawyer, the golden one who triggered my vision of mediocrity, caused panic, and was responsible for my choking collapse on the courtroom floor, was outwardly, physically, a man very much like Vin Farr, though obviously I had recognized they were inward kin, the lawyer what Vin had been above all else, a winner.

The report arrived in a heavy brown envelope stamped with the state's insignia, the flap so well glued I had to cut it with a pair of desk scissors.

The Investigation by Medical Examiner came not in the mail but was delivered by the hand of a state police captain. Despite his blue-gray uniform, the creases of which appeared honed to sharpness, he seemed more of an executive than a law officer, a vice president or chief operative of an insurance or finance company. Compared to him, Sheriff Pickney was as loose and disorganized as a fat man walking on ice.

Blake was the captain's name, his uniform aglitter with the paraphernalia of power, though surely such an antiseptic man never used the whistle on a chain, the polished cartridges pushed into loops of his black belt, the chrome .38 revolver with its ebony grips. Then there were the bars of rank, the badge, the dark epaulets, and the soaped leather of his Sam Browne, which creaked like a well-preserved saddle.

His handshake was quick and abrupt. He did not enjoy touching others. He wore rimless glasses with pearl plastic earpieces. The lenses were as clear as gin. He sat before my desk while I scanned a typed onionskin copy of the medical examiner's report.

Heart: Weighs 290 gms. The left ventricle measures 1.2 cm in thickness and the right ventricle 0.4. The valves of both sides of the heart are unremarkable as is the myocardium. The coronary arteries show an occasional atherosclerotic plaque but not appreciable narrowing of lumena.

Okay, I thought, no heart attack. I went next to his lungs:

Weight 975 gms combined. No emphysema. Lymph nodes antharacotic. There is no bilateral congestion.

Okay, Vin didn't drown. I checked his skull:

No fractures. The sella turcica and air sinuses are unremarkable.

And his brain:

The brain weighs 1260 gms with small and glistening meningeal membranes. No lesions.

Okay, no stroke. From the report I picked out three interesting entries. The first:

G.I. Tract—Esophagus is unremarkable. Stomach contains 50 cc of partially digested food, identifiable as cracklings. Contents have the smell of alcohol. The ileum, jejunum, and large bowel are not remarkable. The appendix is present.

The second:

Blood Alcohol—0.18.

The third:

Genitalia—External genitalia normal circumcised male. The prostate, testicles, and seminal vesicles show no lesions. Recent discharge of semen.

Then one more thing:

Extremities—Small superficial excoriations on the dermis of the middle finger of the left hand and the first toe of the right foot.

I looked at the cause of death:

Pending.

I saw the autopsy had been authorized and performed by:

Dr. Clayborne V. Gaw, M.D., M.E.

When I finished reading, Captain Blake spoke rapidly and to the point.

"What appears to be a perfectly healthy man, no known history of disease or disability, no evidence of bodily disorders, no malfunction of heart, brain, or other major organs, such a man apparently simply stopped breathing."

"He'd been drinking," I said.

"He was drunk," the captain said. "The pathologist, and I add that the state's chief medical examiner performed the autopsy himself because of the station in life of the deceased, does not ascribe to alcohol the basis for life's cessation."

"What's this about the excoriations of the dermis of the middle finger of the left hand and the first toe of the right foot?"

"No conclusion drawn by the examiner."

"Cracklings?" I asked. "Vin Farr had been eating cracklings?"

"We too were surprised. We also found it remarkable that the deceased wore no underclothes. I assume that the wearing by men of underclothes is normal in Howell County, that is, that the lack of them is no local practice."

"We're pretty far out in the sticks, but most men around here have heard of underwear," I said. "It's even sold in our stores."

The captain merely blinked and dismissed my remark.

"Vincent Farr was a person of importance," he said. "The governor's office has taken an interest in his death. That's why I've been sent with the chief medical examiner's report in hand. My superiors would be gratified if you allowed us to assist you and your department in the investigation. Objections?"

"I wouldn't want to stand in the way of the governor's office," I said.

"Thank you for your cooperation," the captain said. "On the street behind this building I have waiting a unit of the state's mobile crime lab. Could we visit the locale where Mr. Farr's body was found?"

"You're assuming foul play?" I asked.

"It's my job to collect evidence, not assume."

"I'll phone the sheriff," I said.

I laid the medical examiner's report in my briefcase, which I carried down the stairs. The captain walked beside me, his step quick, a drill step, the fall of his polished black shoes rapping the corridor. He held a clipboard that, though ordinary, seemed military and part of his uniform.

Pickney waited outside his office, hands were shaken, and we went to the lot where a blue-gray van was parked. It too had the state seal. The van had recently been washed. Two uniformed troopers sat in the cab.

"We'll use my car," the captain said. It seemed an order.

I sat beside him in front, Pickney in the rear. The new Ford was also blue-gray, the siren-flasher reflecting sunlight from chrome onto the waxed hood. There were two radios, each switched on and humming, and under the instrument panel a pump-action twelve-gauge shotgun with a short barrel. I couldn't imagine the captain using such a savage weapon. A scalpel yes, maybe even a high-velocity rifle, but he was much too fastidious for buckshot.

I gave directions to the river. The captain adjusted the air conditioner and repeatedly flicked his eyes to the rearview mirror to be certain the van followed. He drove exactly 55 miles an hour. Pickney scratched an ear and gazed heavenward.

"The department doesn't want you to consider our presence an indication of any lack of confidence in your handling of the investigation," the captain said. "We are simply placing the state's resources at your service."

"We sure appreciate all the help we can get," Pickney said, talking loud and dumb, playing the country yokel who couldn't be expected to understand sophisticated procedures. "Never crossed my mind you was butting in, did it you, Mr. Payne?"

"Indeed no," I said.

We parked at the pines, and the troopers opened the rear of the van to lift out an inflatable yellow dinghy. I glimpsed X-ray equipment, microscopes bolted to a metal table, and a wooden shelf holding black bottles. There was a curtained darkroom. To my surprise a bloodhound bitch pressed her nose against the mesh of her cage and slowly wagged her tail.

The troopers left the bloodhound in the van but carried the dinghy to the river, where one of them used a foot pump to inflate it. The trooper wore high-top black shoes. His fellow officer screwed together aluminum oars. The oars were fitted through the rubber loops of the dinghy.

The captain, a trooper, and Pickney crossed first. The captain held a metal suitcase he'd brought from the van, and the trooper did the rowing. The dinghy floated low in the tawny river, the water reflecting yellowness, the wake splitting a film of pale-green pollen. On the other bank was the all-conquering white oak.

I smoked, adjusted my dark glasses, and eyed the remaining trooper, whose blue-and-white nameplate read Gilley. He was young, heavy in the hips, and wore the brim of his campaign hat tipped low over his eyes. He had brought a canvas bucket to carry water back to the bloodhound.

"They thinking in Richmond this death's a homicide?" I asked, attempting to sound conversational.

"They don't tell me," Gilley said.

"You heard no talk?"

"You work for the captain, you don't have ears."

The first trooper rowed back for us. My feet sank into the dinghy's bottom, making balancing difficult. On the other side Pickney watched Captain Blake work a small battery-powered vacuum cleaner through the wild grass where Vin had been found.

"This area should've been roped off," the captain said.

"We had to get the body," Pickney said.

"There are ways and then there are ways of securing bodies," the captain said. "What's the rise and fall of the river?"

"Depends on a dam sixty miles upstream, which in turn depends on rainfall, but I'd guess no more than six or eight inches."

"A significant difference between six and eight inches," Blake said.

"Especially in my dick," Pickney said and smiled, but he had just informed Blake a line existed past which he'd better not step.

The captain stared a moment before turning to watch his troopers, one now with the vacuum cleaner, the other holding a metal detector he had screwed together.

"The information we have is that Mr. Farr was a golfer, not a fisherman," the captain said.

"Anybody can take a notion to fish," Pickney said.

The trooper sweeping the metal detector above the ground paused, stooped, and lifted a hand for the captain, who walked to him. He and the captain conferred. I opened my briefcase and gave Pickney the medical examiner's report. He squinted as he held it close to his face.

"Nice of you all to let me read this," he said.

With tweezers taken from the metal suitcase, the trooper who had been using the metal detector lifted something from the ground and placed it in a clear plastic envelope held open by the captain.

"According to this, Vin was having hisself a time," Pickney said, lifting his eyes to mine. "Semen, 0.18 blood alcohol, he was on a real tear-'em-up." Pickney continued to read. "And cracklings? Hell, I thought he ate only Russian caviar and French cooking."

"He wore no underwear," I said.

"You telling me what?"

"I don't know what I'm telling you except caviar or not he was wearing no underwear."

The sheriff studied the report. The first trooper put away the vacuum cleaner and at the captain's orders poured plaster into footprints found near the boulders. Pickney returned the medical report.

"Ignorant people like us shouldn't upset geniuses by volunteering that those are our people's prints," he whispered.

While the casts dried, the troopers spooned up soil they fed into test tubes, corked, and labeled. The test tubes were placed in the metal suitcase.

The captain used a tape to take measurements. He was careful no weed or wild grass brushed his uniform. He paced off distances, shot bearings with a hand compass, and wrote on his clipboard. He touched his pen to his nose before crossing back to the sheriff and me.

"How far's the nearest road on this side of the river?" he asked.

"A mile and seven tenths," Pickney answered.

"Ah," the captain said, surprised by any preciseness from the sheriff. The captain noted the information and again moved off to his troopers.

"They think us country boys don't know how to piss down," Pickney said, his finger homing to his nose.

"The governor's office has taken an interest," I said.

"Figures. Vin and Rhea used to be invited to high-hog dinners at the mansion."

With a trooper the captain walked into the woods and examined ground along the way. More notes.

"No way a body could be carried through there," Pickney said. "Too much brier and honeysuckles."

The captain and his troopers worked the area ninety minutes

before loading their equipment and pickings into the dinghy and
rowing across the river. Again we had to make two trips. The dinghy
was collapsed, and we walked through the pine woods to the van,
where the bloodhound thumped her cage. The troopers watered
and fed her pellets.

The captain spoke to the troopers, who without a glance at
Pickney or me drove off in the powerful lumbering van. The captain
returned to us. We were standing beside his car. Pickney's finger
worked in his nose. The nose was soft and fleshy, the finger big,
and it wiggled around like a cat in a sack. The captain stared.

"One of man's greatest pleasures ruined by too much eddikit,"
Pickney said. "Nothing more satisfying than coming up with a juicy
one and rolling it dry between your fingers. How you think such
a pleasure got turned into bad manners? Probably the ladies started
it. They invented eddikit, didn't they? Like belching. I hear belching was once okay, a way of showing how much you enjoyed your
meal. My wife acts like I spit on the table when I belch. That got
ruined too."

He withdrew the finger, on the end of which was a dark, nasty
booger. The sheriff examined it as if it were a trophy before flicking
it into weeds. He was performing for the captain's benefit, and the
captain appeared affected. He eyed Pickney and saw contagion.
The captain was thinking they had shaken hands. He wanted to
wash.

He drove us to Tobaccoton, and this time he broke the speed
limit. In the courthouse parking lot he was careful not to offer his
hand to Pickney, who winked at me, said goodbye, and walked
with his heavy gait toward the jail. Sweat had darkened his brown
uniform shirt, and his tan pants hung loose around his drooping
rear end.

I led the captain through the courthouse to the men's room.
Hot and tired, I went up to my office, slumped in my chair, and
switched on the fan. I turned my face into the airstream. The captain
entered. He appeared refreshed. Creases in his beautifully fitting
uniform were as sharp as ever. No beggar lice dared stick to his
trousers.

"What the voters will elect to enforce their laws," he said.
"There ought to be qualifications for sheriff, some standards."

"There are," I said. "Plenty of kin."

"I'm aware of your meaning," he said and reached to his shirt pocket, which he unbuttoned. From it he drew the clear plastic envelope and laid it on the green blotter of my desk.

I took off my dark glasses to look. Inside was a silver figure no more than a quarter inch high, a robed angel with tiny wings. The angel held a biblical trumpet. Gabriel.

"Mean anything to you?" the captain asked.

"No."

"It did to somebody," he said and reached for the envelope. He fitted it into the shirt pocket, buttoned the flap, and patted it. "How did the deceased get to the river?"

"We don't know."

"His clothes had bits of dried mud on them as well as grass stains. We found wood splinters snagged in his trousers. In his hair was a single small strand of some dark tufted fabric. He may have been dragged."

"We wondered about that."

"The semen may or may not be significant. It remains in the vas deferens some hours. He could've had intercourse with his wife. You've questioned her?"

"Not yet."

"Oh?"

"Her husband's not in the ground."

"I suggest we go now."

"The sheriff's been out there."

"What we have on our hands might well be too large for Sheriff Pickney."

"She's suffering, I know that."

"We all suffer sooner or later. Will you show me the way?"

I reached for my dark glasses.

The captain and I drove out in my Chevy. I felt that his Ford was too official, too threatening to a widow in mourning. Riverview, the estate, lay south of Tobaccoton on the highway to Bannister. I turned left off the highway to steer through a white brick gateway which had black wrought-iron lamps on top.

The farm had belonged to Rhea's people, not that Vin needed her land or money, for he'd made a barnful of dollars before he walked her to the altar, but it was Rhea's father who owned the 2,000-plus acres. His name was Romulus "Blackjack" Gatlin, and he'd been a tobacco planter, a warehouseman, a raiser of pampered purebred cattle, and a banker. The nickname came from an incident at the bank when a raging sawmiller tried to fight Romulus Gatlin for the calling of a loan, and Romulus swung a lead-weighted leather sap against the man's skull.

A forest flanked the white gravel drive, pines mostly, but also poplars, oaks, and red maples, which fired up an October woods. Boys used to sneak in after the first kill-frost to gather persimmons, and the really bold shot squirrels, but the hunters had to be cunning because Rhea's father was a stern man. He'd attended Virginia Military Institute, been a colonel in the army, and wore a British-type mustache. As he sat his prancing horse, he'd send his hounds coursing through the forest to drive out poachers. He collared many frightened youths, black and white, and hauled them down to the courthouse, where he scared them half to death with threats of fines and jail.

The road was serpentine, the gravel somehow softer, whiter, than what could be mined at a mere quarry, a gravel with gentility. Then the forest gave back to make room for English boxwoods planted at least a hundred years ago and now spread and grown together in mass, their leaves shiny dark green because of the cottonseed and bonemeal Old Ben fed them, their odor not fragrant but acrid and even unpleasant to those not born to them. The boxwoods had been thinned to make Christmas wreaths but never shaped. They possessed the wild elegance of a country manor.

Before we reached the house, the road divided to become a long oval which circled to the front entrance. At the oval's center was an iron fountain, the water turned off, though the pond beneath mirrored sunlight. There were goldfish, verbena around the pond, and bluebirds perched on the fountain's fluted rim.

The house was one of the few grand places in the region not built of timber or brick. Rhea's great-grandfather had discovered limestone deposits on his property and brought in an Italian mason who worked for the railroad to cut and shape the blocks. No columns here, no presumptuous antebellum dreams of classical grandeur, but a Mediterranean flair with red tile roof, French windows, balconies, and delicate iron grillwork. Bronze crepe myrtles, not yet blooming, were spaced around the house.

"Like another world," the captain said.

We left my car and walked to the double doors of the main entrance. Each had on it a polished swan-shaped brass knocker and the engraved name Riverview. As we waited, the captain and I watched finches sweep about the fountain like tossed gold coins.

I'd telephoned before coming and talked first to Melissa, the black maid, then to Rhea.

"When can I bury my husband?" she'd asked.

Melissa opened the door, a lifetime servant born on the place. She was thin and old, yet unwrinkled, and wore a dark uniform with a white apron. Her shoes, like ours, were soundless on Persian carpets.

Melissa had been trained by Rhea's mother, who for years was first lady in Howell County. The mother died in church while singing the hymn "Blessed Be the Ties That Bind." When she sat suddenly and bowed her head, the congregation believed she had decided to pray, but she was making her fealty to death. People patted her, rubbed her fingers, and brought a dozen glasses of water for her stilled lips. Rhea was beside her, a young girl wearing a white dress and yellow hat, crying, "Mother? Are you all right, Mother?"

Melissa led the captain and me past a lighted stand holding a book for mourners to sign and through the air-conditioned coolness of the great hall, which had broad pine flooring and golden brown paneling all the way to the ceiling. We entered a room where a harp stood by a concert piano. There were shelves of books, and a view from vast windows gave down over the sloping lawn to the river, whose banks had been trimmed to pool-table felt. Green water seemed only an extension of the grass. Sunlight brightened a white boathouse and the chrome diving board bolted to the pier.

"Any rumor of financial difficulties?" the captain asked, speaking just above a whisper.

"Vin had a genius for dollars," I said.

The captain kept eyeing various parts of the room—the inlaid antique desk, a white satin prie-dieu with a red leather New Testament opened on it, the libretti in a bookcase by the piano, the fireplace which had a marble facing and logs laid on brass andirons, sycamore lengths chosen for their colors, the greenish grays catching tones of the carpet and draperies. Over the fireplace an oil painting of Rhea's mother wearing a lavender gown to match her lavender eyes. From her neck hung a tiny golden cross on an almost invisible golden chain.

Rhea came silently into the room. She wore a dark silk dress, hose, and black pumps. Her only jewelry were her wedding and engagement rings, and a lady's small watch that had a dark leather strap. She was an imposing woman, not only tall but big-boned, a woman people expected to become overweight; yet her size was not a thing she fought but an enhancement of her dignity, as if regality required more in the way of flesh and blood.

Still she was perfectly feminine, particularly in her arms, waist, and hips. Her hair was reddish blond, strawberry, and had a natural lie about it, thick yet loose. She never looked as if she'd just stepped from the beauty parlor. Rather she appeared to be a woman who had just come in from the bracing outdoors.

Like her mother in the painting, her face was wide, the eyes deep-set and lavender. She rarely wore makeup even at parties. Paint on other women only accentuated her tanned, robust loveliness. Though unadorned and grieving, she seemed startlingly healthy.

"Billy," she said and crossed to me, a hand out, the fingers broad and strong, yet that hand joined to a wrist tapered and, in my mind, aristocratic. She'd always been athletic, particularly on horses Blackjack bought her. Later, after marrying Vin, she became a fine golfer, her name inscribed on silver trophies at the country club over in Bannister.

I introduced her to the captain and believed I saw the impulse of a bow in his stiff, correct body, a submission. Men discovered they had an instinct to kiss her hand.

"Forgive the intrusion on your sorrow," the captain said, speaking like a courtier instead of a policeman. He could've clicked his heels Prussian fashion.

She nodded, smiled sadly, and indicated the sofas on either side of a coffee table fanned with magazines, most horsy, all slick and colorful. The one book, unknown to me, was titled *The Sculptor's Hand*. She didn't move like a big woman. There was none of that settling of flesh. She sat neatly, her knees together, her fingers clasped above them.

"Is this a police matter?" she asked. She had the directness of speech only the rich possess. Nobody could fire her or take her house and money.

"Only in the sense that a cause of death must be certified," the captain answered. "It is at this point certainly no criminal matter. Routine questions such as did your husband suffer from any physical debilitations?"

Other times the captain's use of the word "debilitation" would have been comical. Rhea's eyelids lowered slightly, but though she was direct, she was never impolite to servants, and that's what she would consider a member of the state police, even a captain—a servant. She shook her head.

"Did he have checkups?" the captain asked.

"Vin didn't believe in placing himself in the hands of doctors. He thought they are paid to find something wrong."

"Was he ever sick?"

"He suffered infrequent indigestion. He loved hot and peppery pork. He knew he shouldn't eat it, but it was an indulgence. I never served it here."

"Cracklings?" the captain asked.

"Not in this house."

"When did you last see him?"

"The Sunday night we went to bed."

"He must've gotten up sometime during the night to leave. Did you hear him?"

"No."

"Wasn't it an unusual time for him to leave?"

"My husband had many business interests. I'd grown accustomed to his coming and going at all hours."

"He didn't tell you where he was going?"

"No."

"Did he take a bag?"

"I don't know."

"You didn't pack one?"

"I don't pack bags."

She looked straight at the captain as she talked, those lavender eyes not swerving. Her hands were quiet on her lap. I know what the captain wanted to ask—whether or not she and Vin had made love before he left. The captain didn't dare and veered off by changing his line of questioning.

"Have you any idea what Mr. Farr was doing on the river?"

"We live on the river."

"He was upstream from here."

"Yes."

"Did he fish?"

"Not in recent years."

"Can you think of a reason he would be out on the river late at night?"

"I can't, though ordinarily he might be looking at land."

"Buying land you mean?"

"Buying, selling, cruising timber."

"Surely he wouldn't cruise timber at night."

"No."

"Was he bothered by anything, a worry, a business decision?"

"If so, he didn't inform me."

"No anxiety or distress?"

"My husband was always intense about his affairs. I saw no difference."

The captain tapped his gray ballpoint pen against his clipboard. I was admiring Rhea, how calmly she spoke, how serenely. I'd loved her for years. That love had no connection with real life, but it went on within my head. I'd not again allow myself to look at her widowed ankles.

"Have you been through Mr. Farr's papers, the personal ones he would keep around the house?" the captain asked.

"I've glanced at them."

"Anything of interest?"

"Captain, I don't know what you're looking for."

"We're attempting to establish how your husband died."

"I realize what you're attempting. Are you suggesting an unnatural death?"

"Departmental responsibility requires peering down all roads."

"I don't know about your roads. I found in his desk what I expected—canceled checks, business memoranda, a list of securities."

"His will?"

"Is with the United Virginia Bank in Richmond."

"Do you know its terms?"

"Naturally."

"Mrs. Farr, I have to ask."

"I am to receive one half of the estate outright. The residue will be held in trust during my lifetime, with the bank acting as both executor and trustee."

"You have no children?"

"No."

"On whom does the trust dissolve and pay out to?"

"Various organizations and charities—the bank has a list."

"No kinsmen or other individuals?"

"There are minor bequests to uncles, aunts, cousins. Nothing major. Nobody really profits except a boys' home, the church, an orphanage."

"Was your husband a religious man?"

I knew the captain was thinking about the small silver angel he had buttoned in his shirt pocket.

Rhea showed no surprise. "Of late he was becoming so, more than people realized."

Certainly more than I realized. Nobody in Howell County would ever have considered Vin spiritual. He was sharp, always hustling, at times hard-drinking and profane, and if he had a religious side he sure kept it well hidden from the rest of us.

Rhea must've sensed what I was thinking, for she turned those lavender eyes toward me, and I quickly lowered my own. I had never been able to look straight at her more than a few seconds. My breathing would've stopped, and I would've crumbled like salt.

"Did he wear any sort of religious insignia?"

"No."

"There were some slight marks on his body, on a finger, a toe. Would you know anything about those?"

Rhea changed the position of her hands on her lap as she shook her head.

"Also a bit of scar tissue below the navel."

I glanced at the captain. The medical report had mentioned nothing about scar tissue below the navel.

"People die," Rhea said. "All over the world people die. This minute as we sit here they are dying. Allow my husband to go in peace."

"I hope and trust he's already in peace," the captain said.

It was the right answer. Rhea had been at the edge of sorrowing anger, drawing herself up, her fingers working. The resentment flowed from her. She nodded, smiled, and let her hands drop apart. Her smile was gently loving, just enough to uncover tips of her upper teeth.

"I believe he is at peace," she said.

"You've been gracious," the captain said and rose. "At this

time we won't trouble you further."

"You haven't told me when I can bury my husband."

"I'll see what I can do to ensure his remains are returned promptly," the captain said.

"I would be grateful."

She also stood, her arms at her side. She didn't walk us to the door. Melissa appeared to do that. Leaving, I glimpsed another gilt-edged painting hanging in a wainscoted den. She and Vin were together, both dressed in yellow cashmere sweaters, their golfing clothes. Each had a hand laid on clubheads sticking up from a white leather bag. One of Vin's arms was around her waist, and she was laughing. In a palm she held a golf ball.

I glanced back toward Rhea. She still stood before the sofa. Her hands had again joined and lifted to her breasts. She was staring upward toward her mother.

The captain and I walked from the coolness of the house into a wall of heat. It was air that had to be pushed through. A car came slowly around the circle, mourners, women bringing food as was the custom in Howell County, though Rhea would never use it. I recognized Grace Milton, who played the organ at Saint Andrew's Episcopal Church.

The captain and I sat in my car and looked toward the tennis court at the side of the house. The court had night lights and a Cyclone fence. Below it was a putting green with a pole and red triangular flag, the number 19 on the flag. I wondered where Old Ben was. This time of year he ought to be guiding his lawn mower or clipping away at the roses.

"How did she appear to you?" the captain asked.

I started the engine and didn't tell him she was beautiful to me and all I ever wanted in this world. I would've knelt before her. Had she just touched me, a finger against my cheek, that would have been enough.

"I expected her to take it well," I said. "Her way is to take everything well."

As I drove, doves pecking gravel along the drive twisted up and away, uttering their helpless twittering calls, the white undersides of their wings flashing.

"She's contained," the captain said. "Serenity over fire."

"She's a lady."

"Who told us very little."

"She answered your questions."

"Not completely. She slipped around one of them."

"You're talking about the scar tissue?"

"Below the umbilicus 9 cm."

"There was nothing about it in the report."

"Because the medical examiner was instructed by authorities to list the finding separately. The area is a shaved patch of pubic hair. Moreover the scar tissue is a sort of rudimentary tattoo."

I slowed the car to look at him.

"A small, inkless tattoo," he said.

"Picturing what?" I asked.

"No picture, words, tiny printed words, very neat, but amateurish." He glanced at me. "Took some doing to work it out. All magicians those boys in the state lab. Very small lettering. Three words: 'Pull for service.'"

"The three words said—?"

"'Pull for service.'"

I gaped. "I don't believe what I'm hearing."

"Real magicians."

My tires bumped off the shoulder, and I yanked the car back onto the road. I thought of Vin walking along the street in Tobaccoton on his way to the bank, his step confident, his smile and wave quick, laughter close to his mouth.

"You'd be amazed at what we get in Richmond," the captain said. "We just closed the file on a society woman who kept her dead dogs in the refrigerator. She had dogs going back seven years, mostly cocker spaniels."

I was thinking of Rhea. Even sleeping with Vin, being loved by him at night, she might know nothing of that delicate tattoo.

"I couldn't very well force the questioning about it, especially at this time," the captain said. "I don't know that I ever can, she's such an imposing lady. But unless Mr. Farr's death was natural or accidental, somebody will have to eventually. Perhaps you."

"Not me," I said.

We were entering the outer fringe of Tobaccoton where the town's houses gathered, clapboard mostly, a few built of brick, but none large, places owned by men and women who worked in the shoe factory at Bannister. Others of the man-only category cut pulpwood and hauled it to the Southern RR siding at Raleigh Branch.

"After a while nothing surprises you," the captain said. "One gentleman, a comptroller for a major Virginia corporation, choked his wife to death by shoving dollar bills down her throat, five-dollar bills, new, fresh from the bank."

"Nothing to do with Vin Farr," I said.

"Nothing in itself, merely an observation that in police work you can never be sure what's around the next corner. We don't really know anything yet. Strike that. One thing we do know." The precise, immaculate captain for the first time allowed a bit of humor to crack his official mask. He raised a hand as if reaching for a rope. "'Pull for service.' Somebody had to be on the pulling end."

6

It is midafternoon. I am able to tell the approximate time by shadows laid on the cabin floor as shafts of sunlight strike the doorway. Adjusting to one meal a day is no problem. Even before captivity I ate only to live.

A breeze rustles willow oaks, providing more gaps for light. What is difficult to beat down is my yearning for a drink. I have become accustomed to the witchery of drink. I sometimes envision little people inside me, tiny representatives of my body's organs— heart, liver, lungs—all howling upward for the Lord like holy rollers, only in this case the worshipers are pleading for a release from drought. They want a rain of gin or vodka. Those little hands tear me open. Afternoons they rip me apart, and since I am alone I give in and whimper. Cowardly, yes, yet whimpering helps, sobbing, capitulating to weakness. There is less pain in surrender.

Whimpering becomes rhythmic until I hear a sound and sit up from my cot. I stand and move as far toward the door as my chain will permit. I peer out, trying to bend my sight around the cabin and up among the boughs.

A plane, nothing commercial or military, a light aircraft, the engine hardly more authoritative than a chirring of locusts warping over the low ground. The sound fades, returns, and circles slowly,

maybe only a crop duster out to spray corn or tobacco with mala-
thion, or perhaps a student pilot from Bannister.

Yet it can be somebody looking for me. Sheriff Pickney, Captain
Blake, or other officials might have ordered up a search. The state
police own aircraft, and in the sky now troopers could be holding
maps, tracking the area in grids, methodically seeking spoor of a
missing Commonwealth's Attorney.

Still even if the plane flies directly over the cabin, the observers
might not see. There is so much cover—leaves, vines, honeysuckle.
They may glimpse a rusted roof, a mound of tumbled-down bricks,
the rotted beams from the old mill, but those will be meaningless
to searchers. All over Howell County one finds broken sheds and
buildings, fallen dwellings, chimneys stuck up like black fingers,
the last embrace of fire. No reason for this desolation to attract
unless I make a desperate signal.

I rush to the cot where I have a pillow, two sheets, a light
blanket. I snatch them from under the mosquito netting and again
stretch as far toward the doorway as my chain allows. The plane is
closer, nearly overhead. A shadow sweeps the ground. First I heave
the pillow out the door. Next I ball the sheets and throw them.
Lastly the blanket. They glare among weeds.

I imagine troopers up in the plane, big men like those who
helped Captain Blake. They see the sudden whiteness, check their
maps, and reach to a microphone to radio Bannister or even Richmond. "Red Rover, this is Search Unit One and we have a sighting.
Stand by for coordinates. Ground conditions require a team on foot
to investigate."

The plane leaves, a drowsing insect lazily fading, and I picture
it landing. I see troopers pulling on rubber boots to come after me.
They find their way through the swamp on a path which only the
master seems to know. They cross the low ground calling my name,
and I shout an answer. I try to have dignity and will not let them
know how I broke, whimpered, and sobbed.

Finally I am in Tobaccoton, at the house after a bath, a drink
in my hand as I sit in the grape arbor. After the first swallow, I
feel the descent of the unholy ghost upon the upraised frantic hands
within, feel the peace come to them in the rain, the surcease of
writhing, the good shower of gin. I relax as dusk covers me and
lift my chin so my neck catches coolness off the river. I am even
happy to hear my father's Glenn Miller records.

I am crying at the love I have for that small airplane whose
engine merges with the throbbing sea of locusts.

————

As Captain Blake explained, it would be easier for me, a local,
to investigate Vincent Farr's finances in Tobaccoton. The captain
felt his rank and uniform might spook citizens with the majesty of
the state. Successful questioning could involve nuance, sensitivity,
and acceptance.

The town had two banks, the older one, the Planters & Merchants, opened and managed by Rhea's grandfather, a man who
collected businesses as easily as most men pick up winesaps under
a tree—here a warehouse, there a hardware store, farm-equipment
dealership, grinding mill. He owned outlets for just about everything he had to buy, a form of discounted self-sufficiency, yet re-
tained the old traditions too, never appearing in public without a
jacket and tie even if he stepped out his front door merely to look
at the sky for rain. He tipped his hat to white ladies and spoke the
first names only of blacks.

Though a small bank, the Planters & Merchants had made it
through the Great Depression because the grandfather stood at the
entrance and softly but firmly persuaded depositors not to withdraw
their savings. They would have had to push him aside, and there
existed just too much respect for and fear of the Gatlins to do that.
During the panic he bought up bank stock at ten cents on the dollar,
so that at his death he personally owned 87 percent of the shares,
which came down first to Rhea's father and then to Rhea herself.

The bank still loaned money as if dollars were as serious and
solemn as communion. Financial policy had an agricultural bias,
favoring tobacco planters, and only slowly adapted to the industrial
and commercial. The bank remained suspicious of business and
speculation. Borrowers who wanted money to buy automobiles were
treated as if frivolous.

Diagonally across the street was the New Tobaccoton Bank,
created by selling stock to anybody who could put up $25 a share.
Vincent Farr was on the first board of directors, that prior to his
marrying Rhea. Vin believed for the county to develop, a more
progressive money center was necessary. It's what he called a bank,
a money center.

The Planters & Merchants housed itself in a small stone building that resembled a miniature Greek temple, but the New Tobaccoton Bank was all glass and white concrete, the glass glinting a blue tint, the whole so modern among the shabby brick denizens of the street that it stood out like fresh milk in an old bucket.

Vin had been responsible for bringing Alex Poole from Danville to run the New Tobaccoton Bank, Alex only thirty-seven, a golfer. He, his wife, Betty, and their two children lived in a section named the Oaks, a pasture until the land was subdivided, again one of Vin's projects. Old-timers said nobody would ever pay Vin's price for 150-by-200-foot lots, but there were now seventeen houses out there. All the young marrieds wanted to live in the Oaks, where no spinsterish white Victorian monstrosities three stories high, their windows like eyes, seemed to gaze at the modern world as if its odor were coarse and offensive.

Nothing complicated about Alex Poole. He was as simple as money and ambition, two of the most honest characteristics that could dominate a man. When dealing with Alex, all you had to ask yourself was what would the money do. That's what Alex would do.

His was the only private office in the bank. Everybody else had desks in the lobby, where people were tinted blue by the windows as was the color photograph that covered a wall, a panoramic shot of the Dan River with a pristine coal drag running beside it and a bedazzling smokeless textile plant.

I sat in front of Alex's desk, not wood, but made of some shiny pressed material, tan with golden specks. Faint music surrounded us, the melody so soft it could not be identified. The view was to Main Street and the Baptist church, whose steeple had been twice struck by lightning and left truncated. Wags claimed the Lord was attempting to tell the Baptists something.

"When you going to join the club?" Alex asked. A leather frame on his desk displayed a large picture of his wife and children. The colors were too artificially bright and made their lips appear as if they'd just drunk blood. They were not pretty children, yet they sure God looked healthy, like prime calves.

"Have to stay close to Dad," I answered, a lie. Alex was speaking of the country club over in Bannister. I wouldn't explain I had no need of a game like golf or tennis to organize my drinking around.

"I admire your sense of values," Alex said, also lying. "Tobaccoton, the entire community, does."

Standard operating grease Alex applied. Doing it was simple once you learned the world revolved so much easier with a lube job. Alex would stay in Tobaccoton only a few years before moving on to Richmond or another city to shoot the grease at bigger money. To him the town was an outpost, a frontier.

His phone rang, the instrument the color of lemon custard, and he reached for it as if he would punish it. He was, a frown indicated, a busy man being disturbed. Quickly his expression changed again to grease-em-up, and his laughter became hearty. "Yes, Phil, oh yes! And big thanks, fellow! Will we see you at the cup matches? Surely, surely, and my love to Pam." He set the phone in its cradle as if not wishing to offend the person on the other end by transmitting even the slightest jarring through the line.

"Interest rates up again," he said. "Half a point. Excuse me while I get word to my loan officers."

As I waited, I looked toward the street. All the stores had posters in the windows, great outsized slabs of cardboard with pictures of Buster Bovin on them. Buster wore his safari suit and bush hat. His right hand was raised to hurl a moral thunderbolt. REVIVAL the signs announced. The streamer across the street still hung, WELCOME HOME BUSTER, though the material was limp, sagging, and the first rain would cause the lettering to run like mascara.

Alex returned, dapper in a light brown suit, a brown tie with a Windsor knot, and a button-down canary shirt. His hand held a Cross pen, the gold model, and his clean fingers adhered to it lovingly.

"So, Billy, did you come to put the arm on me?" he asked, jerking at the creases in his pants before sitting.

I explained I had questions about Vin Farr. Alex's face became mournful. His mouth drooped, and he touched a finger to the corner of an eye but never let go of the pen.

"I tell you I can't believe it. He was a real friend, not only to me personally, but of this bank, this community. We're going to miss him. Lord God, are we ever!"

"A few inquiries I know you'll keep confidential," I said.

"Surely, but I just still can't accept it about Vin."

"Can you give me the numbers in his account?"

"I'll get them myself. I don't want employees talking."

Again he stood and left. I watched the lethargy of people trudg-

ing through the yellow heat and thought, Pull for service. I'd also
thought of it last night while on a beam reach to Jamaica. I'd
wakened this morning to consider it.

I couldn't reconcile it with Rhea. When I pictured her, I saw
her sitting astride a softly cantering chestnut mare, the pace so
relaxed it was as if the camera of my mind had slowed and the legs
of the horse become ribbonlike. Rhea, her strawberry hair loose,
was a part of the horse's body, growing out of it as they bounded
in gentleness through a field of broomstraw, golden with the autumn
sun on it, on them, the broomstraw a field in my mind where Rhea
was forever gliding, yet she serene as a figurehead, while the horse's
legs were flowing ribbons.

Alex returned with yellow accounting sheets and a bundle of
canceled checks. He sat and studied the sheets before lifting his
face to me. The expression of mournfulness had been replaced by
the briskness of calculation.

"At Vin's death, he had $17,541.20 in his checking account.
He held a certificate of deposit with the bank in the amount of
$20,000. He had a passbook account holding $124.38. That what
you want?"

"What about his business accounts?"

"Several of those," Alex said and shuffled the yellow sheets.
"Shall I read the figures?"

"What I want is for you to look them over and see whether
anything's unusual or out of line."

"I've already done that, and I estimate these are average bal-
ances for Vin's enterprises. You on a fishing expedition because you
don't know how he died?"

"His death may have been natural. The numbers tell you
nothing?"

"Normal stuff you find." He fanned through canceled checks.
"Payrolls, phone company, equipment purchases, a new car, a pay-
ment to Scott & Stringfellow in Richmond for a hundred shares of
International Harvester. A real gamble there."

"Seventeen thousand's pretty high for a man to keep in his
personal account."

"It's an in-and-out account, swinging from about twenty down
to three over a thirty-day period. Probably he just received some
dividends. He has a money-market fund and also bought T bills.
He may have accounts at other banks, though I don't know that.

Vin never told you more than necessary. I do know he liked to keep his money working."

"Does he owe the bank?"

"He always had notes out." Alex shuffled papers. "They came to $65,000, which is in no way remarkable for a person with Vin's range of affairs. At times it's been higher, though Vin, being on the board, never took advantage of his position, partly because he wanted no trouble from the examiners."

"Alex, you're bound to develop a feel for your accounts. Any vibrations whatsoever coming off those papers?"

"None. The money enters and leaves fast, just as Vin himself did."

"Not the slightest hint of business troubles?"

"Vin never made a late payment in his life. He used the bank's money to the last instant but paid on time. He was one hell of a smart businessman and always either working or sleeping, nothing in between."

I again thought of Rhea. If Vin was always working or sleeping, when and where did he take time to uncover that long lovely body?

"He played golf," I said.

"He played golf like it was work. He was out there to win, and mostly he had somebody along to hustle."

"That's admirable?"

"Admire's a funny word if you're talking business. Vin was focused and tough. When there was competition for the same dollar, he usually picked it up."

"I know you're loyal to Vin, but I get this feeling you're saying two things at the same time—one, Vin was great, secondly, nobody better get in his way."

"How confidential are we being here, Billy? Will I have to testify?"

"At present no hearing or legal action is scheduled."

"Still I might have to climb on a witness stand eventually?"

"It's not in my plans."

"But your plans might change. I don't intend to get into that. I don't want to talk at all, yet if I have to, it's off the record."

"I'll do what I can to protect your statement."

"No statement, Billy, remarks strictly off the record. I'm trusting you. Okay, to Vin business was a living and a good one, sure, providing money, cars, his airplane, and the trips he and Rhea took all over the country. But it was also a game to him, a very serious game. He had to win even when it wasn't important, some tacky little deal worth only a few dollars, yet he might throw a body block into a fellow. He made enemies. Not long ago a man took a swing at him right here in the lobby of the bank."

"I want his name."

"Remember, you protect me. We kept it hushed up. Only a few people saw, employees, and I warned them they better not spread it around. The man who threw the punch is named Harrison Adams. Apparently Vin beat him out on a land deal. At least Harrison claimed something like that, but he picked on the wrong guy when he swung at Vin, because he got decked."

I tried to place Harrison Adams.

"Broke the fellow's dental plate, which he spit out onto our carpeting. What's terrible is he was so ashamed he started crying. He didn't want to, yet couldn't help it. Vin left the bank, and we stood Harrison up, some of the tellers and I, and sent him on his way."

"How do I find the man?"

"Haven't seen him since, or before as far as that goes. The word is he's in the construction business somewhere down around Bannister. No account with us. He just must've known Vin used this bank."

I printed the name Harrison Adams on the envelope my electric bill had come in. My sunglasses slipped down my nose, and I pushed them back up.

"Vin was strong," Alex said. "He was complete, you know? Never needed anything from anyone else. People like that aren't always loved."

Yet Rhea had loved him. The only time she was girlish was with Vin. Dancing, she held to him and raised her adoring face. During the term Vin served in the legislature I'd seen a newspaper photo of her gazing at him as he made a speech, her lips parted, her eyes full of wonder, her face illumined at the sight of the marvel who was her man.

"Now a trade-off," Alex said. "Vin's death, was it more than an accident?"

"I don't have enough information to make that call," I answered.

"There's talk around. People saw the state police."

"Routine procedure in the event of an unexplained death, but let's not get carried away."

I stood, as did Alex, and we shook hands across his desk. He wore a fraternity ring, a black onyx inset with the gold Greek letters KA. I was a few years younger, but I felt a lot older than he. All that damn enthusiastic energy.

"Does Rhea keep an account here?" I asked.

"She banks at her own place, and the Planters & Merchants is indeed hers, though a horse-and-buggy operation. What I could do with their assets."

I thought of what he could do—all glass and concrete, tinted windows, consumer and auto loans, money ricocheting around like war while the way at Rhea's bank was slow, slow as crops growing, the wheat, milo, sorghum, above all the thick, coarse tobacco leaves spreading in the hellish heat. Torpid money at the Planters & Merchants. I kept mine, what little I had, there.

"No joint account?" I asked.

"Never. Vin wouldn't want anybody thinking he needed her money."

I thanked Alex, again shook his hand, and told him if he had any ideas to let me know.

"Ideas?" he asked.

"Anything which in your opinion doesn't chime exactly right."

"I'll do it, Billy, and listen, you might consider opening an account with us. We're paying top interest on CDs."

"I intend to, Alex, soon as I get a little ahead," I lied. He wanted his tit for my tat. I walked past clicking machines to the blue lobby and out onto the street, where I stopped on the corner to wait for Tobaccoton's only traffic light to change. It was also Howell County's only traffic light.

Rhea drove past in a black LaSalle. She and Vin had collected antique cars, reconditioned them, and kept them groomed in a garage so clean you could lick soup off the floor and not get grit on your tongue. She was too lost within herself to notice me. Her face was drawn to rigid solemnity by the death of a man who at times lit her up as if she were witnessing the rapture of the Second Coming.

7

I wait for my rescuers. I do not sleep during the night, the heat like hot cotton, the mosquitoes furious around the netting, moonlight reflecting off the algal waters of the mill pond. I hear a cry, some small animal seized by fang or talon, giving its death screech.

The morning is cooler, and a mist unravels around the cabin. Heat spreads like a snake swelling over the land. My blanket, sheets, and pillow are out there on the ground. I hope my rescuers reach me soon because the master will be displeased.

From soil beneath the cabin, milkweed, a single plant, grows up through a floor crack. Valiantly it seeks light. It is thin, etiolated, sickly, yet bends toward the sun. What moisture can it be finding down in that darkness?

I have time before the master comes. Captain Blake and his men will arrive carrying riot guns and two-way radios. I drive my hearing out over the swamp. The troopers can hide in the cabin or crouch among the peeling birches to wait for the master.

By late morning I begin to doubt and fear. Though my ears are so taut they ache, no human sound touches them—insects, yes, the hawk, the cutting of a gray squirrel, the slap of a beaver's tail against a stream, and always the locusts, like a chirring tide flowing in and ebbing.

My rescuers might be lost despite knowing the exact coordinates of the cabin. The terrain looks different down here than from an aircraft. Sightings have to be taken, azimuths, and the men fight the swamp. If they are only a few yards off course, they won't see the cabin.

The sun is high now, the streaks from it that can penetrate the branches and vines vertical. The sickly milkweed seeks it with the longing of a lover. God, not another night now that I know rescue is so near. I cannot endure another night.

Suppose the rescuers arrive while the master is here, while we are having our lesson or I am eating my meal. If they come slogging through the swamp, the master will hear and draw the gun. I think of bullets flying, blood, and death.

At last I hear something—movement, a step, a pacing closer. I stand from my cot and stretch from the millstone to the doorway. I lean against the chain, which bites the skin of my ankle.

The step is nearer now. I hear breathing. The search team will be more than one man, and this just the forward element, the point who stops now and again to give arm signals to the squad that follows.

I'm certain it's not the master's step. That tread I know, and it always comes from the west, while this I hear is from the east. I want to shout, but I wait, standing on one leg because the other is pulled behind me.

The point man is very close now. He is breathing hard with the exertion of fighting his way through the swamp. I extend my arms and show my teeth in a grin. I don't want him to be surprised or think I'm going to attack. Soon as he comes into sight of the doorway, I will call out, "Don't shoot, I'm a friend!"

Yet when he comes into sight, he is no rescuer, no trooper in hip boots, but a mud-caked hound, a redbone so skinny his ribs could be used to scrape paint, his ears ragged, his hind end puny, his tail curved under him in eternal surrender. He stares at me, and I at him. His astonished eyes are terrified. He yelps and slinks away.

I call and whistle to him. If I can coax him within reach, I might be able to attach a message, some item to alert people, my handkerchief on which I'll write with soot from the old fireplace.

But the hound is gone, off on his lonely search for food, game, a place to give up to weariness. I am again about to whimper, yet think it possible the hound can be with someone, a trapper or poacher, a swamp rat lugging a car radiator and copper worm to cover in order to brew a little shine.

"I have money!" I shout. "I'll pay if you come to the door! One hundred dollars!"

No answer because nobody is out there. Sunlight reflecting off the pond shimmers through my eyes as if I'm under water.

———

After talking to Alex Poole, I worked the rest of the afternoon in my office preparing my first court case of the summer term, the bailer theft. Not till five-thirty did I leave for home. In the trunk of my car was a new lawn mower. The garage couldn't fix the old one. Thank you, Eddie Blue, the great All-American mechanic.

Aunt Lettie wasn't in the kitchen, and I sniffed. No smell of food. I looked into the stove's oven. It was empty. Her note lay under a jar of apple butter, the message written in pencil on a cash register tape from the Southside Superette: "David be savd tonit At rivr. Et egs."

Eat eggs. Though Aunt Lettie couldn't spell, she had a pretty hand, the script dainty and ladylike. She'd had to teach herself to read and write in middle age because she'd never gone to school. She and hers had lived too far back in the pine woods for truant officers or school officials to find her, even to care.

David, I remembered, was a grandson, a boy eleven or twelve whose hair grew like frizzy black yarn and whose hips seemed almost as high as his chest. Aunt Lettie was using her big meeting at the church to have him dunked—send him under a sinner, raise him a saint.

I jerked off my tie, rolled up my sleeves, and unbuttoned my collar before climbing to my father's room. His door was shut, and neither his radio nor phonograph played. I tapped three times.

"You're not dishonoring this room!" he called.

"I don't want in."

"You went to the seminary and never even read the Bible."

"I know what's on every page."

"Ha! I'm holding a Bible, the King James. What's on the first page of Isaiah?"

"Words. That page is covered with words."

A long silence, the key turned in his lock, and the door opened half an inch. He still hadn't unfastened the chain of the night latch. Beyond his ruffled white hair I saw the mantel on which were the polished 75-mm shell, the German helmet with swastika, the sheathed bayonet, a disarmed grenade, and, tacked to the wall, the desiccated blue-gray flag with the yin-yang insignia of the 29th Infantry Division.

"The shame to your mother," he said. He wore pajama bottoms and his khaki uniform shirt, the sergeant's stripes on his sleeve below the division insignia. He'd pinned his campaign ribbons above his left breast pocket, one row protected by a plastic casing. Some ribbons had battle stars. "What kind of hypocrite are you?"

"A complete hypocrite," I said. "No sense fooling around with hypocrisy."

"Making fun of everything like nothing's sacred."

"Not much is."

"Joking about men who put their lives on the line. Hiding in a Louisville seminary pretending to be godly just to keep from going where all men should go. Let me tell you, men are measured by war. You think your generation is superior to mine, but I know what I am in the center of myself. Only men who've been to war know that!"

I'd heard it all before. He waxed and waned on the subject, perhaps in phase with the moon.

"How you want your eggs?" I asked.

"I never eat eggs at night," he said and shut the door. "Eggs are day food."

I went downstairs. Later I'd carry up four slices of buttered toast, a jar of honey, and a glass of milk, which I'd set before his door. Eventually he'd snake out a hand for them, though it might not be until late when hunger finally devoured pride.

From the pantry I lifted my bottle and held it to the light. He'd been at it. I sniffed. No vinegar. He sneaked down the steps when I wasn't home. I suspected he stayed downstairs most of the day while I was at my office. Aunt Lettie would never rat on him.

I started to go up, rap on his door, and confront him with the theft, but I realized he now had no choice except to steal my liquor.

Eddie Blue had not been around to make his biweekly delivery of Ancient Age. My father's supply line had been cut, his logistics destroyed. Frantic he was. I'd buy enough for the two of us and allow him to filch what he needed.

"I'm changing my will!" he called. "I'm leaving this house and my land to the Veterans of Foreign Wars. I'll not have a pitiful thing like you for a son!"

"I can break the will!" I called back.

"You so low you could stand under a copperhead's belly without touching!" he shouted and slammed his door.

Another threat, another phase of the moon. He acted as if the house and the ragtag acres around it were of great value when in truth the timber had been cut off the place and the soil had been bled pale and gone sour. One of the pulpwood companies might want the property to plant pine seedlings, possibly pay four or five hundred dollars an acre, but they'd tear down the house to lower taxes, a house which during winter the wind blew through as if walls were mere filters to screen out grit and snow.

I was still seeing Rhea in the black LaSalle, remembering the rigidity of her face, the emotion held in check, sorrow reining her thoroughbred features.

I carried my drink to the grape arbor, no *Sail* or *Cruising* this time because I wanted to keep my mind on Vin Farr, yet I was thinking of her. As I sat, I exhaled long and slowly. To quiet my breathing and the beating of my heart required time. I allowed my head to drop back and looked up among branches to a sky still so light that all color had been crowded out.

I drew in my mind and attempted to focus on Vin. Why had he not kept his money in Rhea's bank? Because that bank was too slow, too hidebound. Also because Blackjack hadn't approved of the marriage, and a new bank was Vin's way of making his own mark.

"Where's Eddie Blue?" my father demanded from his bedroom window.

There was nothing wrong with Vin's background, one better than many in the country. It was just that Rhea's people thought of themselves as members of a landed gentry. They owned property which traced back to a king's grant, and they believed in land first and foremost while Vin was essentially a trader of paper. He would've made millions on Wall Street.

"You tell Eddie Blue I want to see him!" my father shouted.

Vin's father had raised tobacco and been a part-time carpenter, and Vin grew up learning the builder's trade. Before he was old enough to vote, he speculated by putting up a white bungalow on a quarter acre near the high school and made a profit on the sale to his history teacher. He gave off the sweet effluvium of money.

He attended UVA on a track scholarship, served four years in the Air Force, and came visiting flying a smoking fighter plane which he snap-rolled inches over the courthouse. Pigeons caught up in the slipstream were tossed about, hysterical clots of feathers hurled backwards as the terrified birds attempted to flap forward. Local hens didn't lay for a week.

Discharged, Vin started the pallet factory, just a galvanized shed in the pine woods. He worked stripped to the waist to help his black gang erect the shed and install machinery. He drove about the county in a dirty, dented Ford pickup, and sometimes he'd go a day or two without shaving, yet no one believed even for a second Vin had found his place.

He was first seen with Rhea at Waterside before joining the Air Force and then, after his discharge, at the Bannister Country Club spring formal, and the fact Rhea was a member of that club and he wasn't indicated she must have engineered his taking her there. Ladies on straight chairs along the wall shot their eyes at each other because she wasn't squired by her usual dates—the young architect who drove down from Fairfax County or the doctor's son from Tidewater.

Few cut in to dance with Rhea because Vin warned them off by threatening looks over her smooth, uncovered shoulder. His expression was that of a man leveling his eyes to a gunsight, though not dressed in a leather flying suit this time but a rented tuxedo.

They married in October. Blackjack's disapproval of the wedding didn't prevent him from putting on the dog, the reception the largest in county memory with peppermint-striped tents, an orchestra, dancing on a waxed wooden platform, and champagne fountains. Rhea waltzed with the governor.

Old Ben drove her and Vin from the reception in a four-horse carriage. A Cadillac sped them to Danville, where Vin had rented a plane, which he piloted to Sea Island but looped over Riverview first. I stood among guests with upturned faces and thought of Rhea beside him, one hand on her floppy hat, the other holding down the skirt of her white linen suit, laughing, occasionally waving, and finally dropping the bridal bouquet all the unmarried girls stretched up hands for. The bouquet landed in the swimming pool.

Rhea and Vin owned their house only a short while before moving to Riverview. Blackjack needed her. He lived in a wing and still went daily to the bank, driven by Old Ben in the Chrysler that had folding opera seats and sliding glass between the back and the front. Ornate vases held flowers. Like a fine horse the Chrysler never faltered, was, as they say of horses, honest. Some suggested Blackjack would be buried in that automobile, but no, just a regular casket lowered slowly into the ground three days after his being gored by his own prize-winning white-faced bull. The Gatlins of course had their own cemetery.

Rhea was rich, and she and Vin lived out at Riverview like golden people untouched by mortal worries. When I thought of them, I pictured English royalty at a country estate playing croquet on a lawn as perfect and placid as still water. I realized they were not actually like that, especially not Vin, who was too much a son of Howell County to be royal anything, but he possessed strength, vigor, and that certainty which arose out of a fineness of genes, a courage to take up and carry through the speculations and business ventures shaped in his vision. I could never like him—he'd always called me Tone—but I envied much more than his hold over Rhea and her properties.

She continued to ride her chestnut mare through my mind. She played golf, yet it was on the mare I kept her. She belonged to a hunt near Charlottesville and during the season stabled horses there so that on meet days she could rise early and drive her yellow Thunderbird fast to reach the chase. Then she'd stay all night at Farmington, where she was also a member.

When I was a boy, I learned her routine and slipped through the woods at Riverview to lie on dusty pine tags that gave beneath my body. I pulled down boughs to hide my face as I peeked toward the white riding ring and red stable with its belfry and fox-shaped weather vane.

The oval ring contained jumps—coops, fences, oxers. When schooling, she wore fawn leather chaps, a checkered ratcatcher, and a black helmet fastened by a strap under her chin. She trotted the horses three times around the ring in each direction, then cantered them three times, and lastly she turned them into the jumps at a controlled pace. She was joined to her mounts with a sureness of seat I felt could not be learned but come only from a long heritage of blood and bond with things equine.

She jumped boldly, talking to the green horses, speaking confidence into them. I saw her fall when at the last instant a gelding ran out before a spread. Rhea slid down the rump of the dark animal and landed on her back. I stood from my hiding place, ready to go to her, my mouth open in a silent cry, but stable hands and Old Ben were already running from the barn.

They weren't needed, for she pushed up quickly and brushed at her chaps. She was smiling and still talking to the excited gelding. Rhea had never released the reins. She ran a hand down the gelding's sweaty neck and over his chest before stepping back into the saddle, took two turns around the ring at a slow canter, and more with balance than hands directed him over the spread. The gelding flowed into an arc. Rhea slowed him, again patted the neck, and raised her helmet as if saluting the judge's box.

At the house the phone rang. My father might or might not answer it. He was sulking because he'd been forced to dip his beak into my liquor. The odds were, therefore, he would not. It rang fourteen times before quitting.

Before I was able to resettle my mind on Vin, the phone again rang. Emergency. Some big trouble in Tobaccoton or the county. Maybe Captain Blake from Richmond with breakthrough news about Vin. Perhaps Rhea herself—"When can I bury my husband?" I left my drink beside the chair, crossed to the house, and climbed the porch steps to the front hall.

"It's coming to you," the voice said, a slow, deep voice that had hard breathing around the words.

"What is?" I asked.

"You better look up, you better look down, you better look all around."

"You have a name?" I asked.

"My name is trouble. Before you set a foot on the street, you watch for holes. Look for trucks and things that fall out of the sky. Hurt is what you better watch for."

"What'd I do?"

"It's not what you done, it's what you is, which is a red-white-and-blue shit."

That hard breathing continued a moment before he hung up. I stood holding the phone, hearing my father pace upstairs and wondering whether the call had anything to do with the death of Vin Farr.

I hardly slept. I rooted around in a closet to find the twenty-gauge L. C. Smith my father bought me when I was a boy. I intended to keep the shotgun beside my bed but could locate no shells for it. I wasn't about to inquire of him. I knew what he'd reply: "Why I thought you was a pacifist."

At the office in the morning I asked Florene to call down and invite the sheriff up. Out my window everything seemed flat, as if the buildings and steeples had been erected in only two dimensions. Traffic was louder, more abrasive, the truck engines pounding bricks with sooty decibels. Voices carried. Between WPAL gospel numbers—"Take time out for Jesus, He took time out for you"—a car radio announced a 40 percent chance of showers.

Sheriff Pickney arrived, spoke to Florene, and entered my office. He held a bottle of Big Orange, half drunk. While his flesh settled into a chair at the front of my desk, I told him about the threatening phone call.

"So much trash in the county these days," he said. "I'll get the phone company to monitor your line. Probably won't do no good, and it might be nothing more than youngsters having a good time. Or it could be the hay bailer case you got to try. The boys who stole it are loaded with kin. But my guess is it's just trash. The world's overflowing into Howell County."

He lifted the Big Orange and sucked at it. When he lowered the bottle, it was empty, and he rubbed the back of his hand against his mouth. He bumped the bottle against a thigh. Each bump sank the bottle into the thigh.

"You don't mind me reading that medical examiner's report again, do you?" he asked.

"You ought to have a copy."

"That's what I'm thinking."

I got it for him from the locked file, and he set the Big Orange bottle on the floor before spreading the report on his lap. When he read, his lips moved, but he wasn't dumb. He was just careful with words and everything else.

"These ex-what-the-hells on the finger and toe," he said.

"Excoriations, they—"

"I know what it means. To chafe, scratch, or peel the skin. I got me a dictionary, though I can't always pronounce the words. What you make of it?"

"Nothing so far. A little scratch on a finger and toe doesn't have to mean anything."

"Agreed. Could've banged the toe on a chair and skinned his finger counting money. I understand you and the captain went out to visit Rhea."

It was criticism. Pickney should've been asked along. He didn't know yet about "Pull for service" either. I hesitated to tell him. He had a right and duty to be informed, but I was thinking of his nephew who would one day want my job. Pickney could feed the boy material to be used against me. Still, because of the way I was treating him, the sheriff had no reason to award me loyalty. I decided to try a limited openness.

"We learned nothing big," I said. "I would've called you immediately if we had, though there is one finding you don't know. Vin had this sort of tattoo in a very private place." I explained the rest of it.

Pickney stared out of those washed blue eyes and reached to his uniform pocket for a cigarillo. He bit the cigarillo but didn't light it. His mouth opened and closed twice.

"How come Doc Robinette didn't locate it?" he asked.

"Very delicate scar tissue forming the words, and Doc's eyes aren't much."

"Captain Blake could've told me. I'm an elected law-enforcement officer in Howell County even if he don't think I got brains to shuck corn."

"Blame Vin's Richmond connections. They don't want scandal. We don't either."

"But damnit, I like to be informed what's happening in my own bailiwick!" He gnawed on the cigarillo and spat a piece into my wastebasket before shifting in the chair and handing back the medical examiner's report. "What you think of the tattoo?"

"Military men are likely to have them, so I'm guessing Air Force. As for the message, a joke, his or somebody's."

"What happened to the ink?"

"Maybe it wore out or he had it removed, if there ever was ink."

"You reckon Rhea saw it?"

"I consider that immaterial," I said, a short answer because I didn't like Pickney having Rhea in his mind that way.

"Everything has to do with something. Even cow pies grow grass."

I'd intended to tell him about Harrison Adams, the man Vin decked in the bank, but I held back. I was again suspicious of Pickney and didn't want him dogging my steps, coloring my judgment, taking credit for evidence I developed. I'd open no doors for him to run his kin into my office.

"By the way, how's that nephew of yours doing in law school?" I asked.

"Right well," Pickney answered, and his gaze became oblique, a man peeping around a corner. A finger twitched toward his nose. "Fact is he's near the top of his class, though they make fun of his southside accent."

"Guess he's become too high-powered to return to Howell County," I said. "Probably join a big-city firm."

"I don't know, Billy, he's mighty fond of the county. Here his accent seems right, you with me? And as the saying goes, it's easier for a man to get into Howell County than it is to get Howell County out of the man. I'm guessing he'd like to come back if he could scratch up enough lawing to support himself."

"Give him my regards," I said.

"Sure, be glad to do that," Pickney said, reaching for the empty Big Orange bottle as he heaved himself out of my chair to leave.

You conniving bastard, I thought.

Harrison Adams. I found his name in the Bannister County phone directory, only 179 pages counting both white and yellow. Two numbers were listed, one for his office, the second a residence.

I dialed both. No answer. I tried a second and third time during the morning. I then told Florene I was driving to Bannister, seat of government in the county of the same name south of Howell, not just another tobacco town wilting in the sun but a place of industry—a garment plant, a foundry for producing plow points, and the shoe factory. I stopped at a filling station where two bearded white men were changing a tire on a truck hauling crates of chickens.

"Well, Harrison he's kind of hard to find these days," the older of the two men said, banging away at the tire with a sledge. "You try out at his house?"

I got directions to the house, which was just inside the town-limit sign, a one-story residence part brick, part green siding, chimneys at each end and a picture window with a lamp. The grass needed mowing, and a birdbath had been turned over.

I rang the bell and knocked. No answer. I walked around the house to a two-car garage empty except for garden tools and a stack of undressed lumber. A dog, a German shepherd, chained to a clothesline next door barked at me. He ran back and forth causing the wire line to sing. A buxom young woman whose platinum blond hair was wrapped around pink plastic curlers pushed open the back door of her house to shush the dog and look over the hedge at me. She wore a peach-colored halter and shorts. In her mouth were wooden clothespins, which she withdrew and snapped at each other like alligators.

"Hoping to find Mr. Adams," I said.

"Join the crowd," she answered and walked on bare feet to the hedge to tell me she hadn't seen him around for days. There was an aggrieved tone to her voice. She instructed me how to reach his place of business downtown.

Downtown was a community of 5,000 people, the white courthouse at its center. Bannister lay beside the railroad, unlike Tobaccoton, which had only the use of the river for transport and thus lagged the modern world. Bannister could brag about its movie house, six traffic lights, and radio station (WPAL, reputedly controlled by Buster Bovin). It had the country club and a Hardee's.

Though I followed the woman's directions, I didn't find Harrison Adams's place of business. I stopped at the post office, where the American flag hung limply from an aluminum pole and a dusty hound lifted his leg to wet the concrete post of an outside mailbox.

"Behind the International Harvester dealership," the clerk said, an elderly man who wore the gray jacket of the service. "I doubt you find him."

"Why not?"

"His mail's been piling up."

Harrison Adams's place of business was a small frame building, white with blue shutters. The postal clerk was correct about the mail, which overflowed the box and lay on the stoop, the letters held in place by a brick. I rapped on the locked door and bent to a window to peer into dimness. I spotted a desk, a phone, and a map on a wall.

Propped against the side of the building and turned face inward was a sign. I drew it away and read it, black letters on a white background: LAKE HALIFAX ACRES, SALES. Underneath the words a red arrow.

I walked behind the office to scalped land where construction equipment was parked—a dump truck, a bulldozer, a rusting backhoe. Cable lay on the ground and creosoted posts.

I drove up to the International Harvester dealership. Bright paper pennants hung from wire strung over shiny red combines and farm tractors. I talked to a flap-jawed young salesman who became disappointed I couldn't be interested in the manure spreader special. He smelled of barns and cows.

"Harrison might could be out at Lake Halifax if he's anywheres, and I guess he has to be somewhere, don't he?" the salesman said.

I reset my sunglasses and asked about Lake Halifax.

"A place he and people built, dammed up a stream, you just keep going south, almost to North Carolina, and they used to be a sign out that way, though I don't believe so any longer, but if you cock your eye—hold it, well look here, that's old Harrison now."

A car had turned in over the scalped land, a Lincoln Continental, a recent dark blue model, yet dusty and unkept. When it stopped fast, a man stepped out, hurriedly gathered the mail, and unlocked the door. Short and thickly built, he wore khakis and a long-billed cap.

I thanked the salesman and started on foot toward the office. Before I reached it, Harrison Adams came out holding the mail and a manila folder. He yanked the door shut and slid into the Lincoln, whose engine had been left running.

"Mr. Adams!" I called and jogged toward his car.

"I don't know you," he said. He gunned the engine.

"You are Harrison Adams?"

"He's down in Florida. Harrison got him a big job down Miami way."

He drove off, the window swishing up. The Lincoln rocked and squeaked over the uneven ground. I read the license plate—HA 1.

I ran to my car and followed. At the highway I caught sight of the Continental as it smoked south from Bannister. I couldn't keep up in my untuned, plodding Chevy. Though I lost him, I drove on, sitting forward, glancing both to the left and right of the road, which slanted gradually downward among somnambulant sun-drenched pines.

I gave up and searched for a place to turn around. As I slowed, I spotted two posts which once might have supported a sign between them. Beyond was a new asphalt road. I turned into it.

Some dozen houses had been built, none grand, yet all respectable and located on large lots landscaped with maples, forsythia, and Japanese holly. New grass struggled to survive the heat. Under carports charcoal grills and riding mowers were stored.

The houses stopped abruptly, as if a line had been drawn, though the slab of asphalt continued down into more pines and circled, a winding drive along which at exact intervals wooden stakes had been pounded into the ground, the boundaries of lots. I would've made a complete loop except I glimpsed a road unpaved, just two tracks made by the infrequent passage of a car or truck over pine tags.

I parked off the hard surface and walked the unpaved road maybe an eighth of a mile. I was no Indian and couldn't tell whether the tire treads I followed were new or not. Crows called in the pines, though I saw only shadows of fleeing birds. This is crazy, I thought, and would've quit except a glint sped my eyes to deep shade.

The glint was the rear bumper of the Lincoln catching a random ray of sunlight. Farther on I made out a point of land that stuck into the lake, a body of brownish water fringed with green where pines faintly reflected. A powerboat pulled a girl on skis, leaving whitish swells that washed ashore.

Harrison Adams hadn't heard me. He sat on an outcropping of rock near the water, his back curved, blue smoke from a cigarette hanging around his head. His cap was pushed so far to the rear that its bill pointed upward. He was motionless, though his thick physique was not that of a quiet man.

I dragged a foot through pine tags and coughed so he would hear my approach; yet he didn't turn till I was almost at him, and then only a glance. He again leveled his eyes over the lake toward the girl slicking across water. Her skis slapped the surface.

"I owe you money?" he asked.

"No."

"You serving me with a subpoena or court order?"

"Not that either." I stepped around beside him. Again a glance.

"You the law? Everybody seems like the law to me these days."

"I tried to telephone you."

"Phones can be snakes in the grass," he said and flipped his cigarette to the water, where it hissed and bobbed. He had a freckled pug face, the eyes protected by a squint.

I sat beside him on the outcropping, told him my name, and explained I was Howell County's Commonwealth's Attorney.

"So you are the law," he said. "Well, it's gone."

"What's gone?"

"I expect it from all sides now I'm taking bankruptcy. End of the week and it'll be over for me. I swore I'd never do that to my creditors. I always considered bankruptcy cheating, but here I am going through it, and then I got to find someplace to move, somewhere far enough away people don't know me. If there is anyplace that far."

His eyes followed the girl on skis. The white boat turned, leaving an expanding arch on the murky lake. Sunshine did not penetrate the surface.

"Last year this time I was a rich man. The property we're sitting on is where I intended to put my house, a lodge with glass on all sides, decking, a pier and slips, a yardarm with flags, a diving board, loudspeakers all over the place, the stuff you dream about. Had a Richmond architect draw up the plans. At least he got paid. There she is now."

He pointed to the ground and a pit dug to burn trash. Flakes of black residue shifted in the variable breeze. A wisp of smoke drifted off.

"This have anything to do with Vin Farr?" I asked.

He shifted on the rock to look at me full-faced, though his eyes remained squinted. When he spoke, I thought for an instant he meant to spit.

"I hope his death was slow and painful." He did spit, to the side. "Vin Farr was a first-class bona fide sonofabitch. You investigating me?"

"I know you fought in the bank."

"I'll make it simple. Vin and I had an agreement, not on paper because neither of us figured we needed that. We developed land, built houses, and made money. Then we got hold of this lakefront property, paid big dollars, eight hundred acres. I put all I could beg, borrow, or steal in it, and Vin was supposed to come up with more, but interest rates skyrocketed, and people stopped buying. I was left holding land on credit with payments I couldn't carry."

"So you drove up to Tobaccoton."

"I went to talk to him, but he was a prick, and I swung on him. I'd used all my money and my wife's, which was considerable. She got so mad about it she left me. Her brothers told her I cheated her. Took the children to her mother's in Rocky Mount. More than anything in this world I wanted to lay Vin on the ground. The only thing is that sonofabitch could fight. Look at me, I'm in shape and strong. I thought I could handle myself, but that slippery bastard folded me with one punch. I never saw it. I lost a plate and what pride I had left. I should've shot him."

"Instead of killing him on the river?"

"I didn't kill him. I didn't know he'd been killed, only he was dead. I don't know anything about a river either."

"Your whereabouts on Sunday evening June twenty-ninth and Monday morning June thirtieth? Take your time and think it through."

"Am I about to be charged?"

"That's still up in the air."

"God, the way my mind's been working lately I can't remember five minutes ago." He reached to his hip pocket, a movement that alarmed me till I saw he was only after his wallet, pigskin, the leather almost blond. He drew out a card-sized calendar and held it with stubby, battered fingers as he focused on it. "Some of the time I was right here. I been coming to this spot days and nights. It's a place nobody bothers me, except you. I slept here June twenty-ninth, right here on the ground. I heard the church bell across the water, the bell for the Christian Endeavor meeting."

"Witnesses?"

"How could I when I come to be alone?"

"Mr. Adams, when I leave I'm stopping by your sheriff's office to tell him you might be subject to criminal charges. If you attempt to leave the county he will inform me. I will then have a warrant issued for your arrest. I could do it right now, you understand?"

"Joy! Great unbounded joy. I was meaning to go to Florida."

"Not for a while you don't."

"Sure." He spat. "How did Vin die?"

"We don't yet know how or why."

"I don't guess trickiness can kill a man. How about the Lord striking him dead for being a bastard?"

"You ever see marks on him?"

"What kind of marks?"

"Scars, tattoos, anything."

"You think I slept with him? I never saw him with his clothes off."

"You wouldn't know about his underwear, whether he wore it or not?" Harrison stared. "Okay, if he was what you claim, why'd you go into business with him?"

"He could be a charmer. He could outslick oil, and he had the war record and the stint down at the legislature. He could charm scales off a snake, and if you knew him, you knew that."

I knew it all right, though in these last years I rarely saw Vin. I took no trips to Pinehurst or Hilton Head for golf, no flights to Boca Raton or the Caribbean. Still Vin had always stopped on the street to chat. He had the ability to make you believe he was interested in you, even when your reason told you he didn't give two hoots in a high wind.

"You think he went into business with you in order to deceive you?"

"No I don't. Vin played it day by day. As long as things were going right, he was a perfect partner and never showed his tough side. It's just when a dollar bill's lying on the ground and you're standing between him and it that he gets mean—or got mean."

I sat looking at the cigarette he'd thrown into the water unravel and watching the skier, the tan wet young girl, leaning against the curve of centrifugal force. She waved to us on the rock, and I waved back. Wake rolled up against the bank in a loud wash, and a chunk of soil dropped away.

"I don't know what happens to people," Harrison said and adjusted his cap. He wasn't looking at the girl's wet back or sun-bleached hair but out toward the distant shore. "I been studying them a long time, and just when I think I'm beginning to understand something about human beings they change on me. Now I feel dumber than ever. And certainly broker. My advice to you is never like a man who has a hand on your bank account."

"You won't leave the county?" I asked.

"No, I'll be going down to the courthouse on Friday and making my shame legal. Then I'll try to find some work till you let me go to Florida. I was a plumber once, I guess I can still do that. I'll hang my head and shuffle around to keep from having to look anybody in the eye. I won't own this piece of land, but maybe the new owner will allow me to come out here if I promise not to smoke and set fire to the place."

I nodded and stood, yet he didn't notice, and as I moved away, I barely heard his words.

"It's a terrible thing to want a man dead, but, Vin, you son-ofabitch, I hope you're feeling the fire."

8

Sun has burned off mist, and a swarm of blackbirds swirl onto the birches. They quarrel among boughs until suddenly they scatter, their wings sounding like wind rising.

But there is no wind, and I am very nervous. I am close to trembling as I slump on my cot, my forearms resting against my knees. My blanket, sheets, and pillow still lie among weeds beyond the doorway.

I am no longer convinced a search team sent by the plane will arrive. My hope of it has tottered. What I think now is that people in Tobaccoton must assume I have fled. They are not surprised. "The job was too much for him," they agree. "Billy Payne was a local boy and had a good education but no staying power."

Maybe Pickney's nephew is already filling the chair in my office. The wheels of the judicial system will turn. Life will roll on as if I never lived in Tobaccoton, the little gap my absence caused already closed up.

Except for my father. Who is taking care of my father? Probably Aunt Lettie, though there can't be much money. It has been my pay that has held us up. She will not bring him liquor—Aunt Lettie is black death on drinking—so he will be desperate for a source. I feel sympathy for him at this instant because he must want a drink as badly as I do.

Again the blackbirds swirl among the birches. They cause fleeing shadows to form on sunlit patches of ground. The quiet comes down around the cabin. No frogs bellow, no hawk's cry sounds over the swamp, for an instant even the locusts are silenced.

When I hear the master, I stand and brush at myself. I have been kept supplied with clean clothes—khaki shorts, T-shirts, leather sandals. To prevent my hands from shaking, I press the palms against my thighs.

The master, wearing a camouflaged suit and cap as well as the shooting glasses with yellow lenses, steps into my vision and looks at the bedding among weeds. I see disappointment and anger shape features of the face. Fingers shift toward the pistol in the oxblood holster, and the eyes sweep to me in the yellow stare.

"I was scared," I say quickly. "I woke during the night and heard something moving out there. I thought it might be a rabid coon or wild dog. I threw things to frighten it off."

The master's body is tensed, and the hand stays near the gun.

"You know how thinking can trick you in the dark," I say. "So I threw the things, and the animal, whatever it was, ran off."

The master doesn't speak but slowly enters and gazes into all corners of the cabin before lowering the canvas knapsack with the day's provisions onto the table. I am smiling, attempting to appear friendly. My palms sweat against my thighs. The master leaves the cabin to walk around it before collecting the bedding, carrying it inside, and dropping it on the cot. Eyes watch from behind the yellow lenses.

"It was so dark and lonely my imagination ran wild," I say. "I began to think of snakes crawling. Before long I was believing snakes were all over the place. Trouble is I have so much time to imagine at night. I don't sleep, I'm all slept out, and my mind keeps working. It's easy to believe terrible things are out in that swamp."

For the longest time the master doesn't move. I am being weighed. I keep smiling. Finally the hand near the .38 relaxes and slips into a pocket for the key to the lock, the one at the millstone.

"We'll exercise," the master says.

I exhale very softly through my nose so the sound won't be heard. On my leash I do pushups, knee bends, and run in place. Afterward I wash off sweat using a bucket of water from the well. I shave, yet the master never lets loose of the chain, and I feel those eyes attempt penetration to the center of me.

As usual I am allowed to eat before the lesson.

Master: Shall all men die?

Me: Death being threatened as the wages of sin, it is appointed to all men to die; for that all have sinned.

Master: Death being the wages of sin, why are not the righteous delivered from death, seeing all sins are forgiven of Christ?

Me: The righteous shall be delivered from death itself at the last day, and even in death are delivered from the sting and curse of it; so that although they die, yet it is out of God's love, to free them perfectly from sin and misery, and to make them capable of further communion with Christ in glory, which they then enter upon.

Master: I am pleased with your application.

Me: Thanks, I been studying hard.

Master: Don't thank me but One who died for you.

Me: Sure, of course.

Master: Are you feeling the words or just mouthing them?

Me: Oh, I'm feeling them.

Master: Although they die, yet it is out of God's love, to free them perfectly from sin and misery. I love that.

Me: Me too.

Master: Isn't to be released from sin and misery a reward?

Me: In my opinion it is.

Master: Death to the righteous is the most loving gift of all.

Me: I can honestly say I never understood it before.

Master: I didn't like you throwing your bedding into the yard. Don't do it again.

Me: I promise I won't.

Master: Anything before I leave?

Me: I been wondering whether I was in the papers or on the radio.

Master: Not so much now.

Me: What about my father?

Master: He's being looked after.

Me: I'm grateful for that. How'd you get me here?

Master: I used a wheelbarrow.

Me: Thank you again.

Master: Study your lesson and give thanks to God who created us.

————

At my office Sheriff Pickney waited. He stood by Florene's desk chatting with her about a sheep-killing dog. He followed me to my desk.

"Old Ben's missing," he said.

Old Ben, general retainer at Riverview who cut grass, weeded the gardens, and fed the boxwoods. He, like his father before him, had been born out there.

"I went to talk to him," Pickney said. "I figure if anybody knows what's going on around that place he does, but he's lit out. Nobody can tell me where. Just climbed in his pickup and drove off."

Old Ben was an Uncle Tom, no doubt about that, one of the last polite blacks as whites defined polite. He swept off his hat in greeting and made room for them on the sidewalk. He laughed loudly at and yes-sir'd anything whites spoke to him. He drew the deadly contempt of young black eyes.

"What did Rhea say?" I asked, again disliking to call her by her given name in front of Pickney. Mrs. Farr would have been proper for the sheriff, though he'd come a long way from the dirt floor of his father's tenant cabin.

"I didn't get no chance with lawyers and Tom Berry's funeral people out there. The state's released the body, and Tom's making arrangements for the service. Anyhow, the questions are better coming from you."

I raised my eyes to his, but if he hinted at anything, it was lost in the sagging looseness of his face. I had to be careful. Did anybody, everybody, know I loved Rhea or was I haunting myself?

"You're closer to the family, and I thought it'd make it easier on her," Pickney said.

"I'll call."

"That's the way," Pickney said and winked. "You and me'll show those bellhops down Richmond way how to dig taters."

I watched him leave. I'd withhold from him a day or two my conversation with Harrison Adams. No man living on public money as precariously as I was should show his hand entirely.

I waited till noon before calling Rhea. Melissa answered and moved away. Rhea's voice was low and calm.

"It's been a morning," she said. "We're putting Vin to rest tomorrow, at least his body. It seems they did terrible things to that during the autopsy." She paused. "I shouldn't think of it. It's only one's soul that's important."

"I'll call back."

"No, Billy, it's all right. The lawyers were explaining about Vin's estate. So much is in timber. They're hiring experts to assess the value, and some parcels will be sold to pay taxes, at least I think that's what they're saying, though it's difficult to make a lawyer tell you anything definite. Excuse me. You're a lawyer."

"I don't want to bother you at this time."

"You have never bothered me. Don't even think that."

They were just words, polite, ladylike words spoken by a woman under terrible stress; yet they seemed personal too, as if she'd reached through the phone and touched me.

"I want you to be a pallbearer," she said. "The funeral home will notify you, but I'll tell you now. The service is at ten, a graveside ceremony as Vin would've liked. Still you must've called about something else, and please don't feel you're upsetting me."

"I heard Old Ben's missing."

"He's been gone two days, and I have no idea where."

"Grieving?"

"Probably so, during which periods he is usually attacked by a thirst and slips off. When my father died, Vin found Old Ben unconscious in a drainage ditch. If it had rained, Old Ben would've drowned."

"You're not worried?"

"I am worried and have the hands looking for him, but it's just one more thing."

"If you'll let me know when he comes back."

"Oh, I have to believe he'll come back, and thank you, Billy, for being so thoughtful. I appreciate it more than I can put into words. The only good part about any of this is I've found I have many friends to stand beside me."

When we finished speaking, I sat looking at the door first and then my hands. They trembled on the desk blotter. I felt I'd been running or lifting. Rhea could still do that to me. And that evening, though they were burying Vin in the morning, she was aboard the boat, our sloop running across languid swells toward dazzling islands of white sand awash in a turquoise sea.

The funeral was in the cemetery behind Riverview, a plot surrounded by an iron fence whose pickets had recently been repainted black. Each of the simple marble headstones was inscribed with only a name and dates except for Blackjack's obelisk, which carried his military rank and artillery unit.

I was still surprised at being chosen a pallbearer. I suspected the reason was that Rhea had to come up with a list hurriedly and I, because I'd been out to talk to her, was on her mind. Certainly I'd never intended to mourn Vin deeply.

There were eight of us pallbearers—Jason Elliot, Tobaccoton's mayor and a druggist; Thornton Blackwell, a doctor from Bannister and golfing partner of Vin's; Lee Boulden, who ran a trucking business and transported much of Vin's dressed lumber to market; Amos Crafton, owner of a building-supply house; Sam Sutton, a cattleman and leaf auctioneer; Hampton Lightfoot, a planter; and Alex Poole from the New Tobaccoton Bank.

The summer sun was kind. A film of cloud built over it, and a slight breeze stirred from the south. We pallbearers ranked four by four stood at the rear of the Cadillac hearse and waited for Tom Berry to open the door. A green canopy had been erected over the grave, the name of the funeral home, Berry-Burton, lettered in white on the scalloped fringes. Flowers attracted bees and yellow jackets, and the pile of raw red soil dug from the hole was covered by a mat of imitation grass, though a few dry chunks had spilled from under the mat and rolled to a leg of a folding metal chair.

People crossed the pasture but stood back from the canopy. Men shook hands, women drew together, their voices a soughing of whispers. They knew of Rhea's love for Vin and wondered whether she might break.

When Rhea came from the house I adjusted my dark glasses. On one side walked an aged uncle, a man that immigrated to Kentucky years earlier to stake out a coal barony. On the other side was Allison Hopgood, rector of Saint Andrew's Episcopal Church, he, too, elderly and thin, his movements disjointed like a person suffering with arthritis. He wore bright vestments and strode slowly, a Bible under an arm, his face lifted, the chin forward like a prow.

They wished to support Rhea, but she didn't need them. She would never give in to grief like the Baptist widows who wailed and had to be held up as sorrow wrung them limp. She could have been walking through her house or to the scarf or blouse counter at a department store. She allowed her arms to swing freely, turned her head left and right, and nodded to people as she passed.

She was again dressed in black: veiled hat, suit, buttons, gloves, shoes, hose all black. The veil had been lowered over her face, but I saw through mesh which lay like a shadow over her features. On her breast hung a tiny golden cross resembling the one her mother wore in the portrait. I was ashamed I glanced at her legs in those mournful nylons and thought them the loveliest I'd ever seen.

Other members of her family, distant kin from beyond the county, followed to the canopy. Tom Berry opened the hearse door and pulled at the casket, which slid on ball bearings to us eight pallbearers. We grasped burnished bronze handles.

The casket dragged at my arms. Vin had been a large man, and he lay dead inside, close to my fingers. We followed Tom Berry to the canopy and settled the casket on straps for lowering into the hole. The hole smelled dusty.

When we stepped back, people closed in around the canopy. Allison Hopgood's eyes floated upward as if he were in communion with the Lord. Rhea sat on a folding chair, one gloved hand resting on the other across her lap, just a strip of white flesh showing at a wrist.

" 'I am the resurrection and the life,' " Allison Hopgood said. He had not opened his Bible or lowered his face. " 'Whosoever believeth in me shall not perish but have everlasting life.' "

His voice was somber, full of tremolo, as he intoned Psalms and verses from Saint Matthew, Saint John, and Saint Paul. Rhea, however, was serene. She sat as if far away, her eyes focused not on the casket or expanse of flowers but over them and across the pasture toward the river. She could've been sitting on a porch.

At last Allison Hopgood finished his cheerless beseeching of the Lord with the words, "Accept the soul of our dear departed brother and take him to Thy bosom, where he may live delighted forever in the white radiance of Thy grace and love." Allison lowered his chin, crossed around the casket to Rhea, and reached to her.

She rose from her chair, thanked him quietly, and turned not toward the house but the people. She smiled and clasped her hands. She lifted the veil.

"This is not a sad moment," she said. "I know you'll be happy to learn that my Vin found God and came to love Him. We should give thanks."

She spoke so calmly she might have been addressing a group at a garden party. Again she smiled. She allowed Allison to lead her away. She didn't falter at all till she'd taken a dozen steps, and then only an instant when her impenetrable serenity came apart like cracks shooting through porcelain. She glanced back at the casket as if trying to memorize Vin, fix him in her mind for the long and lonely years ahead.

Her heels and ankles wobbled slightly among clumps of orchard grass. That final look was full of deep and abiding love. She collected herself, the sun bright on her now, shining off the blackness of her clothes. She let her arms fall to her sides, turned away from the canopy, and moved toward the house with the leisurely pace of somebody out for a stroll on a summer's day.

Sheriff Pickney had been at the funeral and was waiting when I drove back to the courthouse. We stood in the shade of a dying elm which grew feebly next to the parking lot. The shade just did deny the sun.

"We got hippies," he said.

"Burton, I'm not sure 'hippies' is a term much used currently. Went out of style some years ago."

"Why not hippies if that's what they are with long hair, motorcycles, and whore women? Trash is what they are, riffraff, washing out of the cities like an outhouse overflowing. Call them anything you want, I don't care, but they could be responsible for the recent bust-ins around the county, maybe more."

He had both hands stuck deep in hip pockets and his shoulders braced to support his stomach. His feet were slewed. He smelled of sweat and shaving lotion.

"They bought a nigger farm out in the Hard Times district, almost to the Prince Edward County line, about forty acres of pine and honeysuckles with a shack leaned so bad it's about to fall on its side," he said. "I asked how come I'm just now finding out, and my deputies tell me the place is so far back in the boonies nobody much noticed at first."

"You're thinking there's a connection with Vin?" I asked.

"I'm thinking anything and everything. Who knows what the hell's going on? I want a search warrant so we can move in fast on them before they got time to hide controlled substances."

"You'd like me to get you a warrant."

"It takes less explaining coming from you."

Late in the afternoon I went up to Judge Gareet's chambers on the third floor, the best office in the building and the only one for which the county provided curtains. The judge had just finished trying a civil case in which a farmer sued the Southern Railroad for ruining his grapes by spraying defoliation chemicals over its right-of-way. The farmer claimed the chemicals had been carried by wind to his vines and caused the leaves to shrivel, the fruit to drop. A jury had awarded him $1,500 and costs.

"The railroad could've settled for less but hoped to prevail and prevent further legal action," the judge said. "Now every farmer in the county whose grapes don't produce will be running to lawyers. Good for the lawyers I suppose."

The judge had washed his face and hands and was drying his neck with a towel. He was a proud old Virginian, secure in the long bloodline and kinship with many proud names in Tidewater. He possessed the certainty of quality.

He was a rounded man, no angles, his flesh white and unblemished as ham fat till he laughed, and laughter flushed him pink. After a day in court, he liked a drink or two in chambers and was thus glad to share with me a bit of the I. W. Harper drawn from his desk. He poured into two clean tumblers also taken from the drawer. No ice was available.

"Lordy it's been hot," he said, his hand smoothing gray hair parted in the middle. He sighed and smacked his lips. "I don't suppose good liquor ever cooled a man none in his body, but it will surely send a breeze through his mind. You agree, Billy?"

"I guess you know I'm not opposed to a tod for the bod, Judge."

"Because you're civilized, not a fanatic like some around here who complain about me. I know who they are, though I shall name no names. They write letters to the attorney general and the governor. What's the world coming to if a man can't have a social drink after a day's labor? You aware there's a petition circulating demanding our state store be removed from the county?"

That was Buster Bovin's work, before his African ministry, an outgrowth of an organization called The Ministerial Alliance, which believed the basis of law was fundamentalist morality. They'd already brought out a vote large enough to defeat horse racing in Virginia and were now forming up for an assault on liquor, drugs, and abortion.

"You notice how most of the state-store clerks are Baptists?" I asked. Neither the judge nor I, being public servants, bought our booze in Howell County anyway. We couldn't have touched the doorknob of the ABC store without it spreading in the community like a high wind from Hell.

"Ah, they closing in on us, Billy," he said, leaning back in his chair and sipping. "They making it more difficult every minute for men of good will."

It was his theme, and he draped his slow, liquid voice around it. Beyond his open window was the din rising from the congestion of afternoon traffic—the pickups, cattle trailers, and farm machinery that clogged Main Street. Two of Tobaccoton's policemen were out there waving their arms and blowing whistles. Cows on a semi-trailer lowed in anguish.

"You can have the warrant," Judge Gareet said, "but I'd like to know what it's got to do with Vincent Farr."

"Probably nothing. Pickney's hoping to stumble on evidence."

"Somewhat flimsy justification for a writ. I shall, however, issue the warrant on suspicion that people out there are growing or using dangerous substances. Trust you won't need it before morning."

"Too hot to move now anyway."

"That's it then." He freshened his drink, though I shook my head. "Strange man, Vin. Knew him most of his life, yet never felt I understood him. He was always a person within a person, friendly, helpful to me in getting this appointment while he was in the legislature, but I always had a feeling he was holding back, not being exactly up front, as if we were playing poker and he was hugging his cards close."

"That's Vin," I said. By playing his cards that way he'd won himself a bunch of money and Rhea. "Or was."

"As they say these days, a very private person. You all working with a motive yet?" He sipped. "I hear his wallet's missing."

"Vin didn't have to carry money. Everybody gave him credit."

"Only the poor need to tote money, you're suggesting. Don't go radical on me, Billy. You and I get along too well to cross on politics. I assume you'll be up for reelection."

"Some kind of doing's got to pay for food on my table, Judge."

"Very good. We need you around here. You're a first-rate attorney. I mean it. You just been through a run of bad luck is all, and that luck'll change. Your place is here among your people, not down in Richmond town."

My people, I thought—the rednecks, car freaks, and religious nuts who didn't have talent or ambition enough to break free of the sticks. Tobaccoton wasn't a town, Howell wasn't a county. They were both a slow, dull lane to the graveyard.

"Course you're bound to know Sheriff Pickney is working for his nephew," the judge said. "Now let me be quick to stipulate I like Burton Pickney, think he's a good rural law officer, but I wouldn't want to be surrounded by Pickneys. Get my meaning?"

I told him I did as Rhea walked into my mind and I remembered that last desperate glance of hers toward the casket.

"Billy, you ought to get out more, particularly evenings, do some churching. That's my personal advice to you, be seen at church meetings, and in Howell County you can find one every night of the year. And for the Lord's sake attend services on Sunday."

And give up my sloop, I thought, forswear journeys over the turquoise sea to island sand so white it stings the eyes. Give up the hand on the cooling glass and the pressure of the tiller, the sway and hissing beauty of the bow.

"Press the flesh," the judge said. "Sing the hymns loud, don't matter whether you're off-key or not. When with the Pentecostals, holler out an Amen now and then." He sipped. "Terrible what the public forces its politicians to do. Just terrible. Almost as bad as what it does to preachers. Makes damn eunuchs out of them. Surprised they don't all talk like women. Terrible I tell you."

I had work in my office, but an attorney who wished to stay on the good side of Judge Gareet remained till dismissed even from conviviality. If you were really trying to run up points, you took him to dinner at the General Johnston Hotel and slipped the check under your own coffee cup.

"As to Vin again, I think it likely he died of a heart arrest or stroke," the judge said. "I made it my business to see the medical examiner's report, and what that tells you is precisely nothing. A precise and scientific nothing."

I agreed and wondered whether he knew about the tattoo— Pull for service. I guessed not.

"So much in life is unexpected," the judge said. "A man rubs his hands before sitting down to a fine dinner. Full of delight at the repast before him, he reaches for an iced oyster on the half shell, swallows, and the oyster amidst joy goes down the wrong way. Before anyone reacts, the man is gasping for life on the floor. I'm not suggesting Vin was eating oysters or anything else, but it's the unexpected which living strikes us with that confounds us."

He clucked, shook his head, and sipped. Fingers of his free hand worked into gaps of his white shirt to scratch the curve of his stomach.

"Hard on Rhea I know," he said. "Such a lovely woman. Tell you the truth I believed in the beginning the marriage was a mismatch. I thought old Vin laid a selling job on her. I was wrong. They were a beautiful couple. You ever see them dance? They were the best in these parts, real grace. I would've paid money to watch them ballroom."

He offered to sweeten my drink, but I raised my palm over my glass.

"Such a shame, they had so much," he said. "The thing that impresses me about Rhea is she treats everybody right. Doesn't make any difference who. Somebody knocks on the door selling vacuum cleaners or if it's the governor himself she is nice to them all, genteel. That's the word, genteel."

I kept nodding and held my glass on my lap so he couldn't doctor it. Another drink would've opened a trapdoor under me, and I'd be unable to escape his amber bottle with its slippery sides.

"One thing, just a remote possibility," the judge said. "Vin, I mean. Anybody consider suicide?"

"How'd he do it?" I asked.

"Don't know. Don't actually think it's possible. Vin would

never embrace the coward's way. Not in character. He was too positive."

The judge finished his drink and leaned forward. I quickly set my glass on his desk and suggested we go to the General Johnston for a meal.

"I confess I do have a hunger for a T-bone," he said, and a surge of pinkness spread through him. He laughed out of his pampered softness. "I just wonder what all the poor folks are doing."

Lucy Colette, the judge's secretary, brought the warrant to my office in the morning. I'd slept little during the night. Half in dream, half awake, I'd kept seeing Rhea beside me on a white yawl. She was still dressed in black funeral clothes, a ridiculous imagining. She stood in the blowing cockpit and looked out over the pitching bow, and I reached for a hand, still gloved, to kiss the grief away from her wept-on fingers.

There'd been another threatening phone call, this one taken by my father. He'd loaded his Luger and commenced guard duty at the upstairs windows, limping from front to back, ready for the enemy.

"You recognize the voice?" I asked.

"Think I'd just be waiting around if I recognized anybody? I'd have gone after the bastard!"

From my office I telephoned the sheriff to tell him I held the warrant. He in turn had a plan for the hippie raid to be executed by him and six deputies. No state police would be included. The state police, he argued, were too bound up in regulations, too conscious of procedures. Pickney believed we would have to stay loose. By "loose" he meant we might need to be creative.

"The hippies'll still be in the bed," he said. "Carouse all night and sleep all day. Probably still high, in a daze. They won't expect company this time of morning."

He unfolded a black-and-white Howell County map, which he spread over my desk. His deputies stood in a half circle around him while he pointed out the area of operation.

"There's an old logging trail snaking around the rear of the property," he explained. "Couple of men follow it, not on wheels 'cause the trail's growed up with scrubs and a straining vehicle might alert somebody. Give the men twenty minutes to get positioned. Then call in deputies to both flanks of the place, also on foot. The rest slip up the front lane and rush the house before evidence can be destroyed.

At 9:45 A.M. we drove out toward the Hard Times tract on the Poorhouse Road. A sudden shower patted the Ford's roof, a fall of rain so fine the drops evaporated before spreading over the hot pavement. Steam rose—holes of Hell we used to call them when I was a boy.

The lead car was Pickney's, and I rode in the front seat beside him. Two deputies sat in back feeding double 00 buckshot into their riot guns. Burke, the senior deputy, kept shucking shells out and thumbing them in again. He laid fingers along the gun with the tenderness some men reserve for women.

The Hard Times tract was a cut-over section timber companies had been through, leaving desolation which couldn't have been improved upon by the German army. The land had not been replanted in loblolly seedlings and what had grown up was trash trees—scrub oaks, short-leaf pines, cedars, along with briers and honeysuckle.

Pickney directed the first pair of deputies to park their car off the road, lock it, and move out on the logging trail. Thorns snagged their uniform pants, causing the men to kick and cuss quietly. The second pair of deputies took up positions in the woods at either side of the house. By that time it was almost eleven o'clock, and the slight coolness provided by the flimsy shower had cooked off.

The sheriff, the last two deputies, and I stopped at the head of the dirt lane. From a holster Pickney drew a walkie-talkie, extended the antenna, and, holding the instrument against his jaw, spoke into it:

"Let's do her then."

We moved fast along the rutted lane. Dust rose about us. On either side was a broken barbed-wire fence. A rabbit spooked in front of Burke, causing him to spring sideways. He'd been thinking copperhead.

The lane curved, but we were still far from the house. We spread through broomstraw, and it whisked against our pants. Bent like men on the attack, we reached a garden in which grew cucumbers, onions, snap beans, kale, staked tomatoes, and what at first we believed were melons but turned out to be breasts offered to the sun. Three girls lay on their backs in grass at the garden's edge, arms spread, eyes closed, each naked to the waist.

The sheriff, the deputies, and I pulled up short to glance among ourselves and stare at the sprawled young girls, one of whom flapped a lazy hand above her face to shoo away a fly.

Pickney, unsure, looked at me for advice. I lifted my hands and shrugged. He swept his arm forward, a signal to rush the house. We ran past the girls, who, startled, sat up.

The house had been repaired, seemed in fact plumb. Two-by-sixes supported it like flying buttresses. The plank siding was painted pink, the doorway white. Garden tools leaned against a front porch on which was crude, hand-hewn furniture.

The screen door was unlocked, and, revolver drawn, Pickney stepped in followed by deputies and me. We faced a clean white room whose walls were posted not with rock stars or South American vistas but huge vegetables childishly drawn in crayon—green peppers, ripe pumpkins, watermelons, glistening English peas, yellow corn.

In other rooms were mattress covers stuffed with straw, blankets rolled and tied, wild flowers stuck in Ball jars, cooking utensils, a wood stove, and set on a mantel a thick curlicued root as smooth and clean as a tooth.

We hurried out the back door. From a field at the side three young men walked toward the house. They wore bib overalls of the kind dirt farmers bought from the Howell County Mercantile. They had on no shirts, and their tanned skins were oily with sweat. Around their necks were red bandannas and on their heads straw hats. They carried a posthole digger, fencing tools, and an iron tamping bar.

"Don't you try to run!" the sheriff shouted. He still held his pistol.

The young men weren't trying to run but continued ambling toward the house. The girls had buttoned on blue denim shirts and tucked them into their jeans. Though barefooted and wearing their hair long and straight, they appeared clean, as did the young men, the house, everything.

Deputies ran from the woods and closed around the group, herding it toward a well pump, around which were baskets of snaps, onions, and broccoli. The deputies held their riot guns at the ready.

"We got a warrant," Pickney said to a brawny redheaded youth.

"The doors are unlocked," the redhead answered.

"You got a name?" Pickney asked.

"Cloud."

"Full name," Pickney said as he holstered his .38 and drew a notebook from his hip pocket.

"That's it, Cloud. I had it changed. I can show you papers, though I'll have to send for them."

They had names like Jasmine, Hawthorn, Blue Water, Willow, and Plum. The sheriff peered at them as if they'd crawled up out of holes. The deputies shifted their riot guns and frowned except for Burke, who appeared awed. My guess was that sunlit breasts still raced through his mind.

"Where your cycles?" Pickney asked.

"You see all we've got," Cloud answered.

"I saw plenty out by the garden."

"They were women among women."

"You some kind of religion?"

Cloud laughed, showing fine large teeth and his muscled throat. The others smiled, waiting patiently and unafraid.

"No religion," Cloud said.

"We're searching the place," Pickney said. He sent deputies back into the house and toward ramshackle outbuildings on which raw new boards had been nailed over gaps. The deputies opened everything that had doors or lids. They poked up chimneys, pried loose floorboards, turned over lumber, yet found nothing except a basket of knobby roots in a collapsing tobacco barn. The sheriff smelled the roots and held them out to Cloud.

"Jerusalem artichokes," Cloud said. "They grow wild here along the fence line. Very wholesome and can be cooked or pickled."

"We're taking them in to be analyzed," Pickney said and drew me aside to cedar shade, where he lowered his voice. "If they legit, hogs can ice skate and play the piano. Carousers is what they are, traveling around getting high and screwing like rabbits—you saw the women naked."

He ordered deputies on another search, walked back to Cloud, and circled him and the group as if inspecting livestock.

"You got a deed to this property?" he asked.

"We do."

"Let me see it."

"I'll have to send to Saint Louis for it."

"How I know you'll send for it? You could just be plucking feathers. I'm ordering an aerial survey of this place. If you're growing illegal substances, our camera will find them."

"We grow only vegetables."

"Oh yeah, yeah, you're upstanding," Pickney said and stopped in front of a girl, the one named Plum, a brunette rangy as a boy, yet feminine. She was more like a peach, covered with a sun-bleached fuzz, her face, neck, and arms, I guessed her whole body, fuzzy. "You got a story?"

"Cloud does the talking for us," she said, not insubordinate or sullen, but smiling, sprightly.

"Who does the talking is who I say does the talking," Pickney said. "Where's the money come from you all live on?"

She glanced at Cloud, who nodded permission. "We don't require much. We hope eventually to use no money at all and simply barter. Man has a short number of days and is vain to waste them coveting."

Baffled, Pickney turned away to look out across the broom-straw where deputies searched. Again he drew me to the shade of the cedar.

"I don't believe it," he said. "They got pills and stuff hidden somewheres. Let's split them up, ask the same questions, and see if the answers check."

He used the front porch, sat on the unpainted swing, toed the floor, and called to Burke to send them around singly. Plum was first, her skin darkened by an unstylish farmer's tan. She wore no makeup and smelled of the garden grass where she'd been lying. Her blue shirt was unpressed but freshly washed. Her cleanliness, the cleanliness everywhere, impressed me.

She stood before the sheriff, who toed the swing and stared at her. She was not intimidated and waited respectfully.

"How you get your highs?" the sheriff asked.

"Untainted food, clean air, work, and sunshine provide the best highs of all."

"Shame I didn't bring my shovel. I don't reckon you read newspapers."

"We don't have newspapers, periodicals, radios, TV, or even electricity."

"You wouldn't know anything at all about a prominent man dying in this community."

"No, I wouldn't," she said, undisturbed, her voice gentle, her body relaxed.

"Little angels you are."

This time I stared and wondered whether Pickney had learned of the silver angel Captain Blake found at the river.

"We're pacifists. We don't even kill bugs but pick them off the vegetables." She lifted her hands slightly. "Reverence for life. No one knows where the evolutionary thrust may lead, what form it may choose."

"You want the bugs to take over?" I asked.

"Man may be only an accident," she said.

"Account for your whereabouts June twenty-ninth and thir-tieth last," Pickney said.

"That's difficult to do. We don't use calendars or watches. You own them, they own you. Minutes and hours are man-made. We keep time by our gardens."

"Don't suppose you ever go to the river either," Pickney said.

"We don't take the lives of fish."

"The evolutionary thrust may be piscine," I said to her.

"It may be anything and in a form so transcendent we throw ourselves prostrate before it."

"What you all talking about?" Pickney asked. "You ever been arrested? I'll find out, so you better tell me now."

"I obeyed the law even before my conversion."

"Conversion from what?"

"Being a Michigan public-school teacher."

"I'll find out," Pickney said. "You better be telling the truth. Now you go over and stand by the garden. You wait till I tell you to move. Don't talk to nobody. Don't even look at nobody. Understand?"

"Would you like a carrot? Very refreshing."

"Hell no, I don't want a carrot! What I want is truth!"

"There's a lot of truth in a carrot," she said.

"Get!" Pickney said and stood from the swing. He slapped his notebook against his palm.

She nodded, turned, and walked away, her expression unchanged, her stride womanly without being flirtatious.

"You believe any of this?" Pickney asked and removed his trooper hat to fan his face.

"I'm almost convinced," I said. "It's too wild not to be real."

"I am one hell of a long way from being convinced," Pickney said.

He next questioned the young man named Blue Water, who was small, wiry, with hair the color of straw. He stood with his hands behind his back. On his feet were tattered running shoes, scarred vestiges, I guessed, of another life.

"You ever been arrested?" Pickney asked.

"Yes, sir."

Pickney was surprised by the answer's directness since he'd asked the question routinely, an opener. He required a beat to adjust.

"Where and when?"

"Lima, Ohio, two years ago, petty larceny. It was before I met Cloud and the others."

"What else?"

"My only conviction. I pulled no time but got eighteen months' probation."

"What'd you steal?"

"Cuff links and a dress shirt. '"Vanity," sayeth the preacher.'"

"You have a job?"

"I worked in an auto store but was interested in acting."

"What you steal now?"

"No need for stealing. We make our things. You looked at my feet. In time we'll produce shoes."

"Doesn't hide require modification in reverence for life?" I asked.

"We won't use leather, but rubber, even wood, maybe a combination with a cloth lining. The point is I have no motivation to steal. Even as it is during the summer we can stroll around this country and pick food off the ground, edibles nobody bothers about. We have our garden. Stealing's redundant."

Before Pickney absorbed the words, Jess Elder, a deputy, hurried around the house. He was a former Howell County High School hero, a fullback who'd been the love of leggy, leaping cheerleaders. His life now was settling into his stomach. Those beautiful swift muscles had yielded to time, and Jess's ordinary expression was the distant one of a man searching behind him for a lost promise.

He whispered to Pickney. The sheriff had stopped his swinging with a scraping of his brown leather dingo boots.

"You stay right here!" Pickney told Blue Water and left the porch, Jess trailing him.

I took out cigarettes and offered one to Blue Water, who shook his head.

"Somehow I knew you'd be above smoking," I said.

"You're eyeing my running shoes. I used to be very fast."

"Sure."

"I ran a four-minute mile," he said. "Just me on the cinder track at night, a girl to hold the stopwatch, and a moon so full it washed the earth. Two o'clock in the morning it was, Lima, Ohio, and for a brief spell I became the wind."

"Poetic," I said.

"Toughness is a defense," he said.

Jess Elder came back and motioned to me. I left Blue Water on the porch and walked to the rear of the house, where Pickney questioned Cloud in shade of the cedar.

"You don't have nothing to tell, nothing at all?" Pickney asked.

"I don't understand what you want," Cloud said.

"Tell me some more about how you support yourself out here in the sticks besides lying around naked and picking up food off the ground."

Cloud was puzzled but waited with the patience of one who had stood long in many lines.

"Oh, you so innocent," Pickney said and brought a hand from behind him. It held a black leather wallet wrapped in a translucent plastic bag used by police for evidence collection. He raised the wallet on his palm as if intending to present it to Cloud.

"Am I supposed to react in some fashion?" Cloud asked.

"I think so since it was found under a timber in your shed. Inside here are identifying papers. Like to guess whose wallet this was? Notice I said 'was.'"

Cloud eyed the wallet and looked worried but didn't speak.

"Let's peekaboo it," the sheriff said and was able to open the wallet without removing it from the plastic. "Does she or does she not, according to the driver's license, belong to a man name of Vincent Fallon Farr? Funny thing though. All money and credit cards is missing."

Cloud shook his head and turned to the others, who, except for Blue Water on the porch and Plum coming from the garden, stood by the pitcher pump.

"Who knows about a wallet?" Cloud called.

The group talked among themselves. Blue Water came around the house to join in. Finally the one named Hawthorn covered his eyes, and from the women rose a low moan.

He was the oldest of the three men and had an asymmetrical face as if he suffered from an insect bite or swollen molar. Though not as large as Cloud, he was heavily strong in the manner of a draft animal. His black Indian-like hair had been bound at the nape with a piece of bailer twine.

He walked slowly toward Cloud, one foot scraping dust and leaving a furrow. He closed his eyes, clenched them. It struck me he was simple in some way, lacking. Cloud spoke kindly.

"You, Haw?"

Hawthorn kept his eyes shut as he blushed and ducked his chin.

"Tell us," Cloud said and laid a hand on Hawthorn's shoulder.

"T-the- g-g-greens," Hawthorn said and spit rode his stuttering.

Cloud explained. "Haw had some bad luck during a war. Let me tell you nobody in the whole world can grow October beans like this fellow."

Cloud drew Hawthorn in, hugged him, and Hawthorn was so pleased he stopped twisting and smiled like a child. The women had slipped in behind, and they too were smiling and lifting fingers to touch Hawthorn as if to transfer to him their love and strength.

"W-w-walking the l-line," he said, and under coaching from Cloud we got a story of Hawthorn's foraging the power line right-of-way to pull land cress and dandelion salad, which he stuffed into a croaker sack.

As he stooped, he spotted the wallet, lifted and opened it to look inside. There was no money. He dropped the wallet into the sack, and when he returned with the salad, he pitched the wallet aside.

"We store food in the shed," Cloud said. "A timber might've fallen on it."

"Some story," Pickney said.

"Haw never lies," Cloud said, and the others agreed.

"You think I was sleeping when they passed out the brains?" Pickney asked.

"How do we convince you?" Cloud said. "You can see we don't live extravagant lives. And if we were stealing, we wouldn't bring the wallet back here but throw it in a ditch or the river."

"You go to the river, do you?" Pickney asked.

"We take our baths there."

"Baths and what else?" Pickney asked and turned from Cloud to Hawthorn. "Where'd you really get the wallet?"

Hawthorn stuttered while Cloud and the women tried to make it easier for him by touching and encouraging him. Spit sprayed, eyelids fluttered. He couldn't describe the spot, just somewhere along the power line and near the highway. He was unable to name specifics—a farm, road sign, billboard, country store.

"Haw doesn't hesitate to walk eight or ten miles," Cloud said. "He goes till he fills his sack and concentrates on the job. His mind never wanders."

"You're telling me the place he found the wallet could be anywhere eight or ten miles up or down the road?" Pickney asked. "Does he even know north and south?"

Cloud talked to Hawthorn, tried to coax information from him, but Hawthorn was bothered, disturbed and trembling, his spit flying around words half formed.

Not good enough, I thought, though the wallet could have been thrown out the window of a passing car. Still we had no reason to believe anything they told us. Shooing flies off ourselves, Pickney and I walked away from the group.

"Got to take them in," he said, and his finger homed on his nose.

"All of them?" I asked.

"The Cloud character since he's in charge and Hawthorn, though his bread ain't risen."

"We could wait a day."

"Wait ten minutes and they gone. Come like smoke and leave the same. They the best we got."

We walked back to the group. When Pickney said he was taking Cloud and Hawthorn, the girls shook their heads and made a moaning sound.

"Doesn't there have to be a charge?" Cloud asked.

"How's robbery and felonious assault to start off with?" Pickney said. "You can take toothbrushes if people like you use them."

Burke and Jess Elder walked into the house with Cloud and Hawthorn to get their things.

"Don't let them do this," Plum whispered to me.

"They won't be mistreated." I steadied my sunglasses.

"All they're guilty of is living free."

"Then they'll soon be released."

Cloud and Hawthorn were crowded into the back of a car, a deputy on each side. As the doors slammed, the girls began to clap and sing. Their voices had a black, gospel sound:

> Plenty tired of walking,
> Plenty tired of rain,
> Plenty tired of hurting,
> And a road of pain.
> We love you, Haw!

It was so hot locusts screeched into the night. Thunderheads bunched, collided, and rain fell, a quick shower that caused the grass, fields, and pines to glimmer. Gutters were stopped—Eddie Blue had supposedly cleaned them—and for a few cool blowing seconds water ran over to bang the porch's tin roof and splatter the ground.

In his room my father listened to the news, which was not information or entertainment to him but a personal conflict. He talked to his TV set. He shook his fist at it and stomped the floor. "They ought to put all politicians in the front lines, the sonsof-bitches!"

When the telephone rang, I opened the screen door to go inside. Soon as I lifted the receiver, I knew I'd made a mistake. It was my ex-wife, Jeannie.

"The check hasn't come," she said, more a charge than a statement. In her time she had accused me of lacking the capacity to love and called me a drunk. Before answering, I balanced my weight on both feet as if a wind might rise from the telephone.

"It's in the mail," I said. She lived in Jacksonville. "Sue the post office."

"I don't believe you. It was late last month too."

"I was busy last month and forgot, and you should be mature enough not to expect perfection from a member of the human race."

"If it doesn't come by Monday, I'm getting mad—I mean honest-to-God fire-breathing mad."

"You've penetrated areas of my comprehension."

"You soused?"

"Merely on the doorstep of sousiness."

"Oh, hell, Billy, how are you anyway?"

"Thanks for your concern. It's most gracious of you to inquire after practically threatening me with legal action and death."

"You're swacked all right."

"I am building upon swackiness."

"I'm broke. No barrel even to scrape the bottom of."

"Because of you, so am I."

"Well, fasten your seat belt and hold on to the wheel. There's hope. Are you ready for this? I just might, and I emphasize might, be married again. I'm seeing a man who owns office buildings, races thoroughbreds, and plays polo."

"Offering you all the things I promised and failed to provide."

"Don't be nasty."

"I'll come to your wedding, dance, throw rice."

"You won't be invited, but you can do me a favor. Eat something. I can tell by your voice you haven't been eating. Didn't Aunt Lettie leave anything?"

"She's piqued because I fired Eddie Blue. The last thing she left was a baked chicken, and to be perfectly up front I don't need anything baked since I am baked myself."

"Oh, Billy, my lost, lost love. But don't think I'm growing soft. If I don't receive the check, you'll hear from my lawyer."

"Thanks ever so much."

"Billy, Billy," she said and hung up. Even before I was able to lift my fingers from the phone, it again trembled with ringing. This time it was Alex Poole of the bank.

"Today is my day!" he said. "First time in my life I broke eighty, and I had to birdie seventeen and eighteen to do it. Made a thirty-foot downhill putt. Won twenty-two dollars and had my tods paid for by grown men near to weeping. I'm taking this day and putting it in the vault down at the bank."

I listened to how he'd hit his approach shot on the eighteenth. I'd once played golf, taken it up as part of my program of becoming a wheel in the world. I thought I'd someday be making rounds with industrialists, politicians, financiers. Long since my sporty clothes had been given to Goodwill Industries, and my black-and-white shoes lay amoldering in a damp corner of the cellar. Mice had chewed away the kilties.

"I used a wedge, chipped to the green, and the ball stopped two inches from the cup," Alex said. "Man, I was in Heaven!"

I congratulated him and pictured golf courses in Heaven. No carts necessary. Players would have wings.

"I shouldn't be doing this," he said.

"You shouldn't be telling me about your sensational golf?"

"This is bank business, or Vin Farr business. I'm volunteering it. We cleared a late check today, one of his, dated almost a month before he died, was killed, whatever."

"You consider a month-old check late?"

"I do when it's for $10,000. And when the payee's the Sons of the Father."

"Repeat," I said.

"Got your attention, didn't I? Sons of the Father. Ten thousand dollars."

"Signed by Vin?"

"Signature verified."

"Vin a supporter of the Sons of the Father?"

"First time. I had the girl go back through microfilm." He stopped speaking a moment, and I heard paper rustling. "Vin wasn't a big supporter of religious groups or activities, though he did give a few hundred a year to Saint Andrew's Episcopal."

"You mean you didn't consider him a spiritual type?"

"Hell no. That's why I thought I'd better alert you, that and the size of the check. I don't mean Vin was an atheist. But he was no angel either."

"Hold on to the check," I said and thought of Rhea at the funeral saying Vin had found God and come to love Him.

"I can't turn it over to you without a court order."

"I'll handle the technicalities. In the meantime stop payment."

"Consider it done. Lordy what a day. Wish I had it on film."

I walked back to the porch and sat in the wicker chair. The rain had almost stopped, what's left leaking from a dark swirling sky. It was my responsibility to focus on Vin and the $10,000 check written to the Sons of the Father. My mind skirted the information like a hound circling a blue crab.

The Sons were a black religious community in Howell County run by a man named Father Mercy, who had once been a jailbird, a slicer and slayer of men. After a niggertown brawl in a Danville barroom, Father Mercy, then Jeddidiah K. Poteat, left the floor so bloody the police couldn't cross it without slipping as if walking on grease. There were fingers under an overturned table and an ear lying in front of the flashing jukebox.

He was the meanest man in prison, attacking guards, causing riots, serving most of his time in solitary, but into the blackness of that lonely hole the flaming word descended, an angel of light coming down the golden stairs. Jeddidiah by his own admission quaked and begged for mercy. "Don't drag me off to no Hell!" he pleaded. The angel raised him from the concrete floor, washed away his sins with liquid splendor, and told Jeddidiah he was henceforth to save his brethren, lead them out of evil and darkness just as he himself had been illuminated and lifted from the pit.

At prison he became Father Mercy, the godly man of peace. He calmed blazes of insurrection, laid his strong hand on bodies of rage and revolt, and gathered a congregation which met in the gymnasium and grew to three hundred souls. With eyes alone he dominated a crazed lifer on the loose with a wrecking bar seized from the maintenance shop. The lifer laid the wrecking bar at Father Mercy's feet as if it were a gift from the Magi.

After twenty-seven years Father Mercy was paroled through an extraordinary session of the board convened by the governor. Father Mercy shook the governor's hand, posed for newspaper pictures, and spoke a prayer in a voice like pedal tones of a trombone. "Teach your brother to walk in the golden light of the living God!"

He came back to Howell County where he'd been born, returned to his home place, a crooked shanty, scrub land, fifteen acres of thistle and red clay where he built himself a church, a rickety structure all out of proportion, with odd-sized windows, oblique wings, and a lopsided tower the bell of which clanged off-key.

The church, the congregation, the Sons of the Father had waxed and prospered. Father Mercy bought more land, built cabins around in the woods, and dug an amphitheater by the river where he performed his mass baptisms, the singing and hallelujahing rolling along the water all the way to Tobaccoton and causing people to lift their faces as if the wind were indicating a change of weather.

Recruits came not only from prisons but from all parts of the state and beyond Virginia, arrived on buses or in rattletrap pickups hauling a mattress and a chair or two. Father Mercy took them in, sons and daughters, trained them in the gospel, and sent them out to raise the downtrodden, to sign them up, to show the brethren the golden staircase.

But the Sons of the Father were racists. Part of Father Mercy's theology was that blacks were especially blessed through their suffering, that whites had little chance of salvation because they had not tasted enough rejection and humiliation. In a world of agony, whites were children and had to mature through pain before they were ready for admittance to the promised land. Blacks, however, could carry their suffering up the golden steps like a bejeweled identity card that would allow them to pass singing and praising through the iridescent portals.

So what was Vin Farr doing writing a check for that kind of money to the Sons of the Father? He couldn't have joined up had he wanted, and even thinking of the possibility of his wanting to was absurd. He was no pillar of devotion in his own church. He did accompany Rhea to Saint Andrew's, but within twenty minutes after shaking the rector's hand Vin was out on the links lining up Nassaus. It was said those few players Vin couldn't beat, he usually outbet and that the rare money he lost had the touch of his fingers on it, the reluctance to let go residing in the bills. Yet he had found God and come to love Him. When?

The next morning even before I sat at my desk, I had another call, this one from Captain Blake in Richmond. I told him about Harrison Adams, the bringing in of Cloud and Hawthorn, and the $10,000 check.

"You think the latter significant?" he asked.

"I intend to visit Father Mercy."

"Tread carefully with that man. As to the ones brought in—?"

"Cloud and Hawthorn. They're members of a vegetable cult."

"Keep me informed."

I asked him about the miniature angel found near Vin's body. I was thinking of it and the blazing celestial which had descended to Father Mercy in prison.

"It's been through forensics with no conclusion except that its content is, let's see, 87.9 percent silver. Not something on the market. We checked with several jewelers. The figure was probably a pendant, worn perhaps around the neck. Also it's likely an antique."

"Could it be a badge or insignia of membership in some secret society?"

"If so, we haven't found it, and if it is, we will. One other thing, not about the angel. The lab was able to identify an additional substance in Vincent Farr's stomach. Dr. Pepper."

"One more time."

"No question about it. Dr. Pepper."

And cracklings.

9

Master: Recite.

Me: The sinfulness of that estate whereinto man fell consisteth in the guilt of Adam's first sin, the want of that righteousness wherein he was created, and the corruption of his nature, whereby he is utterly indisposed, disabled, and made opposite unto all that is spiritually good, and wholly inclined to all evil, and that continually; which is commonly called original sin, and from which do proceed all actual transgressions.

Master: Do you understand?

Me: Yes.

Master: You must be convinced man is wholly helpless, that there is nothing he can do to save himself. Good intentions are of no account. He hasn't the will or strength to resist depravity because depravity is in his blood and bones.

Me: I'm convinced.

Fleeting sunlight silhouettes the master's erect body in the slanted cabin doorway and reflects off yellow lenses of the shooting glasses.

Master: In the midst of my despair I received a vision. Alone in the darkness a cube of light appeared before my eyes, and in that light I saw a black building, the largest building your mind

114

can conceive, as if all the apartments in the world were stacked and had their walls stripped away so that what I saw was a honeycomb of existence.

In each compartment of the honeycomb was fire one instant, ice the next. The fire is like the mouth of a blowtorch, only the flame is not yellow or blue but redder than blood and hisses as it hurls through the air.

Then in an instant the fire stops and changes to a blizzard in each of the cubicles—sleet, ice, a ferocious wind, in all the compartments of the gigantic black building this is happening at the same time, lit only by the returning fire.

And in each cell of the honeycomb is a human being, a man or woman, all suffering from fire one instant, shrieking cold the next, all screaming, writhing, begging, and the din flows out of the honeycomb not like sound but serpent tongues, millions of red serpent tongues waving out in horrible howls that have stench and will not cease in an eternity, never to stop, never!

The master is agitated, body stiffened, arms rigid, the words speeding past lips close to seizure.

Master: And the worst thing is neither fire nor ice but the isolation, the separation. Each person in that terrible black structure can plead and howl through all eternity and will not be heard because all are walled off from every other living soul and God himself. All that pain will ring through the eons and count for nothing.

The master, aflame with religious frenzy, is moved and trembling; yet the voice suddenly calms, the control returns.

Master: What is the greatest good you can do for another?

Me: Save them from such a fate.

Master: Isn't any act that saves a person from such a fate justified?

Me: Yes.

Master: Isn't it in essence an act of love?

———

Pickney stood by Florene's desk in my office and chatted with her. Maybe he was attempting to woo her vote for his nephew. She might be considering going with a winner and making a deal for her job. I had to stop thinking like that about my own people.

Pickney swayed into my office and closed the door. Clamped between his teeth was the usual dark cigarillo. It jutted upward as he pushed out his jaw. Vin's wallet, he explained, carried no alien prints and nothing inside except the driver's license, a Blue Cross-Blue Shield card, and a few snapshots of antique cars, the farm, his biplane.

Pickney had located a boat which might have carried Vin to the place on the riverbank where he died—or been found dead.

"Eddied into a fallen sycamore," Pickney said. "And partly sunk."

We rode out in his tan police cruiser to look at the wooden rowboat whose hull was painted white. The boat had wedged into a leafy fork of the fallen sycamore. There were oars but no life preservers. On the bow the number 7 had been painted in green, like the stripes around the gunnel. A line trailed into the water.

"Not Vin's," I said.

"His is still in his boathouse and has an Evinrude on it."

I nodded, thinking Vin would never go anywhere without an engine. He didn't loaf over the waters, tasting the beauty of a summer's day. If he fished, he meant business, and when he traveled the river, he left wake which splashed hard against the sloping banks.

"We got a report from Waterside a boat's missing," Pickney said.

Waterside was a log pavilion and restaurant a mile and a half upriver. Steps led down to a dock where patrons could swim or rent boats. The place was popular on hot choking days when people desperately sought coolness of the river's deepest shade. Saturday nights offered dancing.

"Why would he use their boat?" I asked.

"Hope you don't expect an answer. I'll have it pulled out and dusted for prints, but I doubt we find anything 'cause it's been rain-washed."

"You could call in Captain Blake and his team."

"The day I call in those fancy Richmond sonsofbitches to do my job the sun will rise in the west and crows fly backwards out of their own assholes."

"You're theorizing Vin or somebody stole the boat and what?"

"The boat was definitely taken because Puckett ties them up careful. Now it could've been done by some boys having themselves a good time, but it also might be someone wanting to move a body—a body dead or alive."

"Why would Puckett wait till now to call you?"

"You know Puck, he's always running about two weeks behind in everything. I don't understand how him and Rose ever had children. By the time he got his clothes off and into bed, she'd probably done stood and drove to town for the meat and eggs and Puck would've forgotten what he had on his mind in the first place. Hell, Rose probably had to tell him what it was for and where to put it."

"Let's assume this is the boat Vin was in. How does that help?"

"Everything helps eventually."

We rode back toward Tobaccoton. I considered whether I should tell Pickney about Harrison Adams and the $10,000 check to Father Mercy. If I was withholding information from him, what was he withholding from me? I would cast a line.

"You had any complaints recently about the Sons of the Father?" I asked.

"Nothing except noisy singing. You think of them because of the river?"

"Some of the devotees come in pretty rough, don't they?"

"Father Mercy don't allow no fooling around. They so scared of him their hair stands straight when he walks past."

"Vin ever do any business with the Sons?"

Pickney glanced at me and then looked back at the road. When he was thinking, his face sort of gathered around his nose, as if his brains were centered there.

"Vin wanted that land. He tried to get that land while Father Mercy was still in the bad-boy hotel. But I never heard of any bad blood." He considered. "Father Mercy got no use for Vin or any other white man. He tells his people we got demons in us. He says that's why God made whites white, so everything else can be warned off. White is the color of death, he says, and that's why we're white 'cause we're dead—just walking around mean and dead."

"I'm thinking of going out there," I said.

"Glad it's you, not me. That jig's got no use for my department. Claims we crowd him. Told me it was the demons in us couldn't stand the sound or sight of holiness, and I been a Baptist all my life. If I was you, I'd save the gasoline."

We rode a ways without talking.

"That's what he tells them," Pickney said. "God made people white so they can be seen easy and run from. Well, what'd God make people black for, so they can hide in the dark?"

I drove out to see Father Mercy on a Tuesday, a thick, humid morning when grasshoppers sprang from weeds at the side of the road and pinged against the Chevy's metal.

I was thinking about Howell County, the religious madness of it where the churches ranged from the supercilious through the puritanical to the roaring rollers—from the aristocratic Episcopalians who sipped salvation with sherry to the self-righteous Presbyterians to the dirt-wallowing Pentecostals whose skulls pinwheeled and skyrocketed with hot visions of what they perceived to be the Holy Spirit.

People of our county didn't care to understand that the rest of the nation was trading in old-time religion for a newer model, that old-time religion was like a jalopy dropping parts along a bumpy road—the virgin birth here, the divinity of Christ there, the efficacy of prayer anywhere, all the parts falling off and bouncing along the road into weeds. The new model looked great with beautiful styling, lots of chrome, high gloss, and under the hood everything except the power of faith.

I slowed at the entranceway to Father Mercy's stockade compound, a yellow arch on which a proverb had been painted in black letters: THE WISDOM OF MAN IS FOOLISHNESS TO THE LORD!

The road wasn't paved, but it was cared for, the potholes and dips smoothed, and dust held down by sprinkled crankcase oil. Back among loblollies were unpainted pine cottages that had been allowed to weather into pearliness.

I passed a wooden grocery store with gas pumps in front, a ditch marked by old tires half buried and painted yellow, and a baseball diamond that had chicken wire strung up behind home plate. Children played there, barefooted, all wearing khaki shorts and yellow T-shirts.

The black adults had on sheets, not white, but again the same butter yellow, their heads and arms stuck through holes. They too moved without shoes, their feet coated with reddish dust. The women wore yellow kerchiefs tied about their hair, and some balanced baskets on their heads while others carried open umbrellas to protect themselves from sun.

When I stopped to ask a solemn young man where Father Mercy was, he pointed along the road. I drove till I saw the church, the headquarters, the tabernacle, whatever it was called by Sons of the Father—a yellow frame structure that looked as if it'd been put together by a dozen carpenters working with different sets of blueprints. The building was a series of rectangles sticking out at crazy angles, the windows at varied heights, numerous doors, one halfway to the roof and without steps to it.

The building appeared it might fall from its own elaboration, toppled by the crooked steeple shaped more like a rocket than a belfry. A good wind would roll it onto the red dirt of the parking lot. More partially buried tires outlined the lot.

I left my car, rejecting the impulse to lock it, and crossed toward what I guessed to be the main entrance. Over arched double doorways was another black-on-yellow sign: ONLY BELIEVE! I climbed seven wooden steps and, after opening a door, peered inside a room which was not rectangular but round. The space was lighted by conflicting colors from the many irregular stained-glass windows, and at the center of the room a pulpit had been reared and enclosed by panels of stained pine, the pulpit a square crow's-nest rising among a sea of pews.

Walls jarred the eyes because of slapdash murals portraying primitive flowers growing from agitated soil, the soil not of this earth but a compost of cities—old buildings, smashed autos, washtubs, kitchen sinks, refrigerators, all ground to a kind of mulch out of which the flowers rose in brilliant pinks, reds, violets, each bloom the head of a person, the head and torso, all yearning toward a sun so hot and yellow it would sear the sight of the blind.

As if to mark my timid entrance, an organ boomed deep chords. It too was reared above pews glazed by the rub of ecstatic worshiping bodies. The rounded female organist played leaned back as if holding on to the keys. She wore yellow garb and headdress, and her skin appeared more green than black in the wash of window light. The music must have been liturgical, yet its heavy pulse seemed a relentless drumming not out of Howell County but the jungle.

I stood below the organist and attempted to attract notice. Her face was lifted, her eyes closed. The music became louder. The beat battered my ears and sent vibrations through the sanctuary. I backed off.

I stepped through a doorway and moved into a dusky corridor which zigzagged ahead of me. On either side were rooms with pinned-up crayon drawings of tulips, daisies, and flaming flowers that never existed. Turns of the passage so confused me I thought of going back. Then I saw light ahead.

Before a crooked window stood what first appeared to be a threatening figure. It was a section of tree trunk carved into the shape of an avenging angel, a painted black angel who in one hand held a bloody sword and in the other a sleeping lamb. The angel's teeth, bared to devour, were rocks stuck into the wood, some sort of quartz polished and driven in.

Beyond the angel an office door was ajar. I still heard and felt the pulsing organ. Vibrations rose from my feet through my legs. I peeked into the office to see Father Mercy huge at his desk, his black eyes fired at me.

He was a man so large that the slightest movement of his head seemed to rearrange space around him, change its texture and gravity. The earth dipped under his weight, and all else flowed in.

He wore the yellow garment and a skullcap, though his great arms were bare to the elbows. His immense blackness shone with the richness of wet bottom soil. His features were rudely carved like the figure of the angel in the corridor. Likely he'd posed for the avenger.

I asked permission to enter. He remained unmoving. A scar began under the ragged hairline on the left side of his face and dropped diagonally to his nose and down over his lips to his jaw. Stitch marks had not disappeared and made it seem he had been put together on a laboratory table.

"The mark of evil and sign of destruction," Father Mercy said, his voice deep as a cavern, the words not spoken but proclaimed, causing his jowls to quiver like strings of a plucked instrument. "The living symbol of life separated from love and grace. Look at it and be warned, the walking death where live violence and doom, where demons find soft abode, a comfortable room, a hotel for the damned!"

I stood fearful even to reach to my sunglasses.

"A disorder, distemper, disease," he said, and when he rose, his magnitude traveled through the floor. There was no carpeting, the boards undressed pine, nails visible. Before I could speak, he raised his hands.

"I know you," he said, his expanse making the desk seem insubstantial. He lifted those massive fingers to create waving motions before his face and toward me. The hands became as languid as seaweed weltering at the ocean bottom, and as I watched I felt I was being drawn into helpless acquiescence. Behind the fingers, like glinting eyes peering from black fronds, Father Mercy watched.

"I know your interior, your emanations," he said. "I feel them now. You are no friend to Sons of the Father. You come spreading the white sickness of deceit, despair, and death. Damnation is in the throb of your blood. Only great suffering can cleanse you, and that suffering is coming. It will arrive on chariots of fire and fury. You must pay the price in pain."

"I have a few questions," I said.

His hands ceased their weaving and slowly lowered. He sat ponderously, leaned back in his outsized chair, and interlaced those powerful fingers over his stomach. The office was quiet except for the organ, the beat of it, the locusts, and the whirring of an electric fan on top a file cabinet near a window.

The wedge-shaped room contained no pictures, murals, tapestries, the only decoration being rocks, stones, all sorts and sizes, some polished and gemlike, others brown and oblong as newly baked loaves, a few cracked and tortured.

"The very rocks shall cry out!" Father Mercy said. He swept a ham hand past stones on the floor, a table, the windowsill. "'Help my suffering people!' they shall cry." He sat forward abruptly, and I felt threatened. It was all I could do to keep from stepping back. His blunt fingertips tapped the desk to the drumbeat of the organ. "The rocks shall weep."

"Just a question or two and I'll be on my way," I said.

"Let my people go," he said.

"I'm not holding your people."

"Don't mock me! I know who you are. Your great-grandfather murdered a black man!"

That was my great-grandfather Boyd on my mother's side, the one branch of our family that possessed a little land and money. Great-grandfather Boyd had been attacked by a field hand named Josiah who wielded a hooked tobacco knife. Josiah was drunk on secretly fermented wild scuppernongs; and to escape, my great-grandfather had been forced to gallop his horse over the raging slave. A frantic hoof smashed his face and drove his skull into the red soil.

"The rocks shall cry out, the earth will moan, but on that final day my people will walk with the host of Heaven, chosen for the rapture because pain is the Lord God's special anointment, His precious oil of esteem. Those He favors He bestows martyrdom upon, and when the great terrifying scale swings in judgment, it will be the weight of suffering that settles the balance."

Had I not been so buffeted by his rhetoric I might've told him I was glad to hear it because it meant I had a chance of salvation.

"My people shall ascend the golden staircase to the heavens, where singing angels await them, and the beautiful fingers of the Lord God shall reach to their trembling chins and lift them. 'Raise your eyes, my children, see the feast I have prepared for you. Find your place at my table, eat your fill of immortal food, and take your rest among the green groves of Paradise.'"

His voice had become louder, though still paced and each syllable perfectly enunciated. He would never need a microphone. He dwelt on his words, mouthed them long like succulent sweet candies.

"Bring your pain to me, and it will be blessed a thousandfold. Whites don't know. Since the foundation of the world the greatest suffering has been reserved for blacks. Because of us the world has endured. We have taken unto ourselves the contempt, hate, and injustice of humankind. We accept our mission because Jehovah will anoint our locks with the oozy lavings of spikenard. 'Where are the whites?' we will ask. And the Lord shall answer, 'They are in another place.'"

His hands lifted off the desk to resume their floating ballet.

"A place of darkness and black fire and lightning that singes the darkness, a region of endless wailing and eternal despair, a burning pit so deep that it has no bottom."

Father Mercy's fingers were again weaving their spell, and I had to blink to hold my concentration. Then the hands slowed, stilled, and fell thumping against his desk. He leaned back to eye me. A fly lit on his forehead, and Father Mercy wrinkled such ruts into his brow that the fly fled to escape closing folds of flesh.

"There are those we will plead for," he said. "We shall remember all who treat us fairly. For their sake we will entreat the

Lord God." He stared. "Though your faith is in a bottle."

He was so amused by my surprise and defensiveness that he allowed himself a flickering smile. The scar across his face changed shape. Tips of teeth like cubes appeared.

"You think we don't know?" he asked. "We see everything with a thousand eyes."

"Then you can help me with—"

"—the great Mr. Vincent Fallon Farr. He is in his place."

"I know where he is. What I don't is how he got there."

The piece of smile leveled, and again Father Mercy became impatient and imperial. As if enthroned, he sat without answering. He could have been alone.

"He gave your organization a check for $10,000," I said finally.

"We are not an organization. We have neither charter nor written rules. We draw the world's poison, and the world will be saved through us."

"Why did he give the money?"

"The check arrived by mail, no explanation attached."

"There has to be more, and I'm asking your help. Everybody might be weighed in your heavenly scales one day, but in the meantime some of us have to do the weighing down here."

"Mockery again! White is the color of deceit and deception!"

"And of light," I said.

"Not God's light, not the light of the sun. Of the moon, yes, the moon is dead, but God's light is a golden finger."

"About the $10,000."

"You play your little games, scurry about with your little plans, but here they are meaningless. Here we watch for and wait the judgment."

"Why would Vincent Farr send a check to the Sons of the Father?"

"He sent it to the Lord, not me."

"You received and endorsed it."

"As the Lord's intermediary," Father Mercy said. Before he could speak further, a young black girl dressed in the yellow garb tapped on the door and entered carrying an oval red tray on which was a glass pitcher of iced tea. Halves of lemons floated in it. Slim and grave, she moved quietly, her bare feet silent on the floor. She set the tray to the side of the desk, kept her eyelids lowered, and started to leave. Father Mercy lifted a hand.

"Sister Idel has known the pain and poison," he said. "Tell him."

Obediently the girl faced me, her arms at her sides, her eyes still down, and when she spoke, her voice was a toneless recitation.

"At thirteen I made money with my body. The white devil was husband of the woman who employed my mother to clean, and he led me by the hand to his garage where he gave me a dollar to undress. He brought his friends, and I did it for them. At night men took me in their cars. Their demons lived inside me, and I couldn't cleanse myself until Father Mercy found me and washed me sinless in the river."

"She was beaten and burned with cigarettes, and on the Day of Judgment she shall be seated at a high place of the Lord's table," Father Mercy said.

"I have put my shame behind me," Sister Idel said.

"Another glass," Father Mercy said. There was one already on his desk.

She brought the glass, backed out, and pulled the door to. Father Mercy poured. I didn't want to accept the heavy tumbler from his clublike hand, yet refusing might arouse him. I sipped at the sweetened tea while he swallowed his in gulps, each of which caused his facial scar to bend.

"The divine plan was revealed to me in a vision," he said, setting the glass on the tray in order to refill it. "Think of mankind as a wheel rolling toward the final day, we, the Sons, the hub of that wheel, all others spokes. Can you see it?"

"I'll think about it. Now, Mr. Farr sent you money without telling you why?"

"I don't have to answer."

"I am respectfully requesting that you do."

"We find the lost and bring them here, clean them, doctor them, clothe them in apparel of dignity."

He swallowed and lifted a hand toward the window. The fan whirred, the locusts shrilled, and a faint singing rose, unaccompanied women's voices childishly pure, an innocence rising with the heat of the day.

"We repair them," Father Mercy said. "When they leave here, they never go back to the street."

"Why would Mr. Farr send money for that?"

"I've never spoken with him."

"Has he given before?"

"No."

"And when a check for $10,000 arrived, you didn't inquire?"

"I don't question money. It is used for good."

In drinking the last sugary drops of his tea, he lifted his forearm high, and his sleeve slid down from his elbow. On the mighty lump of his bicep was a tattoo, a coiled blue serpent. He saw me looking and lowered the arm and sleeve.

"From another place," he said. "Once I too was full of demons."

I thought Vin Farr also had a tattoo, the Pull for service, and my mind sought a connection.

"To my knowledge I never saw Mr. Farr, though it's possible we passed on the street," Father Mercy said. He refilled his glass. "As to the $10,000, even the Devil has remorse."

He finished the tea without lowering it and was careful to keep the tattoo covered. He then stood to signal me our conversation was ended.

"You think he was the Devil?"

"He was white."

I too stood and set my glass on the tray. I had swallowed hardly a spoonful. He looked at the glass and at me. Again a partial smile, yet with no friendliness. I was running not only his tattoo through my mind, but also the barbaric wooden angel in the corridor.

"Do the Sons of the Father use any sort of insignia or emblem of membership?" I asked.

"I told you we are not an organization in the usual sense. Our badge of brotherhood is to walk in righteousness."

"What about angels?"

"They come to me in the cool of evening, and on my knees I listen to their songs. 'It is closer,' they say. 'Even now Jehovah is setting his table.'"

He walked out and left me, the world seeming to tilt after him.

I found a door from the lopsided building and returned to my car. Singing came from the direction of the river, possibly where lost women were being dipped into its waters and regenerated.

I drove toward Riverview. The day had become stiller, hotter, the heat visible in rising shimmers. Starlings too enervated to fly sat hunched on fences.

Again my Chevy's tires crunched over the immaculate gravel, which appeared to have been raked only moments before. Old Ben was still missing, but on a money farm like Riverview another black was always available to take up the hoe, broom, or dustpan. Here help was not hired, it was raised.

The heat eased as I drove under shade so dense it had texture. The iron fountain had been switched on, and a bloom of water rose and fell apart to overflow the scallops. The bluegrass lawn sloped to the river. The air around me seemed different, softer, lacking the coarseness of defining objects too realistically.

Melissa in her maid's apron and uniform answered the door. She told me Mrs. Farr was at the stable. I walked slate flagstones toward the outbuildings, all painted the same barn red and trimmed around windows and doors with white.

Rhea was hosing down a horse. She'd piled her strawberry hair up under a black riding cap and wore schooling chaps and a gray shirt. When she saw me, she handed the hose to a young black boy holding the leather shank.

As she came toward me, she took off her hunt cap, stripped perforated gloves from her fingers, and dropped the gloves into the cap. Freed, her clean hair had fallen into place. She pushed at it before lifting a hand to me. Unlike other women of her class, she didn't lean forward to be kissed but always gave men her hand.

Her broad face was sweaty, yet even that made her attractive as if the ladylike beading over her lips and along her temples was deliberately applied and decorative. She wiped at her chin with two long lovely fingers that caused me to think of well-shaped legs.

She wouldn't let me apologize for coming without first phoning. We strolled toward the house. Down the lawn near the willow-shaded river a black man on a tractor cut grass and left fresh pale green swaths that glistened. She led me to a white metal table under a red-and-white beach umbrella near the pool. A hose, a skimming net, and an underwater vacuum lay spread on bright concrete. She didn't have to call or ring for Melissa to appear.

"A shake, thick and cold, with chips of ice in it, made from our own milk and cream," Rhea said. "Fattening it may be, but you're thin enough it won't hurt, and I deserve one after the workout with Miss Scarlet. Don't let me talk you into it. Would you rather have something else?"

I wanted a drink, but she hadn't really offered liquor, only manners. We sat in shade of the umbrella, talked about the need for rain, and watched the red tractor lay strips across the lawn.

Melissa brought the milkshakes in tall glasses on a silver tray. The glasses had silver rims, and the straws were blown crystal that ended in tiny spoons. I fed the silky richness of chocolate into my mouth. There were heavy linen napkins.

I had this feeling I was in my teens and out with a girl from Howell County High instead of sitting across from a fully matured woman I dreamed of sailing to white beaches and loving under royal palms. Of course Rhea had never attended public school past the sixth grade.

She tongued a dab of milkshake from her upper lip and patted it with a napkin. I doubted that paper napkins had ever been used in the house except among servants, maybe not even then.

"Nothing from Old Ben?" I asked.

She shook her head. "So much trouble."

"If you could talk a few minutes."

"Have I ever not talked to you, Billy?"

Her lavender eyes stilled on me, and her voice sounded as if over the years we had built a special relationship, which wasn't the case. My love for her had always been from shadows and bushes. Never in my boyhood had I gotten up nerve to call her. She had a gift for making everybody feel exceptional.

"And no one's ever been nicer to me than you, Rhea," I said and then was alarmed I'd spoken too openly. Blood rising in my face, I hurried on. "Do you know a man named Harrison Adams?"

She was finishing her milkshake and using the little spoon to scrape around her glass. From her neck hung the tiny gold cross. She frowned into glare from the river.

"I might've met him someplace, though no face pops into mind."

"He was a business associate of Vin's."

"Still doesn't register."

"I realize Vin was into lots of things. I learned he gave a check of significant size to the Sons of the Father. Would you know about that?"

"Vin and I talked about supporting Father Mercy. Despite the way he treats whites, the work he's doing in the cities, particularly among misused women, is worthwhile."

"Did you suggest the check or did Vin have the idea himself?"

Again her lavender eyes rested on me. She understood what I was asking, which was Vin's real conviction about good works.

"I suggested it. He could always use a tax deduction and often wanted my advice where to make contributions."

"Is $10,000 a normal-sized gift?"

"Vin had a banner year. In fact, he never had a bad one. Frankly, he wasn't wild about giving his money away, and I'm aware what people think of Father Mercy and his peculiar theology, but to please me Vin sent the check, and I'm convinced the Sons of the Father do good work out there, have, as the record will show, saved many men and women who went astray."

"You know Father Mercy?"

"I've talked to him. There are so many stories, I wanted to see for myself. Goodness takes various forms. Sometimes it comes in coat and tie, but on other occasions it surprises, wearing garments of the poor or yellow sheets. I try to support it no matter how strange it appears."

I remembered her as a girl in a Christmas pageant at Saint Andrew's. Though not reared Episcopalian, I'd stolen into the back of the arched nave to peep at her playing Mary during the manger scene. Lighted by candles she had indeed appeared as virginal as the Holy Mother; yet her Biblical blue robes didn't entirely hide the bloom of her body.

"Father Mercy's intelligent even if he goes to dramatic extremes for the sake of his primitive following," she said. "They expect and need it from him. I don't doubt he's sincere in his attempt to do good. I'm aware the county wouldn't approve of giving him money, but I care little what the county or Tobaccoton thinks."

"It might help if we could reconstruct those last hours before Vin died," I said.

"As you know, a Sunday, we ate breakfast, went to church, and that afternoon Vin played golf while I read a book. He came home for dinner, and we watched TV before going to bed. Next morning when I woke he was gone. I expected him home that evening to attend a party in Bannister."

"You didn't hear him leave the bed?"

Captain Blake had asked the same question. She eyed me before answering, and her expression was not threatening, but it did contain power, the message I'd better be careful.

"We have separate bedrooms," she said. "Before you leap to wrong conclusions, let me explain that Vin snored—a long, loud, manly snore that would wake the dead. Recently we'd been talking about an operation for it. In order to sleep, I had my own room. Often he was up and gone on a business trip before I woke."

"Would you let me look at his things?" I asked. I hadn't thought of doing it till right then.

She nodded, stood, and we walked by the pool, where water spouted from a pipe under the diving board and caused ripples to slide against white concrete siding.

"Where would you like to start?" she asked.

"His office."

We entered through a French window of the dining room, where silver gleamed on a walnut sideboard and a chandelier's pendants reflected quivering light. The table was long and heavy, the dark wood so deeply polished it mirrored three candelabra. High-back chairs had doves, pheasants, and peafowl carved into them.

We walked along a hallway hushed by oriental carpets, past gilt mirrors and family paintings: jaunty Blackjack in riding boots, his wife bowed before daffodils in a garden, and teenage Rhea herself wearing a ruffled pink dress at the ocean's edge. She held a small book in one hand, perhaps a devotional, and with the other she pressed a conch to an ear. She appeared to be listening seriously. On the sea behind her was a distant sail.

Rhea opened a door under the front stairs, and we went down steps into a paneled basement room. Filing cabinets, a TV, stereo, and at the center of the room an antique rolltop desk on which were a calculator and telephone. What startled me were enlarged color photographs hanging from walls, local scenes taken at Riverview—a mare snoozing under a hackberry, a black man tossing hay bales to a wagon, the Wye River beneath a snowfall, a flight of grackles swirling above a field of winter wheat and warping on the wind.

One picture was Vin himself at the pool. He wore black latex trunks and stood postured to dive: arms extended, up on his toes, his face lifted slightly as he leaned into his approach. He appeared trim and fit, his body as hairless as a boy's. His intensity made the dive seem of huge importance. I stared at the photograph. The trunks were cut low, well under the navel, but probably not low enough to reveal even an inked tattoo. At least I could make out nothing now.

"I snapped that one," Rhea said. "The rest are Vin's."

I hadn't known he was interested in anything except money and winning. Again I looked at the room, the tan carpet, the masculine leather sofa and chairs, lamps whose ceramic bases were decorated with wild geese and whistling swans. A box frame held his medals from the Air Force, a cluster on black felt at the center of which a screaming golden eagle hurtled downward grasping jagged lightning in its claws. My eyes stopped at the desk.

"I've been through it," she said. "Also the files. I found nothing out of the ordinary, but if you'd like to try, you're welcome. Take your time. I'll go up and shower. Just call if you want anything."

As soon as she left, I sat at the desk. There were no locked drawers, and he kept his things neat—places for account sheets, deposit slips, canceled checks. I found a list of investments, copies of land titles, a rubber stamp with his signature. A ledger contained row upon row of figures, all meaningless to me.

I stood and crossed to the file cabinets. Manila folders held letters on business matters, many from banks. There were loan agreements and land plats. In one folder lay his discharge from the Air Force at the rank of major. I found tax returns. During the previous year Vin had declared $156,718.94 income even after page upon page of business and farm depreciation and depletion schedules. It was a joint return.

Figures whirled in my head, and I pushed the file drawers shut. I stood looking at the photographs on the wall. Each was framed in blond wood. They were impressive, particularly the nature scenes like snow falling into the dark river. It was difficult for me to accept that Vin along with all else had possessed an artistic side, a sense of atmosphere and composition, a talent. He had money, Riverside, and above everything Rhea. No man should be more blessed.

I heard her on the steps. She'd showered and changed into a white summer dress, hose, and white heels. She'd brushed her hair, though it never appeared untouchably in place but loose and natural. She wore the tiny gold cross.

"What'd you find?"

"I don't even know what I'm looking for," I said.

She showed me his darkroom, where when she snapped a switch a red light came on and an exhaust fan whirred. Photography equipment glinted on a long bench—devices stainless, surgical, esoteric. Plastic trays were stacked in a double sink. A green locker held rows of slots for hundreds of negatives.

"You're welcome to examine them, though they contain nothing mysterious," she said. She hadn't come into the room but waited in the doorway, her hand still lifted to the light switch.

In a cabinet with a glass front secured by a padlock were Vin's cameras, Japanese mostly, some German, and all sorts of lenses, filters, and options.

"The funny thing is I never saw Vin take a picture," I said.

"He came to it late. A few years ago I gave him a Nikon for Christmas. You know how enthusiastic he was. He suddenly wanted to be the best photographer in the world."

As we moved out of his office toward the steps, I again glanced at the pictures on the walls. I had a feeling I was missing something. The photographs were so damned good. Maybe the feeling was simply envy.

"Would you like to go up to his room?" she asked.

I hadn't expected her to offer that, and I nodded. I followed her and tried not to watch the taut shaping of her calves as she set each foot on a step. I knew the real reason I wanted to go up to the second floor was not to find anything about Vin but to poke into her life.

On the divided staircase of the front hall was a rose runner held in place by brass rods. I felt I was rising into a special region, an intimate, secretive, and even sacred area. Along the walls were prints of hunting scenes, and a small penciled drawing of Rhea dressed in her black topper, white stock, and shadbelly. She held a bone-handled crop.

She opened the first door on the left at the top of the staircase, and we entered a man's bedroom centered around a heavy oak fourposter. The room also contained a lowboy and dresser, both with speckled marble tops. Between the two large windows was a cabinet holding rifles and shotguns.

"Vin was able to see the garden from here," she said. "He liked to raise the window quietly and pick off groundhogs."

The windows were closed now, the room quiet and cooled by a faintly humming central air-conditioning system. On Vin's dresser were silver military hairbrushes, each bearing his inscribed initials.

"He used them all through the service," she said and lifted one. It had been recently polished. "Look in the drawers if you like, though everything's been washed and put back. I don't know what to do with his clothes. If there were something to be found, I believe I would have discovered it."

It was like her to use the subjunctive "were" instead of "was," yet she made correct English seem not only proper but natural. She would have had to force herself to speak a flawed tongue.

From walls hung more of Vin's photographs, winter scenes of iced willows weeping over the frozen river, a birdbath piled with six inches of snow, a bluejay pecking at a frosted sundial, a wan sun reflected in bluish icicles formed under white eaves.

I looked at the pictures but thought about Rhea and Vin's sex lives. Surely plenty of that existed between two such healthy, vigorous people. How did it work from separate bedrooms?

The connection was a bathroom, a palace in itself with a his and her green marble sink, a sunken green tub, a shower enclosed by etched glass, a wall completely mirrored, a goose-necked chrome sunlamp, and one fixture I didn't mean to see, and disliked seeing, a bidet, certainly the only one in Howell County.

I quickly raised my eyes to Rhea's bedroom beyond the door. Carpet and drapes were rose colored, the bed white, not a warrior's chunk of furniture like Vin's, but delicate, the posts turned years ago on an antique lathe, the wood again walnut. I smelled a slight perfume.

When I turned, Rhea was watching. Did she sense my excitement? She crossed to Vin's closet and opened the door so I could see his clothes and shoes, which might've been on store display, each suit, jacket, trousers encased by plastic, the many shoes all shined and set with military precision on a three-level metal rack.

"I've had everything dry-cleaned," she said.

We went down the steps, and this time I didn't spy at her legs or hips but at her hair, the springing motion of it as she moved. We walked out the side entrance and toward the stable. In the distance was a white metal hangar hung with a lifeless wind sock. The hangar held, I knew, Vin's bi-wing Stearman trainer.

"Vin didn't much care for horses," she said. "He had natural riding ability but preferred golf."

Past the red stable were old carriages in a shed, each refurbished with black leather. Wheels had been painted bright red and yellow. Oiled harness and drivers' whips hung from hooks at the rear.

Lastly the garage housing the antique cars—a Packard coupe, an MG, the LaSalle, an Auburn, and the yellow Thunderbird. Each vehicle had its bay and was covered with a white throw cloth.

At the back of the garage a workbench, the surface orderly. Chromed tools were bracketed in wallboard above it and gleamed as if only moments before somebody had wiped them. On the bench and around it were a vise, a grinder, a battery charger, coiled wire, an arc welder, grease guns, various electrical equipment, and two pairs of white coveralls, one stitched over the right breast pocket with a red Vin, the other with a blue Rhea.

"He taught me how to tune an engine," she said. "We handled all maintenance ourselves."

She touched a fender of the LaSalle with the same tenderness she had the silver military brush, as if to draw some solace from the metal. There was no question of her breaking down, but pain caused a momentary arrest of her movements.

We left the garage and walked toward my car. She was politely showing me the gate.

"Is there anything else?" she asked.

"A question that may seem ridiculous, but I hope you'll bear with me."

"Of course."

"Did Vin always put on underwear?"

"You're serious?" she asked and stopped walking to face me.

"When found he wore nothing under his clothes."

"He even slept in undershorts, an Air Force habit."

I didn't ask about the tattoo. The question was too daring, too intimate, and Captain Blake, Pickney, or someone else would have to handle that one. Again I wondered whether it was possible for a wife not to know a thing like Pull for service about her husband. Not likely but possible if Rhea and Vin made love only in the dark. Certainly she was a modest woman. I couldn't imagine her acting any way except correctly. Still over the years she had to have seen

him step from a shower or changing his clothes. The tattoo, however, was uninked, faint, and probably Vin had been careful to keep
it hidden. Yet Captain Blake had said a shaved patch of pubic hair.
Vin would shave there?

"Can you think of an explanation?" I asked.

"Not unless he was in some great hurry." She shook her head,
and her fingers rose to the golden cross hanging from the chain
around her neck. "I simply can't explain it." She kept shaking her
head. "A beautiful man like my Vin gone. Who can accept it? I
can't. Yet I know he's all right in whatever existence we go to.
That's a great comfort."

An instant longer she fingered the cross before holding a hand
to me. We said goodbye, I slid into my car, and as I left I looked
into the rearview mirror. White dress against white gravel. She had
stepped to a rosebush and bent to inspect or break off a bloom.
A very genteel scene, one which would have made an excellent
photograph.

Driving home, I was still thinking about Vin's pictures, the
artistic enlargements on his walls. What bothered me about them?
Not just envy. That photograph of him in the black latex trunks
cut so low. Would anything show under a magnifying glass? Not
likely, but I might get the precise information from Captain Blake
and go back to the photograph for a measurement of scale. The
tattoo, he had said, was 9 cm under the umbilicus.

At the house I had a feeling something wasn't right. The air
was still, yet charged. Upstairs my father had on his TV. I walked
through my bedroom to take off my coat and tie, but as I passed
back into the dining room I sensed change.

The silver service, our family's heirloom and tenuous claim to
a cavalier past, was gone from the hunt board. Once belonging to
great-grandfather Boyd, whose horse trampled the knife-wielding
slave, it had been cast from melted-down American dollars. The
date was 1837, the benchmark of a London smith named Beckley.
Our family owned no portraits.

I climbed the steps to my father's room. He shouted at
the TV.

"The blood's on your Walter Walrus and Jane Pain!"

Walter Walrus was Walter Cronkite, and Jane Pain was Jane
Fonda, two on his list of people he believed most responsible for

America's defeat in Vietnam. I knocked on the door. He opened it just enough to peek at me.

"Where's the silver service?" I asked.

"Who?" he asked.

"It's gone."

He held to his chest a small framed picture of my mother that usually sat on his bedside table. The picture had been taken during the first years of their marriage, and she wore a candy-cane blouse, a full summer skirt, white anklets, and saddle shoes. He sometimes kissed the glass.

He stared at me, wheeled, and limped to the mantel for his Luger. He held my mother's picture as if protecting her from attack.

"You're telling me we been plundered?" he asked.

"Maybe Aunt Lettie came while you were watching TV and took the service home to shine," I said. "I'll drive over there."

"What the hell's going on is what I'd like to know. Threatening phone calls and thieving. Can you tell your crippled father what's going on?"

I put on my coat and tie before driving to Aunt Lettie's. She lived two miles down the road in a pink, prefabricated bungalow that had arrived on flatbed trucks and been bolted together. Around the house were flowers she grew to supply the altar at The Healing Springs African Pentecostal Church. The well pump had been painted a bright green. Near the front door a mother rabbit led her three bunnies, all made of chipped white plaster.

Everywhere grandchildren stopped moving to peer at me. They were up trees, behind bushes, on the shed roof, inside a junked car, swinging from tires, running, biting, kicking dirt, eating, drinking, throwing, hollering, laughing, crying. They lurked under the house too, dark eyes glittering through the ventilation grates.

Aunt Lettie stood in her kitchen among more children, in chairs, under a table, licking pans, behind the water heater. Her life had been a series of journeys between kitchens, her own and the whites she cooked for. All those grand odors of her bread baking, her cakes, her pies and pastries had become ingrained, and when I scented her it was like sniffing foods of great occasions—birthdays, anniversaries, reunions, Christmas feasts.

"I been to Dr. Robinette about my kidney stones," she said. "'Yep, you got em,' he says. 'I know I got em. What I going do with em?' I says. 'You going to wait is what you going to do with em,' he says. 'You going to charge me for telling me I got what I know I got and to wait for what I know I has to wait for?' I asks. 'Seven dollars,' he says. 'What I need is a doctor who treats you for going to the doctor in the first place,' I says."

Her carpet bedroom slippers rasped as she moved. If she lifted her feet too high off the floor, the slippers would drop away. Like me she was two-toned, not in her eyes but her skin, a layer of dark loam and under that in certain lights a faint blueness, as if she were laminated. Even in her own kitchen she wore her straw hat, which was attached to her white hair by a long pin that had an ivory bulb at the end.

"You think I been to your house to steal your silver?" she asked. "I don't come to your house no more."

"I didn't think you stole it. I thought maybe you'd brought it here to shine."

"I'm through shining for you after how you treated Eddie Blue."

"Aunt Lettie, I couldn't keep him in lawn mowers, and what's between him and myself has nothing to do with you and me."

"There's no you and me. There's only us. Everybody's us, and if people don't learn that, they don't know nothing. You want to search the house to see if Lettie has your silver?"

"Don't be belligerent, I'm not doubting you."

"Don't you call me no ligerant either. You not talking me into coming back. What I see at your house except dirt and dishes and picking up after white men too trifling to clean after themselves? They meet up with mess, they just step over it and leave it for Lettie."

One of the small boys at the side of the stove pinched a little girl, who started crying, showing wet bits of cookie on her red tongue. The boy grinned till Aunt Lettie casually swatted him aside, and then he too was crying. She turned away as if she didn't hear.

"I'd rather work in the cemetery than your house," she said. "Don't even have stray cats at that place."

Yet she was concerned for my father and me, and her triangular face alternately crinkled and smoothed. She was walking strength, able to work in kitchens or tobacco fields all the day and sing half the night at her church in a voice that made its own rules, a trembling wail no musical notation could ever capture.

"Don't guess you remember this your mother's birthday," she said. "You remember that?"

I hadn't sure enough. My mother meant more to Aunt Lettie than to me. I didn't remember her, yet felt guilty about my lack of loving. I knew now why my father was hugging the picture.

"I been to her grave," Aunt Lettie said. "I laid flowers on it. You been?"

"No."

"Don't tell me. Crabgrass and dandelions all round the head-stone. Hang your head."

"I pay to have it taken care of."

"Pay taking care's not love taking care. Them men don't want to see no weeds. They like to sit in the shade, smoke, and talk about poon. Your mother love you. She was just a pretty little girl, but she love you more than the river's got water. You could care for her resting place."

"I will," I said, shamed. "Saturday I'll be out there with my clippers."

"Mothers ain't nothing," she said, hipping children aside to cross from her stove to the table. "Mothers be less than sticks, grass, and old peanut shells. I know your daddy remembers. Poor old man. He crying up in his room?"

"Yes," I said.

I drove to the courthouse, where Pickney sat in his office listening to the Buster Bovin Gospel Hour. He stood, washed his hands in a sink over which an oval mirror hung from a wire, and walked out with me to my car. We rode back to the house.

He first walked slowly around it, his feet slewed, and studied the ground for tracks. He looked at the windows, which, though screened, were all open. They needed putty and paint.

"The thief could've come right through the front door," I said. "We never lock anything. Daddy probably had his radio or TV on."

"I'll want a description of the silver. I can put it on a hot line to Richmond, Norfolk, and Roanoke. That'll alert the dealers. I figure whoever did it must've had a car around here somewhere."

We searched along the lane to the road and walked the shoulder on both sides, but found no tire marks in the hard, dry soil. We walked back to the house, where he took his kit from my car and dusted the hunt board for fingerprints.

"Your insurance up to date?" he asked, shaking his head.

He wanted to question my father, but by then my father had climbed into a bottle of Ancient Age and sat on his bed aiming his Springfield rifle at phantoms he saw crossing the wall.

"Let the bastards come, goddamnit, let them come!" he shouted.

"You didn't even hear a board creak?" Pickney asked.

"We run them out of their holes at Saint-Lô, them krauts after the bombing, kicked them out like rabbits. They smelled like dirty socks."

He lunged as if the Springfield had a bayonet on the end and almost fell from his bed. We pried his rifle away and laid him protesting on his back. He grabbed for the photograph of my young mother wearing saddle shoes and anklets. The glass was smeared where he'd kissed it. He held it against his face.

Pickney and I went down the steps. Again we walked around the house. He found a cigarette butt in the crackly grass, but it was one of mine. He discovered my lawn chair in the grape arbor, the place I had my drinks and sailed my boats to the dazzling islands.

"Cooler out here," I explained.

We returned to the car, where he leaned his rump against a fender and scratched his double chin with a thumbnail. He wore a big Masonic ring, ruby on gold, and his hands were not hard and rough like a country boy's but had become soft in office, a clerk's.

"Maybe the other hippies," he said. He meant those who weren't in jail with Cloud and Hawthorn.

"That would be pretty dumb of them," I said.

"I'm just considering possibilities. They need bail money, and you been receiving those telephone calls. What I'm wondering now is how it all meshes with Vin being killed."

"We don't know Vin was killed."

"Sure we do. Inside we know."

"Not admissible."

"Yeah, well something better break for us soon. People are talking about what half-ass public servants they got."

"Maybe we'll get lucky and be run out of office."

"Might be funny to you," he said, serious. He'd come from a poor red-clay farm to, in his eyes, an exalted office, a journey that had cost him many a hard and greasy step. He was too proud of his climb to joke about it. "We're going to have to bear down, counselor, or they'll take away our beans. I'd hate to start farming again this late in life."

What about me? I almost asked. You're grooming your hotdog nephew to take my beans.

Yet I didn't speak the words. I drove him back to the courthouse, and when I returned home, my father was stumbling around upstairs, sniffling and trying to center "Moonlight Serenade" on the spindle of his phonograph.

10

The single milkweed thrives in the meager slice of sunlight received behind the broken door. It finds moisture somewhere under the cabin and believes it will succeed in reaching the full glory of day.

The master carries a galvanized washtub—the kind which used to hang on porches of most county shanties—sets it in a patch of sunshine, and draws water from the well to empty into the tub. Eighteen buckets go in, water drumming and splashing. The master places the bucket back on the circular rock wall around the well and walks to the cabin.

For me there are a clean olive-drab towel, GI issue, a bar of Ivory soap, and a pair of fingernail clippers. They are laid on the table.

"Bath today," the master says, eyes indistinct behind the yellow lenses of the shooting glasses. The .38 revolver is drawn from the oxblood holster, and the keys are worked from a side pocket of the camouflaged pants. There are two keys on a wire ring. The gun points toward me. "Lie back on your cot."

I obey, and the chain clinks.

"Put your hands under your head."

I do as I am told and watch as the master aims the gun at me

140

with one hand and with the other inserts a key into the lock at my ankle. The lock snaps open and falls with the chain to the floor. I want to rub my sore ankle but don't move.

"Stand up and take off your clothes."

I don't like removing my clothes in front of the master. The eyes behind the yellow lenses see my skinniness and shriveled manhood. Those eyes make me smaller than I am. I want to hide myself like a surprised female—back bowed, hands fluttering, knees bent.

At a gesture from the pistol, I walk naked through the doorway to the sunlight and washtub. I am afraid but mostly I am embarrassed at how pale and pathetic I must appear. I am a quivering toadstool.

"Get in the tub, then sit."

I step into the water, very cold after foaming up from darkness of the earth, though the sun is hot on my skin. I take a breath and squat. Because my feet can't slide out in front of me, my knees poke upward. The water is so cold I gasp.

"Start at your hair and wash down," the master says and hands me the soap.

I can't bend my hair to the water and have to cup it in my palms and spill it over my head. I see goosebumps along my chest. I soap up and rub my fingers into my scalp. I am shivering both from the cold water and awareness of the master's eyes. As I rinse my hair, the streamings curdle around me.

"Again," the master says.

Twice I wash my hair. Then I do my face, ears, neck, arms, and chest.

"Stand," the master says.

I rise in the sunlight, the suds sliding down my stomach, hips, and legs. I wash the front and back of my knees and between my toes.

"Your private areas," the master says.

I have already turned away from the eyes, and I lather myself. I think of depravity and hideous perversions, of people used and buried, the young men dug up in fields and garages.

"The other," the master says.

Meaning not only the front but also the rear. So degrading. No way it can be done with dignity. Then I must squat a second time to rinse.

"Step out," the master says and tosses me the olive-drab towel.

I stand dripping in sunlight. Locusts shrill in the birches, and an indolent buzzard floats over watching. I pat the towel along my arms and down my chest.

When I am dry, the master has clean khakis for me. They are too large, and I hold them up at the waist as we walk back to the cabin, where I am directed to sit on the cot and clip my finger- and toenails. I throw the clippings into the collapsed fireplace. The gun follows my movements.

I shave at the well. Lastly the master lifts the chain, and I, again lying on the cot, extend my leg. The master wants the other ankle, which is less chafed. The chain is wrapped around it, the lock is pressed closed. The master checks the fit.

I am given a white T-shirt, too large. No belt is provided. The master hands me a book. I am relieved, thinking there are to be no hideous perversions after all. The book is a Bible with a black leather cover.

Master: Read.

Me: "And I will utter my judgments against them touching all their wickedness, who have forsaken me, and have burned incense unto other gods, and worshipped the works of their own hands."

———

The unjailed hippies brought food to their companions Cloud and Hawthorn, fresh vegetables from their garden. Mrs. Harpe, the jailer's wife, didn't want to prepare it for them. Plum, the fuzzy girl in jeans and a blue workshirt, came to my office.

"It'd save the county money, wouldn't it?" she asked. Her long dark hair hung free. She'd carried not only natural foods but also wild flowers for Cloud and Hawthorn to decorate their cells with.

"Bureaucracy doesn't stop at the county level," I said. I knew Mrs. Harpe, a manly humorless woman who wore a tan uniform shirt and skirt. At a Christian Endeavor picnic when I was a boy eight or so, I had flipped up her red-and-white pinafore to see her coltish legs and cotton drawers. Her name then had been Mary Sue Bell, and she had run howling to her mother and the preacher to rat on me.

"The right kind of food's important to Cloud and Hawthorn," Plum argued. "Don't you have an obligation to keep them healthy?"

"I'll speak to Mrs. Harpe."

"You're a nice man. I been asking around about you."

"Why would you do that?"

"Like to know what I'm dealing with. Cloud wants his guitar. He needs it to keep himself quiet inside."

She lounged in the office doorway, her body an S curve, some of the dark hair trailing down her blue shirt. Florene frowned.

"The guitar will have to be inspected, and he won't be allowed to disturb other prisoners."

"Cloud will soothe them. He's a talented musician."

"I'll speak to the sheriff."

"You know you're thin? Why not let me cook you up a meal. I could come out and use your kitchen."

Florene twitched at her desk, but Plum smiled, her face healthy and alert. It'd been a long time since anybody flirted with me.

"Thinness is in my genes, not my stomach," I said and stood to be rid of her.

"Anytime you want some of my cooking, all you have to do is send up smoke," she said and winked. "Nice man."

As she left, I didn't look at her figure. I waited until she was out of the office before raising my eyes. It was a good thing too because Florene was spying on me. That afternoon I spoke to Mrs. Harpe in the jail. I had a feeling she definitely remembered my flipping up her dress at the Christian Endeavor picnic.

"They always standing around in the corridor," she complained. "Can't move a step without bumping into them. I don't get paid for running two kitchens."

Mother of seven children, she was a bitter woman, that bitterness drawn out in her like taut barbed wire. Her husband Mac had been a deputy until his foot was blown off while he was setting dynamite to explode an illegal still. Now he scooted around the jail in a wheelchair, keys rattling against the aluminum armrest. She believed the people owed him more disability pay and a pension. Had she ever worn a pinafore and cotton drawers?

"It'll save the county money," I said, echoing Plum's argument.

"Saving the county don't save me," she said. "Don't I have enough to bear?"

"I intend to put in a word for you at the next budget meeting," I said. "I know it's been difficult for you what with inflation and all."

That quieted her, yet I was fearful of rousing her again by
mentioning the guitar for Cloud. I'd wait a day or two. I left the
jail, walked the courthouse corridor, and started up the steps. Two
deputies passed holding a black man between them. The man was
Old Ben.

He wore a dark suit, a white shirt, a maroon tie, and a gray
felt hat. The way he was dressed it could've been February instead
of July. Sweat made him a shiny mahogany. As old as he was, his
skin had not wrinkled but had stretched sleekly over his bones.

Seeing me, he instinctively attempted to sweep off his hat
cavalier fashion. He had no hair, but his skull was dotted with
round black spots. He almost dropped the hat because, though he
was in no way resisting, the deputies were hurrying him along.

I followed them into the jail and the squad room next to the
sheriff's office. They sat him on a bench against the flaking green
wall. Deputy Hatcher left to get Mrs. Purdey, wife of the county
treasurer. She clerked for her husband and also was a magistrate
who could write up warrants.

Giles Watkins, the other deputy, stayed beside Old Ben, who
sat meekly and stared at the floor. He held his hat between his
knees. I asked whether Old Ben had been read his rights.

"Treated him like the guest of honor," Giles said and turned
to spit into a five-gallon paint can half filled with soil, a country
cuspidor.

"Where you been lately, Ben?" I asked.

The old man sat quietly, his fingers tracing the brim of his
hat, fine dark fingers, the nails clean and cared for. His suit had
been pressed, his white shirt freshly laundered. His black shoes
had a shine on them, and the laces were firmly tied. I glanced at
Giles.

"Forgot how to talk," Giles said.

"Ben, you been knowing me a long time," I said. "You afraid?"

He looked up at me, his eyes not dark, but a butternut brown.
The eyes quickly slid away from my face.

"The Lord's a great gardener," he said.

"Them's the first words out of his mouth since Richmond,"
Giles said.

"I'm certain the Lord is," I said to Ben. "What you doing
down in Richmond town?"

Old Ben looked at his hat, which he had never stopped turning in his hands. A drop of sweat slid off the smoothness of his speckled head into a groove of his neck.

"He was hiding in his daughter's apartment," Giles said.

"That true, Ben?"

He would not look up, and more sweat was rolling into the groove of his neck.

"Ben, I'll help you every way I can, but sooner or later you're going to have to talk to somebody. It might as well be me now."

He flapped his hat between his knees, yet didn't raise his face. As I straightened above the bench, Pickney hurried in, his booted feet heavy and spread, though his knees stayed close. His uniform shirt had short sleeves. He too was sweating.

"Got him, did you, by God?" Pickney asked Giles.

"He was at the daughter's, but he ain't telling nothing."

"Ben not talking to his friends here in Tobaccoton?" Pickney asked and sat on the bench next to the old man. "I can't believe that. Why him and me grubbed taters and stripped tobacco together. Ben, you and me was practically born under the same tobacco plant."

Pickney put his hand on Old Ben's shoulder and kept trying, but Old Ben wouldn't look at him, even when the sheriff stuck two thick fingers under Ben's chin and lifted the face. Old Ben just clenched his eyes as if hit with painful sunlight. The sheriff's fingers came away with Old Ben's sweat on them.

"I expect he's tired," Pickney said. "Probably wore out after that hot trip from Richmond. We'll let him rest a while and, Giles, get him a Big Orange. Turn on the fan for him."

The sheriff and I left the squad room and went to his office, where he closed the door. He shook his head and cussed automatically, worried, I thought, more than just about Old Ben. Maybe it was his wife, a roving-eyed, wheat-haired girl who wore tight red short shorts in hot weather. She was a good fifteen years younger than he, and when you went to Pickney's house, he always took you aside to talk, jealous that any man would look at her.

She was known to spend his paycheck before the money ever reached his wallet. He kept a picture of her on his desk, one of those variety-store bargain specials colored as vividly as intestines.

Pickney sat, blew out his cheeks, and flexed his shoulders as if to make a little slack for his skin.

"What you think?" he asked.

"I think he didn't want to be around trouble," I said. "He knew trouble would spill over on him."

"Maybe, maybe not. He just might know something. He ran, and he was hiding."

"Being with his daughter isn't exactly hiding."

"You're not going to keep us from holding him just because he was Rhea's houseboy, are you?" he asked, his face squinted and sour.

I didn't show my resentment at the suggestion that Rhea's comfort and convenience were more to me than established procedures of the legal system. And I again was unhappy about his using her first name when he wouldn't have dared do it to her face.

"The fact Old Ben works for Rhea is not material," I said. "He had a right to go to Richmond or anywhere else. It could be reasonably asserted he wasn't fleeing the scene but merely visiting kin. So far you're holding him on speculation."

"Hell, more than half of all law is speculation. I think if we turn him loose, he'll run again, and I want everybody in place until we know what's the top and bottom."

He stood, wiped his face with a palm, and moved around the desk toward the door. His hand on the knob, he turned to me.

"I didn't mean nothing in that remark about Rhea," he said.

"Sure you did, Pick."

"Nah, it just come out. I'm a little itchy today, things on my mind other than Vin Farr. I just hope you don't take offense at me calling to your attention here in my office that it's evident you're sweet on her. It could cloud your judgment."

"That evident, huh?"

"Nothing personal. You get a certain sick, lopsided look. I know how it is to be jerked inside out by a woman."

I stood wondering how many others in Tobaccoton had observed my sick, lopsided look.

Florene tapped on the office door, stepped in, and with raised brows whispered I had visitors. They were close behind—Buster Bovin and three other preachers. Quickly I rolled down my sleeves, pulled on my seersucker jacket, and adjusted my tie. I leveled my dark glasses.

Buster was still wearing his sand-colored safari suit with the fluted shell pockets and the matching bush hat, his uniform from the great African crusade. He entered my office as if launched from the wings. A band might've struck up.

Again I was surprised how small he was. On TV he appeared tall and commanding. Here he had to turn his face upward to bring his china-doll button-blue eyes to bear on me. His hand was strong and fast, speeding mine as if priming a pitcher pump. During his boyhood his ears had been jugged, yet now they lay close to his head. He denied ever having a cosmetic operation. His golden brown hair was barbered with machine precision.

I shook the other preachers' hands: Wilton Birdsong, Methodist, who had white hair and a veined face; Wick Bessent, the proud, lank Presbyterian; and Botts Goodwin, a shiny young Baptist who even in July wore a vest with a key chain across it. From the chain hung not a Phi Beta Kappa key but a miniature gold crucifix.

Florene carried in extra chairs so they could all sit before my desk. I laid my legal tablet over the ashtray to prevent them from disapproving of my butts. Buster was smiling. He always smiled. In my mind I had this picture of him being boiled by cannibals on a tropical island, rice, carrots, and wild beans floating in the pot with him, and even as he was pink and cooking he smiled at the cannibals.

"We're here, Billy, to act against crime," Buster said.

"The four of you personally?" I asked.

They laughed because they were cordial men, expansive except in the pulpit, quick to kiss babies or smack their lips over a chicken leg.

"We don't mean we're out with guns to arrest people on the street," Buster said as I noticed except for Wick Bessent how well fed they were, their flesh prime and glossy. Even Wick's leanness had a luster to it. I didn't mean to be critical, although some might argue that men of the spirit ought to embrace denial like John in the wilderness. These fellows couldn't be blamed for eating often with members of their congregations, who heaped plates before them.

"Might not be such a bad idea," Botts Goodwin said. He was about thirty, a healthy youth strong in the width of his hams. He might've been a beauty of a man except his eyes were set too close. He would need to squeeze binoculars to look through them.

"But we didn't come for gun permits," Buster said. He removed his bush hat and held it on his lap as if steering. "What we want is stronger county law enforcement."

Pressure, I thought. They're cooking it up in their churches, stoking the fires so the steam of piety shot out to sear my hind end. I wanted to be on a boat, a Cabo Rico 38, so far out to sea I was past the limits of radio, where all I heard was the wash of swells against the hull and all I saw was the endless roll of a benign ocean.

"After consultation among us, we've agreed on certain realms in which we believe Howell County can improve law enforcement," Wick Bessent, Presbyterian, said. "Our endeavors should be in concert."

Endeavors in concert. Wick was proud of his education. He'd been first-honor man at Davidson and read from the Greek during sermons, always letting his congregation know it was the Greek. He possessed sharp edges, and I had this feeling if I got too close his righteousness might cut me.

"We haven't come to make demands," Wilton Birdsong, Methodist, said. "We just hope to bring to your attention certain activities you and the sheriff might have overlooked."

Wilton had creaky joints. When he moved, his bones sounded like dry sticks being snapped. Yet he was a hunter, a man who could talk turkey so expertly he lured toms right to the blind with visions of lustful hens, only to gape into the blackness of twelve-gauge death.

"Correction of which is certain to be popular with our citizenry," Buster said.

"The majority of whom, needless to say, are voters," Wick Bessent said.

If it was needless, why had he said it unless to remind me I'd soon be wanting those votes? I either cooperated or they would be looking around for somebody else to sit in my chair, perhaps a bright young law student who was Pickney's nephew and also a good upstanding Baptist.

Botts Goodwin had already peered at my shirt pocket and seen my pack of Luckies. I buttoned my seersucker jacket.

"First item is the illegal sale of beer," Buster said. He had drawn a typed list from a flap pocket of his belted safari jacket. Fingers small but not weak unfolded it. Despite his smile and soft tones, I'd always sensed threat from him, the danger of an aroused self-created Jehovah. Were Buster a fighter instead of a preaching man, he would've been a killer.

"Law in Howell County forbids the sale of alcoholic beverages on Sunday, but beer's as easy to obtain as it is for a possum to find yams," he said. "Beer is not only purchased illegally, it is done so by underage youths, making them dangerous on our highways and damaging their self-control otherwise."

"Otherwise?" I asked.

"Alcohol decreases the force of conscience," Botts Goodwin said.

"Boys with girls," Wick Bessent said.

"And girls with boys," Wilton Birdsong said.

"I'm aware of the situation," I said, using words as a barricade. "Unfortunately we don't have the law officers to keep all the county stores under observation. Occasionally we do apprehend a malefactor and prosecute to secure the revocation of the license, but most storekeepers know their customers and sell under the cover of the back room. I shall, however, talk to Sheriff Pickney to determine whether or not we can assign officers to special duty in an effort to address the problem."

I listened to the words frothing from my mouth and thought that with a little application and concentration I might become a proficient government bureaucrat. Maybe that's where I'd go after Pickney's nephew tipped me out of office. The Bureau of Weights and Measures. A man ought to be safe in the Bureau of Weights and Measures.

"I think, or rather this committee thinks, we ought to mount a major offensive," Buster said.

"We'd like to see action taken nigh on to immediately," Botts Goodwin said.

"We're hoping to have a Law Week," Wilton Birdsong said.

"We are in communication with the Board of Supervisors on the matter," Wick Bessent said.

"Grand idea," I said and wished at that very moment I could lay hand on a drink.

"Second on the list is morality," Buster said. "Young people are parking all over the county for the purpose of committing lewd and indecent acts."

"I found a couple fondling in my driveway," Wick Bessent said. "My wife and I had just returned from Presbytery. In escaping, their car tore up part of the manse lawn and left a disgusting thing on the grass. It was pink."

I did not laugh.

"Are you aware they're on sale in the men's rooms of various cafes and garages in the county?" Wilton Birdsong asked.

"I am rarely in those places," I said.

"Dispensers on the walls where for fifty cents you can buy multicolored French ticklers," Botts Goodwin said. "The metal dispensers have provocative pictures of unclothed females in throes of passion."

"I'll call it to the sheriff's attention," I said and thought of Botts and Wilton visiting all the men's rooms around the county to check the rubber-dispenser artwork.

"We'd like to see the county patrol the areas most utilized for these activities," Buster said.

"Patrol all the lanes, fire trails, and lonely roads in the county?" I asked and started to laugh, yet stilled my face before it changed. Buster himself, the great bagger of African souls, had not altered his smile, but his expression was a pool of deep water below which a hungry gliding fish circled, and for an instant that maneater rose toward the surface and showed a deadly danger.

"Yes, patrol them," he said.

"Good idea, though it would be somewhat difficult on our small budget," I said, talking fast. To explain the extent of patrolling which would be required, I unfolded the county map. The lurking fish again sank below the surface of Buster's smile.

"Show them the flag," he said. "Like the days of President Theodore Roosevelt when he sent great white battleships around the world. Howell County could do the same with police cars."

"It's a promising idea, and I'll surely talk it over with the sheriff," I said. Who might shoot me, I thought.

"We could provide volunteer ministers to drive around with the law officers," Botts Goodwin said. "While the iron is hot, preach a sermonette."

"There would be no charge to the county for our services," Wilton Birdsong said.

"The word of the Lord might be quite effective in the presence of a law officer," Wick Bessent said.

I thought of high-schoolers yanked from the torrid clutch of love to stand outside their cars, youths disheveled, bewildered, frightened in the unrelenting glare of a four-cell flashlight as Buster and the others laid a sermonette on them.

"The churches want to help," Buster said. "We await only marching orders."

"We can provide money within limits," Botts Goodwin said. "We'll arrange fund drives and special collections."

"Picnics," Wick Bessent said.

"The effort can make for a closer relationship between the churches and county government," Buster said. "County officers could help by setting examples, that is, by attending church functions. As of now, we calculate not more than 68 percent of public servants attend church activities. We made a study."

I was a statistic in that study. I hadn't gone to church since Jeannie left me, and the last sermon I heard had been on waking up your conscience. The minister had said that each of us should rap on the door of our conscience and rouse the sluggard out of his bed of ease. I'd fixed a drink as soon as I reached home.

Such a hypocrite I was. I should have stood from my desk and told them what I really thought, and what I really thought was they, instead of deviling youths and elected officials, should've been visiting the jail to bring hope and comfort to the drunks, the defeated, the desperate blacks who smelled of sweet wine and old vomit.

"There is one other thing," Buster said and glanced at Botts, who from the inside pocket of his brown glazed summer suit drew a folded paper.

"A member of my congregation found his teenage daughter reading this," he said and handed me the paper. The passage was mimeographed.

Duke slid his tongue from her gasping mouth and wiggled it down her chin, along her throat to her chest, licking each ripe young nipple before lowering himself to her perfumed navel and then the crisp hair which waited between the spread legs, the hot moistness a feast urgently prepared for him.

There was more, but I refolded the paper and offered it back to Botts. He waved it away, indicating I was to keep it.

"A fifteen-year-old girl," Botts said. "She was reading that, a book from the Howell County Public Library, signed out by her and hidden under the pillow in her bedroom. Mr. Commonwealth Attorney, do you believe a fifteen-year-old girl ought to be encouraged at county expense to go to Hell?"

What I thought was, Botts, you deceiver, with your big, ugly wife, wouldn't you love to have your mouth on one of those ripe young nipples?

"There are a hundred books like that in the library," Wilton Birdsong said. "They are paid for by tax money taken from our citizens. Do you consider it right and proper to use tax money to set the feet of the young on the path to perdition?"

"Something must be done," Wick Bessent said. "Each of us has talked to Miss Katie Cullen but received no satisfaction. She continues to buy and display such books for circulation. Our organization, The Ministerial Alliance, doesn't wish to take legal action against the library, which means the county, but if there is no recourse, we will do so. First, however, we thought you might like to talk with her."

I sank a little in my chair as I thought of Miss Katie Cullen, that tall, proud old spinster who ran the library.

"She believes she owns it," Buster said. "It is, after all, ours, the citizens', money."

"Perhaps some accommodation of interests can be reached," I said and sure God hoped so. I didn't intend to get caught in the slimy muck of a First Amendment legal action.

Buster, Botts, and Wilton glanced at one another. They had apparently said what they came to say, for they stood as if on signal and reached across the desk to shake my hand. Wick had missed the signal and was a beat off in his timing.

"We know you'll do the right thing," they said. I stood nodding and envisioning the divine taste of drink deep within the quietness of my shady grape arbor.

Yet only three of the ministers left. Buster stayed in the office. He closed the door, faced me, and smiled.

"The Ministerial Alliance offers everybody help," he said. "We want to punish no one. Our goal is brotherhood."

Not understanding, I stared at his china-doll eyes.

"We all have problems," he said. "God gives them to us to make us understand that we alone cannot make our way in this world. We need His help."

"Right," I said, still not knowing where he was headed.

"You've been seen leaving the ABC store in Crewe," he said. "You were carrying a large sack filled with bottles. We are not making a judgment, but we are asking you the next time you feel you need a drink to call our number and say to any of us, 'Preacher, I am weary of trying to carry this load by myself.'"

Great God, I thought, the load he's talking about is me being loaded! For a crazy instant I had a mental picture of Buster in his safari suit helping me carry a case of liquor from the ABC store.

"We understand how whisky can get hold of a good man, kill his body, and steal his soul. Would you like to write down our telephone numbers?"

"I think I can find them okay, thanks."

"We want you to know you have friends, Billy, both in a personal and governmental sense."

He again shook my hand with his neat, warm fingers. I opened the door and held it for him. He spoke to Florene on the way out. She stood from her desk as if he were the Pope. From my window I watched him amble down the street, waving to all the men, including the blacks, and tipping his bush hat to the ladies.

I unlocked the bottom drawer of a file cabinet where folders of closed felony cases were kept. Behind the folders was a virgin pint of Aristocrat vodka I hid for emergency purposes. I drank the stuff straight from the bottle. I swallowed it as if it were salvation.

I went to church the next Sunday, the Presbyterian, Wick Bessent in the pulpit. Attending ruined the rhythm of my day. I usually slept till ten or so, ate a biscuit and bacon, and carried the Richmond paper and a cold beer to the grape arbor, where I read over the news like a man picking cashews from a bowl of mixed nuts. No violence or disturbing events allowed past my wary eyes. Chiefly I studied the travel page or want ads. I especially bore down on every description of boats for sale.

People were surprised to see me. They welcomed me and spoke in hushed voices as if I were attending my own obsequies. Yet they were essentially happy. In the rural South, religion was not only regeneration but also the main means of recreation.

Singing the first hymn, "When the Roll Is Called Up Yonder," I had the sensation the music was like a merry-go-round, that we were all sitting astride those rising and falling mechanical horses painted gaudy colors, that we could lean out to catch the brass ring of salvation. I realized I was lifting to my toes and lowering to my heels. People eyed me.

"God can tolerate only that which is pure!" Wick Bessent pronounced in a voice undergirded with an authority drawn from his special knowledge of what the Lord was about in the universe. I thought, God must be lonely.

At the end of the service, I half-stepped with the file of worshipers waiting to shake Wick's austere hand, his fingers like claws. He held me, a lost sheep returned to the fold, longer than others. Outside, his pigeon-breasted wife got between me and my car.

"We're having a Pancake Fiesta with lots of good old-time hymn singing," she said. "We tie aprons on the men and let them do the cooking. I'm saving one of those aprons for you!"

I thanked her ten times and promised I'd come to the Pancake Fiesta if I possibly could, which was a lie on the church doorstep. I hurried to my car. Children ran around holding their Sunday-school comics, but an intent little boy pursued a little girl in a yellow dress. He meant to see up her skirt.

I drove home thinking the next Sunday I'd try the Episcopal church where Rhea went. I could sit in the rear and watch her, her neck and hair, the line of her face as she turned it, the contours of her body when she rose to sing, recite, or stride to the rail for communion. Then in later weeks on to the Baptists, Methodists, and maybe some of the black churches, Aunt Lettie's Healing Springs African Pentecostal, where I'd clap my hands and call out an Amen or two just to let folks know I was present.

My father waited on the landing. He carried his cane and wore his Luger in a U.S. Army holster designed for a .45.

"Jeannie's on the phone," he said.

I stopped, touched my throat, and steadied my sunglasses. My ex-wife on the line twice in the same month. The reason had to be the alimony check. I lifted the phone and told her the check was already in the mail.

"I'm not calling about the check," she said. "I have received it, but I'm coming through Tobaccoton and want to see you a moment. Can't we have lunch?"

She was already in Appomattox, just down the road a few miles. I didn't believe for an instant it was only lunch she wanted. It had to be higher alimony. Well, I'd fight her in court. The battle might ruin me with the Howell County electorate, yet even I had limits I couldn't be pushed beyond. She was taking half my salary. She was still young and able to work. God, it was too much, Jeannie and churching all the same day.

My father leaned over the railing to listen, and when I hung up, he shook his head and tapped the cane.

"She's the only good thing happened in this house since your mother, and you had to let her get away."

I met Jeannie at the General Johnston Hotel, a frame building that dated back to the early 1900s, three stories built at the time tobacco was king in the region and the town had so many warehouses that wagons jammed up for miles waiting to display their leaf at auctions. The front was a great white porch, the roof of which was supported by spindly wooden columns. Green rocking chairs of the type used in the old-folks home were arranged each morning by a colored porter named Enoch, who also dusted the railings and wicker tables. If a modern motel were ever built in the vicinity, the General Johnston would expire like air let out of a ball.

The dining room had been the hotel's glory, broad windows which reached from the floor to the high ceiling, blue drapes as heavy as an emperor's cloak, and crystal chandeliers that tinkled when anyone crossed the floor upstairs. Walls were hung with misty pastoral scenes: hills, lakes, fleecy sheep resting in purplish shade. Yet as a boy I'd discovered one picture had a dark shape in a woods, perhaps a large dog or even a wolf, its eyes gleaming from shadows.

Mostly ladies of the community used the General Johnston's dining room, a place for the Daughters of the American Revolution and garden clubs to order tuna salad and mint tea under insubstantial, slowly revolving ceiling fans. Sundays the hotel offered a chicken dinner served with little green peas, spoon bread, and homemade ice cream.

I waited for Jeannie in the lobby. She was on time. Drawing back her short dark hair with fingertips, she came quickly up the steps from the parking lot, a small energetic woman with slender legs, a tiny waist, an impish face. She wore a tan summer dress, hose, and black pumps. When she leaned her cheek to me for a kiss, I smelled the old familiar perfume; yet her fresh, pert attractiveness roused only a small desire.

"You look terrible," she said and straightened my seersucker lapels with her fast fingers.

"You don't," I told her, and she liked that. We walked to the dining room, were shown to our table by an elderly hostess named Miss Bessie Watts, who was also the desk clerk afternoons. She seated us next to a window, the glass shaded by an elm. The window had been raised, and flies walked across the screen, perhaps drawn by the aroma of buttered spoon bread.

"You're sitting there as if you expect me to stab you," Jeannie said. "I haven't come to Tobaccoton to do you in."

"I'm relieved."

"You're thinking I want your money."

"Never crossed my mind."

"You can relax because I'm going to make life easier for you."

Before she told me how, our waiter came to the table, an old black man in a white jacket whose name was Robbie. He was a cousin of Aunt Lettie and had been working at the hotel since as far as my memory went back. His skin had become gray as his hair, the blackness leached out by too many years. Jeannie ordered the chicken special, and I chose a crab casserole. Robbie pushed through a swinging door into a steamy kitchen.

"The crab won't be fresh," Jeannie said. "Takes too long to reach Tobaccoton by stagecoach."

"Tell me how you're going to make my life easier."

"Hold on to your chair. I'm definitely to be married again. You will be set free. No more alimony threats or fear of phone calls in the night."

Her smile made her appear spritely and girlish. She'd had great hope for me, the rising young attorney with a good Richmond corporation. Her father had been principal of a high school in King William County, a serious, devout man with a fine Virginia bloodline but no estate, and what Jeannie really wanted was a place in society and a return of grandeur. She had squandered her virginity on me.

"Thanks for the enthusiastic congratulations," she said. "Knew I could count on you."

"Who's the fellow?"

"You'll love him."

"I don't want to love him. I don't even want to see him."

"Okay, you won't have to, but he's fine. He thinks I'm the greatest thing since running shoes."

"Must be an intellectual."

"Don't be a bastard."

"I suppose he has the capacity to love greatly, which you accused me of lacking."

"He does, and maybe you do too, but I was never able to bring it out." She played with her fork, drawing lines on the tablecloth. "Come to the wedding. Going to be quite an affair. I've decided to invite you after all."

"I would but my dance card is full. And I might cry."

"Why are you acting this way when you don't really care that much?"

"I don't know. Maybe you're right is what, that I do lack something. Anyhow, failing with you wasn't great fun. I regret I didn't do better."

"It's all right, Billy," she said and reached across to pat my hand. She wore her new engagement ring, the diamond not insignificant. I wondered what she'd done with the ring I'd given her.

We ate, or at least she did. She had an appetite for crusty chicken and quivering spoon bread. She was correct about the crab. I drank two cups of coffee, smoked, and looked out the window past the elm to pigeons circling the white spire at Botts Goodwin's Baptist church. Had the birds been immersed?

"You don't even have to send a present," Jeannie said.

She did want to see my father and the house one last time. She and Dad had been thick. He'd taken her side in all disagreements, and most of the time I'd felt they were in conspiracy against me. We drove out in my car, the seat of which she was careful to dust before sliding her neat little rump across.

"Wants paint," she said of the house.

My father limped downstairs to greet her. She hurried up the porch steps to him, her shiny pumps tapping the boards. They hugged, kissed, and cooed.

"God, we've missed you around this place," my father said. "We've fallen apart without you."

While they made over one other, I slipped to the pantry for a belt right out of the bottle. I screwed the cap back, set the bottle on the shelf, and ran a hand over my hair.

Jeannie was upset about the missing silver service. She walked around the house looking at things and extending her fingers to touch the Queen Anne chair, the upright piano, and my bed's counterpane, which had been crocheted by my grandmother.

"I do have feelings," she said, and her eyes wetted.

It was after four and a long goodbye to my father when I drove her to Tobaccoton and the hotel parking lot. We sat in my car smoking.

"I read about Vin Farr," she said. "I couldn't believe it."

"Hard for everybody and causing plenty of stir."

"Killed?"

"We don't know yet."

"I just can't get it through my mind."

"Vin of whom you were so fond."

She smiled, not the spritely expression this time, but the mysterious one, the female one that bespoke compassion for the simplicity of men.

"As you were of his wife," she said.

"Makes us even." My fingers rose to my sunglasses.

"I hardly think so, though I may be mistaken," she said.

"You telling me something?"

"Well, no."

"Your expression indicates otherwise."

"It would serve no good."

"Jeannie, it's absolutely over between us. You're not going to hurt me."

She watched through cigarette smoke curling past her dark eyes. The smoke gathered under the whitish synthetic fabric of the roof.

"You were having very little to do with me," she said. "I always seemed to be waiting and wanting, and you were never there."

"Granted."

"One of Howell County's finest," she said. "He telephoned while you were with your father at the VA hospital in Richmond. He had to be certain you'd gone. He didn't say over the phone he was coming to the house. I had just finished a bath and was drying myself, and he walked right in, put his arms around me from behind, and cupped my breasts. Before I could resist, his mouth was on mine. I'm afraid I lost the power to hold out."

"We're talking about Vin?"

"A very forceful man and expert player of the game, if you think of it as a game. I lack proof, but I have this feeling if you peered into the heads of half the pretty, proper ladies in the county, you'd find memories of sizzling adventures with Vin."

I sat very still and tried to think through my confusion. Jeannie leaned to the ashtray to tap out her cigarette with three rapid pecks. She patted my knee, smiled, and reached to the door handle.

"Hope I haven't shocked you too badly. Buck up, kid, and adieu. I'll see you get an invitation, but, really, don't bother about a present."

I watched her cross to her car, a tan Oldsmobile diesel almost the color of her dress. She belted herself in, looked into the rearview mirror both to catch a glimpse of herself and see what was behind, and drove off with a wave, the Oldsmobile dipping to the street and scattering pigeons.

Vin with Jeannie and other women. I couldn't adjust to the fact. I tried not to let it become personal, to think of Jeannie fresh from a tub and Vin's hands closing over her breasts. What had gone on between Rhea and Vin?

I wondered whether a jealous husband had killed him. Unlikely. Jealous husbands in rural Virginia were not subtle and would've evened things with a twelve-gauge Remington loaded with double 00 buckshot.

When I arrived home from the General Johnston, my father was waiting.

"You made plenty of mistakes in your life, but the biggest was allowing that fine woman to get away. It's when I knew for sure there was no hope for you."

He limped to his room, slammed the door, and switched on his TV.

I sat in the grape arbor. A purplish cloud absorbed the afternoon. Farmers would be fearful of hailstones punching holes in broad leaves of their tobacco. But the storm never arrived, and I snoozed into the twilight. I didn't realize anyone was present till I brought my head forward and blinked to clear my eyes.

The person stood at the arbor's edge—Plum, the fuzzy girl who ate natural foods and exposed her breasts to the sun.

"I apologize for just walking in on you. My van's out of gas down the road. Can you sell me a gallon or two, enough to get to a pump? I have money."

She reached to her jeans' hip pocket and brought out a wallet, which she didn't open but offered as if expecting me to take the whole thing. Her halter was a red bandanna that exposed lots of skin. Her black hair had been braided into a strand at each side of her face. She was again barefooted.

"Didn't know it was your place here," she said. "Not till I saw the name on the mailbox. I told myself, 'That nice man will help.'"

"We'll do something," I said and steadied myself to walk toward the dilapidated disordered garage. I switched on the light, a single bulb around which dirt daubers had plastered their nests. I found the two-gallon can Eddie Blue had used for the lawn mower. It felt half full.

"You have a funnel?" I asked.

"Not so well prepared for breakdowns," Plum said.

The tin funnel had dropped behind a fertilizer spreader. I bent to it and carried it and the can to my car, where I opened the door for Plum. She folded in with boyish grace. She took the can and funnel and set them on the floor between her feet.

Down the road the Plymouth van was aged and rusty, yet still had faint multicolored paintings of oranges, bananas, and tomatoes on the sides. It was pulled off the hard surface, two of its wheels in a shallow drainage ditch. I stopped my car behind it, left my headlights burning, and unscrewed the cap to pour in fuel. Insects zoomed from the dark to our light.

"You're just being terrific," Plum said.

"See if it'll start."

The engine fired on her third attempt. I waited for Plum to drive off, but she cut the engine, opened the door, and stepped out to stand with me at the side of the road.

"I want to pay you," she said and again went for the wallet.

"No charge."

"I'll bring you some nutbread," she said. "I make the world's best, good for you too."

She stood with her hands in her hip pockets, a slim shape against the headlights.

"May I ask you a personal question?" she asked. "Do you need to wear the dark glasses even after sunset?"

"I have to get back to the house."

"They say in town you have eyes of different colors. I'd like to see them. Or are you sensitive about it?"

Bugs were flitting around us, and we both fanned fingers in front of our faces.

"You better get in the van," I said. "Children have been carried off by Howell County mosquitoes."

"I'm not a child, and you are sensitive. Look, I may be rushing it a little, but I do honestly believe you're a nice man, and you're not unattractive to me."

"Would you tell me that if your boyfriend weren't in jail?"

"You think I'd fool around because of that?"

"I realize I have an overpowering effect on the ladies. They call me day and night, and when I walk down the street I hear them sigh and groan after me."

"You're afraid," she said. "I asked about you in town, and they said you're aloof, but I think you're afraid. They say you're going to lose your job."

"It's all right, I have a fallback position in the Bureau of Weights and Measures."

"They say you never win convictions."

"Just you wait, I have a big case coming up involving the theft of a 1977 Model S-4 John Deere hay bailer. I not only expect to win a conviction, but also to lodge the perpetrator in the iron motel for thirty days."

"You have a gentle interior," she said.

"You can see my interior?"

"I sense you've been hurt."

"Everybody's been hurt, and it's my judicious opinion you've been eating too much salsify and turnip pudding. Now please climb into your vehicle and leave so I can go home."

"I may stay a while. I like it here."

"Then I'm afraid I'll have to leave you on your own."

I left her at the side of the road and drove home. In the pantry I fixed a watered drink. My father's TV was playing. I took off my sunglasses. I walked from the house to the darkness of the grape arbor, sat in my chair, and stretched out my legs. My breathing had hardly quieted before headlights swept in along the lane.

It was Plum and the van. She cut her engine, stepped down, and crossed the dry grass. She was carrying the gasoline can.

"You forgot it," she said but didn't leave. Instead she sat in front of me by simply allowing her legs to give way and double under her. It was a graceful move, a dancer's.

"You like my stomach?" she asked and set the can aside.

"What?"

"I noticed you eyeing my stomach."

She rose effortlessly, clasped her hands behind her head, and began a slow harem dance. Her shape was so slim and fluid in the dark. She worked toward me, rhythmically circled the chair, and stopped to lay her cheek against mine. I felt the fuzz. She maneuvered onto my lap and wiggled a finger into my shirt. When she kissed me, I stood hurriedly, but she was still at my mouth.

"The grass is soft in the cool of the evening," she said and pulled me down with her. She reached behind her to release the bandanna halter and fling it aside. She began unbuttoning my shirt.

"Loving helps when lovingly given," she said. She peeled my shirt off and tugged at my belt. In the darkness her breasts seemed luminous.

"What are we doing?" I asked.

"You mean you've gone all these years and don't understand what it is men and women do together?"

She was lying across me now, her breasts pushed against my chest, her mouth at my throat. She shoved my pants down, and I jerked them up. It was as if we were sawing wood.

"I haven't been fair with you," I said. "I was wounded in Nam."

"Poor man," she said, kissing my throat.

"Reconnaissance patrol near Quoc To. Baker Company, an area where no Charley was supposed to be. We had just come over from the States and were laughing and picturing cold Buds back at base. Then Charleys popped out of the ground. All these little lids of soil opened around us, and in the holes were Charleys firing guns and tossing grenades."

"Your wound, was that why your marriage didn't work?"

"I wasn't able to be a complete husband to her."

"You lie!" she said and pressed against me. "You weren't in the service. I found that out too."

She kicked my pants down and lay on top of me. She kissed and squirmed against me. I hadn't been with a woman since Jeannie, and this was beginning to feel very good. She was out of her jeans.

Just then a car turned into the lane, and as it rolled toward the house, its headlights washed over us. I grabbed for clothes and hid behind grapevines. It was a pickup driven by Cleveland Smith's boy who delivered the morning paper to the box at the head of the lane. He'd come to collect. In the rear of the truck stood a lowing calf.

The boy climbed the front steps, knocked, and called through the screen door.

"I never read your trashy paper!" my father shouted. "All lies! I wouldn't have it in an outhouse!"

The boy came down the steps, hesitated, and spoke my name. "Oh, Mr. Billy? Mr. Billy?" When I didn't answer, he got in his pickup, drove back past us, and rattled along the lane, the calf bawling.

"I don't think he saw anything," I said, clutching clothes to me and peeping among the vines. I'd been pushing at Plum to keep her hidden.

"Who cares?" she asked and reached for me.

"I care, I live here!"

"Why you live here is the question. And is it really living? The best thing you could do is get out. How'd you like to go to Arizona with me?"

We were at it again, starting over on the grass. It was exciting having this fuzzy, athletic young woman working above me trying to make a lover out of me. I took it as a high compliment, though I knew her morals were not Howell County Baptist and believed the real reason she'd come was Cloud and Hawthorn down in the jail.

Just as I found myself becoming enthusiastic, about to fit myself to her, a pack of hounds ran howling out of the night. They were after coon, possum, or fox, hot on a trail that led along the other side of the lane. Their cries were like souls in torment, and the world sounded full of them. One that had fiery eyes and the stink of hot manure ran right over us, returned to sniff, and lifted his head to utter a shrill, trembling plaint. He ran on baying to join the pack in the chase.

I sprang up all shriveled and knock-kneed. I still had on a shoe and one leg of my pants. The hounds coursed along the rear of the house and through broomstraw toward the trees. Something thrashed ahead of them, a deer maybe feeding on vines grown up on the broken fence. I hopped about to stick my other leg in my pants.

"Come here," Plum said and wrestled me.

"Listen—"

"I'm deaf," she said and again pinned me. She held me in a very personal way, and we might have managed except I felt not

only the coarse grass against my skin but also stinging on my thighs
and buttocks.

She felt it too, and we both scrambled up, danced around, and
slapped at ourselves. We'd been lying on top an anthill, and the
ants didn't like it a damn bit. I stumbled in my dropped drawers.
Plum's palms smacked skin, but she was laughing.

"There's a mattress in the van," she said.

"Can't you see I'm no lover?"

"I'll teach you."

"I have this picture in my mind of the whole act being ridiculous, some kind of joke the Lord thought up when He created
the race. He assembled the Heavenly Host in Grand Consult and
asked, 'How can we best be entertained by mankind as we sit here
on the parapets?' A wag angel suggested copulation, the way people
do it now, and the idea broke up the Heavenly Host. They laughed,
rolled about on clouds, and called out, 'Oh no! Not that! It's too
crazy!' But a grinning Lord did it to us. That's what I have in
mind, all those angels up there hooting and hollering as they watch
you and me right now."

"Bull," she said and led me to the van and mattress. The
interior smelled of tomatoes. I wasn't so awkward this time and in
fact did pretty well. Plum patted my back.

We were sweaty and rested a while before climbing out and
dressing. We slapped at mosquitoes.

"From now on tomatoes will always have a special meaning to
me," I said.

"You don't need any lessons," Plum said.

Old Ben wouldn't talk sense. Pickney, deputies, and I rotated
questioning him in the sheriff's office, but Ben gazed at his feet
and spoke meaningless words.

"The Lord plants man in the ground and waters him," he said.

Pickney and I closed the door of the squad room to discuss
what next. The squad room was furnished with a kitchen table,
folding chairs, a bench, two ashtrays, and a radiator painted brown.
A fan had been brought in, but the pink ribbons tied to the wire
protector were reluctant to wave as if not believing any coolness
possible.

"You make any sense of it?" Pickney asked.

"None."

"One thing, he might talk to Rhea. She know he's here?"

"No."

"How about calling?"

I did from my office, and Rhea answered as if right by the phone.

"I'm so happy he's all right, and I'll be there in a minute," she said.

A minute was thirty, and I was standing at my window when she drove up before the courthouse in her Thunderbird. She backed into a metered parking space with unerring swiftness. Two moves did it, one in reverse, one forward, and the car was snug at the curb.

When she swung out her legs, they flashed in the sunlight, a glint of dusky nylons. I again thought of her in black stockings. She wore a beige suit and brown-and-white heels. Apparently official mourning was diminishing. She reached back into the Thunderbird for her pocketbook.

She strode up the walk to the courthouse steps as if she owned all she looked upon, yet there was no arrogance in her expression. She was like a person who eyed a tree he'd planted or grass he'd sown. The tree or grass was his, and he had a proprietary affection for it.

I hurried downstairs to meet her at the door. I held it and explained we wanted her to see whether she could coax Ben into talking.

"His mind wanders," I said.

We walked toward the jail, and the authoritative click of her heels sounded and echoed in the corridor. Pickney hastened from his office to shake her hand. He had brushed his unruly sideburns into place and pulled up his trousers. I noticed he addressed her as Mrs. Farr, not Rhea.

Old Ben was in the office, and when Rhea entered, he stood but didn't look directly at her. To my knowledge Rhea never hugged any man except Vin, yet she embraced Old Ben.

"We've been so worried," she told him. "How we supposed to get along at Riverview without you?"

"Trees go up, trees come down," Old Ben said.

"Yes," she said, and she sat him and drew a chair alongside. Pickney and I backed out, closed the door, and stepped into a storage closet. Our jail had no electronic secrets or two-way mirrors, but high on the closet wall was a ventilator which could be opened in order that we might hear what went on in the office. We stood among buckets and mops.

"We miss you so out at the house," Rhea said to Old Ben. "Everybody's hoping you'll come back."

"Put a seed in the ground, and it'll grow," Ben said.

"That's true, Ben, we all know that."

"Man is a seed. The Lord plants and waters him. The Lord looks for the increase."

"Ben, listen, why did you leave Riverview and where've you been?"

"The Lord is a great gardener. He waters and harvests, but some are cast aside."

"Do you understand that my Mr. Vin has left us? He's dead, Ben."

"Taken up."

"But do you know anything about it? Did you see him that last day?"

Old Ben began to hum and then sing. His voice was deep and husky, yet unhurried.

> *I'm walking up the road,*
> *I'm walking to the mountain,*
> *I'm walking to the place*
> *Where I'll see my Lord.*

"That's fine, I always liked to hear you singing, but won't you please try to help us?" Rhea asked.

Old Ben kept singing:

> *Glory, I been walking to glory,*
> *Glory, I going to see my Lord.*

"Do you need anything, clothes or tobacco?" Rhea asked. "If you do or feel you can talk to me, just tell the sheriff or Mr. Payne, and they'll call me to come."

Pickney and I heard the snap of her pocketbook latch and guessed she was leaving money for Old Ben. When she opened the office door, we stepped into the corridor to meet her. Old Ben sat looking at his feet. A new twenty-dollar bill lay on Pickney's desk.

"It's all right for him to have, isn't it?" Rhea asked. Her lavender eyes were wet.

"I'll see he gets it as he needs it," Pickney said and wrote out a penciled receipt for the money.

"I want him treated well," Rhea said.

"We treat everybody fair and square here, Mrs. Farr."

She thanked Pickney, and then she and I walked the corridor to the front entrance of the courthouse. Just as I opened the door, I asked her to lunch. I was surprised I had the nerve and immediately sorry when I saw the conflict on her face. My fingers fluttered at my sunglasses.

"I haven't been out," she said.

"I wasn't thinking. Stupid me. One invitation canceled and one apology tendered."

"Now wait, Billy, you have never been stupid. Best grades made at Howell County High. I'd like to have lunch with you but don't want people stopping by the table to talk about Vin, which would be the case at the General Johnston. Isn't there someplace else?"

We drove in my car to Bannister and a restaurant on a four-lane highway near the hospital east of town. We chose a dim blue leatherette booth at the rear where the sound of buzzing neon around the windows was muffled. The room was air-conditioned, and on walls were mounted heads of slain deer, their glass eyes dusty and stark.

As Rhea read a menu encased in clear plastic, I sneaked looks at her. Her skin was not only tanned, but also lightly weathered, a horsewoman's complexion, yet she wore no makeup other than a faint lipstick. Her mouth was small in proportion to the rest of her face, and the strawberry hair and lavender eyes would've appeared bizarre on anyone else, but she made them as natural as silk on corn. Those eyes were enough to stop my breathing when she caught me peeking at her.

I wasn't just admiring. I also wondered did she know Vin had been a womanizer. I couldn't believe she understood about Jeannie. Then there was the inkless tattoo. Pull for service. What was the answer to the tattoo?

I didn't smoke or drink a beer, afraid she might object. We ordered club sandwiches and iced tea. She pushed at her hair, a completely feminine move that lifted her breasts against the pale blue silk of her blouse. Around her throat were pearls that matched her earrings. The tiny gold cross on the fine chain hung inside the blouse.

"I don't know what to make of Old Ben," she said. "He never acted like that at Riverview. Even drinking he didn't."

As we ate, I kept eyeing her. She could be quieter than any other woman I'd ever known. Most would have been chattering, feeling an obligation to converse, but she seemed totally complete within herself. I was the one running off at the mouth.

I attempted to think up a way to gather information about the relationship between her and Vin. She was too smart for indirection, and I wasn't about to approach the subject head-on. Then she spoke.

"Have the police found anything at all?"

"Not much."

"I guess I don't care about details. Vin's gone, I care about that, but the rest is only aftershock."

Misery rose in her, spread right up through her body to the lavender eyes, where it almost spilled, but she lowered her face so I could no longer see. She worked at swallowing.

"We intend to keep trying," I said.

"I know you'll do all you can, Billy," she said and like Jeannie at the General Johnston reached across to lay her hand on mine. Her nails were short and unpainted, a rider's fingers, lean and competent. Her touch warmed me. I had an impulse to lift her hand and kiss the palm, do it right there in the cafe where Bannister businessmen came for the luncheon special. Then she withdrew her fingers and again took up her sandwich, which she never finished. She drank a little of her mint tea.

On the drive to Tobaccoton, she sat without speaking. No clouds bunched in the pale yellow sky, and people working fields drooped like thirsty corn. Cattle stood in thin shade of hackberry trees. Pond water was low and had a scummy cast.

I held the door of the Thunderbird for her and watched the car move quickly away down Main Street. I walked into the courthouse, climbed to my office, and closed the door. I laid the fingers of one hand against the back of the other, attempting to re-create Rhea's touch of me.

My father brooded about Jeannie. He called from the second floor:

"This house was alive when we had a woman in it. Men should never live alone. Even the dust of men stinks. I hate the smell of this place. She was a fine woman, everybody in Howell County agrees, and you had to go blow it!"

I again thought of Jeannie glowing and rosy from her bath, and Vin slipping behind her and fitting his strong hands to her breasts. What did he do to Rhea?

One minute the sky was a yellow vacuum, and the next a single black cloud rose in the southwest. I heard a feeble thunder. Not much hope, I decided.

"Men were never meant to keep house! When your mother was alive, this place always smelled of flowers."

I stood on the back porch and looked over copper broomstraw to the cloud. I still heard thunder, but I believed any rain would follow the river toward Richmond.

If Vin had been a womanizer, who were the other women? I pictured respectable ladies of the county and wondered how many carried a secret. Wasn't Rhea too intelligent not to know? Yet she would be too proud to put up with infidelity. She'd have locked Vin out of the house or set lawyers on him. Except Rhea was of a trusting nature and possessed a faraway quality. She didn't want to see bad in people.

"God, I'd like to smell a little perfume around here," my father called from his bedroom window. "I'm starved for some woman scent on the air. Your mother was a rose."

I touched the back of my left hand with the fingers of my right. I jerked the hands apart. I was thinking of Rhea here and now instead of her husband dead and buried. Get your mind focused! On what? All Pickney and I had were shards.

"What can be said of a man who won't answer the colors and defend his country?" my father called. "I never believed it would happen to a son of mine. It's not a question of good and bad wars. No war is good when you're in it."

I thought of my year in the Louisville seminary, where I'd sat around evenings in the dorm and agreed with other students that if we were truly Christian, we would never use violence. Rather we would allow anyone to have this country—Russians, Chinese, Eskimos. We'd invite them in and gorge them on brotherhood. Let them take our houses, shirts, women. Afterward we'd love them to death for it.

"You owe me the luxury of your superiority," my father called. "Men like me saved your royal ass!"

Maybe they had. I'd never faced a gun or even fists since a boyhood schoolyard fight. Of course I'd fought legal wars and lost those. But there the violence was to the mind.

"I wanted a son so bad," my father called. "I prayed for a son, your mother and I did. I'm glad she's not here to see what you turned into. I'm happy she's resting eternally instead of having to go through the pain you'd cause her. I just hope she can't look down and see you now."

I hardly heard him. His voice was a constant not requiring attention. I knew the words by heart.

I looked at the cooling sky where the cloud had torn like purple smoke. I thought of Rhea and what she would do now that Vin was gone. In time suitors surely would arrive, men drawn to her both for her beauty and her money.

I thought of myself as one of them. I pictured me stroking her hair and lying beside her in her white bed. After all the sailing I'd done from the grape arbor I was a pretty fair hallucinator. And Plum had given me an A.

"Dying is going to be easy for me," my father called.

11

The master carries white bathroom scales which have a digital readout. Like beef before the market, I am weighed. My eyes are checked, my temperature is taken. What am I being prepared for?

I am unchained for a new exercise. The master hands me a nylon rope to tie around my waist. The line is paid out twenty feet or so, and I jog around the master, who holds an end. I think of Rhea training horses in her paddock.

The first morning I am given five minutes of the exercise. On succeeding days the time is lengthened. The master keeps time by wristwatch. It is very hot. The locusts chirr; the call of crows is lazy and distant.

After exercising, I am allowed to pull up buckets of cold water from the well and empty them over myself. I wear undershorts. In the sunlight I am quickly dry. Next I mount the scales.

"Your weight is constant," the master, holding the gun, says.

"What's to happen to me?"

"No determination has been made."

"Will I ever be released."

"There's hope."

I eat, and we begin the lesson.

———

I sat in my office, but I was on a boat, a Cal 25 painted vermilion, a spinnaker white as clouds set as I ran down the Chesapeake, not before a high wind, just meandering and stopping nights to drop the hook in tidal creeks and rivers of the eastern shore, the serene backwaters where I reclined and lowered my feet to the gunnels as I watched ospreys dip and heard the splash of terns. Darkness slipped in over tranquil waters, and cries of great blue herons were like voices from the age of dinosaurs.

Sheriff Pickney tapped my door and entered, his uniform wilted by heat, drooping around fleshy rolls of his body. Even his revolver drooped, the holster halfway down his thigh.

"Hear you been attending church," he said and let himself down into a chair as if settling into a bathtub of hot water.

"Like you," I said.

"The reverends are really het up. I got two extra men running patrols into the piney woods and scaring hell out of kids with their pants down. It'd be funny 'cept it's happening to my department. One fifteen-year-old got himself hung up in his zipper. Had to rush him to the emergency room at Bannister. I tell you it's a circus every night."

He lifted a heavy leg and scratched the sallowness of his calf. His nails left tracks across his skin. When he dropped his foot, the dingo boot thudded against the floor like a concrete block.

"I know, we got to decide something soon," he said. "Can't hold Old Ben and them grass-eating hippies forever."

"Let them go," I said and thought of Plum. I scratched where ants had bitten.

"What we have then?"

"Same as we have now, nothing."

"You giving up?"

"Stating a fact."

"We'll never see them again. Them lettuce eaters will head West, and Old Ben'll find a hole quicker than a rabbit with a fox snapping at his ass."

"It'll have to be."

"But something might break. There could be something right here in front of us we don't see."

I was thinking of Rhea and Vin, their relationship. I tried to
be careful how I phrased the question.

"You ever hear stories about Vin?"

"What kind of stories?" Pickney asked. He was pinching hairs
from his nose, jerking them out by the roots and examining each
catch.

"Rumors."

"You're not getting through to me, Billy."

"Maybe he played around a little."

He stopped pulling hairs, a hand suspended, looked at me,
and didn't answer. Then his weary blue eyes drifted to the window.
Down the street roared an eighteen-wheeler hauling a red International Harvester combine on a flatbed.

"I never exactly heard anything," Pickney said.

I waited; yet there was nothing else. His eyes didn't come back
to me. The eighteen-wheeler thundered south, and the street quieted. Heat shimmered above pavement and bricks.

"You finished on the subject?" I asked.

"Sure you want to pursue this?" he asked.

"Why wouldn't I?"

He shrugged, again pulled at nose hairs, and held them close
to his eyes. "I never heard no stories, but I saw him once with a
woman not Rhea, at night during the fall. I spotted this Jeep on
the Wye River fire trail. I wasn't lawing but coon hunting. I thought
the Jeep might be stolen and abandoned."

He shifted in the chair but still avoided looking at me. "They
was ducked down in the seats. When I shined my light through
the windshield, he sat up, and the woman covered her face. Hell,
I backed off. Like I said I wasn't working that night. Just wanted
to hear a little hound music, and I never lawed a man yet for getting
himself a slice of poon, not anyway till Buster Bovin come along."

His words dropped off, and I understood his eyes, the evasion,
and what he was telling me. He was saying he knew the woman
with Vin in the Jeep. My ex-wife Jeannie. He wouldn't want to
speak her name and was hoping like hell I wouldn't push him. I
didn't intend to.

"You see any connection or need to follow up?" I asked. "I
mean a jealous husband or the like."

"Nah, that woman left Tobaccoton long ago."

"Others?"

"Not I know about."

"Well then."

"Yeah, well then. Let's hold the little we got a couple more days unless somebody hollers. Take another crack at Old Ben. That Cloud gives me a headache with his damn guitar." .

Pickney left my office as fast as he could without seeming to flee.

As if I didn't have enough to worry me, Uncle Daniel came back, my father's older brother, some claimed the brightest member of the family and surely the one who'd had the most bragging done about him when I was a boy.

I remembered him coming to visit in a Packard larger than any mourners' car owned by the Berry-Burton Funeral Home. Other than Rhea's father Blackjack, Uncle Daniel was the only person in Howell County to have a chauffeur, and Uncle Daniel's was more impressive because his was white.

Uncle Daniel was the one member of the family in his generation to attend college. He'd gone at a sacrifice, the little pile of hoarded money spent so he could study business at North Carolina State. He went to work for Standard Oil of New Jersey, but it wasn't up North he became rich. He used Standard Oil to pump dry the executive minds around him and then lit out for Texas, where he hooked up with a wildcatter named MacMasters to punch holes in arid scrub land so poor even rattlesnakes wouldn't cross it.

Sweetwater Drillers was the company they formed, nothing glorious enough to be sold on an exchange, even the Abilene one, but they brought in sufficient crude to float the big Packard Uncle Daniel's white chauffeur drove him home in. Every head on Main Street whipped around to watch it pass, and children ran after it and squatted to see their reflections in the dazzling hub caps.

Uncle Daniel wore bone-white cowboy hats, golden-striped black alpaca suits, and western boots which had a red-leather diamond pattern in the shank. He sported a black cane with a silver handle, though he suffered from neither rheumatism nor arthritis. He smoked eight-inch Havana cigars, carried his money in a wad, and when he raised a hand in greeting, gems flashed on his fingers like water flowing over sunny rocks.

"I been far away, Lord yes, but I always think of the home

place," he said, having traded his Virginia voice for a Texas one. "I think of Pap, Momma, and those big Sunday dinners we had. After enduring two hours of mean preaching on those hard Presbyterian pews, we'd drive home and Momma would head for the kitchen. She'd have done lots of cooking the night before, but it'd take her another two hours before she hit the gong and we could belly up to the table.

"And the food, my God, the chicken, ham, the hog, the butterbeans, corn, and snaps, the whipped potatoes with brown gravy, and the sugar pies. Why, we staggered away from the table and collapsed on the front porch as if we'd been shot. We groaned and couldn't move."

I was seven years old then, and the next time Uncle Daniel came to Howell County he had an even bigger limousine, a Lincoln this time, and a wife from California—the prettiest woman I'd ever seen. She wasn't pretty the way the local ladies were, but she wore her flaming hair up and tousled. Her face made up was like an enamel doll's. When she walked along Main Street in a short apricot skirt that had a slit in the side, men almost fell out of windows. Her name was Tammy Doe, and she kissed me right on the mouth, causing a scary mysterious swelling in my pants.

Uncle Daniel owned a second and third company by that time, and we'd seen his picture in *Forbes*. None of the family subscribed to the magazine, but they had a copy at the high-school library, and we all sat down at a table to study Uncle Daniel laughing as he stood by an oil rig and held a glass of crude as if it were wine he was about to drink. By then he flaunted a gold tooth. The article said he could sell feathers to birds.

Every time he came home, I'd wait on Uncle Daniel, serve him, stay close in case he needed anything like an ashtray for his cigars or iced tea or the flies fanned off him. We had a big wicker fan, and he would pay me for using it on him while he snoozed, a penny a minute. He also liked me to stand behind his chair when he cocked his boots to the railing and to scratch his head.

He was thin, even more than what I'd grow up to be. He had hair the color of winter broomstraw, though his eyebrows and lashes were dark. He'd learned young to smile, finding the force of it would gain him most anything he wanted from his parents, the townspeople, and the world, including dirt farmers in West Texas who owned land no drill had ever punched through. It was said

Uncle Daniel could turn a charging bull with the gleam of his teeth.
"When you grow up, you come join me out in Midland," he'd
tell me as I stood working my fingers over his clean scalp. "I'll
teach you the business. Starting early you could become ten times
richer than me."

I used to dream of being Texas rich, having my own plane,
houses, at least one of which would be in Hawaii, a wife as beautiful
as Tammy Doe, whom I'd spied in the bathroom just after she
stepped from our old-fashioned claw-footed tub. She'd wrapped a
blue towel around herself, the top of it along her breasts, the bottom
high on her jiggling thighs, and when she saw me gawking, she just
laughed and winked.

"Dream's what you got to do," Uncle Daniel said. "People
everywhere will try to make you small, but no dream is too big, no
shore too far. Raise your sights, son, they always too low."

That was fine with me. I raised my sights to European estates
and countesses with long cigarette holders and African big-game
hunting. I sailed my yacht to the south of France and sipped sherry
at Buckingham Palace with the King of England, who asked my
advice on American investments. I had a box in the golden tier at
the opera, though I'd never heard a living note of that type music
in my life, only the scratchy records in the ninth-grade music class
at Howell County Junior High where Miss Bottles, who was so old
and shrunken she appeared mummified, taught us that Lily Pons
was the greatest singer who ever gave tongue to song.

People pushed money at Uncle Daniel to invest for them. There
weren't that many dollars lying around Howell County, but he could
hardly walk down the street that men didn't come out of doors to
persuade him to take their savings. Even Rhea's father Blackjack
and Louis Booker, who owned the Bright Leaf warehouse, and
Congressman Carrington reached for their checkbooks. Uncle Daniel
would return to the house sprouting money. He could sell fleas
to dogs.

Nobody figured just when Uncle Daniel set his foot on the
bad path, whether he started out straight or from the very beginning
his books were cooked. The first we read was in the Richmond
paper, a dateline not Texas but Wichita, Kansas, and when my
father telephoned all the way out there, he put on a coat and tie as
if expecting formality through the line. Uncle Daniel laughed, said
all the charges were political, and that horse thieves ran the Justice

Department. He claimed the governor of Texas was so ignorant he poured ketchup on grits. Uncle Daniel could sell cats to mice.

The next thing he was in prison, not in either Texas or Kansas, but Oklahoma. There were charges of fraud and a pyramid scheme. Local people like Blackjack, Louis Booker, and Congressman Carrington wrote angry letters out West to inquire about their investments, and after a time the letters came back looking as if they'd been stepped on.

It was the mortification of my father and the family, including myself. Up to then we'd been able to borrow off Uncle Daniel's success. When I walked the street I knew people were thinking there goes Daniel Payne's nephew who when he grows up will be taken into the oil business and own houses, yachts, and pretty women that wear apricot skirts with slits in them. Uncle Daniel brought us glory.

My father took it hardest. He stayed drunk ten days. Aunt Lettie and I ran back and forth to his bedroom trying to do something for him—get him to wash, to eat, to change his clothes, but he shouted us away, and nights he'd cry out as if hot irons burned him.

When at last he limped down the stairs, not sober but able to stay upright by holding the railing, his eyes were demon red and so far back in his head they were shadowed.

"Don't want to hear his name again," he said. "I am making that pronouncement. From this time forth and evermore. He has disgraced us for generations."

So we didn't speak Uncle Daniel's name, though once a year we received a card from the Oklahoma prison. He made the cards himself, drew them in colored pencil, desert scenes with cactus, tumbleweed, and coyotes howling at the moon.

Finally the cards stopped coming. We assumed he was either out of prison and exiled or dead. We wanted him dead. Thus I couldn't immediately trim my mind to what I was hearing over my office telephone.

"I'm telling you he's right out there on the corner," Garnet Ruffin said. Garnet was cashier at the Planters & Merchants Bank. "I went up and looked him close in the face."

I reached for my jacket, walked quickly from the courthouse, and hurried toward the corner. Men gathered, but there were always men on that corner talking crops, prices, land—mostly farmers,

some of whom had been in the fields that very day suckering tobacco. If you shook their hands, you felt the tobacco wax on their
palms and fingers, hateful weedy grease that washed off only with
gasoline or mineral spirits.

I saw the sign, the sort striking pickets carry, or delegates to
political conventions, a big white square of cardboard tacked to a
broom handle. The sign was held up by a man whom at first I
didn't believe was Uncle Daniel. This person wore no gold-striped
alpaca or handmade cowboy boots but scuffed tennis shoes, paint-
splattered Levi's, and a Hawaiian shirt. His gray hair was long, the
strands pulled straight as if weighted at the ends. On his head was
a billed railroader's cap.

He'd gained fifty pounds or more, and his step in the tennis
shoes was heavy and flat. His skin appeared as porous as old cheese
rind. Like me he wore dark glasses, but his had outsized red frames.

It was the sign men talked and laughed about. Cars and pickups
were slowing, and people sticking their heads out windows to look.
Uncle Daniel held it with both hands like the color guard at the
head of a parade. The thing about the sign was nothing had been
written on it. It was just an unmarked white rectangle.

"Ain't he forgot something?" a farmer asked, his hands pushed
under shoulder straps of his overalls.

"What he forgot weren't give out the day he was borned,"
another said.

Reese Prosser, one of Tobaccoton's four town policemen, he a
day man, directed traffic and tried to make a decision what to do
about Uncle Daniel, who had no parade permit but was furnishing
the populace a free show.

"Let him be, he's harming nothing except shoe leather," a
farmer called.

"Which ain't even shoe leather," another farmer said.

I waited for Uncle Daniel to make his turn in front of the
Howell County Mercantile and come back toward the bank. I
couldn't tell where he was looking because of his big sunglasses.
Maybe he wasn't looking. He passed without seeming to see me.

"Uncle Daniel, it's Billy Payne."

The soft squeaking of his tennis shoes stopped, and he turned.
He uncurled fingers from the sign's broom handle to raise the
sunglasses and stare at me out of eyes that appeared to have no lids.
They could've belonged to a fish. For a long time he held those

enormous eyes on me, the color a smoldering amber, smoke from
dreams of lost and burned empires, until finally he withdrew his
grip from the sunglasses and allowed them to drop back across his
nose. The fingers resumed their curl around the broom handle.

"Little Billy. Boy, you've sure shot up."

"Good to have you home, Uncle Daniel. Come on, let's go to
my office."

"Last time I saw you you weren't high as low corn. Too big
to fan the flies off me now."

Men had gathered round as if they had a right to take part.
They smiled and nodded. Kin, reunions, they understood and approved of. Horns honked on the street.

"We could go out to the house," I said.

"Don't expect I'd be too welcome there, Billy, and besides I
got my duty. I am bound to do it."

"What duty's that?" I asked and glanced at the blank sign.

"I made a promise while I was the honored guest of the governor of Oklahoma," he said. "I swore to the Lord I'd bring His
message to the people, the words that came down to me like the
living fire."

"What message?" a farmer in the crowd asked.

"What you think I'm carrying, horse feathers?" Uncle Daniel
asked and turned the sign toward the man. "Read."

The crowd looked at the sign, stirred, and laughed. Men
scratched their heads and squinted. An old farmer drew a pair of
steel-rim glasses from a breast pocket of his overalls and set them
on to study the sign.

"Ain't nothing on it," he said.

"Oh, it's written on all right for those with eyes to see," Uncle
Daniel said. "Maybe your eyes not adjusted to the living word."

He turned slowly so that everybody standing on the sidewalk
and along the curb or sitting in cars and pickups would have time
to read. Then he stepped around me and again began pacing.

"Ain't nothing on that sign, is they?" Reese Prosser whispered
to me, his gaze following Uncle Daniel.

"Not unless we all been struck blind," I said.

"Man, I can tell you I'm glad to hear that."

Uncle Daniel kept walking up and down between the bank
and the Howell County Mercantile. After a while the farmers shook
their heads and drove home to water the stock, eat dinners, do the

milking. But cars and pickups were still arriving, full of men, women, and children who wanted to look at Uncle Daniel and his sign. They even came after dark and watched him march against lights of the store windows.

I convinced Reese and Eustis Goode, another town policeman, that Uncle Daniel wasn't doing any damage, at least not yet, and to allow him to go on with it. He'd eventually tire and have to stop on his own. Then I might be able to drive him out to the house or have him examined by Doc Robinette.

Uncle Daniel paraded on into the night, so late the curious no longer cruised past to gawk, though some truckers, pilots of the big semis headed to Richmond town, as well as occasional tourists on their way to Virginia Beach, spotted him in their headlights and were startled as they peered to read the message not on the sign.

Another victim of the Howell County disease. Symptoms: visions, hot religion, the spirit. God help us. We sure needed all the help He could spare.

Pickney and I were letting Old Ben go. We had nothing to hold him on, and both Rhea and Ben's daughter were calling. Rhea thought it unfair and unfeeling that we kept him in jail. He could, she said, stay at Riverview. He wouldn't have to work. She'd see he was fed and clothed till he was again himself.

Ben's daughter threatened. Over the telephone from Richmond, her voice sounded arch and educated. She told me she'd consulted a lawyer who would bring charges against the county for illegal arrest and detainment.

"We'll be able to keep track of Old Ben," I said to Pickney.

"Sure, but damnit, by releasing him we're just telling the whole world we don't know anything."

"Well, we don't know anything."

"But we were looking like we did."

"I been thinking of driving to Richmond and talking to the daughter."

"Captain-ass Blake and his team of crack investigators has already done it. Hell, if I had their budget, I could find out who invented tits."

Pickney kept wiping his palms. Maybe somebody else in the county was interested in running for sheriff, a man with a family

base as large as his. Or it could be Pickney's young wife again had
him worried by making eyes at the feed and fertilizer salesman.

"I have to take Daddy to the hospital anyhow," I said.

"Sure, well, that way you can at least draw mileage."

That was a cynical statement. The county reimbursed me twenty
cents a mile on travel expenses run up in the job. I wouldn't defraud,
for I intended to measure and deduct the distance to the VA Hospital
and to the liquor store at Southside Plaza.

I had the address of Old Ben's daughter, a Mrs. Leona Poindexter who lived in an apartment below the James River, the
Rosemont. The district was black filtered through money: mowed
lawns, maple and ornamental trees, late-model cars. A public school
at the corner had four tennis courts and a swimming pool. Glistening
kids flipped off the board into sunlight.

The Rosemont was a two-story brick building with flowers
growing from concrete urns on the stoops. I reached Leona's apartment, 4-C, by entering a screen door, passing a row of inset mailboxes, and climbing a flight of steps covered by a brown rubber
runner. The hallway smelled of detergent.

She opened the door. I already knew she worked as a buyer
at Gallitoes, a Richmond department store, but I wasn't prepared
for her perfumed sophistication. She was tall, disdainful, almost
white. She could've passed most places, especially the beach—if
blacks anywhere were still interested in passing. She wore gray
suede heels, gray slacks, and a loose silvery blouse. Her necklace
was many loops of ruby beads, and from her ears hung ruby tri-
angles. Her hair was straight and curled under, her skin had a sheen,
and her eyebrows were plucked to the size of an incision.

"William Payne," I said. "I telephoned."

She was not gracious. She held her thin, chic body like a soldier
at the gate before grudgingly backing off a step and opening the
door farther. I felt I was having to edge into the creamy living room
furnished with Scandinavian pieces, the place high-tech except for
fresh flowers stuck about in painted clay vases and a spinet piano
with a hymnal on it opened to "Amazing Grace."

By a window in a wheelchair sat an old black woman who,
despite the heat, had her lap and legs covered by a red-and-blue
afghan. What little hair remained to her was fluffy cotton. Her face
was so horizontally wrinkled that water from her milky eyes would've

had to run a series of switchbacks to reach her chin. She chewed something, gum maybe, working it in her mouth without moving her pale lips.

"William Payne," I said to her.

The old woman didn't answer or apparently hear. I stood uncertain before her. Leona made no move to ease the situation. She still waited by the door, her posture contemptuously svelte. "Svelte" was a word I hadn't used since I left Richmond for Tobaccoton. *Vogue*? I thought. *The New Yorker*? Bracelets jangled on her wrists, and her nails were scarlet. Where, I wondered, did she get her whiteness? The place was a statement that she wanted no part of memory or the past.

"I've known your father most of my life," I said to her. "I'd never do anything to harm him. We held him in jail because the man he worked for died so suddenly and your father disappeared."

"Not disappeared," she said.

"Went into hiding then."

"Not hiding either. He came to visit me. He has every right to do that."

Her accent was cultivated, fake sure, yet she made it sound right. She used words as if tweezing them from a jewelry box, each syllable as hard as a diamond.

"The way he left caused suspicion," I said. "My office has pressures, and in our state of mind it appeared he was running and hiding. Now he won't answer questions but gives replies that mean nothing to us."

"Known him most of your life?" she asked. "Been intimately associated with him? You ever sat down beside him to break bread, offered him a cigarette, sent him a Christmas card?"

"No, but I have a genuinely good feeling for Ben and believed it to be reciprocated."

"Sure, Daddy knows how to do up white folks. He takes off his hat and bows. They think what a cute little darky he is. I tell you something. My father reads Plato. He's read the complete works of Plato. How many people in Howell County ever heard of Plato? They'd think you mean Mickey Mouse's dog."

I pictured Old Ben shuffling among the flowers and shrubs at Riverview, his shapeless pants held up by suspenders, his sweat-shiny face shaded by a straw hat, mumbling usually, talking to the flowers, telling them they needed a drink of rain or meal of 10-10-10. He smelled of garden.

"I always tried to treat him well," I said. "I think that counts for something."

"You ever read Plato?"

"Only part of *The Republic* in college. I'm not a scholar but merely a Commonwealth's Attorney trying to find the truth about the death of a man."

"A white man. If he were black, you'd never have come all the way to Richmond."

"I hope I would."

"Hope's cheap."

The old black woman seemed to be listening, her face raised, her head perky whether with curiosity or palsy I couldn't tell. She nibbled at her shaky fingers and began to cough. Leona crossed with a fast hard step to the woman, stuck slim fingers into the mouth, and pinched out a clot of yarn plucked from the afghan.

She patted the old woman's back. The woman stopped coughing, and her milky eyes floated around in the sockets as if they'd lost their moorings. Leona carried the clot of afghan to a gunmetal wastebasket and flicked it in.

Her mother, I thought. But that would make her Ben's wife. She and Old Ben ranged in complexion from mahogany to asphalt. Where did Leona's whiteness come from, some reversion to a lonely gene, some cross of chromosomes back in darker, steamier times?

"You want anything else?" Leona asked. She was again at the door, ready to show me out.

"I'd very much appreciate any help you give me."

"You never even saw me," she said. "You passed me on streets, but your eyes went right over me. You never came to a party, wedding, though you did occasionally attend the funeral of a good old nigger who yahsuhed your people. You sat in the pew like honored guests. But you never saw me, black girl in a segregated school. Well, I saw you when you used to hide in bushes and spy on Rhea Gatlin. I saw what you did with your hands while you spied on her."

I stood hot, abashed, mortified. I'd done that with my hand only once when lying on dry pine tags in the resinous heat of summer and watching while Rhea trotted a horse, seeing the shape of her hips and thighs against the tight fabric of her fawn breeches as she posted. I'd imagined being under her, sprawled on my naked back with Rhea on top, posting on me, and after the release I'd become so shamed I bicycled home and took a bath during the middle of day.

"Yes, Mr. Commonwealth's Attorney," Leona said, "upholder of Virginia justice, defender of the poor, I watched you watch her a dozen times. Before I got out I did. Before I begged my father to get me out, which he did, and I love him for it. He saved me because I would've died in Howell County. All the years he sacrificed to send me money, and now you have him in that jail and come expecting help from me. I intend to sue you for it."

"All right, I'm leaving," I said, my face still burning with blood and memory. "I'll see your father's released soon as I reach Tobaccoton."

"I still intend to sue."

"That's your right, but I believe you care for responsibility. You didn't get where you are by not caring."

"You can't oil me, mister," she said and smiled with only one side of her mouth, a twisting up of lips. "Anything happens in Howell County they try to put it on a black man. He won't talk sense, you say? My daddy knows words are tricks. You speak the wrong one, you can't ever take it back. The law has you then, ties you up with your own tongue. Now I intend to change my clothes and go to my tennis lesson. You're leaving?"

I moved toward the door, which she had opened.

"When I was a little girl I used to pass your place and wonder what was going on inside," she said. "My daddy told us it was never a happy house, but I remember your mother who kept a garden. She wore a baseball cap and was usually among her flowers. One afternoon I was passing, she handed me a white peony. That's why I let you in here at all, because of that white peony."

"I never knew her," I said.

"Suppose my daddy didn't want to see something?" Leona asked. I was already out the door and into the corridor.

"Something about Mr. Farr?" I asked.

"My daddy wouldn't want to hurt anybody. He'd sit in jail a long time before doing that."

"Hurt who?" I asked.

"You've used up that white peony," she said and closed the door.

On the drive from Richmond to Tobaccoton, I wondered what Old Ben could've seen. Something to do with Vin. Perhaps Old Ben had caught him with a local woman, maybe lots of women, including my ex-wife.

I again thought of jealous husbands taking care of the score on the riverbank. Mode? We didn't know how Vin had died. Days were passing. Already Vin's death seemed to be fading. Only for Rhea did suffering remain.

My father sat beside me, silent for once, fuming not at me but at the VA doctors and the fact that Uncle Daniel was making a fool of the family by marching up and down with the blank sign tacked to the broom handle.

"Doctors gave you the runaround again, huh?" I asked him.

"He had to come back," my father said. "After all these years he has to bring us one final humiliation. As if he's not done enough to this family. Why does it happen to me? Daniel had the brains. He got the college education. He had the looks, the clothes, the money, the women, and he pissed it all away while I stayed here and grubbed my life out pulling tobacco. Lord, is there no justice in this damn universe?"

I left him off at home and drove to the office to do a few hours' work, but before I got inside the courthouse I heard my name called and turned to see Buster Bovin smiling and waving. He had finally removed his safari suit, changed it to a double-breasted Palm Beach. He wore a white shirt, a brown tie to match the suit, and a Panama hat with a brown band. He also carried a Bible that had a zip-up black leather cover.

"I'm so tickled with the cooperation your law officers have been giving The Ministerial Alliance," Buster said. "We've already achieved remarkable results with the patrols—five arrests, eight conversions, two beer licenses revoked by the Alcoholic Control Board. This county can become a model to the nation."

We stepped into the shade of the dying elm.

"Though I'm told nothing yet has been done about a prime source of pollution to the young minds of the county," Buster said. "I'm speaking of the library. Have you taken action?"

"It's on my list," I lied.

"Good to hear. I hope it's high on your list because the depravity flowing from that place is an abomination to the nostrils of the Lord. The Lord sniffs out sin like a dog winding birds, and He is on point there. The Ministerial Alliance would be most pleased if that action climbed quickly to the top of your list."

The shark did not rise all the way to the surface of the chinabutton blue eyes but circled just beneath that moist fleshy smile, a silent gliding shape.

"Do my best," I said.

"That's good, Billy, because we appreciate our friends. There are those who claim you haven't been zealous in the performance of your duties. But The Ministerial Alliance has defended you. We say Billy Payne means to do it when he can, that he's been awfully busy with the responsibilities of his office, yet will in his time boldly brandish the Lord's sword in the face of the heathen."

"You consider Miss Katie Cullen a heathen?" I asked.

"I think her sense of values has become confused, largely because of her age. With your lawyer skills you might point that out to her. Surely she's in need of a rest. I've checked into it, and she has social security coming. She would make more money from social security than what the county pays hers. She'd be able to sit on her porch and read all she wanted. She could sip lemonade, knit, or tend the lovely flowers in her garden."

"You're asking me to talk her into quitting?"

"The Ministerial Alliance wishes her or no one hardship. We believe this to be an opportunity for her to set her house in order and make peace with her Maker. We would encourage that."

Words were collecting around me, slick oily syllables rising like the tide, and I felt if I didn't move away quickly I'd soon drown in them, an unctuous flood stopping up my nose and mouth.

"I'll look into the situation," I said.

"That's the spirit, Billy. We know you're a good man except for your bondage to the bottle. We're pleased you been attending church and setting a fine example. You haven't, however, called any of us for help with your drinking problem."

"I'm doing better and cutting down," I lied.

"Good to hear, brother, but let me give you this little reminder. No man can do it alone. The Lord didn't mean for man to be able to. He is trying to teach us all that, to force us to reach out to Him and say, 'Help!'"

I finally pulled away from Buster, like tugging my feet out of swamp, and he stood smiling and watching me sidle off. I bumped into the door and stumbled on a step. I hurried to my office, where Florene looked up from her typing.

"You act like somebody stole your candy," she said.

I closed the door, collapsed into my chair, and stared down the street to Uncle Daniel still marching. People were watching him; yet he no longer drew crowds. The way it was going, in a few more days he'd be no more noticed than the shorted-out barber's pole or the torn awning over the flower shop.

I profaned Buster Bovin and dreamed of a job in Washington at the Bureau of Weights and Measures, where I'd weigh all measures and measure all weights. I lifted my eyes over the Planters & Merchants Bank to look toward Tobaccoton's oldest residential section. A lot of those houses were gone now, or stoved and lived in by blacks. Porches sagged, shutters dangled, and bricks had fallen onto roofs. There was more dirt than grass, and during spring the only blooms were splotches of dandelions that worked up not through the hard soil but from cracks in walks and gutters.

Yet one house was repaired, painted, and frilly as a gleaming white steamboat that had paddled up the Wye River from the James, turned left onto Main Street, and then right onto Gaston Avenue, where it had become moored for life. Around three sides ran a porch with fancy fluted columns, wood scrolling, curlicues. There were turrets and oval stained-glass windows, and four chimneys flared at the top.

The house was Cullen-built, the money not from tobacco or trade but cotton, a crop big in Southside Virginia until the 1930s. The family had risen on cotton and declined with it. Now the crop was hardly bothered about in the state, though here and yonder you'd come across isolated patches looking as out of place as snow in July.

The Cullens had been a large family, half a dozen brothers and sisters, but they had all left for good or died except Miss Katie. She was the only woman in Howell County history who'd ever gone to Vassar and been psychoanalyzed in Switzerland. She'd tell you as if those two events were her coat-of-arms or medals of valor.

When I was a boy, grown-ups sat in circles and lowered their voices to speak of Miss Katie. She never married, but there were whispers about an artist, an Italian of all things, who painted what in those days were called nudes. Some reportedly resembled Miss Katie, though even people who wanted to think the worst of her wouldn't believe she'd allow a dark Italian to cast his hot eyes on her alabaster flesh.

During World War II she was a WAC officer, a captain, and afterward she returned to Tobaccoton to reopen the old Cullen house, hired workmen to climb over it with hammers, paint, and new slate. We boys gathered in mimosa shade to watch all the activity, the biggest thing in Tobaccoton since the construction of the cinderblock fire station.

Miss Katie was an imperial woman who wore dresses no longer than any other county female, yet in my mind's movie she always seemed to have on gowns and be standing in a receiving line. Her chestnut hair hadn't lost its luster, and she gathered it high on her head. She didn't appear to walk behind the counter at the library but to sail, as if she resided on a hull and was pushed by a privately directed wind.

She had returned to Tobaccoton because of the town's need for a library. She met with the Board of Supervisors and made them a deal: she would contract to have shelves built in her house if they budgeted money for books and paid a small monthly charge for maintaining the premises. She also asked that taxes be remitted on the house.

It was a county bargain. She worked alone six days a week from 9:00 A.M. to 5:00 P.M. She assembled historical displays such as sad gentle pictures of Robert E. Lee on his way to defeat at Appomattox or letters that told of surveyor George Washington passing through Tobaccoton and staying at a local tavern named The Anvil. The president complained of both the food and the fleas. Nobody ever dared ask Miss Katie about the dark Italian painter.

Not telling Florene where I was going, I walked from the courthouse and avoided the corner where Uncle Daniel paraded. I hiked up the slight incline which was Gaston Avenue. Black children played kick-the-can in the street and spun a red Frisbee over a clothesline. A truck engine hung from chains wrapped around the limb of a sassafras tree. Then the whiteness of Miss Katie's steamboat, a house that indeed seemed in motion.

She needed no bell over the doorway to tell her somebody had entered since the frosted, swan-etched glass always rattled. Inside, the air was still and cool. She was usually among the stacks or in her crammed office behind the counter. She lived upstairs and never entertained.

She was tall, spare, and straight. Her chestnut hair, full and billowy, seemed a crown. When she spoke, you expected her voice to be loftily disapproving, but it was warm and womanly.

"Why, Billy, I'd come to believe you'd given up reading books," she said as I stood before the counter. She walked from her office, not wearing a gown at all, but a pale cotton dress simple and neat. Her flat brown shoes had rubber heels and soles.

"Winter's my reading time, Miss Katie."

"There are summer and winter books, just as food has its seasons. One doesn't expect fresh local lettuce in February or Thomas Mann during a Bermuda high."

She had to be seventy, but her skin was fair, the few wrinkles adding lines of character. She nibbled a smile when she spoke, a sort of mischievous working of her lips as if she shared some amusement with whomever she talked to.

Nobody knew how much money she had. She didn't bank locally but drew her checks on a Richmond trust company. Perhaps she was rich, though she was quick to cash the small stipend paid monthly by the county. She owned no automobile and walked to stores.

"You used to read them all," she said. "I watched you on those afternoons it was raining. You liked the chair by the window, and I'd peek to see you living the words. You kicked, your hands jabbed, and you squirmed. I thought you might be our writer, especially when you won the essay contests. I believed Howell County might at last have an author."

The two contests I won had been sponsored by the DAR, the first paper titled "John Randolph, Eccentric Virginia Gentleman" and the second "The Agricultural Genius of Thomas Jefferson." The prize in both cases had been $25 and a shake of my hand by Senator Harry Flood Byrd the elder.

"One day we'll have our writer out of this poor soil," Miss

Katie said. "Perhaps he'll creep from under a tobacco plant, and we may revile him because he shows us too clearly what we are. I hope I live long enough to witness such an event."

"That's a nice thought, Miss Katie, and I hope you do too."

"May I bring you something? I just finished cataloguing two novels and was about to put them on display."

"You suppose we might have a private word?"

She unlatched a gate through the counter. She led me into her office, a place that must have once been the dining room, for there were plate railings, a brass chandelier, and a china cabinet stuffed with books and periodicals. A bay window looked down over decay of the town's east side to the river, the water flat and motionless under the strike of summer sun.

At the center of the room her desk was stacked with catalogues, books, paste pots, scissors, an electric gun for burning Dewey decimals. From white plaster walls she'd recently hung oil paintings, not family portraits like at Rhea's but flamboyant city scenes of what I supposed to be New York, garish views of low life where in the bloody glaze of neon drunk or dead men sprawled on sidewalks under elevated tracks, birdlike hookers smoked beneath the halo of a corner streetlight, and a five-piece Salvation Army band played in a shaft of moonbeams wedged between buildings that appeared more like tombstones than inhabitable space.

"You're developing a real gallery back here," I said, noting all the canvases carried the same signature—A. Bonelli.

"Fragments from another time," she said. "Though I'm told Bonellis are coming into their own, not his street scenes done in an earlier period but his nudes."

She looked right at me as she said that, and I had a sensation she knew exactly what was in my mind about herself and the Italian painter. I coughed, cleared my throat, and reached for my handkerchief.

"You all right, Billy?" she asked, her mouth tight with amusement.

"I smoke too much."

"And you don't want a book or is it you're nervous about asking for one where the public might overhear?"

"Miss Katie, I have to tell you I'm embarrassed. I didn't want to come here at all."

"Why, I thought you loved the library."

"I do, and if I had any money to give away, I'd bring it here to you. I hope you understand at times I'm made to act in ways I dislike because my office, its duties, requires it."

"Buster Bovin and his Ministerial Alliance," she said.

"Yes."

"I knew it was coming. They had a delegation at the last meeting of the Board of Supervisors."

"I'd rather take a beating than be here."

"I realize that, Billy. Just what is it you, or they, would have me do?"

"Certain books they object to, the language, the sex. I expect they have a list."

"Do you have names of any books on that list?"

"Buster was passing this around," I said and drew the folded mimeographed quote from my pocket. She took it with slim fingers, opened it, and read. I felt hot, suffocated. I was damn embarrassed.

With no change of expression she laid the paper on her desk and left the office. I again inspected Signore Bonelli's art. Canvases which hadn't been framed leaned face inward to the wall. I peeked at a scene of roused blacks fighting inside a blue honky-tonk cafe. All the blacks wore cowboy clothes, and women were dressed like dance-hall girls, and knives and razors were carried in holsters like six-guns. I heard Miss Katie returning and quickly stepped away from the picture to her desk.

She held a book, a novel entitled *Light the Sun* by an author named Henry Williams, which she handed to me.

"I want you to read it," she said. "He's a young writer with the talent of a Crane."

"Miss Katie, you know I'm on your side in this thing, but I have to look at the situation from The Ministerial Alliance's point of view. They don't see whole books, just the parts considered dirty."

"The group and oral sex in this novel are absurdly disgusting," she said.

"You mean you think so too?"

"Of course I think so. It's the point of the passage. You're supposed to be satirically repelled. The scene is artificial, hyperbolical, and there's no way it could be rendered without exaggeration of coarseness, perversion, depravity."

I stood holding the book, turning pages without actually seeing words, wishing I'd never come.

"I don't need to read it, Miss Katie. If you speak for it, the book has to be good."

"Yoo hoo!" a voice from the stacks called. It was Inez Bopart, wife of Howell County's only dentist. "Katie, do you have the new Billy Graham, the one on angels?"

Miss Katie glanced at me with a face firmed by long suffering and left the office. Again I crossed to the pictures turned inward along the wall. I looked at the knife fight among blacks staged as a shootout in the Old West. It was high noon in a blue cafe.

There were more street scenes, the elevated crouched above like a hungry spider. A river flowed between skyscrapers whose lighted windows reflecting in black water resembled eyes peering from depths. A dead boy lay in a moon puddle.

The last picture was at the room's far corner. When I drew it from the wall, I glimpsed a seascape, swelling combers rolling in, only the water wasn't green or blue but red, the foam and scud yellow and jagged; yet the shock was not those but the body being washed in, a long, thin woman white like marble with great breasts and seaweed hair, also red. She lay high on her back, her arms flung out, smiling and holding on one palm a blue crab and in the other a pair of dancing sea horses. It was a young Miss Katie.

I heard her coming, set the painting in place, and stood by her desk. My face was on fire. As she entered in her sailing manner, I glanced at her breasts, thinking A. Bonelli must surely have exaggerated those.

"So what will you have me do?" she asked and dangled her fingertips against the desk top. "Billy, is something wrong?"

"Just the heat. You'd think I'd be used to it after all these years."

She stared at me, and then her eyes moved to the pictures along the wall. Those eyes were sea green and slowly came back to me. She wasn't disturbed. As she folded her hands, her smile nibbled back into place.

"Yes you would," she said.

"I'll take the novel," I said, raising it as if she didn't realize I held it. "I wonder if in the meantime you could keep things here at a minimum till I figure out the best way to proceed."

"You mean remove volumes from circulation?"

"At least don't display certain ones too prominently. I'll try to come up with something to satisfy The Ministerial Alliance and at the same time allow you to circulate your books."

"Billy, the First Amendment was still part of the Constitution when last I read it."

"But we don't want a court battle royal and all that publicity. The Board of Supervisors wouldn't like it, and the first thing they'd do is cut your appropriation. Best to be low profile and reasonable."

Her hands pulled up along her stomach and were clenched. I thought of her white marble body on a red sea.

"Reasonable, how I hate that word!" she said. "Long ago I gave up being reasonable. It can wash away your life like a piece of soap. I understand you've been put in a difficult position. I will, therefore, promise not to wave flags or climb barricades. I will also not thrust books on anyone, nor will I withhold them. I shall be circumspect but not cowardly."

"Thanks, Miss Katie, and after I read this novel maybe I can show it to one or two of the supervisors and explain what the author was getting at."

"You have to sign for it," she said.

I nodded and slid the circulation card from the back of the book. I glanced at the names: local ladies, English teachers from the high school, Buster Bovin, but it was an unexpected signature which jolted me—Vincent F. Farr.

"I didn't know Vin came to the library," I said.

"He did often and read a great many books."

"I'm surprised. Can you tell me what kind of books he liked?"

"I can but won't."

"Why, Miss Katie?"

"To know a person's reading preferences is to see inside him. You would be invading the personality, and I would be abetting it."

"Wish you'd help this once."

"No."

"Miss Katie, I'm an officer of the court investigating Vin Farr's death. I need your help and am asking for it as a friend. I hope you won't force me to try to force you."

Her hands dropped to the desk, and her short unpainted nails tapped the wood surface. She was a strong woman, her fairness stretched over steel, not bone. All the fallow years she'd endured in Tobaccoton; yet I thought of her standing in the bow of a ship.

"You haven't exactly brought happiness to my day," she said. "I'll do it under protest, and if you misuse what I tell you I'll hound you. I'll write letters to editors, nail up posters, and contribute every dollar I can raise to unseat you from office."

I stood holding the book and wishing I'd known her when she posed for A. Boñelli.

"Vincent usually came early in the week and went right to the rack where I keep the display of new novels. He would leaf through them, glance at the dust jackets, and sometimes read the ending, a practice I detest. He signed out three or four books at a time."

Why would he be reading so much when he had a woman like Rhea at home? I asked myself.

"Vin was intelligent, a fast reader. They take *The New York Times* at Riverview, and he knew what he wanted."

"What sort of books?"

"War novels were his first choice, which war not making any difference. His love was planes. All books with aircraft he seized."

"What else?"

She nibbled her lips, and her nails scratched the desk. She didn't like the question.

"He preferred novels set in a cosmopolitan milieu, lots of action, and what some might describe as sexually exciting and explicit."

"Thank you," I said.

She walked me from the office to the door. Her hands were again folded and pulled against her waist. I would've liked another look at the painting of her on the red sea.

"Did I ever tell you about Joyce?" she asked. "I knew him when I left Vassar for Geneva."

"No, Miss Katie, you didn't."

"He pinched me in Geneva. Don't you think that an odd place to pinch one?"

She smiled teasingly as she closed the door which held the oval of rattling frosted glass etched with preening swans.

Plum appeared as I sat in darkness of the arbor. She set her feet down so softly I didn't hear her behind me. Maybe she believed it a crime to damage grass. She slid her fingers along my temples and over my eyes. I was so startled I spilled my drink.

"Knew where to look for you this time," she said and stepped around the chair to stand in front of me. She wore jeans, a tanktop, and a bandanna about her hair. Her feet were shoeless. She handed me a small heavy package wrapped in aluminum foil. "My nutbread."

"Oh, the hope we had for him!" my father shouted from his bedroom window. He didn't know Plum was here. "We were happy to sacrifice, to wear last year's clothes and never own a new car or decent piece of farm machinery. We never got to go to Richmond and stay at the Jefferson Hotel. We lived on hog and hominy, but it was all right because he was out there becoming a legend. He was going to put the Paynes on the map!"

"Kind of you to bring it," I said to Plum.

"Kind of you and the sheriff to be letting Cloud and Hawthorn out."

"Fastest growing corporation in Virginia!" my father shouted. "A congressman went to bat for him, and he had to throw it all down a rathole!"

"He talking about you?" Plum asked.

"Me and an uncle."

She listened to him rave, smiled, and sat at my feet with the same graceful retraction of legs.

"I knew you'd let them out," she said. "You're no chitlin-eating redneck lawman who chews up so-called hippies for breakfast."

"We didn't have enough to hold them."

"You walk around like a man trying to hide under a lawyer's dark cloak, but I happen to know that's not what you really are. You just need to be released. In fact I'd be helping you get released right this minute except I have this fellow I've sort of developed a thing on."

She fingered my ankle, rubbing upward to the calf. It was both exciting and calming at the same time. Yet I would've braved the ants for her.

"You screwed it up good!" my father shouted from the window.

"He's pretty excited," she said.

"Actually not so much for him."

"What I'm thinking is driving to Arizona. Fellow out there believes I'm the sun and the moon. Want to come along?"

"Appreciate the invitation, but I guess not."

"I didn't want to leave without telling you."

"Somebody else around here's nice," I said. "Hawthorn and Cloud going?"

"You don't have to worry about them running. They plan to stay at least till cold weather. My fellow out in Arizona's got an adobe hut and a garden. He irrigates the garden from a mountain stream and grows lettuce large as pumpkins. I like the picture, big heads of iceberg lettuce growing in the desert, long green rows clean and moist under the sun."

"I like it too. Almost as good as boats."

"You could carry me home," she said, still rubbing my calf. "The van's in the shop."

I walked her to my car, and we skirted Tobaccoton because I didn't want anyone in town to see me with her. She ducked whenever another vehicle passed or approached. When she lit up, it was a second before I realized the smell was marijuana.

"Not in here with me!" I said. "Thought you didn't believe in that stuff."

"Slight modification of philosophy."

"Put it out!"

"Oh, quiet down, it's not that serious, and besides I've something to tell you about Mr. Vincent F. Farr. I'm not supposed to. Our bunch is essentially law-abiding, yet as a rule we don't consort with the man. We don't as a rule even have rules, but we know you need help to keep your job."

As she turned to me, she drew her legs up on the seat between us. Before speaking, she inhaled, finished her roach, and dunked it in my ashtray, which I would be sure to empty.

"He used special sugar," she said. "Other than his wife, I mean."

I thought she meant ex-wife Jeannie. Plum could've found out. I gripped the wheel, straightened a swerve, and felt white lines of the road were speeding into me like arrows out of the night.

"Details," I said.

"He was seen, Mr. Farr was, by one of us who shall remain nameless, seen down in Richmond town in the company of a slinky black lady. Time: shortly before his death."

When I pulled to the shoulder, weeds whipped the underside of my car. I cut the engine and switched out the headlights. Leona

Poindexter, I thought. Old Ben's daughter. That's why Ben had
run. Vin and the chic buyer for Gallitoes could've known each other
for years. But wait a minute. Leona could pass for white.

"You sure she was black, not just tan?" I asked.

"Definitely not tan, but dark ginger and fancy."

"Fancy how?"

"Exact description by observer at a motel, who stopped to buy
ice: hair spiked, black lashes long enough to cause wind, mouth
purple, earrings like gold coins, heels so high you could run hounds
under them, a short red dress shiny enough to see your face in."

I remembered Vin at the center of men standing on the corner.
Most of his jokes had an ethnic slant reflecting upon the ignorance
and concupiscence of blacks. He'd been able to mimic the patois
of the billet woods, the rapid punchy cadences of speech, a private
language local white people puzzled over as if they'd stepped into
a foreign country.

"Mistaken identity," I said.

"We know what Mr. Big looked like. He cruised timber on
property adjoining ours. Observer saw him park near the ice machine of the motel—"

"Name of motel."

"The Jaybird. He parked close to the ice machine and didn't
need to go to the office because he already had a room key. He
helped that slinky black lady out, and she showed leg up to her
you-know-what."

"You mean she was—"

"—a friend of man for money."

"I can't believe this," I said, thinking of Rhea.

"You don't have to. You don't have to do anything at all. We
thought it might help. We voted to tell you."

I drove her to the farm, where kerosene lamps burned, their
reflectors beaming an unnatural whiteness around the house. She
walked to my side of the car, leaned in the window, and kissed me.

"Grown kind of fond of you," she said. "Well, beware of ants."

Driving home, I felt the nutbread still warm in aluminum foil
at my side.

During the night I stood at my bedroom window and waited
for a breeze to stir air which pressed around me like hot wool. I
felt that air would settle and so harden I'd be unable to breathe.

My father had gone to bed without leaving his TV on. I heard him snoring. I also heard raucous night insects and a hound baying with a tragic wavering cry.

I considered Vin Farr, his choice of books, and the black gal. Definitely not Leona, but what did Old Ben see to make him run? I again tried to figure why anyone with a rich, cultured, sexy wife like Rhea would want anything more. Did Rhea know? I wouldn't tell Pickney, at least not till I had information more definite than what Plum had brought me. As long as I could I'd protect Rhea.

I smoked at the window. Southside Virginia, a simmering kettle with lid, was cooking me. My father stopped snoring. "Bastards!" he shouted. Moths collected on the screen a few inches from my face. One fluttered downward, a corkscrew dive, and I hoped he pulled up before he struck the ground.

All night I wrestled sleep. I pictured Rhea in a white bathing suit, though I'd never seen her in any bathing suit or even shorts. I wondered what Old Ben had run from. I thought of lewd books and a slinky black lady with spiked hair and lots of leg. How long had Vin been unfaithful? I puzzled over that rudimentary tattoo, and a body otherwise unmarked except for excoriations on the dermis of a toe and finger, both superficial. Then Rhea appeared again, this time wearing a black bathing suit.

I drove to the office without eating breakfast. Though tired and rumpled, I wanted to talk to her. I personally needed it. I had no wish to go to Riverview as Commonwealth's Attorney but simply as Billy Payne.

I smoked, drank coffee Florene brought, and wondered whether Rhea a second time would eat a meal with me, something more formal than a club sandwich at a Bannister cafe. I thought of a dinner in Richmond.

It was early afternoon before I worked up courage to call. I talked fast so I wouldn't falter or second-guess myself.

"I been feeling the need to get away a few hours and thought maybe you did too. Dinner, a play, something to beat the heat."

From her a moment of silence. I imagined her holding the phone and wondering what in the world she would do with Billy Payne, how she would handle and not hurt him.

"You haven't given me a lot of notice," she said. Then before

I could apologize, "Won't we have to leave early to make the curtain?"

I was certain I heard pleasure, even enthusiasm, in her voice, the first I'd detected since Vin died, maybe the first she'd allowed herself. I felt privileged and even exalted. I realized I'd stood from my chair as if she'd entered my office.

"Five at the latest," I said.

"Billy, I can't wait."

When we hung up, I did a little soft-shoe routine around my desk till I remembered I had no tickets. I went out for Florene's folded *Times Dispatch,* turned to the Leisure section, and began picking plays and telephoning. The first three—*Blithe Spirit, I Love My Wife,* and *Good News*—were booked up. The fourth theater, named the Coffee House, offered a show called *Rainy Day on Cornelia Street.* I knew nothing about it, but rain sounded attractive in the fiercely hot dry weather. The reservation girl explained the play was a musical drama.

"We've had very favorable responses," she said. "We're holding it over an extra thirty days. I do have a cancellation for two if you'd like."

I took the cancellation and sat thinking that though in my mind I'd been intimate with Rhea for years, I'd never gone on an actual honest-to-God date at her side. I would mention nothing about police business or Vin. I laughed. She was coming along because I was Billy Payne and she liked me.

I frowned. Once a suitable time passed and the Vin investigation ended, eligible males would swarm around her. I thought of those suave Richmond slickers with their tweeds, Mercedeses, and polo mallets arriving to court her. I pictured them pouring wine aboard yachts, dancing, and kissing her. I was so disturbed I shot up out of my chair and protested.

Florene stuck her head in. "You called?"

"Bumped my shin."

She withdrew unreassured, and again I sat, faced my desk, and tried to work, but I worried about my clothes. I had bought none since Jeannie left. She had always gone with me and made the final judgment in stores as I stood before the triptych mirrors.

"I want you to appear assured, prosperous, and a bit English," Jeannie had said.

Well, now I looked baffled, penurious, and a lot Howell County. It was too late to buy a suit off the rack and have it altered, but I could still get a haircut.

Uncle Daniel was carrying his sign past Waldo's shop as I entered. I spoke, and Uncle Daniel dipped the sign, though I wasn't certain he recognized me. Aunt Lettie had been feeding him. I wondered where he slept. He'd exchanged his dirty tennis shoes for battered cowboy boots.

Waldo's barber chair was empty. There were only two chairs in the shop, the second used on Saturdays when he hired a cousin to come in and help. Waldo was a Hamlin, a big family in the lower end of the county, and the men generally pulpwood cutters. Waldo himself claimed to be seventy-four, but standing most of his life had kept him healthy despite a tremor in his scissoring fingers and the need to lean close to see through his bifocals.

"You ahead of schedule," Waldo said and set my dark glasses on the shelf among his tonic bottles. He tucked a paper collar tight around my throat before settling the striped cloth over me. He smelled of plug tobacco and the sweet tonics.

"Grab a cut whenever I can," I said.

"See your Uncle Daniel out there. How he walks in them boots I'll never figure. Must have pointed feet. Reckon he'll ever paint anything on that sign? I remember him and the Packard, his tailored suits, and how he'd give the chaps a dime to run errands. Dime meant something then, all brand new and shiny. Things change, huh?"

I agreed things change and watched Uncle Daniel pass under shade cast by the faded green awning. A black woman drew her little girl in, wary of allowing the child too close to him. Aunt Lettie brought him an ice cream cone, which he thanked her for and licked as he carried the sign one-handed.

"We all grass, we all get cut down, that's what the Good Book tells," Waldo said. "Look at Vin Farr. Healthiest man ever walked the streets of Tobaccoton and yet mowed down. Question is, ain't it, how he was mowed?"

"Can't talk with you while the case is still under investigation."

"You don't have to talk. The courthouse has cracks in it. Anybody says anything, it comes on down the street like water from a broken jar. But Vin was sure God mowed. Me, I'm ready when the blade comes. Made my peace with the Lord. Glad to hear you been going to church."

I started to ask for a shave, but that would alert Waldo. I'd never had him razor me. He would suspect a special occasion. I didn't need it talked around that I was going out with Rhea. I imagined the grins that would greet me.

I drove home instead of returning to the office. Let Florene take the helm. My father had come down from his room and sat on a wicker chair in shade of the front porch, his cane held between his legs. He was in his undershirt and wore a straw hat. When I spoke, he said nothing.

I washed my hair, had a bath, and shaved not once but twice. I meant to slice every prickle of beard off my face before I went after Rhea. I took a second bath. Luckily a clean seersucker suit hung in my wardrobe, an old one washed by Aunt Lettie weeks ago, though the cloth had been in her hands so many times it possessed the fragile feel of silk. Silk, that's what Rhea was.

I kept brushing my hair until my scalp ached and slapped on some Lilac Vegetal that had been sitting in the medicine cabinet so long the top had crusted.

At twenty minutes to five I looked in the mirror over my bureau for at least the tenth time. I was like newly unwrapped soap I appeared so clean. I also thought I resembled a gawky country jake out on his first date with the prom queen. I wished for face powder to take the sheen off myself and rooted around in the wardrobe till I came up with talc meant for feet. Using fingertips, I dabbed my cheeks.

I set on my Panama hat, smiled at myself in the glass, and breathed as if I were about to dive off the high board.

"Stink like a French whore on Bastille Day," my father said as I passed.

"Thanks very much and good evening," I said and went down the front steps to my car. His cane tapped angrily against the porch.

"Lover boy!" he called. "Maybe it's my fault I never told you what to do with it. I always supposed anybody with sense enough to know water runs downhill could figure it out."

I drove away seeing him in my dust, up on the porch waving his cane, his mouth moving, though I could no longer hear. He had caused me to start sweating. My car wasn't air-conditioned. I hoped

Rhea wouldn't mind. I slowed and stretched my neck to look at myself in the mirror.

At exactly five o'clock I turned in between the white brick gateposts at Riverview. Howell County was thirsting, but the grass here was as green as jungle. No pall of dust lay on the white gravel or leaves of oaks and maples. Maybe Blackjack's agitated ghost kept dust from settling.

I believed Rhea would be the sort of woman who never kept a man waiting, yet I was wrong. Melissa opened the door and led me to the parlor dominated by the painting of Rhea's mother in her lavender gown. I was to fix myself a drink if I wanted. On top an antique walnut cellaret was a silver tray loaded with an icebucket and cut-glass decanters, each identified by a sterling badge hung from its neck. Everything had been provided, even rye.

I wanted a drink all right but intended to prove to Rhea I didn't live in a bottle. I turned away from the liquor, stood flapping my hands behind me, and crossed to the white satin prie-dieu. On it was not Holy Writ but the book *The Sculptor's Hand*. I gazed upward at Rhea's mother. She was smiling and beneficent.

I thought about the photographs on the wall of Vin's basement office. I had never felt exactly right about them. I assumed it was the fact I couldn't marry Vin the flinty businessman to Vin the artist. Using a magnifying glass to search for a trace of the tattoo, I would've liked another look at the picture of him in his low-cut bathing trunks. I shook my head. None of that tonight.

Rhea came down the front steps and turned into the parlor. She held out a hand. "Billy, how nice." I thought of kissing her hand as a European might. "Melissa, did you offer him a drink?"

Uniformed Melissa opened the door for us, and I tripped over the sill. Melissa giggled while Rhea caught my arm to steady me. I hurried to my car to open that door. God I was ashamed of my dusty Chevy. At least I could have hosed it down. I thought of the immaculate vehicles in Rhea's garage.

Yet she didn't grimace or flick an eyelash as she sat and smoothed her dress over her legs. She would never intentionally make a person feel bad. She appeared so beautifully fresh and healthy I had difficulty breathing in her presence, like the time in the Richmond courtroom that ended my career as the great attorney. I imagined myself staggering, clawing at my throat, and turning blue.

"Your dress, lovely," I managed to say, speaking like a man

who had a dead horse lying across his chest.

The dress was dove gray chiffon and simple, just right for a woman in transition from mourning to life—modest, unadorned, classic. She wore hose and gray heels that matched the dress. Other than her engagement ring and wedding band, a silver bracelet and silver earrings shaped like miniature daisies were her only jewelry. Then I spotted the fine gold chain low on her neck. The tiny gold cross had to be inside her dress, perhaps lying between her breasts.

That was the thing about Rhea, she gave elegance to simplicity. I loved her. I didn't have to run it through my mind to test it. For me she was an absolute.

"Hurt your finger?" she asked, leaning to look at a Band-Aid I wore where I'd nicked myself slicing the seal from a vodka bottle the previous night.

"Actually I skinned it repairing the air intake of my chain saw," I said, a miserable lie and attempt to convince her how manly I was.

"You can fix chain saws?" she asked.

"Well sure, every Howell County boy has to have one, a rite of manhood and all that."

"Two stroke?" she asked.

"What?"

"Your saw has a two-cycle engine?"

"Right," I said, though I owned no saw and hadn't the slightest notion how many strokes any engine had. I knew I'd better get off the subject quick. Out at Riverview they learned all about machinery. Vin and she had repaired cars. "You notice how many ants are around this year? Must be the dryness."

I babbled on about ants while she sat quietly, her broad face set in polite receptiveness, ready to be kind. She'd had her hair cut recently, not greatly shortened but the ends clipped so it was more controlled.

I became afraid to stop talking, fearful not to carry the conversation and amuse her. She might hold up a hand, tell me this was a mistake, and ask me to carry her home. No ants, I thought, would crawl on her, no insect violate that aristocratic skin. She would be hallowed ground even to bugs.

"Where'd you learn all this?" she asked finally, her first words in miles interrupting my bewildering discourse on ants. I'd been dredging up stuff on them I didn't know I knew.

"Sorry. Got a little carried away on the subject," I said.

"Billy, all this talking and you haven't mentioned Vin."

"I hoped we could forget a while and relax."

"I'm for it, but at least tell me what's going on. Then we'll drop the subject and enjoy ourselves."

"Nothing new, Rhea. Nothing at all."

"The state police?"

"Captain Blake hasn't been ringing my bell lately. They might be letting go."

"Dropping the investigation?"

"Not officially, that is, nobody will order them off, but other cases will draw them, and Vin's file might come to rest as 'pending.'" I resisted reaching for a cigarette. "Old Ben making any sense yet?"

"He's gone back to Richmond and his niece Leona. I notified the sheriff."

"You mean his daughter Leona."

"She's not his natural daughter. Ben's sister is her mother." Rhea hesitated. "Her father was a trashy white man who worked at Riverview. My grandfather ran him off the place. Ben took the baby in."

I thought of the old woman at Leona Poindexter's high-tech apartment. Her mother and Old Ben's sister. Anyway, Leona's whiteness had been explained.

"There are moments I expect Vin to walk in the house as if he's been away on a business trip," Rhea said. "When I shop, I sometimes forget and buy for the special dishes he liked."

She stared ahead, her face unchanged, her voice not about to break. She was past breaking now, speaking as if remembering events years ago, happenings of childhood.

"I wish I could do more," I said and very nearly reached to her.

"I know you do, Billy. You're a kind man, and there's no one I'd rather be with."

For an instant I felt like a boy who'd received his first kiss from his true love. But wait a second. A kind man, is that what I wanted to be in her eyes? Maybe kind meant safe and sexless.

The highway led bright and straight through lowland farm country, where sun-sapped cattle roamed dry pastures nibbling at short grass. Trucks coming toward us raised dust and trailed diesel smoke, the sun on their windshields glinting like dragonflies.

As we passed Powhatan Courthouse, she glanced right to a secondary road. I peeked at her legs.

"I was here just yesterday to visit Vin's mother," she said.

I hadn't heard of Vin's mother in so long I'd forgotten she was alive.

"A private nursing home," Rhea explained. "She's healthy in some ways, though she's seventy now and her mind wanders. She remembered her birthday all right. She wanted her cake." Rhea paused. "She doesn't know about Vin."

"You won't have to tell her eventually?"

"I don't think so. Her sense of time is confused. Ten years ago is like yesterday."

On down the highway we glimpsed Richmond's industrial haze and white towers catching the rosy afternoon sunlight. I drove over the James and turned off a ramp onto a brick street among warehouses. The theater itself had been a warehouse at the edge of a canal where river water once spilled through cuts to allow barges to move around chalky rocks.

The place appeared grubby, but the parking lot held respectable cars, and over a doorway a bright banner announced the play. The area had scents compounded of grit, alluvial soil, and curing tobacco.

The owners of the theater hadn't done much decorating inside the warehouse, just cleaned, put in chairs and tables, and taped playbills to walls. The waiters and waitresses were also the actors. They wore running shoes, Levi's, and orange T-shirts. Our waiter, a young black man who asked us to call him Jerry, turned out to be a dancer. He became less cheerful when I told him we wanted neither drinks nor wine.

"He was hoping for big spenders," I said as Jerry left us for another table. "I should have checked out this place before bringing you."

"Billy, it'll be fine. Believe me, I'm happy."

We went for our food cafeteria style—ham, chicken, crab cakes. Jerry brought us bread and iced tea. I was relieved the food was passable and Rhea hungry. She didn't fool around with a meal either, pretending she was a delicate little bird who lived on crumbs. Single candles sticking from empty wine bottles on every table created a low roof of gentle light in the soaring emptiness of the warehouse.

Jerry served us peach cobbler for dessert, and then a girl walked through the dining area striking a gong which reminded me of the one Uncle Daniel had carried home from China. We left our table to walk to another section of the warehouse. Unpadded benches were raised in tiers around a stage on which were a few chairs and a black upright piano.

"Are you familiar with the play?" Rhea asked.

"The reviews have been good," I said as if a devotee of theater. I was conscious we were overdressed among the young, informal audience. Not that it bothered Rhea. Foremost she wore her composure.

People sidestepped between the benches. Rhea and I squinted to read the mimeographed single sheet of paper that was the playbill. *Rainy Day on Cornelia Street* had been written by a drama student at Virginia Commonwealth University who hoped next to carry the production to Washington's Arena Theater. I wanted a cigarette.

I was very much aware of Rhea beside me, her arm near mine, her knees toward me, her perfume slight yet definitely feminine. Members of the arty young audience watched her too. Eyes of those looking over the house stopped on her.

The benches weren't anywhere near filled. Cancellations hell, I thought. The actors, black and white, walked down among the audience to the stage—three young men, three young women, and a piano player, also a girl. Like rag dolls, they sat in chairs, knees together, toes turned inward, heads hanging, and faces idiotic. People laughed, and Rhea seemed pleased.

The pianist came to life and began to play the upright. The others sprang from their chairs into dance, a kind of boogieing shag, suggestive, each male shuffling forward and bumping his pelvis against the girls, who bumped back. The dancers' arms were thrown behind them, their faces lifted as the piano banged away.

Abruptly the music stopped, and the actors plopped into chairs and resumed the rag-doll posture. Sounds of rain and thunder. Lightning flashes. A girl and boy rise. They mime the scene, the girl ironing, the boy painting a canvas. He struggles to do the picture, becomes angry, throws his brush to the floor, and stomps about. The girl turns from her ironing. She pounds on an imaginary wall and shouts, "Knock it off!" "Fuck you!" the boy shouts back.

More rag dolls jump into life. The plot involves Greenwich

Village artists, each of whom does his dance and tells his story: a poetess, the painter, an actress, a singer, a trumpet player, and a sculptor, the latter striking with an imaginary hammer and welding with an imaginary torch.

Romances formed, everybody coupled, the actress with the painter, the poetess with the sculptor, the singer with the trumpet player. The lights went out, and a girl's voice spoke:

"Get your hand off that!"

"Sorry, lady, I thought I was petting your cat," a male voice answered.

Uproarious laughter in the dark. A youth down the bench from me could hardly draw his breath and kept saying, "God yes!" The girl beside him gripped her fingers and called out, "Too much!" When the lights came on, the female actors had on the men's clothes and vice versa. They formed a high-kicking chorus line.

Lights out again and then on. Clothing had been straightened out. Everybody was a rag doll except the poetess and sculptor. She was a fragile white girl with long pale hair to her hips, and he was black, towering, and bearded. He tore away his shirt and lifted her off her feet to kiss her. The fragile girl pulled her lips free and bobbed her brows at the audience in the style of Groucho Marx, causing riotous laughter. She then kissed the sculptor so enthusiastically her cheeks drew in. His tongue wiggled in her mouth.

Calmly Rhea leaned to me, touched my wrist, and whispered, "Billy, do you mind?"

We stood and sidestepped among the howls of these young southern cognoscenti proving they could be just as liberal as anyone in New York, Chicago, or San Francisco. As we pushed out under the red Exit sign, we heard the poetess exclaiming, "O blackbird, blackbird, find your nest in me!"

Rhea and I walked through the dining room, where people cleaned tables and swept. A young blonde, wearing a chef's hat and apron but barefooted, laughed, her expression amused and patronizing.

"Too rough for the old folks, huh?" she asked.

"I hope you live to be a hundred and fifty," I said as I opened the door for Rhea and me to escape.

We stepped into the sultry abrasive night. Gulls along the river were excited and screeching. To the south a siren wailed. A gap of sky between darkened sooty buildings was covered by haze. I kept apologizing to Rhea.

"Billy, it's not your fault, you couldn't have known," she said. But she was upset, and I wondered how much of her reaction was due to the play's obscenity and how much might be racial, harkening back to Old Ben, his adopted daughter Leona, and the trashy white Rhea's grandfather had run off from Riverview.

I drove west along Hull Street, where my tires bumped brick pavement and blacks paraded in mottled garish light from bargain stores, hair emporiums, and food markets. The dirty window of a bankrupt discount house displayed an unclothed, headless mannequin.

"I am not a prude," Rhea said.

I agreed she wasn't, but I also wondered about Vin and the slinky Negress Plum had reported. Maybe Rhea thought of Vin kissing a black woman. No, I couldn't accept that because Rhea wouldn't accept that.

"But if having standards is prudish, then I am," she said. "Billy, as a nation we're going to need so much forgiveness."

We were leaving Richmond, and my headlights pushed darkness before us. I glanced at her. In the blue glow from the dash she wasn't just stringing together words but deeply serious. She had raised a hand to finger the tiny gold cross.

"God's mercy will indeed have to be infinite," she said.

Howell County had hold of us. Instead of being relaxed and happy on a summer night, she was conjuring up images of the Last Judgment and sinners hurled flaming into the pit. None of us natives escaped the disease, not even the rich and aristocratic. Yet I was thinking her theology and the shape of her legs didn't go together.

"I'm sorry I'm talking so much," she said, crossing those legs and adjusting the hem of her skirt. "Vin used to become bored with me on the subject."

"I'm not bored," I said and thought Vin also used to read sexy books checked out from the library.

"It's such an important question. My mother often tried to conceive of infinity. She would take me by the hand, and we'd walk out into the night to look at the sky. We attempted to push our vision past the stars. As a child I thought if I tried hard enough, I'd be able to see the edge of Heaven."

I wanted to stop the car, lift her skirt, and kiss her thighs.

"One thing consoles me when bad thoughts descend," she said. "Vin was in a state of grace when he died. I know absolutely he was saved. It's a great comfort."

I wondered how she knew that and how Vin could be in a state of grace while fooling around with paid black stuff in Richmond. Vin had connived to best many men. Obviously deception hadn't stopped in his dealings with his own wife. The sonofabitch.

We were close to Tobaccoton and the entrance to Riverview. Bugs splattered on my windshield diffused beams from the wrought-iron lights atop the gateposts. I circled to the front entrance of the mansion where the brass carriage lamps on either side of the door-way cast shadows of boxwoods across the white gravel.

She didn't ask me in nor did I expect her to. Instead we sat a moment, and I felt the pressure of words I'd carried bound in my head most of my life. She gathered herself to leave.

"I hope you'll believe I enjoyed myself despite *Rainy Day on Cornelia Street*," she said.

"Rhea, I love you," I said.

The words were out. I'd never planned or intended to speak them. They had escaped up through my body and sped over my tongue. Like the Ancient Mariner, I was forced to confess. I was also afraid to look at her.

"Why, Billy, I guessed that about you a long time back," she said. "Don't you think I knew you were sneaking around to watch me? I wanted you to call, to ask me out, and if it hadn't been against etiquette of the day I might have phoned you."

I sat regretting, thinking if I'd been bolder I could've hit it off with her, made her love me, married her, fathered children, and lived at Riverview. Like a jerky movie the story slanted through my mind.

"I thank you for bringing the gift to me now," Rhea said. "It's precious, and I treasure it, though we can't do anything about it presently, can we, not with Vin and all."

She leaned to me, removed my tinted glasses, and pressed her mouth against a corner of mine, the kiss a compromise between lips and cheek. She then set my glasses back on and turned away. I hurried around the car to help her out. I felt weightless. Arm in arm, hip to hip, we walked to the house.

"You'll call again?" she asked.

I stood nodding till she released me and slipped through the doorway. She touched her mouth with her fingertips. When the door closed, I walked dizzily to my car, drove out, and shouted. I raced home so fast I skidded off the road into weeds and bounced back. I didn't go into the house, where lights burned at my father's window. Instead I spun among the rattails, my arms extended like a man attempting to whirlybird himself into the sky.

The telephone rang. I wouldn't have answered it except I believed it could be Rhea needing something or wanting to impart a last endearment. I ran into the house.

"Your ass on fire, brother," the voice whispered.

12

I sit on the floor and rub a link of my chain against an edge of the millstone, an action that is futile, yet I have to do more than just sit watching the milkweed grow up through the crack. The milkweed bends toward light and is forming blooms. It is thriving, though I am not. My skin is sore from hours of lying on the cot. I feel no hope.

I think of my funeral. Surely a memorial service has been held. I picture who would be there. My father, perhaps wearing his American Legion cap; Florene; the courthouse crowd; Pickney and his deputies; maybe Uncle Daniel; Jeannie; Rhea dressed in black as she was for Vin, the combination of her mourning clothes and arousing body causing contradictory emotions in men attempting to hold spiritual thoughts. She would be brave and beautiful.

As I work the chain link against the millstone, I look past the milkweed to the crooked doorway and the tangled clearing before the cabin to thistles and the algal pond where bulrushes grow and glittering blue dragonflies sweep in. The algae appears as thick as fabric.

It's almost time for the master, and I stop rubbing the link. With my fingers I brush the white grit from the millstone through a floor crack. The stone's edge shows wear, an indentation and lighter cast. I spit on my fingers, run them over the floor, and transfer stain to the millstone.

The master emerges noiselessly from birch shadows into sunlight. I not only must exercise on the chain but also am directed to sweep up. After I wash, shave, and eat, we have our lesson, which I have prepared. I sit on the cot while the master stands in front and above me.

Master: Is there any use of the moral law to man since the fall?

Me: Although no man since the fall can attain to righteousness and life by the moral law, yet there is great use thereof, as well common to all men, as peculiar either to the unregenerate, or the regenerate.

Master: Of what use is the moral law to all men?

Me: The moral law is of use to all men, to inform them of the holy nature and will of God, and of their duty binding them to walk accordingly; to convince them of their disability to keep it, and of the sinful pollution of their nature, hearts, and lives, to humble them in the sense of their sin and misery, and thereby to help them to a clearer sight of the need they have of Christ, and of the perfection of his obedience.

Master: What does the moral law mean to you?

Me: Makes me know that of myself I'm nothing.

Master: Anything else?

Me: Teaches me that misery has a purpose.

Master: Tribulation is the hand of God modeling us. Can you give thanks for yours?

Me: I'm trying.

Master: You have no understanding of God until you can thank Him for misfortune equally with the good that befalls.

Me: I can see that.

Master: Is there anything you need?

Me: I'd like to know what you're going to do with me.

Master: That isn't a need.

Me: From my point of view it is.

Master: I'm preparing a place for you.

Before I can question further, the master moves to leave. The camouflaged clothing is clean, but the boots have a crusting of swamp muck around them. The master adjusts the shooting glasses, examines the cabin with a slow sweep of yellow lenses, and stops to stare at the millstone where I've been rubbing the chain. Fingers curl toward the pistol.

Me: It's not what you're thinking. I can't move around without the chain scraping.

I go through a crippled pitiful act of walking in such a way to force the link to rub the millstone. The master isn't convinced.

Me: I wouldn't try to escape. I know you want what's best for me. I like what you're doing.

Master: What am I doing?

Me: You're saving my soul.

Threat eases from fingers, and the hand lowers from the gun. The master nods, again adjusts the shooting glasses, and leaves. I sit on the cot. I hold to it as shaking takes over. I have to lie down to keep from toppling.

Again a sea of sound covers the swamp like the tide's rising. The master is preparing a place for me. A grave, I think. The fanatic is going to kill me.

———

I drove my Chevy from Tobaccoton westward toward Father Mercy's and the compound belonging to the Sons of the Father. The evening was no cooler, the air as humid as a wet dishrag.

Ahead in the blue darkness I saw the yellow arch and stockade fences of the entrance, but the slatted wooden gates were closed, though flames flickered back among pines and I heard drums and singing. Torches moved, causing shadows to flow, and the tabernacle shone in the distance like a disordered castle. A layer of whitish smoke hung motionless over thatched huts.

I left my car, walked to the gates, and found them bound by lock and chain. When I rattled the chain, a shape stepped from darkness on the other side.

"No entrance tonight," a young black said. Bearded, his face a shimmering plane, he wore the yellow robe of the order. His turban made him seem unnaturally tall. He stood as still as stone, and he held an ebony spear.

"I want to speak with Father Mercy," I said.

"Father Mercy speaks with no devils during the Week of Festival."

Drums and singing were louder now, and like a golden snake

a procession of torches wound among pines. Trees appeared on fire. I tried to make out the song, but it was no hymn I'd ever heard. I wasn't even sure of the language.

What I'd hoped to get from Father Mercy was a name. He dealt with fallen women, and I thought perhaps he could learn from one of them information about a slinky ginger-colored Negress. It was stupid to think he would help me.

"Take your poison away," the young black said.

I stepped back from the gates and walked to my car. Torches twisted among the pines, drums beat faster, and the singing rose in a compression of joy.

I drove home. Aunt Lettie had visited my father and brought him cold chicken and buttermilk. He allowed her in his room, where they would sit and talk of my mother. She made his bed for him and straightened his things. She carried home his dirty laundry. She would touch nothing of mine.

For once I went to bed without a drink, slept well, and as usual woke thinking of Rhea. The locusts were quiet, but doves and rain crows called in melancholy tones. I wasn't melancholy. My imagination built upon my developing relationship with Rhea. I took her, in my mind, to a formal dance, maneuvered her onto a moonlight terrace, and asked her to marry me.

I pictured our life at Riverview. Summer mornings we would breakfast by the pool, our food served by Melissa, her uniform starched. At the door Rhea kissed me as I left to drive to my law office. She'd be wearing jodhpurs and a ratcatcher, and I might take a minute at the ring to watch her school green horses over the jumps.

Two or three times a day we would telephone each other, and when I returned home afternoons, she'd be waiting cool and perfumed. I'd shower and join her on the lawn, where she'd have a drink for me. We'd look toward the river as it darkened and hear the first whippoorwills of evening. My drinking would be no problem, no more than three ounces of whisky a night, sipped genteelly while we chatted and reached to one another.

I might learn to ride, nothing like Rhea of course, no fox hunting, but a slow gait beside her around the estate as we looked over crops or checked the fences and woodlands. I'd wear a white shirt, fawn breeches, and black boots. We stop by a stream, tie our horses to a weeping willow, and lie on violets as in romantic novels.

In my bed I turned on my right side and gazed to the window with its limp white curtains washed to sheerness. Bluejays were strident among locust limbs, feathers gaudy in flashes of sunlight. Bluejays. Jaybirds. Naked as. The Jaybird Motel, Plum, who had gone to Arizona, said.

Surely with Rhea I'd become an accomplished lover. I pictured myself bringing her to heat and then thrusting with such manliness that she gasped and moaned. She clutched my back, sobbed, raised eyes wet with devotion. "Thank you, Billy, oh yes, thank you, thank you!"

My father clomped around upstairs and switched on the "Today Show." I pushed from the bed, shaved, and combed my hair. I walked back into my room to find my father standing by the bed. He wore his slippers, pajamas, and leaned on his cane. His white hair was brushed.

"I reckon you think you're something," he said, but it was a charge without the usual anger.

"It's true, I do consider myself composed of some substance."

"King of the hill going out with Blackjack Gatlin's daughter."

For an instant my fingers stilled on buttons of my shirt. How could he know already? Aunt Lettie of course. How did she know? Easy. Black people had developed an intelligence network over the years. They kept track of whites who could hurt them. They watched from shadows of pine woods, from cracks between weathered boards, from behind shades lifted with a finger. Leona Poindexter had seen me.

"Blackjack would be having a howling fit if he knew," my father said. "He'd come runing over here with a hoe handle. His sweet preciousness going out with a Payne who can't control his drinking, keep a wife, or even get a conviction. Why, he'd chase you out of Howell County."

"What about you controlling your drinking?"

"My life's over. I'm just waiting to leave, but by the time I was your age I'd killed men. I'd stared death in his ugly face. I didn't slip into the bottle till your mother, bless her, died."

I stood at the mirror tying my tie and thinking I should take more pains with my hair, shampoo and have it trimmed more often.

"I knew Blackjack," my father said. "He used to ride a horse to school from Riverview and keep it in a stall behind Miss Katie Cullen's house. A dandy he was, but he could sure fight. He wasn't a big boy, yet he always seemed big and nobody could take him."

"He carry a blackjack then?"

"That was later. He had his clothes tailored in Richmond with a special pocket, a slot of cloth, for the blackjack. Not his dress clothes, but the suits he wore to the bank. When the blackjack made him uncomfortable, he set it on his desk. People saw it and accorded him respect."

It occurred to me my father was being cordial, and I wondered whether it was Rhea or the fact I'd been out with any woman.

"There's another reason too," he said. "For calling him Blackjack I mean. Course nobody called him that to his face. I sure as hell didn't. Even when he wasn't around, I lowered my voice to speak that name."

"What other reason?" I asked.

The room had once been his and my mother's, and as he talked my father limped about touching last traces of her: the painted globe of the glass lamp, the cherry wardrobe, a Victorian mirror whose gilt flaked like golden dandruff, and the bed itself where I'd probably been conceived.

"I used to play baseball for the Howell County Hornets, second base, and I had a friend named Amos Elliott who was killed at Iwo Jima, a Marine sergeant. Amos was also a friend of Blackjack, and their senior year in high school they drove their girls home after the spring formal. Those days girls didn't drop their drawers at the snap of a finger, and you had them home by twelve. Blackjack produced some liquor he and Amos began drinking. When they got fired up, Blackjack took Amos to Riverview, not the big house but one of the dirt roads along the rear of the property. They left the car parked in the woods and slipped up to a tenant cabin where Blackjack scratched on a window. This black woman came out and serviced them both in the grass. Amos worried for a month he might've caught something. He was sure he was going to break out in sores."

My father laughed as if it were a dear memory, but I was thinking of Old Ben's sister and Leona Poindexter. Should her name be Leona Gatlin? Not necessarily. Leona could have been fathered, as Rhea told me, by a trashy white hand run off the place. Regardless, what Blackjack did happened long before he married the stately woman in the portrait who wore the lavender gown and garden-party hat. It was a hot-blooded Howell County escapade unconnected, as far as I could see, with what had happened to Vin.

"Black plus Jack equals Blackjack," my father said. "But nobody ever spoke it to his face."

I finished dressing, drank orange juice and coffee, and drove to Tobaccoton. Pickney and his deputies stood in the parking lot behind the courthouse. They conferred in shade of the sick elm, but Pickney detached himself and crossed to me using his rolling, foul-weather gait. He smoked a cigarillo.

"Out with revenuers to break up a still," he said. "Care to join the party?"

"I better get at my desk. You know anything about the Week of Festival out at Father Mercy's?"

"Big time of year for the Sons. Go back to their origins. That's what Father Mercy claims. Rediscover their origins. Whatever that means. My origin was a tobacco plant. I'll fill you in on the raid when I come back."

Pickney clamped his teeth on his cigarillo, reset his trooper's hat, and joined the deputies, who then moved toward three washed police cars. The deputies carried shotguns. The federal men weren't with them, and I assumed they had a staging area arranged.

I climbed to my office, spoke to Florene, and hung up my seersucker jacket. I had no sooner settled to my chair and turned to the mail before the phone rang. It was Allison Hopgood, the Episcopalian minister, and he wanted me to come by his study.

"I think you should try to make time for me," he said.

I hung up the phone and looked out my window past the pigeons on the flat dark roofs of the stores to the steeple of Saint Andrew's and the wan sky beyond. The steeple was so slim and pointed I thought of spears belonging to Father Mercy's warriors. The slate had an algal cast and no pigeons. The cant was too steep for pigeons.

My eyes followed a curved descending flight of the birds headed for the Tobaccoton rolling mill, where they would bob under farm trucks and around the loading docks in search of grain. I shook my head. I had to get my mind back on business. Which was? Vin, survival in office, Rhea.

I wanted to call her. At the same time I didn't wish to crowd her. I thought of her waking, pulling on a bathing suit, and taking a morning dip. I pictured her slanting down from a dive through bubbling water. I saw us meeting and kissing under the surface.

All right, Allison Hopgood. I stood from my desk and reached for my jacket. Allison's great shame was not being English. He felt socially and theologically superior to all that was southern and even American, but in his soul he believed himself deprived. Had he his way, there would be no Declaration of Independence or United States. His vision was of flowing sacerdotal robes, boys' choirs, greensward, cathedrals, tea before vespers, and beatific bishops.

I left the courthouse and walked past Uncle Daniel and his sign. When I spoke, he smiled but didn't answer. I stayed on the shady side of the street, my soles grinding dust.

The small Gothic-style church had ivy growing up around its arched windows. A strip of yard needed weeding, and the vaulted interior showed neglect, understandably since so few Episcopalians remained in the area. Allison Hopgood was past retirement age. He'd been allowed to reside in the vicarage, but after he left, Saint Andrew's would be demoted to a mission, an outpost with two sermons a month provided by a visiting priest or seminary students.

I walked through the empty nave and along an unlit corridor that smelled of chalk, mildew, and more dust. Allison sat in his study. He wore his clerical collar, though his dark shirt had short sleeves and uncovered flesh as richly white as Jersey cream. Except for fuzzy tufts, he was bald.

He had been drinking tea. Cluttered about him were old sermons, biblical commentaries, and lexicons. He cleared a chair for me. On walls were framed sketches of British abbeys he had brought back from a two-week vacation, his only trip to England. Two weeks was enough to reinforce his accent.

"Beastly heat, though I try not to complain," he said. "No tea then? I'll have another cup. I suspect I was meant for cooler climes, but the Lord puts us where He wants us, eh? Things all right at your place? Your father? Give him my hello, will you? I'm not a person to grouse really. One works with the timeless nature of mankind. That doesn't change, only the scenery. Make the best of it. I try to but must confess I don't consider myself a law-enforcement officer like some members of the ministry who ride about in squad cars to scare the pants off youngsters. Well, perhaps in some cases the pants are already off; yet I can't believe for a moment such public policy will bring anyone to Christ."

So it was Buster Bovin and The Ministerial Alliance he wanted to see me about.

"I wish to announce I disassociate myself from their activities," Allison said. "I will have no part of it. It is mockery of the faith and will make us the butt of a thousand ridiculings in the press and elsewhere. I intend to speak against it in a sermon. I am no liberal, but men cannot be herded into Heaven like cattle. They are drawn by the goodness of God."

He went on about it. I looked out his ivy-fringed window to the oak-shaded street where two grimy boys fenced, pussy willow branches their swords. Rhea came to this church, as had Vin. When Allison ran down, I told him I agreed with him but had to be careful because of the voters. I also inquired about Vin.

"Would you consider him devout?" I asked.

Allison set his cup in the saucer and drew his face long.

"That is a question, isn't it? Who knows about people like Vin? He was his own person, self-contained, affable, helpful, pleasant to deal with, yet, Billy, surely you're aware there are men who lack spiritual depth, individuals born without it just as others enter our world without hands, hearing, or sight. I used to bewail my failure to reach them, but as I've grown older I realize it's like castigating myself for not being able to change the color of my hair by willing it."

He touched his baldness and smiled. Beyond him and the window a sprinkler swished lazily, fed by a green hose snaked across grass.

"It's enough to convince you the Presbyterians are right to put emphasis on predestination and the elect," Allison said. "People born with little sense of the divine. What happens to a spiritual primitive when, to use the vernacular, the roll is called up yonder? Should a man be doomed for being born with a clubfoot? Certainly not. Then what if he enters the world lacking a talent for God? The answer defies reason. The Lord will have to reveal that mystery to us in His own time."

"Rhea," I said.

"Ah, now, there's a lady. Just like her mother, a saint. All I have to do is hint from the pulpit we need a new carpet or the baptismal repaired, and she sees to it swiftly and anonymously. Rhea affirms my belief in the goodness of man, or in this case, woman. I've pondered whether certain people have enough virtue to compensate for its absence in others. We might surmise she carried Vin spiritually."

"You heard her say at the funeral Vin had found God."

"Well, that can happen in the blink of an eye, don't you see. It is never too late to receive the Lord's forgiveness."

"Funny, I don't remember her as being particularly religious."

"You make it sound as if she contracted a disease. Rhea is sincerely and quietly devout."

"I don't mean anything's wrong with her. I just never thought of her in terms of piety." I reflected a moment. "You notice any change in her before Vin died?"

I was attempting to put together Vin's running around with paid black stuff and how much Rhea knew about that side of him, if she knew anything at all.

"She's graciously steadfast, though placed upon her is the curse of beauty," Allison said. "It's a cross most women cannot bear. Think of what Rhea could have become: a kine of Bashan, a country-club specimen, a voluptuary drinking liquor and oiling her body beside the pool. She chose to subordinate herself to her church and God."

"Never a crisis?" I asked.

"If you mean did she undergo a sudden transformation or spiritual struggle, no. She's a woman who has grown in the faith, one of those rare individuals who develop in the spirit apace with mind and body. There was a time—"

He stopped speaking and tapped fingers against his wrinkled forehead.

"—a brief period when I believed she might be drifting away. Several years ago. She was in the county but missed services. I thought something said from the pulpit might have upset her. Then she returned as faithful as ever. If displeased by me, she never spoke of it. We did talk of God. I have a tendency to be academic and preachy, but she never intellectualized or complicated Him, though she's extremely intelligent and capable of deep thinking. Her beliefs are clean and pure, uncluttered by complexities of the day. It is as if all else drops away and she's left with the unencumbered Word."

As I stood, I thanked him.

"In another time, despite her loveliness, she might have been a nun," Allison said. "Have you noticed how she downplays her body. She's rightly fearful of it, what it might betray her into. An amazingly good woman."

Before I could leave, he again dissociated himself from The

Ministerial Alliance. We walked to the door, where I shook his slender white hand. On the way back to my office, I pictured Rhea in combat with her body, she dressed like a lion tamer, holding a whip and pistol, while up on a circus platform she stood naked, female, sleek, a tigress gathered to jump through a flaming hoop.

That afternoon as I worked in my office Pickney came up, closed the door, and sat. He held a brown paper bag, which he positioned on his lap. As usual he was sweaty, and seeds stuck to his sweat, the seeds from growth he'd brushed while running through fields and woods in pursuit of two blacks fleeing the illegal still.

"I ain't built for chasing," Pickney said and slapped at his uniform pants with his trooper hat. I wouldn't have been surprised to see steam rise from him.

"You bring them in?" I asked, thinking I'd surely be able to win a conviction for men taken at a still where fire burned and the evidence bubbled in quart Ball jars.

"They made it to the swamp. Had an escape route already figured. Some of my boys got stuck. The Feds are bringing a chopper, though they so dumb they wouldn't recognize pies dropping from the south end of a cow."

He saw my disappointment as he fanned his face with his hat, and his washed blue eyes met mine for an instant, showing me openly he well knew how rickety my position as Commonwealth's Attorney was. No cunning or malice fired those eyes, just a weighing of reality. A man had to be for his kin.

"We did bring in something," he said. "Come across a shack out on the edge of the swamp, just pine boards tacked together and a tin roof made from a Big Orange sign. Sleeping inside on an old school-bus seat was a fellow used to work down at your place name of Eddie Blue."

He handed me the brown paper sack. Inside was the sugar bowl from the stolen silver service.

"He was packed up to run," Pickney said. "He didn't have nothing to do with the still, just used the shack as a hiding place for what he light-fingered." His own finger itched to get at his nose. "Now, first thing I wondered is could Eddie Blue be connected with what happened to Vin. Eddie had over two hundred dollars on him. If we believe what hippie Hawthorn told us, Vin's wallet had no money in it when he picked it up off the power line. That means somebody took it, which might've been Eddie Blue. Eddie's so strong he could easily snuff a fellow while emptying pockets."

"Vin wasn't roughed up."

"We don't know how it was done. Maybe Eddie Blue lifted and squeezed him good."

"Vin would've fought."

"Except he was drunk, maybe too drunk to fight. Eddie Blue's been robbing houses, including yours. He could've come on Vin helpless, lifted his wallet, and thrown it on the power line after helping himself to the money. Just what he did to kill Vin we don't have to know yet."

"Not good enough," I said and shook my head.

"Agreed, but we got something else. You recall a tie Vin used to always wear, a blue job with little white swans on it? I never saw another like it around here. That tie was in the shack. And if you remember, Vin didn't have one on when found."

For the first time I began to believe and felt excitement. I didn't want anything bad to happen to Eddie Blue for Aunt Lettie's sake, but I thought of a trial and conviction. There would be state-wide newspaper publicity and TV coverage. I could make a repu-tation for myself and appear worthy in both Rhea's and the community's eyes. I pictured her smiling and meeting me at the door to Riverview.

"He give any explanation?" I asked.

"Claims he bought it. Not likely, but why don't you try?"

We went down to the jail. I had Eddie Blue brought from his cell to the sheriff's office. I knew Pickney would be standing in the utility closet where he could listen through the ventilator.

Deputies had handcuffed Eddie Blue, who wore loose-fitting mechanics' coveralls and high-top workshoes crusted with mud. He needed shaving and gave off an odor of sweat and swamp. The coveralls couldn't mask his strength, the collected muscles. He might heave himself across the desk, take me in his teeth, and shake me as a dog does a rat to break its neck.

He wouldn't sit but stood pulling against the bind of the cuffs and glaring. His body bunched, his shoulders thrust forward, and his lips drew flat against his teeth.

"Sorry to see you under these circumstances, Eddie Blue. Won't you take a chair?"

He still strained against the cuffs. Steel surely had to give. His fists tightened, and the tautness of his muscles brought a sheen to his skin's blackness. No, I thought, if he killed Vin, the body would've displayed violence. There was no gentle death in Eddie Blue.

"Surprised and disappointed you stole from my father and me," I said. "What's Aunt Lettie going to think?"

Obscenity hissed from his mouth in spit. I'd been cussed in my time, all the words, but never lashed with such continuous abuse, such repetitious and various stringing together of those words. I held to my chair as if I might be blown away. From the furious phrasing, from the tone and accent, I understood who'd been calling the house with threats.

"Had no idea you hated me all that much," I said when he stopped to breathe. "Sure I deserve it?"

"You shit is what you is, the way you treat me, pig shit!" And he went on. The profanity came in waves. How could he hate me so explosively? His face was boiling blackness. I waited for him to quiet.

"Eddie, I want to understand. What did I do to you to cause this?"

"Pissy little money you pay me," he said, his eyes outraged and bulging. I hoped Pickney would come running if I hollered. "I never liked working for you. You never cared no more about me than bird crap in the yard. You and your shitty house and your crazy daddy up there sucking down juice and listening to the soaps. You ever ask me inside for a sip of water? I had to swallow my water out of your yard faucet like a dog. You paid me on the back porch, not in the house. You bought them cheap lawn mowers and blamed me cause they was no good. I could see you thinking nigger and blaming me. Why should I give a fuck about pig shit like you?"

I began to feel guilty as well as afraid. I hadn't cared about him, but how was I to explain I hadn't cared about anybody?

"I'm sorry, Eddie. I never meant to treat you badly. If you'll give me a chance now, I'll try to help."

He laughed, and the laugh was a cry of a youth who had lost all belief in goodness or truth. Again he tugged at the cuffs and then let his head drop forward, his chin against his chest. His eyes closed.

"You sold our silver?" I asked.

"I used a hammer to beat it into lumps and melted it down in a lard can. You seen the last of that silver. I liked doing it. It was the funnest thing I ever done. I was pounding you and all the whiteys. Man, it was fine."

"You kept the sugar bowl."

He lifted his head, not fully, not his whole face, but just enough for his eyes to see under his fallen hair. The wild black hair was speckled with seeds.

"I never had no piece of silver," he said. "I come from a big family, lots of brothers, sisters, cousins, uncles, and nobody owns one piece of fucking silver. I wanted it, something I could hand down. You and your crazy daddy drunk half the time, yet you got silver to hand down. I wanted to start something to hand down."

I sat thinking of the deep urge any man would feel to pass something on, not a sugar bowl, but a vessel holding his courage and accomplishment, his manhood and nobility.

"You earn what you hand down, Eddie, not steal it."

"You didn't earn it."

"But somebody in my family did."

"Black sweat earned it for your family."

"That's not the question here. You'll have to be prosecuted, and I can go after you tooth and claw or I can be gentle. That's your choice."

"What you want from me?" His chin had again dropped, his eyes closed.

"Where'd you get the tie with swans?"

"I bought it."

"No."

"Fuck you."

"Stealing's one thing, that tie another. It belonged to Mr. Vincent Farr."

"If I'd killed anybody, it'd been you."

"Tell me again about the tie."

"I ain't telling you no more nothing," he said. His face jerked up, and he struggled against the handcuffs. His knees bumped the desk. I stood quickly and called for Pickney. The sheriff rushed in with deputies, who held their hands on their guns. They hustled Eddie Blue back to his cell.

"What you think?" Pickney asked as we stood in the corridor and looked after Eddie Blue.

"I don't make any connection between his housebreaking and

Vin," I said and used my handkerchief to wipe sweat from my face.

"What about the tie?"

"Let's see what we can find out about that tie."

I climbed the steps to my office and dialed Rhea. She answered on the first ring. I pictured her wearing white silk and standing in the rose bedroom. I asked about the tie.

"Yes, I gave that one to Vin," she said. "He liked anything with birds."

"Is it still with his clothes?"

"I've been burning Vin's clothes. I can't bear to think of anyone else wearing them. Melissa and I made a pile behind the stable."

"You saw the tie burn?"

"I think so, but I'm not certain."

"Could Vin have been wearing it the day he died?"

"I'm just unable to tell you. Are you going to explain why you're asking?"

"When I can, I will."

"I know you're looking out for me. You do plan to call again, don't you, I mean on other than police business? I'm thinking of cooking you a dinner. Do you like lamb?"

By the time we clicked off, I didn't care about the tie or anything else except Rhea. I stood and circled my desk. I opened the door to smile at Florene, who stared. I had made a giant step from hope into belief.

During the afternoon I leaned back in my chair, closed my eyes, and envisioned my life. My God, Rhea and I could have children! As I watched from the terrace I saw them ride their ponies across the lawn.

Florene tapped at the door to tell me Captain Blake was on the phone from Richmond.

"I finally was able to break through the Pentagon's bureaucracy," he said. "I wanted to check on Vincent Farr's history with the Air Force. I talked to a General Ryerdon who was Farr's squadron commander during the Vietnam conflict. At that time Ryerdon was not a general but a colonel.

"He gave Farr a glowing report. Said Farr was a person to go bear hunting with, a man of great spirit. Said Farr on a training flight did a snap roll in an F-14 under the Bay Bridge. General, then Colonel, Ryerdon attempted to convince Farr to sign up for another hitch, but Farr was always talking about Howell County and the woman he later married. According to the general, Farr could've gone all the way in the Air Force."

I listened and doodled on my legal pad. I thought of Rhea preparing a lamb dinner, of us sitting in candlelight on the terrace, no mosquitoes allowed.

"I asked what he was like when not flying," Captain Blake said. "'On the ground or in the air an ace,' was the general's answer. I tried to get more personal, but the general was reluctant to talk about much other than flying. He believes in protecting 'his boys,' as he calls them."

I doodled, listened to him recite in his official voice—he must've been consulting notes—and again pictured Rhea and myself with children. Why had she and Vin never had them? With such health between them, impotency seemed impossible.

"He gave me a lecture on military life in the combat zone," Captain Blake said. "He told me civilians have to understand that men at war live in a different dimension than ordinary people. One life has no connection with the other. He was saying something I hadn't asked for. I pushed a bit in that direction. Defensively the general said Farr had the drives of an extraordinary man and what he did in Saigon or anywhere else should not be judged by non-combatants' standards. We all loved him, the general said. Farr made a strafing pass so low across a paddy he sucked rice into his air intake. He would, the general said, have flown right up Charley's ass if permitted."

"Did you ask about a tattoo?" I said.

"I did. The general remembers none. Major Farr in a run to Saigon after a raid might have erred. Though advised against it, a lot of men got tattooed. The general said many of those slanty-eyed little ladies could use a needle. It was, he also said, a different planet. Then the general became somewhat disturbed. I quote: 'I don't want him dishonored. You reading me? Vinnie was the best, and he's not to be dragged through civilian muck. I am going to be very upset if that happens, and I'm not without recourse in the halls of power.' I told him we were not attempting to blacken Major Farr's reputation but merely hoping to discover how he died. I promised we would protect Farr's record, particularly for his wife's sake. I gather Farr must have been a hell-raiser extraordinary in

Vietnam. During your investigation have you found indications of like conduct in Howell County?"

"Might have," I said.

"You mean you've come up with something?" he asked. I detected surprise, even disbelief, in his voice. He no longer expected anything from Pickney or me.

"Apparently he cared for the ladies," I said. I didn't want to tell him all I knew, not yet. If he learned of the slinky black gal in Richmond, we might not be able to shield Rhea from great hurt.

"I'd appreciate any information you have," Captain Blake said.

"Give me another day or two, and I'll drive down your way for a talk," I said. "You have files on paid black stuff?"

"They come in all varieties," Captain Blake said.

Next morning when I walked barefoot into the kitchen for my coffee, Aunt Lettie was standing outside at the foot of the back steps. She wore a blue dress uneven around the hem and lumpy brown shoes. Her straw hat was decorated with a few last waxy flowers. She held her paper shopping bag by its string handles.

"People thrown out like bathwater," she said. "Like potato peels and eggshells. Who cares? Only the Lord."

"Come on in," I said and opened the screen door for her, but she didn't move.

"I wish I's a bird in the trees, even a buzzard," she said. "I'd fly on up, just keep going to glory. I'd beat my wings against the golden gates."

More churching. She never had enough. She would've slept in that ragtag unpainted little meetinghouse under the pecan trees had they let her. Her squirming little body had worn a dip in the pew.

"Who's preaching?" I asked. I walked out onto the steps and let the door close.

"Beautiful man, tall, hair like licorice and skin the color of bright leaf tobacco. Speaks fancy and fast. Says God loves all men, but nobody going to understand how that love work till Judgment Day."

"If He loves all men, why judge them?" I asked. "Just fit them with wings and let them find themselves a cloud to stretch out on."

"You don't believe nothing that's not in a bottle."

"How come you're picking on me so early?"

"You get up and go to work and don't see people who is thrown
out like old bones. Your daddy's been after me to come back to
work here, but I ain't ever going to clean up your mess again. If
your house fell in, I wouldn't help. You remember my second
husband Jimmy Joe?"

I tried to picture which among the procession of husbands
Aunt Lettie had led to the altar was Jimmy Joe. Possibly the bent,
soft-stepping one who'd been a master poacher, a man who read
and tasted the winds and slipped through the woods so silently that
birds didn't stop singing. In all his life Jimmy Joe never bought
meat in a store.

"Sure, he could talk turkeys out of trees," I said.

"That was Grover," Aunt Lettie said, her little face squeezing
in disgust. "Your brain's gone. Jimmy Joe had the bees and sour-
wood honey he used to bring your mommy. He done the grass here
a while too."

"Old Jimmy Joe, sure, didn't he get—"

"Killed by a train. Jimmy Joe could think so deep he didn't
hear nothing, and he was walking the Southern tracks and never
even turned around. That's what the engineer testified. Said Jimmy
Joe was just walking along with his hands behind him, his head
down, thinking hard. Even in bed I could feel him thinking."

I was certain now where she was going. Jimmy Joe, if my
arithmetic was correct, had been Eddie Blue's grandfather.

"Aunt Lettie, I'll help Eddie Blue all I can, but he's making
it difficult."

"Ate at my table and slept under my roof. His little head's
been on my knee. People think Eddie Blue's dumb because he so
big and strong, but he smart. He could count to a hundred before
his sisters. He can write pretty too."

She dug around in her crackling brown shopping bag and came
up with a paper she thrust at me. It had been folded twice, the
creases as thin as wafers and translucent. It was a report card from
Howell County High School, Eddie Blue's, and he had received a
D in English, a C– in History, an A in Mechanics, a B– in Civics,
and an A in math. The report card was two years old.

"I'm impressed with the math," I said.

"You never looked at him," she said and reached for the report,
which she tenderly folded and fitted back into her shopping bag.

"You never even seen him. He come here and wanted to do good work, and you treated him like he was dumb. You fussed at him about that old lawn mower that should've been junked ten years ago. They don't even make the parts no more, and he kept it running longer than anybody in town was able to, but you laid it on Eddie Blue so you could buy liquor instead of a new mower. You should've helped and kept him out of trouble."

I had treated Eddie Blue the way most white men in Howell County would a young black, like a borderline member of the human race. All I'd wanted was somebody to cut grass, not a relationship.

"You could've showed him with your education, talked to him, found out, but you don't care nothing except about climbing in that bottle. He could've gone to college or got a government job, but you never took ten minutes to explain to him about that. Now you stuck him in the jailhouse. That make you feel good, to have a smart, hard-working boy you never talked ten minutes to in the jailhouse?"

"He stole from me, Aunt Lettie, and from others. And he had in his possession, besides lots of money, a necktie which might have belonged to Mr. Farr."

"You stole from Eddie Blue, every day he was here you did with what you paid," she said. "He tried to save his money. He was going to Norfolk when he had enough to get him a job in the shipyard. That tie you talking about, you afraid to use Vin on me instead of Mr. Farr? They might kick you out of the county if you use a white man's first name on me? I can tell you about that tie. Melissa had her Little Hertel helping carry out them piles of clothes to burn. He just a boy and sneaked that tie into his pocket when nobody was watching. He sold it to Eddie Blue in the woods. Eddie Blue was going to wear it to Norfolk. Paid a dollar to Little Hertel for it so Little Hertel could go to the Five-County Fair in Bannister. You going to stick Little Hertel in the jailhouse too?"

I told her I wasn't and tried to get her to come inside, but she kept shaking her head.

"You don't know everything about Mr. Vincent Farr," she said. "People do things in the dark. I ain't supposed to see nothing. I just supposed to go around picking up after messy men who live in the bottle, but people, even the high and mighty, they move around in the dark."

I wondered whether she was talking about Vin and Jeannie. I stared down into her purplish shiny eyes. Everywhere else she was leached by time, but if life were in the eyes, she was stoked with living. Stubborn, hurt, defiant, she looked back, a tough little lady who carried so many sorrows of others—the husbands, the children, the grandchildren, all that terrible weight—on those dwarfish shoulders.

"Night's big, like a tobacco sheet," she said. "You lift it, you don't know what you going to find underneath. God made black people black so they could have the night around them. He made white men white so they can be seen in the dark."

"What happened in the dark?"

"Where I go? Ever seen me anywheres except the kitchen and the clothesline? What I know?"

"Tell me, Aunt Lettie."

"Some people live different in the dark. That's when you see what they really is, proud people, people own banks and ride horses and live in big houses on the river."

"Who?" I asked, wondering whether she was talking about Vin or Blackjack.

"I tried," she said and felt into the shopping bag for her red umbrella, used to protect her not against rain but sunshine, as if her skin were delicately fair. She opened it over herself. "I going to reach down and pull rest over me. I tired of all the troubles people bring me. Sometimes I'd like somebody to hand me a big dish of ice cream, nothing more than a big dish of peach ice cream so I could sit on my porch and eat that ice cream cold and sweet without no hungry eyes watching and waiting."

I tried to keep her from leaving, but she went, carrying her own shade down the sunny lane. Her hat was crooked, her back straight, and her misshapen shoes sent up tiny spumes of dust. I thought man didn't accomplish much. It was women who did the real work of the world, the significant stuff like feeding, clothing, worrying, nursing, healing, birthing, and, above all, loving.

As I drove from Tobaccoton, Buster Bovin gave me a friendly wave from the corner in front of the Planters & Merchants Bank. He too wore dark glasses. I was headed east, the sun a blood globe slanting rays into asphalt, softening it and causing my tires to hiss. Prison gangs worked in ditches, swinging brush axes and raising heads to watch every car, thinking of themselves speeding into freedom.

Whether Aunt Lettie had been talking about Vin or Blackjack, she hadn't revealed anything I didn't know. So a young Blackjack had slipped out at night to visit a tenant house or two behind Riverside and Vin chased women of all shades and styles. The information provided no answers I needed, chief of which were how and why Vin had died.

I drove north of Powhatan and parked at the side of a modern cinderblock structure, pink with a white roof. Flowers grew in borders around the building, and in front an ancient magnolia tree dominated the lawn, its bark pocked by woodpeckers. The name of the place was the Magnolia Nursing and Convalescent Home.

I talked to a starched nurse named Miss Bosley, who was young, prissy, and pigeon-toed. She reminded me I hadn't come during visiting hours. I showed her my Commonwealth's Attorney identification.

"She doesn't know about her son," Miss Bosley said, speaking of Vin's mother. "You mustn't tell her."

Miss Bosley stood in an office behind glass which had a round speaking hole like the ticket cage of a theater. She came out to me, and her uniform swished as she led me past an area where chairs were lined up before a TV console that flickered with no sound.

"Physically she's fine," Miss Bosley said. She held a metal clipboard against her stomach. "A delightful patient, living out her life in her own world. The staff loves her."

We walked the waxed corridor where tubes of light reflected in pale-blue flooring and aluminum handrails. From rooms like lairs men and women peered out, aged, shrunken people wearing white nightgowns, their eyes set in corroded faces displaying both hope and alarm—hope for a kinsman's visit, alarm at fear of the death angel. The smell was decay, not that the Magnolia Nursing and Convalescent Home hadn't been scrubbed, but no amount of astringent, antiseptic, or disinfectant could defeat the relentless dissolution of bodies.

Miss Bosley's rubber-soled shoes made squeegee sounds on the tile, her legs moved rapidly against her uniform. She stopped before a room, tapped once on a door left ajar, and entered with a glance back at me.

"Mrs. Farr, you have a visitor!" Miss Bosley said, smiling and crossing to the bed, where she put an arm around a woman propped up and fingering through snapshots the way a person will collect cards after a hand has been played.

I remembered Vin's mother from Tobaccoton as a neat, pleasant woman, but here she had become heavy and soft. She wore a rose gown, which had slipped off a shoulder, a gown maybe Rhea had brought. Her hair was not gray or white but startlingly blond and thick. I realized she had on a wig. Her smile was childlike. Miss Bosley arranged the gown over the flabby shoulder.

The room had photographs everywhere, dozens of them, on walls, the windowsill, stuck in the mirror, all of Vin—Vin as a boy holding a fishing rod, Vin riding a bicycle, driving a Ford pickup, among members of the high school track team, on brick steps beneath the insignia of his fraternity house, wearing a leather flight jacket and leaning against the wing of a fighter plane whose engine cowling was painted like a shark's mouth, Vin holding golf clubs beside palm trees, Vin tanned and dressed in a perfectly fitted tuxedo.

On a table to the left of the bed another color picture of him in his full-dress Air Force uniform. He grinned at the camera: crew cut, rock solid of face, threateningly handsome, spermy. The photograph was in an ornate silver frame at the sides of which were small silver vases, each holding a freshly cut red rose. I stood at a shrine.

"You know my Vinnie?" Mrs. Farr asked, her fingers busy with the deck of snapshots like a lady saying her beads.

"Billy Payne, Mrs. Farr, you might remember me from Tobaccoton," I said, speaking loudly.

"She's not deaf," Miss Bosley said and placed a chair at the side of the bed. Obediently I sat in it.

"Everybody knows Vinnie," Mrs. Farr said. "He was in the legislature. He brought the governor to lunch and shook hands with President Johnson. I got the picture."

She pointed, and I looked to the wall where President Johnson pinned a medal on Vinnie.

"You ever seen a prettier man? When I went to the hospital, getting him borned was so easy I wasn't sure it'd happened. I had to ask the nurses, and they laughed he was so beautiful. I knew he was special. No pain came with him, and I knew the Lord's hand was on him. I told his daddy this boy's going to be a Jonathan. He's going to be a David."

As I sat listening and wondering how to put in a question, I realized no pictures of Rhea hung here, not even one where she waited in the background. Could Mrs. Farr be a mother so possessive she wasn't willing to share her son even in marriage?

"He was never bad," she said. "His father and I never had to lay a finger on him. You told Vinnie to bring in wood or feed the stock, and it was done. Cleanest boy you ever did see. Dirt just wouldn't stick on him. He'd play nine innings of ball, and his uniform didn't need washing. I tell you dirt was afraid of him. He'd shine in the dark, Vin would. I been blessed, I can tell you. O Lord, how I been blessed. Dutiful Vinnie is. Not like some people's children who don't come to visit. He comes every day."

"That often?" I asked.

"Was here just minutes before you. You must've almost bumped him when he left. Fire and snow can't keep him from visiting his mother. Here's a snapshot of him when he made the speech at school. See how he shines?"

Her freckled, overfleshed hands shuffled the deck of pictures, and she offered one stained around the edges—Vin standing at the podium in the Howell County Consolidated School auditorium, an arm raised for emphasis, his face serious, and indeed he did seem to give off an aura. The speech must have been post-Vietnam, for he was wearing his major's uniform.

"Was he ever sick?" I got in when she took the snapshot back and returned it to her deck.

"Not Vinnie. He didn't even have measles. No germs lit on him. You clean inside, you don't get sick. Sickness comes from the Devil, not the Lord. The Devil can't get on clean. Vinnie was a hero. He ran faster, jumped higher, and swam fartherest of any boy in the county. His medals would sink a ship. He shook the President's hand. Lord, I been blessed, and I thank you."

She looked to the color photograph in the ornate silver frame, and I thought she might cross herself.

"So pretty and beautiful, they all wanted to marry him," she said. "They set their caps for him, but Vinnie was my boy. I told him he could be a David and a Jonathan. Keep yourself pure for the Lord, I told him. He knew traps was set all over the ground, but he never stepped in one." She laughed delightedly.

"Rhea Gatlin?" I asked.

"She was the worst, but Vinnie's smart. I taught him. He knows how to look at the ground. All those gals set their traps for nothing, Miss Gatlin too. Oh, she wants him worse than candy. She still thinks she can have him, but none of them will ever catch Vinnie. He don't belong to me or to her, but the Lord. That's why he's been so favored in his life. The Lord touched him."

"I heard he and Rhea Gatlin were keeping company," I said.

"Vinnie'll go with them. He learned his manners, and Miss Gatlin comes here to visit, trying to get at him through me. I'm nice to her. I try to be nice to everybody. I explain Vinnie has a mission in this life, something special. God sent him for a wonderful purpose."

She laughed and shuffled her snapshots. As I stood, I thanked her. She would never see anything except her son's shimmering youth and glory, holding him to the light like a flawless white diamond. She laughed softly, nodded, and her fingers worked the snapshots as if about to deal a hand of solitaire out over the sheet.

I left the room, spoke to Miss Bosley, and walked to my car. As I drove toward Tobaccoton, a thunderhead built in the west, a soaring cumulonimbus with an anvil top. When rain swept in, hailstones banged the car, and jittery lightning ignited purplish darkness. I slowed, pulled to the side of the road, and waited for the storm to pass. The end, I thought, of the world.

Just as quickly as it struck, the squall washed away, leaving a lingering thunder. Fast bright heat soaked up wetness. Asphalt steamed. By the time I reached Tobaccoton, the land had dried. Broken limbs lay about.

I left the office at five, drove home, and climbed the back steps to the house. My shoes crunched shards of glass. In the kitchen, chairs and the table had been overturned, dishes and pans thrown to the floor, bottles smashed, cups pulled from cabinets to the linoleum, flour and cornstarch heaved about, leaving a pall over the wreckage.

I found my father crumpled at the bottom of the hall steps among his war flags and souvenirs, which had been hurled down and torn or broken. I thought he was dead. He'd drawn up on his side, an arm limp behind him, the other clutching the picture of

my mother against his chest. From his temple leaked a zigzag of
blood. I knelt, rolled him to his back, and centered my ear against
his mouth.

He was breathing, but I feared moving him. I snatched the
telephone and called Doc Robinette's office and then his house. No
answer either place. I dialed the Rescue Squad. They would send
an ambulance.

As I waited, I sat on the floor beside my father and wiped at
his temple with my handkerchief. I wondered who could have done
this. Eddie Blue was in jail. I looked at the violence which had
struck the rooms. Only the sideboard appeared unharmed, the tar-
nished silver sugar bowl undisturbed on top.

My father's eyelids flickered. He hugged my mother's picture,
swallowed, and clenched his eyes.

"I'm dying," he said.

"Who did this?"

"I feel death at the door," he said and slowly slid the picture
of my young mother in saddle shoes to his face to kiss. "Son, I
want to tell you I'm sorry. I want to tell everybody I'm sorry."

"Lie still. Help's on the way."

"Too late. That's what you learn, it's always too late. I want
you to believe I loved your mother. No man ever loved a woman
more."

"I do believe it."

Again he swallowed, coughed feebly, and had difficulty breathing. As he wheezed, I looked out the screen door to the lane for
the ambulance.

"You don't know," he said. "All these years I been living lies.
I want you to understand I'm sorry."

"Sh-h-h, breathe easy."

"But I got to tell you, son. I don't want to die with it on my
conscience. I was never in the fighting. I wasn't in the infantry, not
even the artillery, but drove a six-by-six for the Quartermaster
Corps. I wanted to fight, I did till it hurt, and kept trying for a
transfer, begged for it, yet I had to drive that truck, and it didn't
even carry ammunition."

His voice faltered, he choked, his body bucked. He's gone, I
thought, but the wheezing renewed.

"I always wanted to be a hero," he said, his voice whispery.
"I wanted to be an infantryman, and they stuck me in a damn truck

carrying shoes, blankets, and crates of rations. I was so shamed. I never got wounded. I tripped over a fifty-pound sack of navy beans and broke my hip. The bones didn't set right. More shame. When I came back stateside, I couldn't tell people the truth, that I never got shot or even missed a meal. I never went a single night the whole war without a roof over my head."

"Dad, it's okay."

"Naw, your mother, that's on me too, that sin, your pretty kind mother that I drove from the house with my drinking. Out of shame I'd started drinking, out of all the lies. I never saw a German holding a gun except in a newsreel. All the stuff I carried home, the souvenirs, I bought those from the Limeys. I even lied to your good mother."

He hugged the picture and was crying now, the tears squeezing from under his clenched eyelids. His voice fluttered away and came back.

"I started drinking early one Sunday morning, a freak day, terrible with rain and hail the night before, and though July, it was cold, damp, and mean, causing the tobacco to droop and draw up. I never went to church with your mother like she wanted. I got that on me too. You was just a little bit of thing, and your mother didn't go to services that day because she was afraid I wouldn't look after you right. She knew when to walk around me and fade. She stayed down in the kitchen cooking and kept a playpen for you in the dining room. I got so drunk, so bad drunk. I had this crappy job at the Planter's Warehouse grading tobacco during the season, and I was trying to do a little farming on land so poor not even a starving rabbit would bother to cross it. I didn't have enough money for fertilizer or lime, and the scrub cattle I was running looked so skinny and disreputable I hated anybody to see them. With reason I was drinking serious."

I raised from him and turned toward the screen door, thinking I heard the siren, but it was only the shrill of locusts, taken up by others and crossing the land.

"I was full of lying and hurt," my father said. "I kept thinking I should've become something. I told myself I deserved an office and a decent car, some fine clothes like other men I knew. Blackjack Gatlin had just built hisself a swimming pool, and I couldn't afford an overhaul on my tractor. So I was drinking hard and mean and began to shout at your sweet mother. No reason except I was hurting so bad because I'd told all those lies and knew I'd never become nothing at all in this life."

Spit gathered at a corner of his mouth, and his eyelids batted the tears. Please don't die on me, I thought, and wiped his mouth with my handkerchief.

"I was full of poison and put it on your mother. I banged around the house hollering. I broke one of her vases with marigolds in it and kicked over a chair. She was afraid for you. She picked you up out of the playpen and carried you down the back steps to the yard. She'd do that when I got mean, go walking till I quieted down. I stood on the back porch yelling at her, cursing that good kind woman from all the poison in me. God, I want to die. The memory of it's too terrible. No man should have to live with it."

As he lay hugging my mother's photograph and crying, tears filled the lines of his face. I dabbed at them and prayed for the ambulance. He kept choking and bucking.

"Your mother had on a sweater I'd given her for her birthday, a blue angora sweater, not real wool but the fake stuff they make at the mills. She carried you away from the house and down along the fenceline toward the river. I don't know how she got into the hornets in that fencerow all grown up with honeysuckles. Maybe she was trying to avoid thistles or stumbled, but somehow she roused them out of their nest, and they came after her."

As he talked in the wheezing voice, he rolled his head from side to side as if to negate the pictures flaming in his mind.

"I heard her screaming. Drunk as I was, falling-down drunk, I heard that and reeled outside. She was running through lespedeza holding you, and the hornets were swarming around her. She tried to protect you, kept her arms around you so they couldn't get at you, but hornets were all over her, stuck in that fake angora, tangled in it, yet able to sting. She was screaming and crying, and I stumbled toward her. To save you she threw you, underhanded like a bundle, to me and kept running herself to draw the hornets away from us, away from you and me, to protect us!"

He wept, and I'd never seen such tears come from man or woman, water flowing off his face and pooling on pine boards under his head.

"You and me got stung, though somehow I'd caught you by an arm, and you were dangling and howling. I rushed you inside, stripped off your clothes, and rubbed you all over with butter. By the time I reached your mother she was lying in the lane. Hornets were still tangled in that fake angora sweater. I brushed them off and carried her into the house. You was crying in the playpen. Your mother could hardly move. She'd been stung so many times she was bad hurt, yet I never thought she'd die on me. She looked beat up. I undressed her in the kitchen and began smearing butter on her too, using my finger, she in the chair, and she died under my fingers."

He moaned and turned his head from side to side. I heard the keen of the ambulance and saw red lights flashing in front of a rooster tail of red dust rising in the lane. The ambulance skidded around the circle to stop before the steps. Lester Peck, who worked night shift at the shoe factory, and Wayne Mears, rural mail carrier, ran up the steps. They wore white coveralls, hardhats, and carried a folded canvas stretcher. Gently they fitted my father onto the stretcher and lowered him to the ambulance. The red lights clicked off and on. Lester and I climbed into the rear with him while Wayne drove.

The siren rose and fell. We were hit by another shower with more thunder and lightning. Lightning seemed to be in the rocking ambulance with us as I held my father's hand and Wayne steadied the stretcher. With each bolt my father's bloodless face emerged from darkness.

At the Bannister hospital, the orderlies slid my father off the stretcher onto a stainless steel dolly and rolled him away through swinging doors. I smoked in the waiting room. A TV set was being watched mournfully by an elderly couple and a sleepy child. Magazines in a wooden rack had lost covers. A vase of cut flowers drooped on a windowsill.

When the doctor came from the emergency room, he took me aside. He was a young man, tanned and athletic, his name Warren. He had on a white medical jacket, checkered pants, and docksiders. He seemed amused.

"No, not his heart, but drunk, dead drunk," he said and smiled at a passing young nurse. "Your father is bombed. Blood alcohol shot right off the scale. Those Rescue Squad commandos should've caught it. You can go up and see him, though he's passed out. He do this often?"

I stopped by the business office first to give information and guarantee payment of my father's bills. I took the elevator to the third floor, where I walked a long warm corridor to his room. He lay with eyes closed, mouth open. His white hair was messed, and he needed a shave. I sat on the second bed in the room to watch his face, the skin and stubble silverish in light from the hall. My father groaned, tried to push upright, and fell back. He twisted and whispered a word I couldn't understand.

I stayed on the other bed through the never-ending night. My mouth dried. My eyes burned. When finally a morning mist condensed over the window, I sat up and rubbed my face. My father's head was turned on his pillow so he could look at me. He had again been crying.

"I going to die?" he asked.

I shook my head, smiled, and stood to reach to him, but he didn't want to be touched.

"I need to die," he said. "Bring my Luger."

"That's foolishness."

"Nobody in the house," he said, closing his eyes. "Not Aunt Lettie, you, not your mother. I get this feeling I'm all alone in the world, and I been ashamed so long. I couldn't suffer it no longer."

He pulled the sheet to his eyes to wipe them. He was small, sick, and helpless, like an underfed child.

"God, I keep trying to figure what it's all about, but you know what? It's not about anything, that's what I think, or at least I can't figure it. How's a man supposed to live in this world and not know what it's about?"

A black nurse came in, took his temperature, pulse, and blood pressure. She brought a capsule which she fed him by lifting his head. I left him dozing, his mouth working. I was very tired. I felt hot and raw. I'd call Florene and tell her I wouldn't be in to the office till afternoon.

At the house I looked at the wreckage. I gathered my father's guns, helmets, torn flags, all his war souvenirs, and carried them down to the basement, where I piled them among empty canning jars on the dusty concrete floor.

I didn't go to the office but slept, visited my father that evening, and told him he'd have to stay in the hospital another day or two. He didn't argue. They were feeding him pills, causing him to slide in and out of sleep.

On the way home I stopped by Aunt Lettie's to try to persuade

her to help me clean the house. She was at church. I left word with
a grandson named Richard for her to come. I righted furniture and
swept glass; yet the most sensible act seemed to be to fix a drink
and rest on the horsehair Victorian love seat of the parlor, where I
tipped over and dozed till the telephone rang. It wasn't Aunt Lettie
but Sheriff Pickney.

"Eddie Blue's loose," he said. "Grabbed Jesse carrying him
supper. Pulled Jesse so hard against the bars it broke his nose.
Eddie Blue got the key and's gone. We think he's headed to Black
Swamp. The boys are taking hounds down there, but hell, what
can you do in a swamp at night?"

I didn't know what anybody could do. First thing in the morning I rose from my bed and called Pickney. The hounds had treed
a coon. Pickney wasn't certain Eddie Blue was still in Howell
County.

After visiting my father at the Bannister hospital, I was again
on my way to Richmond in the heat of the day. My father hadn't
wanted to see me and requested no visitors be allowed. When I laid
the morning paper on his bed, he pushed it to the floor.

I drove to downtown Richmond, where white office buildings
were ghostly in the haze, the new money of Virginia, no longer
agricultural but financial and industrial—big-engine fast money,
not leisurely like the growing of leaf tobacco. People here walked
almost as rapidly as they did in New York.

I stopped at a self-service gas station to call Captain Blake. I
intended to invite him to lunch and tell him about Vin Farr and
the paid black stuff. Chances were good the captain already had a
file on the Jaybird Motel and a ginger Negress with spiked hair and
lots of leg.

The receptionist at state-police headquarters told me Captain
Blake wasn't in his office. When I explained who I was and asked
to speak to someone else in authority, she switched me to a Lieutenant Wiley.

"The captain won't be back today," Wiley said. "There was
an attempt on the governor's life at the Crab Festival. It'll be on
the news any minute now. Everything else has been dropped."

I thanked the lieutenant and asked him to have Captain Blake
call me when he could find time. I drove to McGuire's, the VA
hospital, to talk to an assistant admissions director about their al-

cohol rehabilitation program. The program, a retired army lieutenant colonel explained, was full, the waiting period sixty days. Papers
would have to be filled out and mailed in along with a doctor's
certification and an honorable discharge. I was given a mimeographed sheet of instructions.

So far I hadn't accomplished much. I'd been counting on Captain Blake and the VA. I borrowed the lieutenant colonel's phone
book to find the address of the Jaybird Motel. It was in south
Richmond, as was I, so I decided to have a look.

When I asked the lieutenant colonel for directions, his left
eyebrow twitched only slightly. The street was named Gardenia and
had once been a main artery from Richmond to Petersburg, but
with the completion of the interstate, Gardenia had become a truck
route through the city.

Fancy motels had operated along Gardenia, some built in plan-
tation style with columns and boxwoods, but no quality traffic
moved past them now. Many had closed or become ramshackle.
Weeds grew in lawns, neon was smashed, windows boarded. The
area was a sore spreading into the neighborhood surrounding it.

The Jaybird sat back from the potholed highway, and in the
hot glaze of afternoon sunlight did not appear altogether shabby.
It was an orange two-story stuccoed structure with black railings
along the walkways in the Mediterranean fashion. Water of a small
fenced-in swimming pool had a beer can floating in it. Willows grew
from holes drilled through paving, one of the trees dead. An unlit
electric sign displayed a strutting bluejay atop a red heart pierced
by a neon arrow.

I sat in my car at the curb across the street from the motel.
Not much was happening. A black man pushed a broom along a
deck. A linen-service truck drove to the office to leave towels and
sheets. A TV repairman wheeled out a set and lifted it into the
back of his van. I spotted the ice machine, the sign ICE red on
white.

Beyond the office was the restaurant, it too orange and with
flashing beer signs in the oval tinted windows. Go home, I thought.
You're no detective. Send in Captain Blake or his investigators. Or
take it to the city police. Yet I'd have to tell a lot to involve the
city police. I could cross to the restaurant and have a quick look.

The air conditioning was noisy and too cool. People were not
eating at this hour of the afternoon but drinking at a bar around a

tropical island of hooch, the exotic bottles lighted from beneath as if burning. I sat on a chrome stool to order a beer from a slim black waitress who wore tight red slacks and a sleeveless white blouse.

Men drinking were black and white. They had bets on the outcome of a TV baseball game. They looked me over as if I'd slipped from under a rock. Their voices, languid between pitches, raucous at the crack of the bat, were tidal. The game was interrupted by news of the attempt on the governor's life.

"Too bad they missed," one of them said.

"Fucker anyway," another agreed.

I moved to a red booth to order a second beer and draw the waitress apart.

"What does a stranger do around here for entertainment?" I asked, speaking quietly. "Besides shooting at the governor, that is."

"Happy Lanes down the street," she said and lifted an elbow to point. Through the oval window I saw Happy Lanes was a bowling alley.

"You happen to know a ginger-colored girl with spiked hair?"

"I don't get paid to know," the waitress said, turned, and left.

I finished my beer before using the men's room and crossing back to my car, where I sat and smoked in the heat. A false twilight set in, caused by the car and truck traffic, a diesel blueness through which the sun filtered. The neon motel sign, the jaybird, heart, and arrow, switched on. Magenta it was.

I drove into the Happy Lanes parking lot, drank another beer at the counter, and ate a hamburger. Few people were bowling. A black girl passed, and her shiny eyes appraised my value. I did not impress her. She too wore slacks and heels so high she seemed to be climbing instead of walking.

A young man sat next to me at the counter. In black letters on the rear of his white bowling shirt were the letters Southern Bread. He had close-cropped red hair, and one pale eye was slightly cocked.

"This a good place for girls?" I asked.

"No place is good for girls," he said. "Try Forsythia Avenue after dark." He gave me directions.

I was two short blocks from Forsythia, fronted on one side by small stores, on the other by begrimed townhouses with high stoops and overhanging gables. It wasn't dark yet, and no girls cruised. I smelled bread before I reached the end of the brick-paved street and saw a bakery, a white three-story building with a smokestack and delivery vans backed to a loading dock.

I parked, removed from my wallet everything which could identify me as Howell County's Commonwealth's Attorney, and smoked. Darkness dropped quickly. Streetlights switched on. Windows had no curtains or blinds. I saw naked bulbs. Children were called in by their mothers.

Girls didn't appear till ten—in pairs mostly, bizarre angled shapes lit by storefronts. High-heeled and stiffly silhouetted, the girls resembled cranes or herons. They loitered in doorways and at curbs. The girls were black, and the men who drove by to eye them white. Some cars stopped, negotiations were held, girls slid in to be driven off. All the while I smelled the bread baking.

I tossed my cigarette to the bricks, started the engine, and drew up to a girl who stood in the doorway of a closed furniture store. She wore a short yellow dress and yellow shoes. Apparently she heard music within herself, for she bent her knees and snapped her fingers. Her heels made her at least six feet tall. She was crooning.

"Can you help me?" I asked, leaning across the seat toward the car window.

"Help you what, boy?" she asked. She stepped unhurriedly toward the car and ducked forward to see me. She wasn't ginger but absolutely black.

"I'm looking for a girl."

"Maybe you didn't notice, but I'm a girl," she said and straightened, relaxed a knee, and breasted.

"You're a joy, but I have my sights set on a particular lady after what a friend told me."

"What she can do for you I can't?" she asked and lifted fingers under her breasts as if they needed rearranging.

"You understand how it is when you hanker after a special dish," I said. "This ginger-colored lady wears her hair—"

"I don't fill up talking," she said, dropped her arms, and stepped back toward the furniture store doorway. "Now you spending my time, mister. You can get me or you can just get!"

I raised a hand to her, put the Chevy in gear, and drove on. I rode up and down Forsythia peering at girls, trying to make out their features in the shrouded light. A few were very young. I slowed to squint at a girl on a corner, but she was what in Howell County the men would've called a "yaller." Her hair was conked to straightness, like black wire.

"Who needs you?" she called.

I drove back to the Jaybird, parked near the unlit pool, and walked to the office. Behind the desk stood a smiling young clerk whose barbered sandy hair was parted boyishly. He wore a white shirt, blue tie, and a newly pressed light summer suit. He appeared so unthreatening and respectable I thought I must be wrong about the Jaybird.

"I don't want a room," I said, glancing at the office, like him neat and perfectly maintained. It was furnished with two vinyl armchairs, potted plants, tangerine carpeting, and a large color TV quietly giving more news of the attempt on the governor's life.

A couple entered, the black girl the tall one wearing yellow dress and shoes I'd talked to earlier. With her was a white man at least sixty-five in madras shorts and a primrose sport shirt. He kept grinning. The girl looked bored and rolled her eyes at the clerk. When she recognized me, she stuck out her pink tongue.

"What's happening, Jenette?" the clerk asked in his modulated, respectable voice.

"With luck the world'll end tonight," Jenette said and yawned while the man signed the register and paid out thirty-five dollars plus tax to the clerk, who then handed over a key. The couple left, the man still grinning.

"Sir?" the clerk asked me, polite, accommodating. At the end of the counter sat a brass can with a long spout for watering plants. His trim fingers rose to touch the can's handle.

"I'm looking for a ginger-colored girl," I said.

"You from the police?" He wasn't alarmed.

I told him I wasn't and slipped a twenty-dollar bill from my wallet. As I laid the money on the guest register, I was able to read the name the elderly man had written: I. M. Dong. The clerk watched, his expression benign. He did not reach for the twenty.

"Sorry, I don't have that information," he said and, acting as if I weren't present, lifted the brass can and came around the counter to water the plants.

I picked up my twenty and left. Again I got in my car to patrol Forsythia. My tires bumped over bricks and an abandoned trolley track that ended abruptly. Lights in store windows stretched the girls' shadows. They recognized my car and watched with a cool malevolence. One had a peacock talking to her, a black man who wore a broad white hat, a white suit, and white shoes. I thought of razors and switchblades.

I'd go on home, catch some sleep, and be up early to visit my father and make out the papers for his admission to the VA hospital. At the bakery I turned for one last pass along the street and almost missed the girl. She was coming down from an apartment over a closed donut shop to a narrow brick entranceway lighted by a low-watt bulb. Several dented mailboxes were nailed to a wall on which graffiti had been sprayed with scarlet paint.

I stopped, reversed, and leaned to the window. She wore a black shirt unbuttoned at the neck, a tight black miniskirt of slick satinlike material, and heeled black boots. She carried a large black pocketbook held up by a shoulder strap. She was giggling, her head bent forward, as if she'd just seen something very funny. When she saw me, a hand slid fast into the big pocketbook and came out with an object that glinted. She is, I thought, going to knife or shoot me.

She brought up a flashlight, the kind you flip the top off to make it switch on, and shone it over my face. I still hadn't seen her clearly. Again she giggled, as if that's how she breathed.

"Kitten you don't know, and this is some sorry limo," she said.

"Shine it on yourself," I said.

She started at her boots and lifted the beam to her thighs and pelvis where she made a thrusting motion with the flashlight and giggled louder, then to her breasts, neck, face. She was ginger, all right, and her features were catlike and Asiatic. Her short hair had been twisted and stiffened into lacquered spikes. Japanese or Korean she was partly, I thought, the child of some black GI and a mama-san.

"If Kitten don't know, Kitten don't go," she said.

"I'm crazy for you," I said.

"Give us thy book and we take a look," she said, still giggling.

She meant my wallet, which, after I fingered out the money, I let her have. She used the flashlight to examine my identification but squinted as if reading perplexed her. Suddenly she opened the door and hipped in beside me. She began patting my body in search of what—a badge, gun, tape recorder? She was sweetly and strongly perfumed. She sat hard against me and laid a hand on my lap.

"Your mouse got no house?" she asked.

When I leaned across her to pull the door closed, she nipped my ear, and it hurt. I drove quickly to the Jaybird. She drew cigarettes from my shirt pocket. In light of the neon her lipstick appeared violet.

"Give Alvin my hello and say from Kitten the love doth flow."

"Alvin?" I asked.

"Keeper of the keys and fleas."

I had my wallet back and took my car keys before going into the office where the accommodating young man, Alvin, smiled and had me sign the guest register. For my name I wrote Joshua Howell, used Ashland as my address, and put down a fake license number. When I paid thirty-five dollars plus tax, Alvin presented me the room key. I didn't give him Kitten's message.

"Up steps to your left," Alvin said. "Enjoy your stay at the Jay."

Back at my car, Kitten sang to herself in a tiny voice. When I opened the door, she swung out thin shiny legs and closed arms around my waist. "Your way is my way any way," she sang.

I locked the car as she shifted her large pocketbook to hold my arm and guide me toward the steps. At the bottom were the ice machine and coin dispensers of confections and canned drinks: Hershey bars, potato chips, Dr. Pepper, Life Savers, Coke, packaged cracklings. Cracklings and Dr. Pepper! I thought of Vin's stomach contents.

I followed Kitten up the steps, her hips swinging, her black slick shirt and skirt catching a gleam from yellow bug lights. We walked the deck to the room, where I unlocked the door and stood aside. She knew the location of the lamp switch.

The room, like Alvin at the desk, appeared respectable. No mirror on the ceiling, no vibrator on the bed, no special fixtures in the john. Mediterranean furniture, orange draw drapes at the window, two clean glasses wrapped in plastic, and new cakes of soap above the sink. On a metal platform bolted to the wall a color TV.

Kitten turned up the air conditioning, swung the big pocketbook from her shoulder to the bed, and crossed to the vanity. Before the mirror she drew a finger along an eyebrow little more than a slanted black line. She wore gold bracelets, a gold necklace, and dangling gold earrings. She approached to lay hands on my shoulders and lift her mouth to my throat where she again nibbled, painfully pinching my skin between her tiny teeth.

"No pie, no thigh," she said and removed my sunglasses. She giggled at my eyes.

"What's the fare?" I asked and reached for my wallet. She laid the sunglasses on the vanity and worked her body against mine.

"If this is your basic lay, fifty you pay. You order the special dally, up goes the tally."

I gave her fifty dollars, which left me less than ten. She wadded the money and jammed it carelessly into her bag. Again she pressed to me. I looked at her eyes and saw darkness within darkness. At the very center was a pupil so contracted it was like a black puncture, but erratic, surging and diminishing.

"How we going to fly to the sky without a plane to Jane?" she asked, working her body. For a moment I didn't understand.

"I don't have anything else," I said.

"Surely you stashed some quicker from liquor, boy."

"I meant to buy a pint."

"A pint is not a giant, and Kitten don't become no cat for that." She had let her hands fall away from me and stepped back.

"I'll make you a deal," I said. "You can keep the fifty if you'll just talk to me a few minutes."

She was reaching for the pocketbook, but her face came back fast, a jerk of the head, the electric eyes pulsating, a feral animal.

"I'm writing a book," I said. "All I want is some information from you. We can just sit here and talk and you could rest. You won't even have to take off your clothes."

She came to me and again felt all over my body for a wire. Watching me, she backed off. From her pocketbook she drew what appeared to be a compact with a mother-of-pearl cover, but inside was not face powder but dark-green gelatin capsules striped red. She unwrapped a glass, carried it to the bathroom to fill it, and popped two of the capsules into her mouth before drinking. She then came back and sat on the bed. She crossed her legs and closed her eyes, her expression concentrated like a person listening for a sound in the distance.

I stood waiting. Somewhere along the floor a TV played, and despite the closed room and air conditioning, I still smelled baking bread. Suddenly her hands gripped the ocher coverlet of the bed, her eyes opened wide, and she laughed. She laid a hand on her breast and breathed as if she'd just come up from under water.

"Oh nice, so nice!" she said. "Para...dise...!"

"No notes or anything," I said. "Just a friendly little talk between us about some of the men who come visit you, for the book in which no names will be mentioned, not yours, not anybody's."

"So nice in paradise," she said and giggled. Her hands had clawed into the ocher coverlet but now relaxed. "You skinny, boy, a giraffe, you eat off the ceiling? Don't talk to me about books. I got a regular writer comes to see me, had his picture in the paper and all, teaches at William & Mary, though he ain't hairy." She giggled. "Brings his own heels and panties."

"Your men are mostly white?"

"My boys is toys, everything, all the way from fourteen, a little pink virgin so scared he shook, and an old man on a crutch who just wanted me to parade around and rub it in his face a little. Black, white, yellow, brown, they all go down. Rich man, poor man, beggar man, thief, some got gums, some got teeth. One john brought his wife to watch so she could learn how to do it."

All the while the giggling, the relaxing, her body becoming longer and looser. She recrossed her legs and allowed me to light her cigarette.

"Mostly locals?" I asked, hoping to work my way to Vin.

"I've had New York actors, college boys from Boston, a man who claimed he owned the biggest hog farm in Virginia and laid a thousand-dollar bill across my stomach, people whose language I couldn't even recognize, maybe Russian, and the French owner of a restaurant who liked to be walked on. I didn't have to undress, just stroll around and drop my ashes down."

She flicked cigarette ashes to the floor, and her giggling became more excited. In her hilarity her crossed leg kicked.

"The men who come to see you have more than just the basic lay in mind," I said.

"I'm a girl with a pearl, and the word is heard."

"A specialist."

"Treats is my beat," she said, and she reached to her pocketbook, peered into it like an oriental cat, and teasingly brought out a little whip, two pieces that could be screwed together, both decorated with red-and-white peppermint stripes, the thong white silken strands.

"Men do what Kitten say, little boys best obey."

She turned to the side to lash the sateen coverlet. Again and again she did, the thong hissing and smacking the fabric. As she giggled, she glanced at me to see whether I was joining the fun. She laid the whip on the bed, again slid fingers into the pocketbook, and came up with a bright pair of handcuffs.

"Got to be had when they bad," she said. "Oh, the tunes they sing for the strokes I bring."

She opened the handcuffs, stood to show them to me, and before I realized what she was doing snapped them closed around my wrists.

"Wait just a minute," I said, trying to open the handcuffs, but they weren't for children who wanted to play policeman. They were made of steel. When she approached me again, I believed she was going to take them off, but suddenly she shoved me to the bed. I fell on my back, and before I could struggle up, she was at my feet and fastening a second set of handcuffs around my ankles. I rocked to a sitting position while she stood in front of me and giggled.

"Do what Kitten say or you got to pay," she said.

"I mean it, I don't want any of this."

"You bad, giraffe, bad, bad, bad, and everybody knows bad has to be had."

I was able to rock to my feet and take mincing steps despite the handcuffs around my ankles. Giggling, she reached to my belt and jerked it, spinning me toward her. I tried to pull away, but she loosened the belt and unzipped my seersucker pants, which slid down over my shoes.

"Okay, get business out of the way," she said and stooped for my wallet, took the rest of my money, and stuffed it into her pocketbook.

"I know you probably don't believe me, but I honestly don't want this," I said, feeling the coolness of the air conditioning on my legs. "You see, I have a war wound. I was badly shot up in Nam, and even if I wanted to make love, I couldn't."

"Lay your head on that bed."

"I'm serious. You can keep the money. The money means nothing to me, but I'll have to shout if you don't unlock me. Bring the management."

"Gi-*raffe*," she said, giggling at my legs.

"Somebody'll hear. The police will come. Just free me, keep

the money, and I'll be on my way."

She slapped my face, shoved me onto the bed, and before I could right myself she brought something else from her pocketbook, a straight razor with a pearl handle, the steel blade as clean and cared for as a scalpel. She climbed over me to hold the point at my throat.

"You listen to Momma and listen good or she make you sad and bad. Are you hearing me, dearie?"

Because of the razor I was afraid even to nod and whispered the word "yes."

"I know what you want," Kitten said, astraddle me. "Kitten understands what all you little white mothers' boys like when they come to her. All the little baby men who knock on her door, big little men who own the money and cars and houses and pale runty little wives who can't do nothing for them. The wives got ice in their boxes and need real men to thaw them out, and you bad for not doing that and come to Kitten to be spanked. Don't you move, Jack, from you back, hear?"

As she drew the razor away, I gave the slightest nod. She crawled off and kept the razor held in front of her as she unzipped her boots and kicked them away. Next she worked her black panties over her legs and tossed them to a chair. She lifted the whip.

"You going to beg Kitten 'fore she punishes you?"

"Kitten, I can help you, I know a man, Father Mercy who—"

"I know that God gabber. To his bed the ladies is led, and he's praying while he's laying. No giraffe going to help me. Each day I fly to the sky. Oh, but you rank and got to be spanked."

She held whip and razor in her left hand while with her right she reached to my undershorts and yanked them open. She giggled at what she saw.

"No wonder no woman respect you, you bring that bitty thing," she said and shoved my shirt above my stomach. "Now you bad, hear, bad!"

She pushed my shirt to my neck. The whip swished as it lashed my chest and stomach. The sting was at the edge of real pain. With each stroke she brought the silk thong closer to my genitals, and when she reached them she quickened the action. To my shock, I began to erect.

"You been mean, you feel this thing!" she said and holding

the whip in one hand, the razor in the other, she stepped onto the bed. She moved over me till her feet straddled my head. I looked up her legs beneath her short skirt to her black pelt. Behind herself she whipped at me.

"Boy, you my toy!" she said and jerked up that skirt as she squatted over my face. I clenched my eyes and turned my head, but she settled that spreading perfumed slit on me and worked it.

"Get that thing!" she commanded.

I heard no one enter the room. Wiry pubic hairs rasped my face, riding it, but the rhythm stopped abruptly, and the skirt dragged off me.

She'd risen to turn and look at a black man who was tall and solemn, his long hair curled. He had a moustache and goatee, both finely trimmed. He wore a pink summer suit and vest, a ruffled white shirt, and a broad white hat with a black velvet band. His hands glittered with rings, which were both adornment and weaponry. He carried a pink umbrella.

"Catch the show, Beau?" Kitten asked, but she was afraid.

The man crossed to her, curved spidery fingers to her neck, and hauled her off me and the bed. She stumbled and caught herself on a chair. The man raised his umbrella to twist loose its rubber ferrule. The tip of the umbrella had been sharpened to a spike, which he lowered to my right nipple and held there as he faced Kitten. It pricked the skin, and a bead of blood rose around it.

"I told you nobody you don't know!" he said.

"I check him," she said and reached for her panties. Whip and razor lay on the carpet. "He no man."

"Dumb bitch, you can't even read."

"I can smell man."

"Did you smell the Howell County sticker on his car, bitch? I told you nobody but regulars. And not to call me Beau in front of johns."

She had a leg in her panties, and he slapped her, his hand so fast I heard the blow before I understood. She'd been bent to the panties, and her hair quivered with the violence. She fell, righted herself, and worked the other leg into the panties.

"Give me his wallet!" the man ordered. She extended it to him warily, fearful of being in range of his hand. The man held the wallet with the same fingers gripping the crook of the umbrella, its spike still against my nipple, and one by one he removed cards

from my wallet, studied them, and flipped them over me. Lastly
he tossed the wallet to the bed and increased the spike's pressure.

"Ten seconds to explain your act," he said to me.

I decided to go with the truth. "I'm William Payne, Howell
County's Commonwealth's Attorney, and I'm here trying to gather
information about a man who used to visit Kitten at this motel."

They looked at me as I lay on my back, my knees drawn up.
More blood formed around the umbrella's spike. The man again
slapped Kitten without ever moving his eyes from me. She stumbled
and reached for her razor.

"Bitch, you never learn nothing! I taught you but you quit
listening and started hearing sounds from another band. We needing to do something about you. First we got us a little problem on
the bed."

"Little is right as light," Kitten said. She had picked up the
razor, which she was about to fold into her pocketbook. She crossed
to me and lowered the blade edge to shivering skin between my
navel and pubic area. "Jelly of the belly," she said and delicately
shaved away hairs.

I thought, Pull for service.

"That's enough!" a voice said from back near the door. I couldn't
see past the looming Beau, but I saw obedience on his and Kitten's
faces. Maybe the voice belonged to Alvin, the accommodating desk
clerk. It would explain how Beau got in the room. "Unlock him!"

Kitten closed the razor, dropped it into her pocketbook, and
came up with small keys on a silver ring. First she freed my ankles,
then my wrists. I was still unable to move because Beau hadn't
withdrawn the point of the umbrella from my nipple.

"Get out, Kitten," the voice said, and she zipped up her boots,
unscrewed the whip, and put it and the cuffs into her pocketbook.
Spikes of hair had been knocked askew, causing her face to appear
out of line. She moved away from my vision, but I heard her leave,
the sound of her boots dying on the deck.

"Ask what he wants," the voice said.

I told Beau, who drew the umbrella point down to the center
of my chest. The spike left a thin broken line of blood behind. I
talked into dark, shiny eyes as unblinking as a judging God's. I
explained how Vin Farr had been seen with Kitten and was now
dead. Then I lay waiting. Beau looked toward the doorway.

"Answer him," the voice said.

"Don't sound smart to me," Beau said.

"He knows how close he is to leaving this world," the voice said. "He understands all you need to do is give a little loving push with the umbrella, and he's gone. We could carry him to the river. Ask if he understands that."

"I understand it," I said and felt I was going to wet myself.

"Ask whether he'll deal," the voice said.

"I will," I said.

The umbrella spike eased from my chest, though Beau didn't draw back but stood straighter. His left hand rose to his goatee and stroked it downward. I heard a siren out on the street and thought the police might be coming to rescue me, but the shrill faded. I still smelled Kitten's perfume and the baking bread.

"Your questions," the disembodied voice said.

"Do you know Vincent Farr?" I asked.

"We know he was here," the voice said.

"How did he meet Kitten?"

"She used to work the hotels during sessions of the legislature. He was at the John Marshall."

The John Marshall Hotel was near the capitol, but Vin hadn't served in the legislature for years. Had he been deceiving Rhea that long?

"His relationship with Kitten was a continuing one?" I asked.

"Not so much at first."

"Did she do for him what she was doing to me?"

"It was what he wanted."

"Did Kitten tell you his reasons for coming to her?"

"No reasons needed below the belt," Beau said, stroking the goatee.

"I'll do the answering," the voice said. "He wasn't satisfied at home."

I lay on my back, my pants down, my shirt up, thinking of Vin leaving Riverview, that emerald expanse of lawn and trees, leaving Rhea, the most exciting woman I'd ever known, to drive down here to the Jaybird and immerse himself in the depraved and obscene.

"How often did he visit Kitten?"

"Now and again. He had her number and called ahead of time. They usually kept company several hours. Look, Mr. Payne, we read about Vincent Farr in the papers. Kitten had nothing to do with that. We questioned her, and neither she nor Mr. Farr used drugs that last night. They didn't try anything different. He was drinking, he always did that, but he left the motel before eleven. What happened happened in your county, not here. Further questions?"

"No," I said.

"Do you feel you've been dealt with honestly?"

"Yes."

"If we walk away from this room, will you dress and leave without bringing the police or causing trouble? I want your word."

"Yes."

Beau must have received a nod from the man at the door, for he pulled the pink umbrella away from my chest like a swordsman freeing his saber from a pierced victim. I expected him to take out his handkerchief and wipe off my blood, but it was the rubber ferrule he twisted onto the tip.

"Don't want to see you again, my man," he said and backed toward the door. The other person, whether Alvin or not, had gone. Beau cockily reset his white hat, touched two fingers to the brim in a casual bejeweled salute, and ducked away.

I rolled free from the bed, jerked up my pants, and stumbled to the bathroom. I ran hot water and peeled paper from soap. I washed my face, neck, and chest. I dabbed a corner of the soap into the puncture of my nipple. In hurrying to my car, I broke to my knees only once and righted myself on the Dr. Pepper machine, which glowed as red as panic.

13

Rain at last, a summer squall that blows in during early evening and renews at night. I lie on the cot hearing the rain advance across the swamp, striking the sloughs and birches, tapping the thickened pond, and finally banging the cabin's tin roof. The racket keeps me from sleeping.

Not that I need sleep. I have slept out. I watch lightning lash the blackness and wind whip the landscape. Cattails are beckoning. Thunder is instantaneous with flashings. A tree is hit, groans, and falls. I smell burned wood.

At dawn the low ground is flooded. The millpond has overflowed, leaking its algal spill around wind-blown rushes and elders. I am lucky to have remained dry, for on the floor are puddles. The milkweed which has grown up behind the door thrives in the moisture. It is in flower, its pinkish-white blooms spread for light.

When the sun comes, puddles on the floor dry fast. Birds sing, and dragonflies dart among the rushes. I have a rash from lying so long on the cot. The master has brought me another plastic bottle of skin lotion, which I rub over my body several times a day. The lotion is scented and draws sweat bees.

The master doesn't arrive until late afternoon and wears rubber hip boots, the kind duck hunters use. To hold them up, leather

255

loops are fixed to the belt. The master has brought provisions. After
I exercise, wash, shave, and eat, we have our lesson, which I have
again diligently studied.

Master: What doth every sin deserve at the hands of God?

Me: Every sin, even the least, being against the sovereignty,
goodness, and holiness of God, and against his righteous law, de-
serveth his wrath and curse, both in this life and that which is to
come; and cannot be expiated but by the blood of Christ.

Master: You speak words. Do you believe them in your heart?

Me: I do.

Master: You're too quick to give what I want. I need to hear
your theological thoughts. Don't lie. I won't punish you if you tell
the truth.

God help me, I thought.

Me: Until you I forsook thinking theologically. My views lacked
steadfastness. For a while I was caught up in what I believed was
faith; yet that faith could not withstand the stresses of life. I became
contemptuous of man, considered him stupid and hypocritical in
his search for a God relationship. He built his temples, but God
was always beyond him. God could be there, like the sun is there
and the milkweed yearns for it, but nothing ever reaches the sun.

The master watches through lenses of the yellow shooting glasses
and crosses to the milkweed.

Master: And I saw heaven opened, and behold a white horse;
and he that sat upon him was called Faithful and True, and in
righteousness he doth judge and make war. His eyes were as a flame
of fire, and on his head were many crowns. And he was clothed
with a vesture dipped in blood. And the armies which were in
heaven followed him upon white horses. And out of his mouth
goeth a sharp sword, that with it he should smite the nations. And
he shall rule them with a rod of iron. And he treadeth the winepress
of the fierceness and wrath of Almighty God.

The master reaches to my companion the milkweed, tears it
up from the roots, and tosses it out the doorway.

Master: God plucks.

Me: I understand that now. I know too I have been terribly
confused. Lately I've changed my way of thinking. I've come to
admire man's search for God. It's noble and heroic, and to be
contemptuous of religion is to be contemptuous of all that's best in
man's history and achievement.

I am talking fast, and the master watches with an expression stern and set in judgment. I believe if I throw enough words between us I might insulate and protect myself from this aroused fanaticism.

Me: I have learned here from your instruction. I don't want the wrath of God. Nothing could be more terrible. The greatest love one person can show another is to save him from that. I think of an eternity of fire, of flames crackling forever, of pain and agony without ceasing, of screams and bursting flesh. Anyone saved from those has been given the greatest gift of all. I want God's love!

The master removes the shooting glasses and crosses to the cot, where I sit trembling. The master raises my chin before leaning down to kiss my mouth.

————

Still feeling disordered and tainted the morning after returning from Richmond and the Jaybird Motel, I doctored my chest with Merthiolate and arranged to have my father moved from the Bannister hospital to a treatment center for alcoholics in Danville. I couldn't wait sixty days to receive VA approval.

My father no longer spoke. When I entered his room at the hospital, he turned away his face. As attendants pushed him down the ambulance ramp, he tried to escape from the wheelchair, and they were forced to strap him onto a stretcher.

The center was named Land of Goshen Lodge, a cluster of cottages under yellow pines. A paved drive led to a clinic of brick and glass. Each cottage had six men or women in it, a nurse counselor, and a game room with card tables, Ping-Pong, and TV.

My father was locked in a private room that had bars shaped like wild vines over the window. I looked through a peephole in a white door to see him lying face down on his bed, his nose pressed into the pillow as if he hoped it would block his breathing.

"He'll adjust," Dr. Randolph said. Dr. Randolph was a woman, a stout brunette who wore a white smock and modern glasses, the frames indigo and slanted at the corners like an oriental. They made me think of Kitten and the Jaybird. "We'll keep him medicated till he's ready for therapy. The men learn to rely on each other, to draw strength from collective support."

I made financial arrangements with the business office. The charges were more a month than I netted as Commonwealth's Attorney. I'd need a loan from the bank. I drove to Tobaccoton, climbed to my office, and told Florene no interruptions before closing my door and sitting at my desk.

I'd had another call from Burley Speas at the Bannister *Bee & Messenger*. He was still after me for the exclusive on Vin and becoming even more disappointed and impatient that I had nothing to give him.

Pickney entered puffing, his boots and uniform legs wet. "We sighted Eddie Blue trying to break out the swamp, hiding in a slough, just his head up and he paddling through the reeds. Hounds got wind of him. We chased him back, but he bound to come out sometime. I left deputies and hounds down there."

When Pickney had gone, I felt guilt for not telling him or phoning Captain Blake about events at the Jaybird. To reveal anything would be humiliating to Rhea and myself, yet I was withholding evidence. Still I had made a promise to Alvin, if it were Alvin. But a contract made under the duress of a spiked umbrella was neither valid nor enforceable. I held hands before my eyes. Jaybird tremors still lived in my fingers.

"I told you no calls," I said when Florene tapped on the door.

"Mrs. Farr," she said and looked at me in such a manner I knew there was more talk around town concerning Rhea and me. I picked up the phone, and as soon as I heard Rhea's voice, everything bad dropped away.

"I have negotiated the purchase of a leg of lamb," she said. "I want you to know I don't usually call men I have dinner with."

She asked me to come to Riverview at seven. I left the office early to drive to Bannister and The Hub to buy myself a new seersucker suit, which I talked the woman who did alterations into fixing immediately. I bought new shoes, a new shirt, and new socks. When I reached home, I found I had no clean underwear, so I washed out a change and dried it by ironing it in the kitchen. I went through my elaborate rituals of shaving and anointing myself with Pinaud's Lilac Vegetal. Ten times I stood before the mirror. No tripping on anything tonight.

I was ready forty minutes ahead of time. I tried to read the Richmond paper, but words were like bugs on the page. I shaved again. Finally I drove back through town and stopped at the light. Nobody was on the sidewalk except Uncle Daniel, who paraded his sign through the last grinding heat of day. His legs moved with slow steadiness.

At seven exactly I turned in at Riverview, made the circle in front of the house, and left my car on the white gravel. Rhea herself opened the front door. Her sleeveless coral dress with its V-neck set off her tan. Again she wore no jewelry except her wedding and engagement rings. She was cool elegance.

She took my hand, and I believed she would offer her cheek to me, or maybe I should have leaned to her, but the moment was awkward, and she disengaged the hand to lead me through the parlor to the terrace. It was as I had pictured it: on the clean flagstones a round white table covered with a linen cloth; two chairs; and a silver tray, holding bottles, ice, and glasses, which had been wheeled out on an antique tea cart. Around Rhea's neck I spotted the fine gold chain of the tiny cross hanging inside her dress.

"We'll catch a breeze from the river," she said. "At least we will if the mosquitoes don't eat us alive, though I had the area fogged."

I smelled a faint odor of insecticide as well as the scent of her perfume. She offered me a drink, and I'd already decided to have just one in order to show her my control. I watched her sure fingers crab up and drop ice cubes into the two cocktail glasses. Each had a broad silver rim and horsehead on it, stallions. There were also white knitted boots to fit the bottoms of the glasses.

We sat looking over the stone railing and beds of red and blue verbena to the lawn and river. Sprinklers twirled curls of water to grass that had been freshly mowed. The air was fruity with the rich moist smell of earth. The sun had shed most of its yellowness, the rays long now, baffled by willows at the river's edge, allowing only bars of light to lie across the darkening flow.

Melissa in uniform carried out hors d'oeuvres on a silver platter. I thought how much of Riverview was silver. I'd eaten caviar in my Richmond days of glory, but never anything better than this spicy cheese served on tiny buttered biscuits with bacon chips and slivers of mushroom. I again thought of myself as master of this house and making love to Rhea in the perfumed silkiness of her hushed white-and-rose bedroom.

"What is it?" she asked.

"A thought, nothing important."

"You were smiling."

Melissa served vichyssoise, lamb, vegetables. In the dusk she
also lit the white candles and lowered hurricane chimneys around
them, though the quiet air did not even tilt the flames. Rhea talked
of her horses, particularly the weanlings, this year's crop—three
fillies and two colts.

"One mare aborted," she explained. "Rhinopneumonitis."

I grasped only bits of her equine talk. I was again thinking of
Vin, how he could have betrayed this lovely place and woman for
the depravity of the Jaybird and Kitten. I smiled for Rhea, nodded,
spoke a yes or no, but I was also attempting to comprehend, though
I didn't wish to share this night with Vin.

He wouldn't stay in his grave. I thought of the photographs
he'd taken, enlarged, and hung on walls of his basement office.
Nothing further to be learned from them now that I understood
about the inkless tattoo incisions made by razor in Kitten's gleeful,
agitated fingers. Yet my mind wouldn't let the photographs rest.

"I'm planning a riding clinic for local children," Rhea said.
"In conjunction with the county agent and the 4-H. Invite them
for the day, feed them lunch, attempt to teach the rudiments of
horsemanship."

Melissa brought dessert, a chocolate mousse topped by a cherry.
Green of the lawn had given way to darkness. Fireflies rose and
glowed. The river was only a blacker gleaming where frogs began
to sound, the great bulls whose ba-romp boomed over water like
warring bass drums. Cattle lowed, and from the stables came neigh-
ing and the halfhearted barking of a hound.

Such peace, I thought. Such grace and style. I am sitting here
with Rhea, and she treats me as if I'm worthy of her. I had to keep
reminding myself to believe it. Melissa served us coffee in delicate
gold-rimmed porcelain cups. I looked across the table at Rhea.
Would she expect me to make a move on her, take her hand, lead
her to her silken scented bed?

"I visited Vin's mother at the nursing home, and the nurse,
Miss Bosley, told me you'd been by," Rhea said.

"A hope, groundless, that I might learn something," I said,
and even as I spoke I remembered the woman dealing snapshots
like cards across her lap. I also remembered she kept no pictures
of Rhea in that room.

Something else clicked. I knew what it was that had been

bothering me about the photographs down in Vin's basement office. None was of Rhea. I was positive of it.

And the wallet found by Hawthorn on the power line. Again no pictures of Rhea, though Vin carried snapshots of the farm, old cars, and his biplane—a glossy of his Stearman trainer but not his wife.

"You're getting that fretted expression," Rhea said, her face ivory in candlelight.

"I was thinking about horses," I lied. "Can adults attend your clinic?"

"You I'll give private instructions to," she said and laughed, her teeth catching the flame's gleam. I should have been soaring but felt I had to work out the puzzle of the photographs.

Rhea excused herself to speak with Melissa. I stood smoking at the stone railing and looking toward the river, which could no longer be seen for darkness. I strolled to the French window that opened into the parlor. Over the fireplace was the lighted painting of Rhea's mother. They shared a correctness of carriage, a ramrod posture, perhaps the conformation necessary to bear the burden of old family and primacy.

The tiny gold cross hung from her neck. I stepped closer and saw something else. About the upraised wrist of her hand steadying the beribboned garden hat was a bracelet. I needed something to step on and glanced at the white satin prie-dieu holding *The Sculptor's Hand*. I couldn't use the prie-dieu, but what was it doing here? I felt the area in front of the painting was like the altar of a chapel.

I drew up a leather footstool, positioned it, and climbed on to peer at the bracelet. A silver chain with pendants. Were the pendants figures, and the figures angels?

I heard Rhea calling. Quickly I stepped down, slid the footstool back to the wing chair, and walked out to the terrace, where I almost bumped into her.

"What were you doing?" she asked.

"Admiring your mother," I said, dryness of my throat causing my voice to sound harsh.

"Sovereign lady, isn't she?" We moved toward the portrait illuminated at the top by a bulb in a tubular brass shade. It was the only light in the parlor, resulting in dimming and loss of all else in the room. "I sometimes come here and gaze at her. How she could sit a horse! I used to watch her cantering in on her mare.

I was happy I never had to compete with her."

With a last look at the portrait, she took hold of my arm, and we walked back to the terrace and our chairs. She blew out the candles, and after my eyes adjusted I was able to see the river, a denser line in the darkness below the willows. The land pulsated with night insects. Great frogs beat the drum. Across the river a pack of hounds bayed in giving chase. I thought of Eddie Blue slogging through the swamp in frantic escape.

"Melissa's gone," Rhea said. "We have the place to ourselves."

Her face and form were enveloped by night so I couldn't make out her expression, but her words were definitely an invitation. I should've stood and crossed around the table to her; yet I was thinking about the bracelet. Not necessarily angels. My throat felt tight. A plane flew over, its red lights blinking. I sensed her waiting.

"You've become very quiet," she said.

"Rhea, when I came here tonight, I intended to put Vin out of my mind."

"So serious you are."

To gain a moment and order my thinking, I lit a cigarette. In the match's glow she sat with legs crossed, hands on her lap. I coughed to clear my throat.

"He was a fine photographer who took hundreds of pictures," I said. "Yet I haven't seen the first one of you."

For a moment she didn't speak.

"He did take pictures of me and hang them around the house, but when he died, I removed them. I didn't want to look at myself being happy."

"You took them down right after he died?"

"You think it's so strange a grieving woman would roam the night lifting them from walls of her house? When you can't sleep and are near hysteria, you'll do anything. I felt my life was over and there was no use keeping pictures around meaningless to anyone else."

"What'd you do with them?"

"You are pressing," she said, and though I couldn't see her face, I felt her displeasure. "I carried them to the pile behind the stable and burned them with Vin's clothes."

"Frames and all?"

"Frames and all. Should I have saved the frames? What would I do with them? I can get a flashlight if you'd like to sift the ashes."

"No ashes, Rhea, and I guess I've just about ruined it for us tonight."

"Yes, I'd judge you pretty nearly have."

"So I might as well go on with it. There were no pictures of you in Vin's wallet or his mother's room at the Magnolia home."

"If you visited her, as I believe you did, you had to notice there's no person in her life except Vin. No mere woman could be good enough for him, not even a Gatlin. Vin's mother would consider the royal princess beneath her son."

"I was looking at the portrait of your mother."

"Is that why you came tonight, to snoop?"

"I came because I love you," I said and realized I'd been able to speak the words without the world lurching.

"Rather a change of pace there, Billy boy. What about the portrait?"

"I happened to notice the bracelet on her wrist."

"Her salvation bracelet, given to her at her confirmation by her mother, the bracelet with little angels. It's been in the family a hundred years."

"Is an angel missing?"

"Why?"

"One, I believe it's Gabriel, was found near Vin's body."

"I don't think so, unless Vin—" She stopped speaking and sat forward to clasp her hands. A breeze was moving up from the river now, causing the willows to rustle.

"Vin what?" I asked.

"Do we really have to delve into this? Can't we just let him go in peace?"

She stood, came around the table, and reached down to draw me up. She was almost as tall as I. I moved my mouth to hers awkwardly, but her body took charge, her arms strong against my back, her shape pushed into an astonishing fit fronting mine. I was dizzy with the sensation and holding to her. She moved her forehead to mine.

"I'm very fond of you, Billy. You're one of the truly nice people I know, and I think as I heal from Vin there will be a life ahead for us. But if you're not careful, we mightn't be able to come back to this point."

I stood trying to switch off my mind.

"I want you to make love to me," she said. "Now, in this

house, in my bedroom. Think you can manage that?"

She drew her face away to look at me, though we still held each other. My fingers touched her warmth through the fabric of her summer dress, my nose was full of her clean scent, and my vision again expanded to the life of a country gentleman, the farm, children playing on the lawn. No more drunkenness in an unkept grape arbor where I sailed boats I'd never own across turquoise seas to shimmering islands that never were.

Yet I felt wooden, inarticulate, as my throat closed just as it had in a Richmond courtroom, choking off the brilliant future of a young man who'd made the highest SAT scores of any student graduated from the Howell County Consolidated High School. Rhea knew.

"All right," she said and released me. "If you must unearth family skeletons. Vin had a side people weren't familiar with."

I followed her into the house, where lamps were stained globes in darkness. Maybe she'd turned down those lights for me. I was rueful and walked clumsily. I'd undoubtedly wrecked it for us, taken us past the moment when we could've reached across loneliness, touched, and joined.

She switched on the chandelier in the front hall so we could climb the steps with their rose carpeting and graceful curved railing. The chandelier sent out not a wash of light through crystal teardrops but pale gold speckles that shifted on white plaster walls. Rhea neither glanced back at me nor hurried. I trailed her, eyeing the hips and aristocratic legs, the elegant body so honestly offered, which now I'd not have.

We walked the second-story hall past the closed door of Vin's room to hers, the warm pinkness of femininity, the white tester bed with its frills, the rose drapes hanging to the floor, a white dressing table where lampshades too were rose, that color shading into walls to create an aura like the interior of an oyster shell.

"I did all I could to protect him," she said and crossed to the dressing table, where she opened a drawer to lift out a red leather jewelry case. The golden latch snapped up, and when she raised the case's lid, rings, brooches, and earrings were revealed on tiers of black velvet. She fingered into the bottom of the case to find the bracelet.

"His habits couldn't be controlled, and he was in mortal danger," she said.

She extended the silver bracelet to me: Michael and his flaming sword, Raphael strumming a harp, Uriel experiencing rapture, but there was an empty mooring and no Gabriel.

"Danger how?" I asked, turning to her from the lamp where I'd leaned to inspect the bracelet.

"I didn't want to have to show you this," she said, and I only glimpsed the second item taken from the drawer. She gripped my arm to move me back from the mirror in which I did see descending what she'd lifted, another of the family heirlooms, this one her father's, the leather dark and oiled, the stitching neat and decorative, the weapon limber—Blackjack's blackjack.

14

"I saved him," she says.

Rhea and I lie on the cot covered by the swarmy heat of late afternoon, our arms about each other, our faces cheek to cheek, my nose shoved into fragrance of her hair. We do not remove our clothes but embrace as if for us there is nothing else to hold to in this world.

"This is the way it should be," she says. Aroused, I try to kiss her breasts through the soft pink broadcloth shirt, but she stops me by pressing her palms against my temples and bringing me back.

"Not now," she says. "When we've worked things out."

Work things out. Is that what we're doing as we lie tangled in the August heat which drifts through the crooked doorway like a dog's hot breath? We hear crows, woodpeckers, the cries of hawks, always the locusts. Whispering, we fit ourselves, though I know I must start thinking straight and consider realities; yet I've never felt such ease and lassitude. I forget the chain around my ankle.

"I loved Vin," she says at my ear, her voice low and distant, as if she's not actually speaking words but merely forming them with her lips and exhaling lazily. "I loved him too much, a heritage of the Dillon women. But I saved him."

The Dillon women, her mother and that family from down in Yancey County, women who in generations past honored the Confederate dead not only once a year on Lee's birthday, but monthly by placing flowers at the base of the Johnny Reb infantryman forever treading the courthouse lawn, a ritual as solemn and sanctified as the taking of the wafer and drinking from the chalice.

"My mother used to tell me it was a failing of the Dillon women to love too deeply," Rhea says, her cheek rubbing mine. "So lovely she was, yet she had the Dillon strength. Horses knew, the rogues. They felt her in the saddle and understood there was no nonsense here. She would've faced a charging lion."

We shift our bodies slightly, and the cot squeaks under us. I see strands of hair curl into her scalp. She speaks against the skin of my neck.

"My father always stood for her," she says. "She never crossed through a room that he didn't stand. They treated each other with elaborate politeness. She had such presence she could've gone on the stage, but she would never have made herself public. The Dillon women didn't do that anymore than they would've appeared in church without hats."

We move our legs to remesh them. She has taken off her boots and socks and set them on the cabin floor. She runs the edge of a foot along the inside of my free ankle. Her yellow shooting glasses and the pistol she has left on the table.

"My father had a reputation for hardness at the bank," she says. "He was that way because when he inherited Riverview from his father, there wasn't much cash money. He had to hold the bank together and the farm. He kept his word and forgave no one who didn't. No man ever faced him down."

Not with the blackjack they knew he carried, the one she handled so expertly in the oyster pinkness of her bedroom.

"At first I didn't understand about my mother," Rhea says. "It was always my father I ran after, who rode with me in front of him on his saddle when he inspected fences or drove me to the bank where I sat on a stool beside his desk as he did business. He took me to lunch at the General Johnston, and all the men came by the table to speak to me as if I were a grown lady. I believed him the closest thing to God on this earth."

As we lie there, something comes into her, a transformation from softness, as if the femininity were replaced by muscle and

WILLIAM HOFFMAN

bone. She is no less gentle with me, her voice remains calm; yet she is not the same woman.

"I rode out one afternoon on Cherub, my pony, given to me by my father. Instead of staying on trails he'd ordered cut for me through the woods, I followed a path among the pines, a deer trail I believed until it came out at a tenant house on the place. The house needed whitewash and had weeds, yuccas, and honeysuckle growing around the porch. I meant to lead Cherub to the well and draw a bucket of water, but I heard somebody in the house. When I stopped to listen, I recognized my father's voice.

"He walked onto the porch and lit a cigar. He wore riding breeches, a blue shirt with a black tie, and a hat. Even in farm clothes he always appeared formal. I still stood at the edge of the woods and would've called to him, but he glanced into the cabin, and a black woman came out. She was barefoot and had on a flimsy little red dress over her shameless body. She held something, money I saw, dollar bills my father had given her.

"I knew by sight all the tenants at Riverview because on Fridays they came to the house for their pay. My father sat at a card table under the portico, consulted his ledger, and counted out the bills and coins. I'd seen the woman there and working in the fields. She flirted with every man she met."

I think of Old Ben's sister, Leona Poindexter, and what my father told me of Blackjack's sporting with black women. I wonder how many other half sisters and brothers of a dusky race Rhea has.

"When my father saw me, he began giving the woman orders to get the bucket and broom to clean the place. He pretended he brought her there to fix things up so he could rent it. He stepped down from the porch and came through the weeds. 'How's my lady today?' he asked, and as he hugged me, I smelled that black woman's perfume on him, the orange-blossom kind his little store on the highway sold from dusty glass cases along with Ingersoll watches and toenail clippers."

I feel the disturbance in Rhea, the hardening of her body, and I tighten my hold on her. I lay my lips against her temple. I think of the gun on the table, but I don't move. I taste the saltiness of her skin.

"That night at dinner I watched him with my mother. He treated her with respect and politeness, and he joked with me, saying he'd seen a jackrabbit chased by a hoop snake rolling down a slope behind the stable. I kept looking at my beautiful mother and wondering whether she could know.

"The next afternoon I rode Cherub to my father's store, an unpainted frame building with one gasoline pump and a rusty tin overhang. He'd had it built for his tenants, a place where they could buy seed and salt on credit. He carried them till crops came in. He was rarely there himself, a black man named Allan ran it, and on hot days I'd tie Cherub's bridle to a post and go inside to buy a nickel bag of candy and a soda. I'd share the candy and soda with Cherub, who liked to lift his head and drink straight from the bottle."

I remember the store and tenants. During Vin's time, the store closed and gradually fell in on itself. Most tenants are long gone. Vin brought machinery and efficiency to Riverview.

"Riding home from the store, I followed the trail through the woods and met the black woman. She was dallying along in the shade, her hands behind her, humming. She wore that skimpy red dress, and her body was developed in ways no decent white woman's ever is. We looked at each other as we passed, and she smiled and spoke to me.

"I didn't speak to her. She went on toward the road and the store. A farm wagon with blacks on it rolled by, and they hollered to her. She waved and laughed. I waited in the pines till she came back. Then I rode at her. I had a little leather crop my father had given me, and I galloped Cherub at her and tried to beat her. She was frightened and ran behind trees, calling, 'Child! Child!' and finally she pushed me off Cherub to protect herself, but I threw rocks at her, chased her along the path throwing rocks and pine cones and her crying, 'Child! Child!'"

Rhea breathes hard as she relives the memory. Her eyes wide, she stares across the years.

"I walked home that afternoon. Cherub had run on, and when I reached Riverview my mother was about to send out and look for me. I had a place I hid, in the low ground behind the stable, a grove of birches with a little branch running through it. I'd creep in under the vines. That's where I fled, where I lay on the moss and wanted to die.

"I heard my mother calling. She came down from the stable wearing her lemon dress and hat. She had on white gloves. I lay looking at her through the leaves and thought her the most beautiful woman in the world, all I wanted to be when I grew up. She must've known about my hiding place, though she pretended not to. She acted as if she'd just accidentally spotted me, shielding her eyes with a hand to peer into shadows. 'Rhea, dear, is that you?'"

I remember when we in Howell County thought of gentility, we pictured Rhea's mother. At Christmas she gave away new silver dollars to those who sang carols at Riverview's door. She possessed the style of a woman from another time and place.

"She had to stoop and touch her fingers to the ground to reach me, and I didn't cry until she sat and put an arm around me. 'What's the matter with my darling?' she asked, and I never cried so much. I thought I was going to cry my life out. She held me and rocked me, all the while singing a wordless tune she'd made up in the nursery. Her voice was sweet and gentle, and she stroked my hair and rubbed my back. 'You going to be brave and tell Mother what's the matter?' she asked.

"I could only look up into her face and let her see into me, all the way in, like a stream to the bottom. She did see, and I believed she too was going to cry. But she held me tight and said, 'We are the Dillon women, you, I, my mother, and hers, and we are very strong. It used to be told in Yancey County that the Dillon women would put their hands through fire for their families. That's what we have in us, little Rhea, you and I, that strength of the Dillons. It's my gift to you, and if you ever bear a daughter, it will be your gift to her.'"

I envision it as I lie holding Rhea, the hand coming through fire, the fingers graceful, feminine, the white palm deflecting flames, yet no cry of suffering. I also see a little girl and her mother wearing white gloves in a hutch of woods, each holding the other and rocking among ferns, moss, and a pure running stream.

"She told me there are humiliations women must endure, have always had to endure. Men can't help weakness, some can't, those really alive can't, but for women it's opportunity to be brave and show strength. 'God expects it of women,' she said, 'and I have borne it for years. You should never think your father doesn't love us. Oh, he does and would rush forward to give his life to protect us, but he suffers the weakness, and we Dillon women are strong enough to bear it, aren't we, my little Rhea, who is having to learn before her time.'"

Rhea stops talking and is crying. I lie holding her, seeing pores of her temple, thinking it was too much to have a father and then a husband driven not simply by lust for other women but for the traditional lowest of the low, for blacks. I remember *Rainy Day on Cornelia Street*, the interracial sex, and understand the real reason we walked out of the play. I kiss her forehead and wait, knowing at the last we will get to Vin.

She sits on the side of the cot and rubs lotion over my chafed skin. I love feeling her fingers. I think of her graceful hands in white gloves. Nothing is as beautiful as the arch and give of a woman's fingers dispensing kindness.

"You can take off the chain," I tell her. "I won't run."

She doesn't answer but stands to set the plastic bottle of lotion beside her pistol and shooting glasses on the table. We eat together now, sitting across from each other, though I stay chained. She is considering what to do. I ask about my father.

"He's still a patient at the Land of Goshen Lodge," she says. "Don't worry about the bills. So much money comes in. The lawyers and bankers keep finding it. Vin had business interests all over the state. Not a day passes checks don't arrive."

"Did the police question you?"

"Sheriff Pickney and Captain Blake. I told them we had dinner and you left early. They found your car, which I'd driven into a ditch on a back road west of Tobaccoton. I wore gloves to keep my fingerprints off the wheel and ran back through the woods."

We sleep, we wake, and again she speaks of her mother:

"The Sunday after I found out about my father she died. I sat beside her in the church. With her last breath she had words for me. She said, 'Believe in God's goodness and I'll always be with you.' She has been with me. Every night and day. I could talk to her. I still can."

I think of the mother's lighted portrait, the prie-dieu before it, the feeling of altar and chapel which pervades the parlor.

She exercises me. She has me carry the chair out by the well so she can cut my hair. When I ask how much longer she intends to keep fastening me to the millstone, she repeats that she is preparing a place for me.

"The basement at Riverview is being fixed," she says. "What was Vin's office and studio. You'll have a bath, kitchenette, a TV."

"You'll keep me locked underground?"

"Something must be done before fall. You'll need a warm place. The basement has heat and a sun lamp. Billy, I'm working this out as best I can. Try to be patient."

Though I am again alarmed, we lie on the cot, the shifting of our bodies, the fit, familiar. I smell skin lotion and her perfume. Locusts shrill around the cabin, a rising and falling sea. As long as I am holding her, I feel quiet and secure.

"I saw Vin pole-vaulting," she whispers. "I was on spring break from Saint Catherine's. I drove a little car my father gave me on my sixteenth birthday and passed Howell County High, where they were hosting a track meet. Everybody was cheering and seemed to be having so much fun. I parked by the wire fence around the athletic field.

"Vin was ready to make his run at the bar. I knew who he was but had never seen him in his white track shorts and black shoes. He sprang up and up into the sun, and right at the top he looked at me. Everybody shouted, and before he dropped out of the sun he stared at me as if to declare he'd done it just for me."

I remember Vin's beauty not only on the track field but also simply walking along a school corridor or dumping his books into his locker. He could make adjusting his sweater an act that would cause other students to pause and watch, as if the world were affected by the position of the pullover's roll above his hips.

"He telephoned that night," Rhea says. "Wanted me to go dancing at Waterside. I'd never been to a dance with a local boy. I left the phone off the hook while I went downstairs to ask my father, who was in the den reading his Richmond paper. 'The Farrs are good people and pay their bills, but I don't think you ought to encourage any familiarity there,' he said and shook out the paper.

"Finally he allowed me to go, though when Vin arrived in a washed-and-waxed pickup, he had to stand inspection before my father, who looked him over the way he might a head of stock. He gave Vin instructions—don't exceed the speed limit, no drinking, have my daughter home by eleven. It was the only date I had with Vin that year. He was a good dancer, very formal, and so proud of being with me. The glare he gave other boys kept them from breaking in. I wanted him to hold me even closer then he did."

I remember Vin dancing with her after they married, when Jeannie and I were still together, how on the ballroom floor Rhea wearing a gold lamé gown and Vin in tails had shamed our woodenness with their bold gliding style. Always other dancers left space around them.

"Then he went to war," she says. "He became a pilot because, in his mind, flying was the hardest, most heroic thing to do. I was a sophomore at Sweet Briar and hadn't seen him for months. He turned up on a Saturday afternoon wearing his Air Force uniform. I broke a date with a Saint Elmo from the university to drive with Vin to a Lynchburg movie. Afterwards we sat in his car, he kissed me very correctly, and said he hoped I'd write him in Vietnam.

"I wrote once a week. He answered in his neat engineer's script and sent snapshots of himself and his planes. I grew used to those letters. Vin was good then, innocent, sweet. I thought of him as a little boy with a deadly toy in a big war.

"When he came back, I was out of college and showing horses on the circuit. He appeared wearing his major's uniform, a full man now, his face and body filled out, no longer afraid of anything, not even my father, who suddenly looked smaller to me, as if his clothes fit badly. He didn't want me to marry Vin. He believed some gentry would appear to carry me off. In Daddy's thinking, nobody in Howell County was good enough because everyone was below the Gatlins. He growled and rumbled, but it didn't scare Vin. Vin had killed men I guess and was learning he possessed a talent for money. He wouldn't back down.

"I went to Daddy and told him when Vin proposed. My father and I'd been growing apart for years. He must've hated what I knew about him, what I learned that afternoon years before when I caught him with the black woman in the tenant house. Our relationship was correct, but we'd stopped kissing and embracing. I could love him, and did, yet never the way I loved my mother. 'You going to defy me?' he asked, and though angry, he was unable to meet my eyes more than a moment. He threw up his hands and let them slap his sides.

"I had to make arrangements for my own wedding. Daddy sulked or drank at the barn. He didn't want to give me away. On the afternoon of the ceremony he tried to pretend he was sick. As we walked down the aisle, his hands shook, and during the reception he went up to his room with a bottle and closed the door."

I remember the wedding when I stood in Saint Andrew's balcony beneath the vaulted ceiling, up with the black servants from Riverview. I wasn't envious of Vin in his gray cutaway and cravat,

had not even thought life unfair for endowing some with more
beauty, talent, and intelligence than others. I felt it right they should
marry, and as I watched Rhea at the altar, her face veiled and misty
in candlelight, she seemed to have a spiritual, nunlike quality as if
we weren't in Tobaccoton at all but some ancient Spanish cathedral
where blood and royalty had gathered for a coronation.

"Yet Daddy wanted us to live at Riverview," she says. "Vin
wouldn't allow it. He insisted on a small house in town paid for
with his own money, two bedrooms and one bath. Each day I'd
drive to the stables to school the horses. Daddy was always trying
to slip me money and couldn't believe I didn't need or want it. In
his way he was attempting to buy me back. With Momma gone too
he became very dejected. Finally he and Vin struck a deal whereby
we would have a separate part of the big house and he would live
in a wing.

"That summer Daddy was gored by Thunder King Maker. He
loved his white-faced bull and would walk out to the pasture anytime
to lay hands on Thunder's muzzle. He'd do it for guests while they
sat around on the terrace drinking. Daddy liked to lead Thunder
up and brag about his potency and get. Then one hot evening he
crossed the pasture carrying his drink and didn't come back for
supper. I went after him. I believed he was just sitting under the
hackberry tree resting and watching the herd. He was already dying,
his white suit spreading crimson. He took off his hat to me before
closing his eyes."

I remember the funeral, when people came in from Richmond,
the legislators, the governor, the military. Gatlins were drawn all
the way from the Kentucky coal fields to the lush South Carolina
savannas. Men who never spoke a word to Blackjack felt him one
of themselves because he was Howell County. They stood on parched
grass around Saint Andrew's unable to hear the preaching but truly
sorrowing, knowing without verbalizing that a portion of their heritage had departed, a way of life, the last of a rural elite they both
feared and respected.

"Vin began running Riverview then," Rhea says. "We never
considered selling the place. He'd learned to love it and put his
mind to it. He set up new methods of bookkeeping and operating.
Things began to pay as they never had for Daddy.

"Oh, Billy, I loved Vin so much in those days. You don't know
how much. I don't think it's possible for a man to love the way a

woman does. I understand it can be wonderful or terrible for a man but never the sun coming up and the air and very breath of the body. I'd look out a window and see him returning from the fields driving his pickup, his khakis sweaty, his arms bare, and he came together with the Gatlins and Riverview in such a way I was struck dumb by my love for him."

She cries a while and touches the back of a hand to her nose. Then she breathes deeply as if righting herself.

"And I saved him," she says.

Because she is to be gone two days, she brings extra food and water. Bank trust officers in Richmond need her to decide questions concerning the distribution of income and the sale or retention of property.

"Do your exercises without me," she says.

While she is away, I sleep and study my lesson. We still have lessons. I don't object, they keep my mind functioning in an attempt to understand the strange syntax and unrelenting condemnation of man: "The imperfection of sanctification in believers ariseth from the remnants of sin abiding in every part of them, and the perpetual lusting of the flesh against the Spirit; whereby they are often foiled with temptation and fall into many sins, are hindered in all their spiritual services, and their best works are imperfect and defiled in the sight of God."

I must have the lesson straight before the hardness goes out of her and she will lie beside me. She is religiously infected and feverish. At the slightest theological deviation, lavender flames lap at her eyes, yet I would rather be chained and have my arms around her than a free man. I should be making plans, plotting, but I lie unresisting and listen for her. She holds me even when gone.

And she has yet to tell me what happened to Vin. She is preparing the soil, I feel that. She has to be connected to his death, but I cannot think it through as to how. I will wait till the words come on her breath.

I stand by the cot to exercise not because she has ordered it but because I will not betray her belief in me. I lift my arms to the horizontal and circle them forward and in reverse. I perform knee bends and run in place, the slap of my feet spinning old dust upward and jarring a dirt dauber's nest loose from a ceiling beam. Mud cracks apart on floorboards.

During my afternoon nap, I picture Rhea and myself leaving
Riverview in a Buick to attend church. With us we have our young
son William. We wear our Sunday best and sit in our pew nodding
and smiling to the approving people around us. Very respectable
we are. At the doorway we shake the preacher's hand, and he says,
"Thank you for your generous contribution to the organ fund."

When I open my eyes, I think it is evening the light is so dim.
A cloud passing over the sun, but no rain falls. The swamp has
quieted and stays hushed till the sun returns hot and fast as a knife
stroke. All life starts again.

I sit on the cot's edge, drink tea from the thermos, and look
out the doorway. I believe movement I see among rushes is some
deflection of light caused by a blown bough. The contradiction is
that no air moves. It is not even air but atmosphere so heavy and
humid that chunks could be axed and stacked.

An animal, I think. I hold up my thermos and offer to share
tea with him. "Come on, Mr. Fox," I call. "Or you, Mr. Coon."
Before I again lie down, I rub lotion on myself. Resting, I think of
Rhea crossing the lawn at Riverview to watch foals in the paddock,
the spring crop who prance and play while patient mares eye them
and swish their tails. I smile to myself.

Again the afternoon darkness, but this time it's no cloud. It's
Eddie Blue holding a broken limb like a club and ready to swing
down at me. He is shoeless, shirtless, his jeans torn and rank with
scum and stink of the swamp. Long tangled hair strings over his
bearded face. His blackness is misshapen by stings and welts of
insects which had fed on him till he's pitted. He's clawed himself
to scabs. Blood has crusted in his snarled beard.

The club uplifted, his deadly jet eyes burn at me, the chain,
the millstone. He spies the food on the table and lunges to it. He
snatches bread one-handed and shoves it into his mouth till his
cheeks bulge. Next potato chips, a whole tomato, a Hershey bar,
the latter still wrapped. He spews out paper.

He is thin and coated with swamp muck nearly as dark as his
skin. Scratches run blood. His feet are wet, and each time he moves
they leave imprints on the floor. As he eats, he burps, and food
dribbles from his swollen lips. He catches it in a palm to cram it
back. He belches and grabs the thermos of tea. When he drinks,
the tea overflows his mouth and streams down his body. He reaches

for more bread. The force of his chewing causes thick muscles of his face to coil and twist.

All the while he glares at me and holds the club. He finishes the food, drinks the last of the tea, and belches like an animal roaring pain. He rubs his eating hand against wiry clotted hair of his chest. He bangs the club against the table.

"Who around here beside you?"

"Nobody."

"Don't tell me no tales now." He looks at the chain and millstone. "You somebody's dog?"

"Eddie, you can help me, I can help you."

"Help you?" He snarls laughter. "Lawyer man, I thinking of playing a tune on your roof." He approaches me, holds the club with both hands, and raises it over my head. He brings it down quickly but stops just as it touches my hair.

"I'll go to the authorities and plead for you," I say. "I'll tell the judge you've been treated unfairly. Get you probation instead of jail. I'll help you find a job."

He stares, and a long growl rises from deep within him. Crumbs and spill have lodged around his mouth and in his beard. His body is rancid with the stench of the putrid swamp. Again he lifts his club and lowers it to my hair. He rests it against my scalp.

"You think I dumb enough to believe a lawyer man drunk half the time anyway?" he asks.

"I'm your best hope. You leave the swamp, the sheriff will be waiting. Without me they connect you to Mr. Farr's death. They're nervous to find someone to lay a killing on."

He walks around me and the cot. He becomes angry, growls, and swings the club over my head. I hear and feel the air of it. He pushes his agonized face toward mine.

"What you asking me to do, give myself up to the sheriff? You think me and him'll drink tea? Shit, I know what they want me for, and I'll get out the swamp. I'll move by night till I find California."

"But it's dumb, Eddie, there'll be warrants, you'll have to hide and won't know from one second to the next when the law's on you. You'll have to take ratty jobs dishwashing and dumping trash. Somewhere you'll slip up, be caught, and they'll lower the jail over you. You'll never see the outside again."

He is scared, and fear makes him furious. He has thought of all I tell him, has had too much time to think as he lay starving on hummocks of low ground while insects sucked his blood. He's been picturing sunny California as the promised land, yet wandering through muck which never releases, swinging his club at briers, vines, and snakes, maybe howling like a lynx in the night.

"What you want from me?" he asks.

For a moment I'm unable to say. I don't want him bringing the sheriff and deputies back here to take Rhea. I mean to help her. What I need for her sake is an option.

"There's a path out front that leads to some part of Riverview. It's been used so much lately you should be able to follow it. I'm sure no sheriff's deputies are in the area. Sneak to the garage where the cars and tools are and find me a hacksaw. Will you do that?"

He doesn't answer. He stares at me from his wild dark eyes, eyes that belong to a fleeing animal that has been too long pursued. He turns to the table, lifts a silver spoon Rhea brought from Riverview, and grips it as if to crush it. Instead he places it back on the table.

"Where the path?" he asks.

I move as far as my chain permits and point out the doorway to the elders and green rushes where Rhea always appears. He leaves the cabin, glances back at me from the rushes, and pushes among them, holding his club ready, and then he has stepped beyond my view.

"Have you found it?" I call.

He doesn't answer. For a while I listen and hear nothing. I don't know whether he's standing out there or has gone.

I sit on the cot. I again think of protecting Rhea. I will make up a story for Pickney and Captain Blake, confess to them I have been away on a binge. I am already sorry about the hacksaw. Even if Eddie Blue were to bring it, I will never use it. I believe in Rhea.

Then I have another thought. I can use the hacksaw to free myself of the chain and be waiting for her, proof the chain was never needed. An act of trust and love.

It's not Eddie Blue but Rhea who walks softly through morning mist. She wears the knapsack, camouflaged hunting clothes, boots, and the hat with net to shield her face from insects. When she sees all food is gone, she smiles, removes the hat, and kisses me.

"You must have been starved," she says.

"I was hungry all right," I say and wonder what has happened during the night to Eddie Blue.

She unlocks me, and we clean the cabin. I use the broom, she wipes the table. She carries more food in the knapsack—a loaf of bread, lunch meat, a white plastic bowl of fresh salad. There is another thermos of tea. We touch hands as we eat. After the lesson she relocks me, sets the pistol on the table, and unlaces her boots before lying on the cot.

We doze, her breath warm at my throat. Lightly I rub her back and feel tension dissipate under my hand. I'm only half awake when she speaks into me.

"The Air Force, Vietnam, ruined him," she says. "Vin was good once, even innocent, but over there they corrupted him. He learned to need excitement. With everything he learned to love the cliff's edge. That's why I was so patient—because I remembered the person he used to be."

She shifts slightly and lays fingers along my cheek. I think of Eddie Blue, not wanting him to come while she is here. Slight chance he will come at all. I don't care because I don't need him. With Rhea I am complete.

"I believed him as happy as I was," she says, her voice low and languorous. I rub her back. "Vin worked hard, and I was showing horses on the circuit and winning. We talked about children and decided to put that off a few years so I could continue to ride.

"Vin drank, but I was accustomed to men drinking, my father, all the Gatlins. I didn't worry. Vin never became sloppy, though a mischievousness began to come out. He was a member of the Air Force Reserves, and he drove to Richmond for meetings. After one of those meetings, there must have been a stag evening, for he brought novelties home."

"Novelties?" I ask, not moving.

"Sexual contrivances, items men laugh and joke over. He wanted to use a thing on me."

A thing? I was afraid to ask what. A rubber with a tickler at the end, a vibrator, harness and pulleys?

"I wouldn't allow it," she says. "The next morning he was sorry. He apologized and sent me roses. He acted boyishly contrite. I put it out of my mind, but it wasn't out of his, for when we came home after the Governor's Ball he wanted me to undress in front of him. We were downstairs, and I tried to joke about it, mugging, posing, ready to go up with him to the bedroom, but he insisted I do it right there in the parlor where the portrait of my beautiful mother is. He wanted a striptease and parade. He kept saying I was his wife and nothing was wrong with it.

"I walked to the kitchen, and he followed. He was holding a drink. He wouldn't leave me alone until I began to do it. I was embarrassed because lights were on, and I thought of servants passing the window. I thought of my mother whom I often stood before and talked to. Yet I took off my organdy gown and paraded for him, trying to appear sexy, crooking my finger and hoping to lead him upstairs. I felt humiliated and full of dread while he sat on a kitchen chair smiling, nodding, applauding."

She stops and draws away her face only to push it deeper along my neck into the pillow.

"Billy, I'm having difficulty telling you this, so please don't look at me. Keep your eyes closed. Are they closed?"

I say they are, and she breathes as if about to plunge under water.

"Vin stood and made me watch while he removed his tuxedo. He wanted to dance, the two of us naked. I was still trying to coax him upstairs, but we danced from room to room all over the first floor. Vin turned up the hi-fi and switched on more lights, the music so loud it rattled the dining-room crystal.

"We whirled into the parlor, and he drew the piano bench to the center of the room, right before my mother. He sat on it, turned me to face him, and tried to make me sit on him. I wouldn't because I was seeing my mother, who still came alive for me. He wanted to shame me in front of her and tried forcing me, but I broke loose and ran upstairs to the bathroom. I locked the door."

I am seeing it and hating Vin for acting like a drunken flyboy on a Saigon knee-walker, the bastard swaggering among slanty-eyed ladies in their shiny slit dresses. Did he never understand what he had in Rhea?

"He came upstairs, stood outside the door, and called me a sexual prude. He used words I can't repeat even in my mind."

Vin, you sonofabitch, to attempt to debase her in front of her mother. Revenge, I think, for the fact her family was better than his. But perhaps more too. Again I picture the parlor, the prie-dieu, the chapel atmosphere. Did she kneel before her mother to talk to her?

"I was hunched against the bathroom door crying. To me sex is not a carnival, a sideshow, but a sacred joining. God doesn't stop outside the bedroom. I felt I'd not only been defiled, but also the house, Riverview, my heritage. I felt God had seen us."

I hate Vin but am disturbed too. God in bed with them?

"Again Vin apologized, yet he resented me. I made him ashamed of himself. We weren't sleeping in different rooms then, and I'd feel his anger as he lay beside me. I couldn't sleep at all sometimes and would read or go down to the garage to work on the cars. Physical action calmed me. He complained about my waking him and leaving lights on. One night when he was drinking, he used a guest room. I wanted him with me but couldn't make myself go ask."

No Gatlin understood how to do that. There was no bend in the Gatlin knee, at least not before mortal man.

"I believed he'd come back. I thought we were having a married couple's quarrel which would resolve itself. Maybe Vin thought that too, but his clothes began to accumulate in the guest room, his suits, hairbrushes, his magazines. Melissa and the servants knew, so I made up a story about his snoring. Vin wouldn't give in. Neither would I."

Vin was just as proud as Rhea, a man used to dominating. He'd been up in the sky, a streaking demigod with lightning at his fingertips. He believed his feet alien to the ground.

"When you're playing these games you cross a line and can't get back," Rhea says. "That happened to us. We stayed in the house together, invited friends to dinner, spoke politely in front of servants, but when alone we hardly talked at all, the words as impersonal as ones you'd use to somebody you met in a store or on the street. And Vin would be gone for days."

I think of the grand house, how it contained them, a magnificent box not to keep the world's blast out but to hold pain in.

"I considered leaving him. I went to a Richmond lawyer, yet couldn't go through with divorce because my mother would never have. I was a Dillon woman. We won by lasting. Besides, I still loved Vin. At moments I hated him, terrible moments, but I loved him too because I remembered what he was. I couldn't get the good out of my head."

She shifts to lay her face against my chest. I look past her to the cabin's ceiling, where dirt daubers bump rough beams. I think of what she must be going to tell me.

"I knew there would be women finally," she says. "Vin had strong desires. From the very first he was that way. In time I believed that desire would bring him back to me, and when it didn't, I guessed he had to be seeing someone. I began to wonder about every female I met—ladies I golfed with, friends on the riding circuit, girls who clerked in stores."

My Jeannie, I think, and move my face so I can press a cheek against the top of her head.

"Occasionally I'd smell women on him, a lingering perfume. There were other signs—lipstick, rumpled clothes, stains. Bills arrived for gifts I never received. I'd hear him late at night, his step clumsy as he climbed the stairs and flopped onto his bed without undressing or brushing his teeth. He'd groan sometimes, and I'd almost go to him. Once he fell off the bed. Yet he was always up early, fresh from his shower and ready to work. He had amazing vitality and recuperative powers."

I remember Vin striding along Tobaccoton's streets as if he owned them, quick to smile, moving with energy, his jacket open, his tie swinging from his speed.

"I was often alone. I had golf and my horses, though I was growing too old to show, to give my best. Nights I roamed the house in the dimness of lamps. I read a lot, even did a little private drinking, nothing like Vin's. I'd sit in the quietness of the parlor sipping whiskey and looking at my mother's portrait, trying to draw courage from her."

In the portrait the mother wears the bracelet, the salvation bracelet with the tiny archangels strung to it. I will soon know about that.

"Books in the library belonged to her, religious books mostly. One titled *The Sculptor's Hand* was written by a Methodist bishop who believed the world is God's studio and that suffering is His hand molding us to shapes worthy of His presence. I drew comfort from the book, the knowledge that what was happening to me had a purpose, that pain is something needed to bring us to a better end."

I see her in the great empty house as she sits in slanted lamplight to read books by divines who have attempted to figure out God. I picture loneliness pressing around her like blackness.

"Vin was drinking more all the time. One night while I read on the library sofa, he came in, and without seeing me staggered to the kitchen. I heard the refrigerator door open and a crash. He'd knocked over a glass pitcher of orange juice and stood weaving and staring at the floor. His suit was messed, his tie gone, his collar unbuttoned. On his throat were teeth marks, and I smelled the stink of perfume, a whore's sweetness so strong it filled the kitchen, the perfume and sourness of his sweat. He staggered, cursed me, and stumbled up the steps."

Kitten, I think, her perfume and teeth imprints on his throat as well as other places. Vin must've run through the local ladies, the respectable ones like Jeannie, women too conventional. He needed the brink, and that in the end served him up to Kitten.

"I was again considering a child, a son, which might change Vin and bring him back," Rhea says. "I'd go to bed for that, but in a fit of fury I hired a private detective in Richmond to find out what Vin was doing, what woman he'd taken up with. I shouldn't have. I was ashamed till I read the report. Then I became horrified. I might have guessed she'd be black. After my father I ought to have suspected that. She also had a police record and worse. I can't even tell you how much worse. I realized Vin might be diseased. I didn't want a child from a diseased father."

She is crying, and I feel her tears on my neck. I flatten my hands on her back and press her to me.

"I decided he had to leave. I caught him at a sober moment and told him if he didn't, I'd go to the lawyers. I said I already had the evidence to defeat him in court. He broke down. We were in the breakfast room, and he begged me. He said he loved Riverview and me as well, but that he had this sickness he was fighting and I should help him fight it. He promised to reform. He was so disgusted with himself. He wanted to give money to the church to prove he was sincere. I suggested Father Mercy. That's when Vin sent the $10,000. Father Mercy saves fallen women. It seemed appropriate."

She rolls away from me to her back and stares at the ceiling. Tears overflow her unblinking eyes. They slide down her face, yet she doesn't wipe at them.

"I let him stay. I wasn't feeling well, some sort of virus which caused a slight fever, and wasn't up to a battle. Vin called Doc

Robinette, who came and put me in bed. Vin remained home instead
of driving to work in order to wait on me. He was very attentive,
and I began to believe there was a chance we could go back and
start again. I prayed it. I would forgive him his awful things."

Her eyes are open and staring upward. I have turned to my
side and lie against her. I rest an arm across her stomach and grip
her wrist. I know I am about to hear it.

"I woke during the night," she says. "I was hot and tossing.
I couldn't get comfortable. I sat up to drink water. Despite the air
conditioning, I was choking from heat. Vin lay in the other room
sleeping. I didn't like bothering him, though he had left a little bell
for me to ring if I needed him. I pushed to my feet and crossed to
the window, which I opened. It was dark outside, no moon, and
as I stood gazing at the ground, my sight seemed to go down through
the lawn and soil, down and down through the earth till I was able
to see into Hell itself, into the fire which is not quenched!"

"The fever," I say. She has begun to shake, and I hold her
close.

"No, more than fever, a vision! I was hot yes, sick, but it was
too real for just fever and the medicine Doc Robinette left. All that
howling and screaming, I heard it, the damned in compartments
writhing among fire, shrieking. They were freezing too and burning, the sound of eternal agony like red serpent tongues waving in
screechings that have stench, all reaching out for mercy; yet nobody
could touch anybody else, and in one of those black compartments
was Vin!"

She is wild now, touched with fright and panic. Her head turns
from side to side. I see that terrible blaze in her lavender eyes and
become afraid myself. Maybe I have been wrong about her, and
she has gone too far. She burns with God fire.

"I rushed to him, made him get out of bed and kneel to pray
with me. I clutched him till he prayed what I prayed. He wanted
to telephone Doc Robinette, but I held his hands and forced him
to speak the words. I didn't care what he'd done in the past. All I
wanted was to save him from one of those burning compartments.
I could never live with myself if I abandoned him to that!"

I do not like her eyes. They are fanatical beyond what I have
ever seen before. Lavender flames they are. Instead of looking into
them, I kiss her forehead, which is hot.

"For a few weeks it was all right, though we were like two

new people meeting. Each morning we ate breakfast across the table and talked formally. He came timidly to my bed, and I allowed it. He was so tender I again thought of a child. Still I had concern for him, his soul, and tried to persuade him to study books from my mother's library. I wanted him to read the lessons you and I've been over. I constantly wore the salvation bracelet."

I think of her and Vin in the tester bed after loving, perhaps lying on their backs and holding hands, and her asking Vin, "What is sin?"

"I believed we would be able to repair our marriage," she says. "I thought I could love him so hard he couldn't resist goodness. Then he drove to Richmond for another meeting of his reserve squadron, and when he came back at one in the morning he was drunk, drunker than I'd ever seen him. I lay in the dark and heard him banging his way through the house. He talked to himself, shouted, sang. He came staggering into my bedroom, switched on lights, and stood weaving. He'd already taken off his clothes, left a trail of them up through the house, and he was grinning, leering out of his nakedness. He tried to get in bed with me, but I smelled the sickening sweet stink of his black slut on him. I shoved him away.

"He became evil. He began saying awful things to me. He called me a Puritan. He said I was warped and needed a doctor, that what I wanted was a priest, not a husband.

"In his anger he attempted to make me do disgusting things. He dragged me from the bed and became perverse. He tried to force me to my knees in front of him and to use my mouth. I fought. He was so drunk I could handle him. I pushed hard, and he fell. He crawled about cursing.

"I pulled on my coveralls and shoes to go downstairs to the garage. I intended to stay till he passed out. Earlier I'd removed a tie rod with a hairline crack from the Thunderbird and laid it on the workbench. I rolled the arc welder to the bench and adjusted my goggles.

"Vin came from the house so drunk he had to walk sideways to reach the garage, and he giggled and was playing with himself. I pushed him away, but he grabbed me from behind, tripped me, and again attempted to force me to take him in my mouth. I butted him, and he stumbled against the LaSalle, held to it, and cursed. He said he was leaving, that he couldn't stand to live any longer with a nun. He said I was ice and he had to recite his Sunday-school lesson before I'd let him love me. He shouted he would buy his own farm, make it better than Riverview. In the morning he was packing and leaving and would tell the whole world what sort of person I really was."

She is crying and covers her face with her fingers as she turns her head from side to side. Her body is rigid, her breathing shallow and fast.

"He slumped against the LaSalle. In catching himself, he pulled the dust cover from it. He was able to open a rear door, tumble in, and lie on the seat. His legs were still out, kicking, and he squirmed like a bug on its back. He began singing a dirty Air Force song, but it wasn't the obscene song or his disgusting nakedness or what he'd tried to make me do or even his threat to tell people about us that terrified me. I saw if something didn't change him, he was lost—finally and totally lost and destined for an eternity of fire. I had to try to save him!

"Connected straight to the circuit-breaker box we have a rheostat used to run tools at variable speeds, and from it I stretched electrical wire to Vin lying on his back. He was singing and fondling himself. I split the wire, twisted one section around his finger, the other around a toe. He cursed and swam up as he tried to understand, and when his feet touched the concrete floor grounding him, I set the rheostat for 175 amps and flipped the switch."

Small superficial excoriations on the dermis of the middle finger of the left hand and the first toe of the right foot.

"He jerked and yelped. I switched off the current, but when he attempted to free himself, I cut it on again. He shouted, kicked, and threw his arms as he rolled on the floor. I told him if he didn't confess his sins and truly repent, there was no hope. He lunged at me. I had to increase the amperage.

"He flopped on the floor and begged till at last came surrender. He was weeping and confessing, asking God's forgiveness, praying to Jesus. I didn't want to hurt him, but I had no choice. He had to feel pain. He needed pain, the sculptor's hand. Even after all his dissipation his body was strong and required so much current. When he stopped moving, I believed he was just resting and had found peace. He looked serene."

I have raised my head to stare. I draw apart, my body as rigid as hers while she rapidly turns her head from side to side like a person experiencing a seizure. The horror of it fills me, the picture of Vin with electricity coursing through his body acknowledging God, his legs kicking, the fright and agony, the spasms and screams. I think of Old Ben in his small cottage near the stable who must have heard and fled.

She slows her head and sets eyes on me, and I see it is in them, that compartment where during a mad vision Vin has burned.

"I saved him," she says. "Do you think it was easy for me? I almost died too, but his death was his victory, don't you see, because he was in a state of grace. I gave him an eternity of life and love with the Father!"

I'm so aghast I can't move. My throat closes, and I am slimed with sweat. Her head stills. She is calmer, yet I am shaking.

"I had to think what to do with him—not him, he was gone, but his body. I couldn't call you or Sheriff Pickney. There might've been a trial and Vin's memory dragged through scandal and shame. I wasn't going to allow a press circus. I spread the LaSalle's dust cover on the garage floor, worked Vin's body onto it, and wiped him clean with a rag. I then ran to his room for clothes to dress him, clothes that didn't have the stink of slut on them. I forgot underwear and hated not having him attired properly, but I was too frantic to run back into the house. I pulled him up onto the floor of the LaSalle and drove from Riverview."

God, Rhea!

"I didn't know where to go. I was wild, praying, weeping, still talking to him. I must've driven a hundred miles an hour through the night, and suddenly I was at Waterside, where Vin first took me to a dance. The log pavilion was closed and dark, but I parked in the empty lot, got Vin out, and dragged him to the dock. I lowered his feet first into a skiff and then the rest of him.

"On the river years ago he proposed to me. I rowed to that same spot, able to find it because of the white oak, its size and shape huge in the moonlight. I pulled Vin up the bank. I again cleaned him with a rag from my coveralls. I arranged his body and features of his face."

Oh God, Rhea!

"Finally I stood, spoke a last prayer over him, and said goodbye. The skiff had floated off. I dove into the river, swam it, and made my way back through the woods to Waterside. On the LaSalle's seat was his wallet, which I'd snatched from his pants left on the house steps. As I drove, I removed the money, wiped the wallet, and threw it out the window. At home I swept the garage before turning off lights and hurrying to my bedroom, where I threw up and kept praying for Vin.

"I discovered then that Gabriel was gone from my salvation bracelet, but I couldn't go back to the river to try to find him. Vin was all right, I knew that. I felt happy for him. He'd accepted God and Christ and been received into fellowship and love by the Father. I'd saved him!"

For a moment she doesn't speak. Slowly her fingers slide from her face. When she sees my expression, she pushes up to look at me.

"I did the best I could for him," she says. "I gave him the greatest gift of all. Only out of love was I able to do it for him."

"Rhea, I want to help you."

"I don't like the way you're staring at me."

"I love and will protect you."

"I have prepared you," she says and smiles. "Together we can live a holy life. One night soon I'll move you to Riverview. Then we'll be together every day and in grace."

I think of myself in Riverview's basement, a prisoner never to glimpse the sun, my father, anybody except Rhea. Once even that might have been alluring, the giving in absolutely to her, but now I've seen too far.

"Let's leave together," I say. "You unlock me, and we'll walk to Riverview."

"Not yet," she says.

The struggle begins with my attempt to work a hand into the pocket of her camouflaged pants for the keys. She holds me, and at first we are not fighting but only pulling at each other. Then she jabs an elbow into my chest. I shoulder her beneath me on the cot. She hits a cheek with a fist and claws at me. To break loose I will have to strike her, and I can't. Even twisted in a grimace of fury, her face is still dear.

She topples me from the cot. She is strong, strong enough to have dragged Vin down to the dock at Waterside and have rolled me here in the wheelbarrow. All the riding she's done, the golf she's played, have put muscle on her firmer than my own. She escapes my grasp to reach the table and her gun.

I look into the swift darkness of the .38's barrel and fires of her eyes. I remember my father has chided me for never having faced death. He can no longer do that. Bleeding, shaking, I wait for the bullet.

"I trusted you," she says, her hair awry, a cheek smudged. "You're the only one I did."

"I've loved you so long," I say, torn mosquito netting draped about me.

"We could've had a life, a life decent and holy, the two of us. I would've taken care of you."

"You killed Vin and now me?"

"I didn't kill him. I gave him all that matters! Pain is just a drop in this great stream which flows to the sea. What's a moment's hurt in the light of eternity? Hardly more than a child's being spanked."

She holds the pistol with both hands and points it at my face. I am still on the floor. I taste blood from her clawing. I am trembling and hoping the bullet won't hurt too badly.

Rhea stands straighter and backs away. She looks at the chain locked around my ankle and its connection at the millstone. She steps into her boots. She reaches to the table for her hat, sets it on, and adjusts the netting down over her face. Veiled, she watches me as she leaves through the crooked doorway and is gone.

I hear doves cooing and fluttering in trees of the swamp. I lie waiting. She has not returned. I've eaten all the food, drunk all the tea and water.

She doesn't plan to come back but will leave me to die. I stand from the cot and shout. I beg. I know I won't be heard, but I think of myself dead and undiscovered. I picture a chain attached to bones.

I pull at the chain and wrestle the millstone. It will not give. I lie on the cot and draw up my knees against hunger. My beard grows through scabs on my cheeks. I wonder how long it takes for a man to starve. Have I read thirty days? But those people had water. Without water it's quicker. I allow whimpering to escape from me.

I worry about my father, whether Rhea will continue to care for him. And our house. Unless Aunt Lettie is doing something, it must be surrendering to dust. I am surrendering. I rise, shout, and jerk at the chain. I feel my growing weakness. I sniffle and whine.

Then I hear her coming. She finally returns but to do what? I sit on the cot and stare out the doorway toward the motionless cattails. I hear the plop of a frog into the pond.

Sun brightens the doorway, but the shape which slides into it is not Rhea. For a joyful instant I believe it must be a member of a rescue team, Captain Blake and his men. When the figure stills and blocks the light, I see it is a savage, swamp-torn Eddie Blue. His caked feet leave wet tracks across the floor.

"What train run over you?" he asks and stands holding something in a proffered swollen hand, not a hacksaw but just the blade. I don't move, and he tosses it on the cot. "You buzzard bait," he says and starts away.

"Stay and help me!" I say.

"Nah, lawyer man, got to move it, but you remember I come back. I take a chance stealing and being caught to get back to you. You never done nothing for me in my whole life, and that makes me better'n you, don't it?"

"I'll help you, I swear it!"

"Can't have a thing like you slowing me. I got a plan to 'scape. You be all right if you follow the path just like me. It come out of the woods behind a Gatlin hay barn where I been sleeping and sucking pigeon eggs. Sneaked last night to the garage, but when lights switched on, I ran. I going to run tonight too, the other way. They shoot me, you get 'em. You owe me big since I come back for your skinny white ass."

"Reach a telephone and call the sheriff for me."

"The day I start calling sheriffs rain'll fall up."

"Eddie Blue, wait!"

But he is gone through the weeds and among the rushes. I sit on the cot, draw up a foot, and begin using the blade on the loop of chain around my ankle. Without the saw frame, the blade is flimsy and difficult to grasp. The chain is a squirming snake, and my hands, slick with sweat, lose their grip. I work frantically but see only tiny flakes of steel gather on my shin.

Each time I rest I listen for Rhea. She's not coming. I don't want her to. If I can free myself, I'll run along the path to the rear of Riverview, circle wide through the woods at the rear of the house, and find the highway. Then I'll go to Pickney, make him sit and understand before we drive after Rhea. We'll take Doc Robinette, who'll make arrangements for her at Richmond's Saint Mary's Hospital.

I work the blade. I saw the rest of the afternoon and into the night. I rest only to rise and continue sawing. In the depth of night I succeed in cutting through one side of a link. The other side will not give. I moan, pound the link on the floor, and feel exhausted.

I again saw, working by sense of touch, my eyes closed in the darkness. My grip is loose, and I stop to flex my fingers. When the blade slips, I saw into myself and then have the slippery stickiness of blood.

If she comes before I finish, I will have to hide the blade and drape the blanket over the chain. I'll lie on the blade and pull the blanket to my chin. I'll tell her I'm sick, which is true.

Even if she doesn't hurt me, if she intends to unlock and take me with her, she will discover what I've been doing. Lavender will again flare in her eyes.

I use the entire top of my body, not just my arms, to push the blade forward and draw it back. My breathing becomes part of the sawing rhythm. The chain is made of high-quality steel, but then Rhea is accustomed to buying the best of everything.

I think of her in a private institution. I will protect her. Nobody will humiliate her, I'll see to that. She's suffered beyond human endurance, and step by step doctors can restore her. We will still be able to have a life together.

Sawing is instinctive and automatic. I no longer think. My mind spins. Never has there been a time I wasn't sawing. Like a galley slave I row the blade. Blood is thick on my fingers. I am so tired. I will not finish because I am so tired.

I fall to my side and sleep. Light wakens me. When I push up to eye the link, I am dejected at the sight of the little groove I've managed to cut. Quit, I think. Go on, just lie back and quit. Yet bloody fingers lift the trembling blade, and again my body rocks. I sing a muddled count: one more, two, three—until I lose the numbers and start over. My eyes sting and blur with sweat. I realize I'm grunting. I'm no longer certain what part of the day it is. I drop the blade, lift it, and drop it. What does the light tell me? The light tells me nothing, and all sounds I hear come from myself.

When the link parts and the chain slides to the floor, I am so weary and dazed I'm not sure it has happened. I finger my eyes to clear them and stare at my ankle. I lift my foot to feel its weightlessness. I push up from the cot, throw my arms out to balance myself, and start toward the door.

I hear crows cawing and the hawk's cry. Somebody is coming. I hurry back to the cot, sit on the blade, and wrap the chain around my ankle. Then I cover my bloody foot with the blanket. I smooth the blanket over my lap.

The sun is low, and its beams stretch horizontally through tree branches, striping weeds with shadows. There is a swishing, and Rhea parts the rushes. She too is striped till she steps into the doorway.

She holds the gun and stands looking at me. She wears the netted hat, camouflaged pants, boots, and is as beautiful as ever, herself again, calm, contained. She won't hurt me. She can't do that. She carries my dress shoes, the laces tied and the shoes hung over a shoulder.

"We're leaving," she says. "We'll go to Riverview, clean you, feed you. We must move quickly so we can use the path while it's still light, though we'll have to wait till dark before crossing from woods to the house. I intend to unlock you. Lie on your back and place your hands under your head. Why are you using the blanket?"

"I felt chilled," I say.

She lifts the netting over her face. When I lie back, she slides the .38 into the holster. She brings the keys from a pouch pocket. After she lifts the blanket and sees what I've done to the chain, she will believe I've betrayed her a second time. She is stooping with the keys. I wait till she touches the blanket before I rear.

I shove her so hard she falls and her hat rolls across the floor. I'm off the cot, grab at the gun, and yank it from her. I step away holding the gun. I fumble it as I cock it. As she stands and backs off, I aim at her. She looks at the gun, my bleeding ankle, and chain on the floor. She drops the keys to the table.

"How'd you do it?" she asks.

Careful to keep the gun pointed at her, I show the hacksaw blade. She nods and appears undisturbed.

"I'll take my shoes," I say. They are still carried over her shoulder, and she removes them to hang them across my quivering fingers.

"Will you tell everyone?" she asks.

"Not everyone, Rhea. Together we'll work it out."

"I don't think so," she says and shakes her head.

"Believe in me."

"No, Billy, it's impossible."

"I love and will do all I can for you."

"I know you love me," she says and smiles. "You love me so much you couldn't ever shoot me."

"Rhea, don't!"

She steps toward me, and I do shoot, not at her, but into the floor. The bullet splinters old boards and spins up violent dust. The sound of the shot pounds from wall to wall. She is surprised but not frightened. She has never stopped smiling.

"Billy boy," she says.

"They'll never send you to jail," I say. "I'll see to it. You might have to undergo some short-term psychiatric treatment."

"I wouldn't care for that."

"It's worth it if we can have a life together."

"We can have that my way," she says and backs off to the chair to sit. She begins unlacing her boots.

"Rhea?"

"Oh you know," she says and removes the boots and her white wool socks. She folds each sock neatly across the top of a boot. Smiling, she stands and unbuttons her blue broadcloth shirt. Under it she wears a white brassiere. She unbuckles her leather belt, zips down the camouflaged pants, and steps out of them. Like her brassiere, her briefs are satiny and have a lacy design around edges.

"We'll do it any way you want, Billy, even like that slut nigger bitch of his if that's what you feel you must have."

"No!" I tell her and think, It's no longer Rhea in that body.

"I've tried to remain a moral woman," she says and curves hands behind her to unhook her brassiere. She allows it to slide down her arms to her fingers and drops it on the table. Her breasts released are startlingly fair and heavy, untouched by any sun, the rounded nipple area pinkish brown. I've never thought of her as possessing such great breasts. Has she kept them bound all these years, considering them shameful? The breasts, their bareness, the expanse of flesh along her arms and stomach are shocking. "All my life I've tried, yet the men I love won't accept it."

Her body is a crescent of beauty as she bends to push the briefs down her fine strong legs and steps out of them. She drops the briefs too on the table, raises her palms to either side of her shoulders, and continues to smile as she moves toward me. Lastly she removes the tiny gold cross and dangles it back to the table.

"No closer!" I say, knowing if she touches me I'm lost.

"I understand how to be fully a woman," she says, her palms again lifted, her step dainty. Again I will shoot into the floor, though I want her, even this way I do. Had she kept on in the teasing, maidenly little step, she might have reached me, but she springs, and my finger is already tensed to the trigger. When the gun fires, I intend the shot to go wide, yet her quickness has plunged her in front of the muzzle.

The blast knocks her sideways. She is still on her feet. The awful wound blooms on her inner left thigh. We stare into the shiny clean redness. From the puncture the blood spurts so richly red it is like new nylon.

We gape as if observing something beyond ourselves. She straightens to place both hands above the wound and squeeze the thigh to stop the astonishing pumping of blood. She drags the leg to the chair and sits.

"Billy?" she asks, her voice full of wonder.

Sickened and terrified, I throw the gun on the cot and rush to her. I jerk her belt from her pants, wrap it around the thigh, and draw it tight, but the wound is high, and though bleeding slows, it doesn't stop.

"Oh God, Rhea!"

"Sh-h-h, I'll hold the belt, and you help me dress."

"We don't have time."

"I have to wear clothes, at least my shirt," she says. She is able to smile, and when I look into her eyes, the fire is gone.

As she sits bleeding, I work the shirt onto her, button it, and then she insists I help with her briefs. The white silkiness soaks up blood as it passes the wound. We untangle and retighten the belt. She must have boots.

"I'll stand and hold to you," she says. Around her neck she refastens the cross.

I lace her boots and wipe blood from my hands on my khakis. I jam my feet into the shoes she brought and help her move. With her right arm over my shoulder, we step from the cabin into weeds.

Her other hand keeps the belt tight around her thigh. Blood flows down her leg into the boot.

We push through rushes and cattails and pass the algal pond. I see the path easily. She has worn it down during my captivity, but overhanging branches create a dimness, a shadowy twilight. In darkness I could lose the way among sloughs and hummocks. Already my feet are wet, the muck sucking at my shoes.

"How far is it?" I ask.

"A little way," she says. "I never thought you'd shoot."

"Please believe I didn't mean to hit you."

"Poor Billy."

"Can't you hold the belt tighter?" I ask. God, the blood, the blood!

"I'll try."

She is able to carry most of her own weight, her body dropping slightly against mine only when she lowers the foot of the wounded leg. I'm thinking how's the fastest way to deliver her to Doc Robinette. The path leads out of the woods behind Riverview. I'll take her to the house and telephone him and the Rescue Squad.

The path is soft, the ground uneven and at times slick. She stumbles, and I feel the fullness of her weight. I now have to hold her up. The blood, our sweat, attracts insects. I brush them off her, but they spiral up and resettle.

"Rest," she says, her breath rapid.

"No time. How much farther?"

"Almost there," she says as if half asleep. "And Billy boy really shot me."

"I love you so much, Rhea, I don't care about the law or myself or what you did to Vin, but I had to try to help you."

She is nodding, dreamy, and the blood still flows, not squirting, but a pulsing stream that has filled her boot. I hear the squish of the blood in the boot. I tighten the belt and shoo away green-headed flies. She is leaning heavily on me.

"Poor Billy," she repeats.

"Are we close?"

"I'm so sorry," she says.

"We're going to make it," I say, yet I stumble. She is a big woman clinging to me. I am not strong. My own breathing labors in gasps. Mosquitoes gather at my eyelids. I can't release her to rub at them.

She is giving way. Her legs are out of control, though she's trying. She's trying hard. Her arm slips from me, and she grasps my shirt. Her fingers won't hold. I stop, turn her toward me, and tighten the belt. Then I let her fall forward across my shoulder in the fireman's carry. I stagger under her weight but lurch onward along the path.

Her dripping leg is near my face. Her blood slides over me. I keep reaching to tighten the belt. Her strawberry hair hangs. Somehow blood is there too, and the flies, the gathering flies.

"We'll make it, we're on the way," I tell her.

"Thank you, Billy," she says as if I've served her tea.

It's becoming dark, the night seeping in under trees like murky water rising. I can just see the path and don't know how far we have to go. I ask her, but she thanks me again. Not the night, I pray, not the darkness. I talk to encourage her, and for a while she answers politely. Her hair brushes my body. Is there about her still a faint perfume? Then she stops talking, though she sighs and once reaches to my waist and squeezes it.

Blood drips, an arm dangles, I'm afraid to rest. I shove through thickets of marsh elder and clawing briers. I take several steps before I realize I have lost the path. I backtrack, but in darkness I can't find it.

Rhea is motionless except for the dangling arm and her hair swinging. I have to rest. I set her against a swamp willow growing from a soggy hummock and lay an ear to her breast. Her heart is beating. I tighten the belt all I can.

"We're bound to be close now," I say, and she gives an answer, an exhalation.

I struggle to stand her. Again she folds over me in the fireman's carry, which I learned during first-aid class at Howell County High. The fireman almost drops her, and my feet race around beneath us. She raises her head.

"Vin?"

"Fine," I say. "Everything's fine."

My feet spread, my body near to tipping, I push on. I don't know whether I'm circling or not, but I can't quit. Mosquitoes swarm. A veil, they cover my eyes and face. I try to keep them off Rhea as I talk to her.

I no longer attempt to watch where I'm stepping, and my feet slip into a slough. Muck sucks off my shoes. The stink of it is sulphuric and biting. I am forced to crawl out with her and slide back once, but I prevent Rhea's head from going under.

I talk to her. Thank God the bleeding has slowed. The belt is holding. A human has lots of blood. How many quarts I can't recall, but it is a large and amazing amount. The belt is holding, and the wound could be closing itself. The body possesses marvelous defense mechanisms.

I am tripped by thorns, go to my knees, and again rise without losing her. I fall several more times, the impact cushioned by slimy muck. For a space I move on my knees before staggering up with her. I've got to be close to some habitation. I begin to call. Why do I have to be close? I have to be close because I have to be close. I shout, and a dark bird flaps from a cedar, its great wings batting the air.

Why am I whining? I am whining, I am shouting. The goddamn mosquitoes. I am wearing mosquitoes like a veil. Is there a lesson on why God invented the mosquito? I wade out of black still water to an insubstantial hummock. My feet are bleeding, my pants and shirt shredded by thorns. I try to see stars in gaps of trees, take a bearing on Polaris as if I'm a boat on a turquoise sea, but I can't find the sky.

I hear someone answer my shouting. I scream, hurry forward, and fall. I am up with Rhea, but it is no one, an owl perhaps, the screech of an owl or other night creature. I whimper and blow mosquitoes from my mouth.

Rhea is bleeding very little. The wound has to have closed, and she is sleeping. I can't go much farther, but at least the wound has closed. I must stay on my feet. If I fall again, I won't be able to rise with her. I am praying. I am saying, God, you have no right to do this to a lady like Rhea. But that is not a prayer.

Then, as if my not-a-prayer is answered, my numb, wobbly, bleeding feet sense a difference in the lay of the ground. It slopes upward to firmness. Vines and briers drop away as do ragged cedars. I weave among pines that stop suddenly at a fenced pasture where frightened horses wheel and dash into darkness.

I lay Rhea across the rail fence, talking to her, climb it myself, and drag her into the fireman's carry. My knees almost give. I stumble over the pasture and beside the fence till I find a gate. It is aluminum and rattles when I slide the latch. I smell pine resin and sweet fragrances from a flower garden, but the house is dark, a black shape without dimension. No light burns in the stable, garage, or outbuildings.

I yell for help. I stagger to the front door, lean on it with Rhea, and bang the brass knocker. No one comes. I move along stones of the house to a window above rose bushes, which snag me. I will break the window and get to a telephone. With a fist I beat on the glass, a storm window thick for security and to protect the efficiency of central air conditioning. Even if I break it, I won't be able to lift Rhea or myself over the jagged edges.

I try other doors. They are all locked. I am shouting. Where are the servants and hands? She has let them go for the night so she could bring me in. God! Stumbling, half running, I carry Rhea over white gravel of the drive toward the highway. Between shouts I talk to her. Then I realize I'm not shouting at all. My voice is a wheezing squawk. My bloody feet crunch gravel. I hardly feel the sharpness. It seems I am running without advancing, as if the drive is moving under me.

I reach the dark entranceway to Riverview. The gates are closed, but flanking them I slip among trees to the road. The asphalt is more darkness, which my feet slap as I reel toward Tobaccoton. I see light emerging, a car or truck, and I maneuver Rhea and myself to the center of the highway. I straddle the broken white line as headlights shatter the blackness into sparklers.

The car doesn't stop. It brakes, swerves, and the horn sounds loud and long. I see the flash of frightened ashen faces as the car speeds past and away. I think of what I must look like, my clothes torn, my body gashed, carrying sleeping Rhea with her bloody hair dangling.

I shout, yet hear little sound. I trip, one leg in a broad weave catching the other, and fall forward on the road. I twist to keep Rhea from hitting the blacktop. I crack my own head, and she rolls off and lies crumpled at my side. I am shouting and making no sound. A tide of insect shrillness washes over us.

I collapse and lie touching her. She is so still, so calm, not wanting to cause trouble. She has always been a great lady, especially during adversity. I move my face close to hers. Because of darkness I can't see her features, yet I know she is smiling. She will never consider me a young Vin, but she loves me in the manner a lady loves. That is enough. That is more than I believed I would ever have.

I hear thunder, a slow drumbeat of it, and in a jab of lightning I glimpse the paleness of her face. Her eyes are closed, and she is resting. I check the belt. It is tight. She deserves rest. I'll see she's not disturbed. I wipe insects off her brow.

A little rain falls, warm and gentle, a slight late summer shower to cool the steamy earth, though Rhea is already cool. I lower my cheek to hers. I love you, Rhea. Don't worry, somebody's bound to come. You rest. Take all the rest you need.

The rain passes, the clouds slide away in retreating thunder, and we lie on the road till lights explode from the direction of Bannister. The lights are a farm truck carrying lowing cattle, and the truck skids, blows its horn, and curves into a ditch as I lift an arm without rising. The oily heat of the engine and burning stench of hot tires remain close to my face.

A door opens, a man comes running. I tell by his voice he is black.

"Lord God!" he says.

"It's all right now, Rhea," I say.

15

My view from the Bannister hospital is between white slats of Venetian blinds and over roofs and steeples to concrete strips of interstate highway leading west. The concrete's brilliant newness hasn't seasoned to the land it crosses, old land drawn to wanness by a longer burden of giving suck to tobacco. I watch cars silently slide away, their metal carrying the glint of an evening sun.

"Rhea?" I ask.

"She's being looked after," Captain Blake says.

Sibilant nurses enter and leave. Doc Robinette has wiped his smeared glasses to peer at me. My feet and legs are wrapped, and his palsied fingers unwind gauze to dress the bites and lacerations with a cooling yellow ointment.

Reporters from Danville, Lynchburg, and Richmond are kept out. Captain Blake has posted state-police guards at my door. Underneath he is a kind man, though duty requires he ask questions and provide a uniformed male secretary to take down answers.

"Rhea?" I ask.

"In good hands," Captain Blake says.

I will not tell them what she in her loving pride and desperation did to Vin. In her sickness. Nobody except me will ever know that. Captain Blake, resplendent in his glittering blue-gray, and a lawyer

from the investigative division of the attorney general's office sit by
my bed. The latter requests permission to use a tape recorder. I
look past him. Captain Blake lays a hand on my arm. He is fatherly.

"You can't hurt her now," he says. "No one's left who can be
hurt. Only distant kin remain, and they're gone from Howell
County."

"Rhea?" I ask.

"A service at Riverview, the family plot."

I turn my head to stare, and when I understand, I don't know
what I do, but it brings nurses with needles. I sink into a dark
drifting sea which has no bottom.

When I rise to light, Captain Blake, his secretary, and the
attorney general's man with his tape recorder are again sitting by
my bed. A nurse cranks me up, and two pillows are adjusted behind
my head. I watch cars slip west between slats of the blinds.

"We've located the cabin and chain," Captain Blake says. "Also
the gun. But we don't understand what she did to her husband."

I close my eyes.

"Will you tell me in confidence off the record?" the captain
asks after his secretary and the attorney general's man leave
the room.

I shake my head.

"You're an officer of the court!" the captain says, momentarily
threatening. "You have responsibilities!"

"Were people at her funeral?" I ask.

He gazes at me, his eyes nearly the pressed color of his blue-
gray whipcord shirt. His face softens. He sits and settles his hands
on his knees.

"Just about everybody in Howell County," he says.

"She was loved," I say.

For a time questions from Captain Blake and the attorney
general's man cease, and people are allowed to visit. Florene, her
hair in spitcurls, is first, and she carries a cake. When I ask about
the office, she's embarrassed to tell me Pickney's nephew is filling
in for me.

Buster Bovin and members of his Ministerial Alliance arrive.
They pray over me. "The Lord be with you," they say.

Miss Katie Cullen, the librarian, comes bearing books of colored photographs, mostly pictures of shore birds. Beyond them is
a dazzling turquoise sea.

"You can get well in books," Miss Katie says.

Roses arrive from Jeannie, who is honeymooning in Italy.

The most surprising visitor is Father Mercy wearing his butter yellow robes and tribal cap. At first he does not speak. Massively he crosses to the bed and lays his immense black hand on my forehead. The hand is warm and heavy. He acts as if he's listening through his arm into my body. He draws the hand away.

"You are on the threshold," he says and leaves wild flowers wrapped in yellow paper.

Sheriff Pickney accompanies his nephew, the honor graduate from William & Mary who is tending my job. He's a boyish young man, serious, his off-blond hair groomed, his tan summer suit neat, his button-down blue-and-white striped shirt fashionable. He wears a golden class ring.

He's quick to tell me he is only helping out in my office, that he doesn't intend to stay.

"I'm joining a Norfolk firm," he says. "I love Howell County and agonized over the decision, but I can't fight the money."

"They going to discover he's hick underneath and toss him back," Pickney says. "Though he don't talk like us no more. He gotten Howell County out his mouth."

"Took seven years," the nephew said. "Had to give up chitlins, fatback, and plug tobacco, though I still slip out to the barn occasionally for a chaw and spit."

They are pleasant and concerned, but I am tired. Before they leave, Pickney stands by the bed and takes my hand. He asks me to call on him for anything, anything at all, he can do. Like Captain Blake, he means it. The law at its best is motherly.

Aunt Lettie arrives, driven to Bannister by one of her grandchildren, not Eddie Blue. She wears a green dress and her rickety church hat. She too has flowers, daisies wrapped in newspaper. She sits on the chair by the bed, and only toes of her new white tennis shoes touch the floor.

"Did they catch him?" I ask of Eddie Blue.

"That boy's just disappeared into air," she says as if peeping from under a lid, a look which makes me know he's safe long miles from Howell County. I hope he's reached a sun-splashed California where the sky drops forgiveness.

She tells me she's gone to the house to sweep, wash windows, beat the rugs. I thank her. She's been to see my father, who's still at the Land of Goshen Lodge but will be coming home because Rhea no longer pays the bills.

"I brung a pie," Aunt Lettie says, a brown-sugar pie, the specialty of our region, so sweet it causes ache through the teeth to pierce the skull. When Aunt Lettie leaves, I give the pie, as I have Florene's cake, to the nurses and orderlies.

I am allowed up and walk about my room. Church bells ring for Sunday services. The bells alarm pigeons, who sweep wide into the sunny haze and circle back. Siren sounding, a red fire engine races along a street and speeds from view. On the sidewalk burnished children carrying bright balloons run after it. In the distance smoke.

Hands in my bathrobe pockets, I stroll to the end of the waxed corridor where soft-drink machines hum. I avoid haunted eyes peering from rooms. The eyes are searching for something I don't bear. I buy a root beer to give a towheaded boy in a wheelchair who has broken his left femur by falling from an apple tree.

During the second week Doc Robinette walks the hallway with me. His glasses are again smeared, and he bumps along unable to hold a straight course. Nurses smile at him. We light cigarettes as we pace. The same nurses don't like our smoking in the corridor.

"Want to leave?" Doc asks. His gait is disjointed, and his shoes squeak, old shoes dimmed by Howell County dust. "I can arrange a discharge."

I finish drawing smoke deep before I shrug.

"Like you to talk to a colleague," he says. "To be on the safe side."

"Safe side of what?"

"Shrinks got to eat too. I hasten to add nobody believes you're unbalanced despite your ordeal." He bumps the wall. "I'll drive you home."

Later I dress and thank the nurses and orderlies. The business office informs me it will mail my bill. Doc has a new air-conditioned Buick, but the ashtray overflows, and the blue velour is already holed by careless cigarettes.

On the asphalt road I am all right till we approach the entrance to Riverview, its black gates closed and chained, grass and weeds already pushing up through white gravel. I break forward to the padded dash. Doc slows, reaches to my shoulder, and gently rights me.

Tobaccoton's the same, a runty town baking away in sunlight through which hot yellow dust spirals, the shade without deliverance, a dark fire. Uncle Daniel continues to parade his sign, only at last he has words on it, has had them, I realize, all along, and those words are what every man writes on his own sign. Each man does carry one. Mine is like the religious lunatics in cartoons: THE END IS NEAR! Uncle Daniel understands and is over the threshold.

At the house Doc raises windows. The air is heavy, fierily abrasive and worn as if breathed before and exhaled. Doc leaves capsules on the kitchen table and offers to bring someone to stay with me. I decline, thank him, and stand on the front porch to watch him drive off down the lane between dusty locust trees.

I sit at the dining room table, where Florene has neatly stacked my accumulated mail. I don't open it. Though Aunt Lettie has washed, ironed, and cleaned, dust resettles. On the sideboard is the sugar bowl, the last of the silver service. She has polished it.

My palms leave sweaty prints on the round mahogany table. Chirring locusts are a sound like the lifting of a sheer scarf by the stirring of sullen air. I hear a vehicle and look out the window. It is a Rescue Squad ambulance bringing my father home. Men in hardhats and coveralls carry his suitcase and help him up the porch steps. He uses his cane. He still wears pajamas and slippers, and his white hair needs cutting.

I thank the men. They drive away, dust of the lane curling after them. My father has limped past me directly to the pantry. He is pallid, thin, brittle. He hooks his cane over the counter and bends, holding onto the counter to open the cabinet beneath and lift out the fifth of Ancient Age. He unscrews the cap and drinks from the bottle.

I go to him. We both take pulls from the bottle. Then I work my arms around him. I look into his anguished sepia eyes, and it's like gazing down a long dark corridor to the emptiness at the center of myself. For an instant he resists, but slowly, shakily, his hands touch my back and creep over it until they come to rest. We are as two bereaved women given to grief and weeping at the edge of the grave.